SNOWED
IN FOR
Christmas

CAROLINE
ANDERSON

PATRICIA
THAYER

SOPHIE
PEMBROKE

MILLS & BOON

Published in Great Britain 2016
By Mills & Boon, an imprint of HarperCollins*Publishers*
1 London Bridge Street, London, SE1 9GF

SNOWED IN FOR CHRISTMAS © 2016 Harlequin Books S.A.

Snowed in with the Billionaire © 2013 Caroline Anderson
Stranded with the Tycoon © 2013 Sophie Pembroke
Proposal at the Lazy S Ranch © 2013 Patricia Thayer

ISBN: 978-0-263-92690-3

24-1016

Our policy is to use papers that are natural, renewable and recyclable products and made from wood grown in sustainable forests.
The logging and manufacturing processes conform to the legal environmental regulations of the country of origin.

Printed and bound in Spain
by CPI, Barcelona

SNOWED IN WITH THE BILLIONAIRE

CAROLINE ANDERSON

*For Angela, who gave me insight into the
harrowing and difficult issues surrounding
adoption, and for all 'the girls' in the
Romance group for their
unstinting help, support, and amazing
knowledge. Ladies, you rock!*

Caroline Anderson has the mind of a butterfly.
She's been a nurse, a secretary, a teacher, run
her own soft furnishing business, and now she's
settled on writing. She says, 'I was looking for
that elusive something. I finally realised it was
variety, and now I have it in abundance. Every
book brings new horizons and new friends, and in
between books I have learned to be a juggler. My
teacher husband John and I have two beautiful
and talented daughters, Sarah and Hannah,
umpteen pets, and several acres of Suffolk that
nature tries to reclaim every time we turn our
backs!' Caroline also writes for the Mills & Boon
Medical Romance series.

CHAPTER ONE

'Oh, what—?'

All Georgia could see in the atrocious conditions were snaking brake lights, and she feathered the brake pedal, glad she'd left a huge gap between her and the car in front.

It slithered to a halt, and she put on her hazard flashers and pulled up cautiously behind it, trying to see why they'd stopped, but visibility was minimal. Even though it was technically still daylight, she could scarcely see a thing through the driving snow.

And the radio hadn't been any help—plenty of talk about the snow arriving earlier than predicted, but no traffic information about any local holdups. Just Chris Rea, singing cheerfully about driving home for Christmas while the fine, granular snow clogged her wipers and made it next to impossible to see where she was going.

Not that they'd been going anywhere fast. The traffic had been moving slower and slower for the last few minutes because of the appalling visibility, and now it had come to a complete grinding halt. She'd been singing along with all the old classics as the weather worsened, crushing the steadily rising panic and trying to pretend that it was all going to be OK. Obviously her crazy, reckless optimism hard at work as usual. When would she learn?

Then the snow eased fleetingly and she glimpsed the tail lights of umpteen cars stretching away into the distance. Far beyond them, barely discernible in the pale gloom, a faint strobe of blue sliced through the falling snow.

More blue lights came from behind, travelling down the other side of the road and overtaking the queue of traffic, and it dawned on her that nothing had come towards them for some minutes. Her heart sank as the police car went past and the flashing blue lights disappeared, swallowed up by the blizzard.

OK, so something serious had happened, but she couldn't afford to sit here and wait for the emergency services to sort it out with the weather going downhill so quickly. If she wasn't careful she'd end up stranded, and she was *so* nearly home, just five or six miles to go. So near, and yet so far.

The snow swirled around them again, picking up speed, and she bit her lip. There was another route—a narrow lane she knew only too well. A lane that she'd used often as a short cut, but she'd been avoiding it, and not only because of the snow—

'Why we stop, Mummy?'

She glanced in the rear-view mirror and met her son's eyes. 'Somebody's car's broken down,' she said. Or hit another car, but she wasn't going to frighten a two-year-old. She hesitated. She was deeply reluctant to use the lane, but realistically she was all out of options.

Making the only decision she could, she smiled brightly at Josh and crossed her fingers. 'It's OK, we'll go another way. We'll soon be at Grannie and Grandpa's.'

His face fell, tugging her heartstrings. 'G'annie now. I hungry.'

'Yeah, me, too, Josh. We won't be long.'

She turned the car, feeling it slither as she pulled away across the road and headed back the way she'd come. Yikes. The roads were truly lethal and they weren't going to get any better as more people drove on them and compacted the snow.

As she turned onto the little lane, she could feel her heart rate pick up. The snow was swirling wildly around the car, almost blinding her, and even when it eased for a second the verges were almost obliterated.

This wasn't supposed to be happening yet! Not until tonight, after they were safely tucked up with her parents, warm and dry and well-fed. Not out in the wilds of the countryside, on a narrow lane that went from nowhere to nowhere else. If only she'd left earlier...

She checked her mobile phone and groaned. No signal. Fabulous. She'd better not get stuck, then. She put the useless phone away, sucked in a deep breath and kept on driving, inching cautiously along.

Too cautiously. The howling wind was blowing the snow straight off the field to her right and the narrow lane would soon be blocked. If she didn't hurry, she wasn't going to get along here at all, she realised, and she swallowed hard and put her foot down a little. At least in the fresh snow she had a bit more traction, and she wasn't likely to meet someone coming the other way. She only had half a mile at the most to go before she hit the other road. She could do it. She could...

A high brick wall loomed into view on the left, rippling in and out like a ribbon, the snow plastered to it like frosting on a Christmas cake, and she felt a surge of relief.

Almost there now. The ancient crinkle crankle wall ran alongside the lane nearly to the end. It would give her a vague idea of where the road was, if nothing else, and all she had to do was follow it to the bigger, better road which would hopefully be clear.

And halfway along the wall—there it was, looming out of the blizzard, the gateway to a hidden world. The walls curved in on both sides of the imposing entrance, rising up to a pair of massive brick piers topped with stone gryphons, and between them hung the huge, ornate iron gates that didn't shut.

Except that today they were firmly shut.

They'd been painted, too, and they weren't wonky any more, she realised as she slowed to a halt. They'd always hung at a crazy angle, open just enough to squirm through, and that gap had been so enticing to an adventurous young girl out for a bike ride with her equally reckless older brother.

The gryphons guarding the entrance had scared them, mythical beasts with the heads and wings of eagles and the bodies of lions, their talons slashing the air as they reared up, but the gap had lured them in, and inside the wall they'd found a secret adventure playground beyond their wildest imaginings. Acres of garden run wild, with hidden rooms and open spaces, vast spreading trees and a million places to hide.

And in the middle of it all, the jewel in the crown, sat the most beautiful house she'd ever seen. A huge front door with a semi-circular fanlight over it was tucked under a pillared portico that sat exactly in the centre of the house, surrounded perfectly symmetrically by nine slender, elegant sash windows.

Not that you could see all the windows. Half of them were covered in wisteria, cloaking the front and invading the roof, and the scent from the flowers, hanging delicately like bunches of pale lilac grapes against the creamy bricks, had been intoxicating.

It had been empty for years; with their hearts in their mouths, she and Jack had found a way inside through the cellar window and tiptoed round the echoing rooms with their faded grandeur, scaring each other half to death with ghost stories about the people who might have lived and loved and died there, and she'd fallen head over heels in love with it.

And then years later, when her brother had started to hang out with Sebastian, she'd taken him there, too. He'd come over to their house one day to see Jack but he'd been out, so they'd gone out for a bike ride instead. His idea, and she'd jumped at it, and they'd ended up here.

It had been their first 'date', not really a date at all but near enough for her infatuated sixteen-year-old self, and she'd dragged him inside the still-empty house just as she had her brother.

Like her, he'd been fascinated by it. They'd explored every inch of it, tried to imagine what it would have been like to live there in its hey-day. What it would be like to live there now. They'd even fantasised about the furnishings—a dining table so long you could hardly see the person at the other end, a Steinway grand in what had to have been the music room and, in the master bedroom, a huge four-poster bed.

In her own private fantasy, that bed had been big enough for them and all their children to pile into for a cuddle. And there'd be lots of them, the foundation of a whole dynasty. They'd fill the house with children, all of them conceived in that wonderful, welcoming bed with feather pillows and a huge fluffy quilt and zillion-thread-count Egyptian cotton sheets.

And then he'd kissed her.

They'd been playing hide and seek, teasing and flirting and bubbling over with adolescent silliness, and he'd found her in the cupboard in the bedroom and kissed her.

She'd fallen the rest of the way in love with him in that instant, but it had been almost two years before their relationship had moved on and fantasy and reality had begun to merge.

He'd gone away to uni, but they'd seen each other every holiday, spent every waking moment together, and the kisses had become more urgent, more purposeful, and way more grown up.

And then, the weekend after her eighteenth birthday, he'd taken her to the house. He wouldn't tell her why, just that it was a surprise, and then he'd led her up to the master bedroom and opened the door, and she'd been enchanted.

He'd set the scene—flickering candles in the fireplace, a thick blanket spread out on the moth-eaten carpet and smothered in petals from the wisteria outside the window, the scent filling the room—and he'd fed her a picnic of delicate smoked salmon and caviar sandwiches and strawberries dipped in chocolate, and he'd toasted her in pink champagne in little paper cups with red hearts all over the outside.

And then, slowly and tenderly, giving her time even though it must have killed him, he'd made love to her.

She'd willingly given him her virginity; they'd come close so many times, but he'd always stalled her. Not that day. That day, when he'd finally made love to her, he'd told her he'd love her forever, and she'd believed him because she loved him, too. They'd stay together, get married, have the children they both wanted, grow old together in the heart of their family. It didn't matter where they lived or how rich or poor they were, it was all going to be perfect because they'd have each other.

But two years down the line, driven by ambition and something else she couldn't understand, he'd changed into someone she didn't know and everything had fallen apart. Their dream had turned into a nightmare with the shocking intrusion of a reality she'd hated, and she'd left him, but she'd been devastated.

She hadn't been back here in the last nine years, but just before Josh was born she'd heard on the grapevine that he'd bought it. Bought their house, and was rescuing it from ruin.

She and David had been at a dinner party, and someone from English Heritage was there. 'I gather some rich guy's bought Easton Court, by the way—Sebastian something or other,' he'd said idly.

'Corder?' she'd suggested, her whole body frozen, her mind whirling, and the man had nodded.

'That's the one. Good luck to him. It deserves rescuing, but it's a good job he's got deep pockets.'

The conversation had moved on, ebbing and flowing around her while she'd tried to make sense of Sebastian's acquisition, but David had asked her about him as they were driving home.

'How do you know this Corder guy?'

'He was a friend of my brother's,' she said casually, although she was feeling far from casual. 'His family live in that area.'

It wasn't a lie, but it wasn't the whole truth and she'd felt a little guilty, but she'd been shocked. No, not shocked. Surprised, more than anything. She'd thought he'd walked away from everything connected to that time, as she had, and the fact that he hadn't had puzzled her. Puzzled and fascinated and horrified her, all at once, because of course it was so close to home, so near to her parents.

Too close for comfort.

But a few days later Josh had been born, and then only weeks after that David had died and her whole world had fallen apart and she'd forgotten it. Forgotten everything, really, except holding it all together for Josh.

But every time since then that she'd visited her parents, she'd avoided the lane, just as she had today—until she'd had no choice.

Her heart thudded against her ribs. Was he in there, behind those intimidating and newly renovated gates? Alone? Or sharing their house with someone else, someone who didn't share the dream—

She cut that thought off before she could follow it. It didn't matter. The dream didn't exist any longer, and she'd moved on. She'd had to. She was a mother now, and there was no time for dreaming. She dragged her eyes and her mind away from the imposing gates and the man who might or might not be behind them, flashed her son a smile to remind her of her priorities and made herself drive on.

Except her car had other ideas. It slithered wildly as she tried to pull away, and the snow swirled around them, the wind battering the car ferociously, reminding her as nothing else could just how perilous their situation was. Gripping the wheel tighter, her heart pounding, she pressed the accelerator again more cautiously and drove on, almost blinded by the blizzard.

Before she'd gone more than a few feet she hit a drift with her right front wheel, and her car slewed round and came to rest across the road, wedged up against the bank behind her. After a few moments of spinning the wheels fruitlessly, she slammed her hand on the steering wheel and stifled a scream of frustration tinged with panic.

'Mummy?'

'It's OK, darling. We're just a teeny bit stuck. I need to have a look outside. I won't be long.'

She tried to open her door, but it wouldn't budge, and she wound the window down and peered out into the blizzard, shielding her eyes from the biting sting of the snow crystals that felt as if they were coming straight from the Arctic.

She was up against a snowdrift, rammed tight into it, and there was no way she'd be able to open the door. She shut the window fast and shook the snow out of her hair.

'Wow! That was a bit blowy!' she said with a grin over her shoulder, but Josh wasn't reassured.

'Don't like it, Mummy,' he said, his lip wobbling ominously.

Nor do I. And I don't need them walking in a winter wonderland on the radio!

'It's fine, Josh. It's just snowing a bit fast at the moment, but it won't last. I'll just get out of the other door and see why we're stuck.'

'No! Mummy stay!'

'Darling, I'll be just outside. I'm not going away.'

'P'omise?'

'I promise.'

She blew him a kiss, scrambled across to the passenger side and fought her way out into the teeth of the blizzard to assess the situation. Difficult, with the biting wind lashing her hair across her eyes and finding its way through her clothes into her very bones, but she checked first one end of the car, then the other, and her heart sank.

It was firmly wedged, jammed between the snow-drift she'd run into on the right and the snow that had fallen down behind them, probably dislodged as she'd slid sideways. The car had embedded itself firmly against the right bank, and there was nothing she could do. She could never dig it out alone with her bare hands, not with the snow drifting so rapidly off the field in the howling wind. It was already a few inches deep. Soon the exhaust pipe would be covered, and the engine would stall, and they'd die of cold.

Literally.

Their only hope, she realised as she shielded her eyes from the snow again and assessed the situation, lay in the house behind those beautiful but intimidating gates.

Easton Court. The home of Sebastian Corder, the man she'd loved with all her heart, the man she'd left because he'd been chasing something she couldn't understand or identify with at the expense of their relationship.

He'd expected her to drop everything and follow him into a lifestyle she hated, abandoning her career, her family, even her principles, and when she'd asked him to reconsider, he'd refused and so she'd walked away, leaving her heart behind...

And now her life and the life of her child might depend on him.

This house, the house she'd fallen so in love with, home of the only man she'd ever really loved, was the last place in the world she wanted to be, its owner the last man in the world she wanted to ask for help. She didn't imagine he'd be any more thrilled than she was, but she had Josh with her, and so she had no choice but to swallow her pride and hope to God he was there.

Heart pounding, she struggled to the gate, lifted a hand so cold she could scarcely feel it and scrubbed the snow away from the intercom with her icy fingers.

'Please be there,' she whispered, 'please help me.' And then, her heart in her mouth, she pressed the button and waited.

The sharp, persistent buzz cut through his concentration, and he stopped what he was doing, pressed save and headed for the hall.

This would be the last of his Christmas deliveries. Hurray for online shopping, he thought, and then glanced out of the window and did a mild double-take. When had it started snowing like that?

He looked at the screen on the intercom and frowned. He couldn't see anything for a moment, just a swirl of white, and then the screen cleared momentarily and he made out the figure of a woman, huddled up in her coat, her hands tucked under her arms—and then she pulled a hand out and swiped snow off the front of the intercom and he saw her clearly.

Georgie?

He felt the blood drain from his head and hauled in a breath, then another one. No. It couldn't be. He was seeing things, conjuring her up out of nowhere because he couldn't stop thinking about her while he was in this damn house—

'Can I help you?' he said crisply, not trusting his eyes, but then she swiped the hair back off her face and anchored it out of the way, and it really was her, her smile tentative but relieved as she heard his voice.

'Oh, Sebastian, thank goodness you're there. I wasn't

sure—um—it's Georgie Pullman. Georgia Becket?
Look, I'm really sorry to trouble you, but can you help
me? I wouldn't ask, but my car's stuck in a snowdrift
just by your gateway, and I don't have a spade to dig
myself out and my phone won't work.'

He hesitated, holding his breath and staring at her
while he groped frantically for a level surface in a world
that suddenly seemed tilted on its axis. And then it
righted and common sense prevailed. Sort of.

'Wait there. I'll drive down. Maybe I can tow you
out.'

'Thanks. You're a star.'

She vanished in a swirl of whiteout, and he let go
of the button with a sharp sigh. What the hell was she
doing driving along the lane in this weather?

Surely not coming to see him? Why would she? She
never had, not once in nine years, and he had no reason
to think she'd do it now—unless it was curiosity about
the house, and he doubted it. Not in this weather, and
probably not at all. Why would she care? She hadn't
cared enough to stay with him.

She'd hated him in the end, and he couldn't blame
her. He'd hated himself, but he'd hated her, too, for what
she'd done to them, for not having faith in him, for not
sticking by him just when he'd needed her the most.

No, she wasn't coming to see him. She'd been going
home to her parents for Christmas, using the short cut,
and now here she was, purely by chance, stuck outside
his house and he had no choice—no damn choice at
all—but to go and dig her out. And that would mean
talking to her, seeing her face, hearing her voice.

Resurrecting a whole shed-load of memories of a
time he'd rather forget.

Dragging that up all over again was the last thing he

needed, but just moving here had done that, anyway, and there was no way he could leave her outside in a blizzard. And it'd be dark soon. The light was failing already. He'd dig her out and send her on her way. Fast, before it was too late and he was stuck with her.

Letting out a low growl, he picked up his car keys, shrugged on his coat, grabbed a shovel and a tow rope from the coach-house and threw them into the back of the Range Rover he'd bought for just this sort of eventuality. Not that he'd ever expected to be digging Georgia out of a hole.

He headed down the drive, his wipers going flat out to clear the screen, but when he got to the gates and opened them with the remote control, there was no sign of her. Just footprints in the deep snow, heading to the left and vanishing fast in the blizzard.

It was far worse than he'd realised. There were no huge, fat flakes that drifted softly down and stayed where they fell, but tiny crystals of snow driven horizontally by the biting wind, the drifts piling up and making the lane impassable. He wondered where the hell she was. It would have been handy to know just how far along—

And then he saw it, literally yards from the end of his drive, the red tail lights dim through the coating of snow over the lenses. He left the car in the gateway and got out, his boots sinking deep into the powdery drifts as he crunched towards her. No wonder she was stuck, going out in weather like this in that ridiculous little car, but there was no way she'd be going anywhere else in it tonight, he realised. Which meant he *would* be stuck with her.

Damn.

He felt anger moving in, taking the place of shock.

Good. Healthy. Better than the sentimental wallowing he'd been doing last night in that damn four-poster bed—

Bracing himself against the wind, he turned his collar up against the needles of ice and strode over to it, opening the passenger door and stooping down. A blast of warmth and Christmas music swamped him, and carried on the warmth was a lingering scent that he remembered so painfully, excruciatingly well.

It hit him like a kick in the gut, and he slammed the lid on his memories and peered inside.

She was kneeling on the seat looking at something in the back, and as she turned towards him she gave him a tentative smile.

'Hi. That was quick. I'm really sorry—'

'Don't worry about it,' he said crisply, trying not to scan her face for changes. 'Right, let's get you out of here.'

'See, Josh?' she said cheerfully. 'I told you he was going to help us.'

Josh? She had a *Josh* who could dig her out?

'Josh?' he said coldly, and her smile softened, stabbing him in the gut.

'My son.'

She had a son?

His heart pounding, he ducked his head in so he could look over the back of the seat—and met wide eyes so familiar they seemed to cut right to his soul.

'Josh, this is Sebastian. He's going to get us unstuck.'

He was? Well, of course he was! How could he refuse those liquid green eyes so filled with uncertainty? Poor little kid.

'Hi, Josh,' he said softly, because after all it wasn't

the child's fault they were stuck, and then he finally let himself look at Georgie.

She hadn't changed at all. She had the same wide, ingenuous eyes as her son, the same soft bow lips, high cheekbones and sweeping brows that had first enchanted him all those years ago. Her wild curls were dark and glossy and beaded with melted snow, and there was a tiny pleat of worry between her brows. And her face was just inches from his, her scent swirling around him in the shelter of the car and making mincemeat of his carefully erected defences.

He hauled his head out of the car and straightened up, sucking in a lungful of freezing air. Better. Slightly. Now if he could just nail those defences back in place again—

'I'm really sorry,' she began again, peering up at him, but he shook his head.

'Don't. Let's just get your car out of here and get you inside.'

'No! I need to get to my parents!'

He let his breath out on a disbelieving huff. 'Georgie, look at it!' he said, gesturing at the weather. 'You're going nowhere. I don't even know if I can get your car out, and you're certainly not taking it anywhere else in the dark.'

'It's not dark—'

'Almost. And we haven't got your car out yet. Just get in the driver's seat, keep the engine running and when you feel a tug let the brakes off and reverse gently back as I pull you. And try and steer it so it doesn't go in the ditch. OK?'

She opened her mouth, shut it again and nodded.

Plenty of time once the car was out to argue with him.

* * *

It took just moments.

The car slithered and slid, and for a second she thought they'd end up in the ditch, but then she felt the tug from behind ease off as they came to rest outside the gates and she put the handbrake on and relaxed her grip on the wheel.

Phase 1 over. Now for Phase 2.

She opened the car door and got out into the blizzard again. He was right there, checking the side of her car that had been wedged against the snowdrift, and he straightened and met her eyes.

'It looks OK. I don't think it's damaged.'

'Good. That's a relief. And thanks for helping me—'

'Don't thank me,' he said bluntly. 'You were blocking the lane, I've only cleared it before the snow plough comes along and mashes it to a pulp.'

She gulped down the snippy retort. Of course he wasn't going to be gracious about it! She was the last person he wanted to turn out to help, but he'd done it anyway, so she swallowed her pride and tried again. 'Well, whatever, I'm still grateful. I'll be on my way now—'

He cut her off with a sharp sigh. 'We've just had this conversation, Georgia. You can't go anywhere. Your car won't get down the lane. Nothing will. I could hardly pull you out with the Range Rover. What on earth possessed you to try and drive down here in weather like this anyway?'

She blinked and stared at him. 'I had to. I'm on my way home to my parents for Christmas, and I thought I'd beat the snow, but it came out of nowhere and for the last hour I've just been crawling along—'

'So why come this way? It's hardly the most sensible route in that little tin can.'

She bristled. Tin can? 'I wasn't coming this way but the other road was closed with an accident—d'you know what? Forget it!' she snapped, losing her temper completely because absolutely the last place in the world she wanted to be snowed in was with this bad-tempered and ungracious reminder of the worst time of her life, and she was seriously leaving now! *In her tin can!* 'I'm really sorry I disturbed you, I'll make sure I never do it again. Just—just go back to your ivory tower and leave me alone and I'll get out of your hair!'

She tried to get back in the car, desperate to get away before the weather got any worse, but his hand shot out and clamped round her wrist like a vice.

'Georgia, grow up! No matter how tempted I am to leave you here to work it out for yourself—and believe me, I am *very* tempted at the moment—I can't let you both die of your stubborn, stiff-necked stupidity.'

Her eyes widened and she glared at him, trying to wrestle her arm free. 'Stubborn, stiff-necked—? Well, you can talk! You're a past master at that! And we're not going to die. You're being ridiculously melodramatic. It's simply not that bad.'

It was his turn to snap then, his temper flayed by that intoxicating scent and the deluge of memories that apparently just wouldn't be stopped. He tugged her closer, glowering down into her face as the scent assailed him once more.

'Are you sure?' he growled. 'Because I can leave you here to test the theory, if you insist, but I am *not* leaving your son in the car with you while you do it.'

'You can't touch him—'

'Watch me,' he said flatly. 'He's—what? Two? Three?'

The fight went out of her eyes, replaced by maternal worry. 'Two. He's two.'

He closed his eyes fleetingly and swallowed the wave of nausea. He'd been two...

'Right,' he said, his voice tight but reasoned now, 'I'm going to unhitch my car, drive into the entrance and hitch yours up again and pull you up the drive—'

'No. Just leave me here,' she pleaded. 'We'll be all right. The accident will be cleared by now. I'll turn round and go back the other way—'

His mouth flattened into a straight, implacable line. 'No. Believe me, I don't want this any more than you do, but unlike you I take my responsibilities seriously—'

'How dare you!' she yelled, because that was just the last straw. 'I take my responsibilities seriously! *Nothing* is more important to me than Josh!'

'Then prove it! Get in the car, shut up and do as you're told just for *once* in your life before we all freeze to death—and turn that blasted radio off!'

He dropped her arm like a hot brick, and she got back in the car, slammed the door unnecessarily hard and a shower of snow slid off the roof and blocked the wipers.

'Mummy?'

Oh, Josh.

'It's OK, darling.' Hell, her voice was shaking. She was shaking all over—

'Don't like him. Why he cross?'

'He's just cross with the snow, Josh, like Mummy. It's OK.'

A gloved hand swiped across the screen and the wipers started moving again, clearing it just enough that she could see his car in front of her now, pointing into the gateway. He was bending over, looking for the towing eye, probably, and seconds later he was dropping a loop over the tow hitch on his car and easing away from her.

She felt the tug, then the car slithered round and followed him obediently while she quietly seethed. Behind them she could see the gates begin to close, trapping her inside, and in front of them lights glowed dimly in the gloom.

Easton Court, home of her broken dreams.

Her prison for the next however long?

She should have just sat it out in the traffic jam.

CHAPTER TWO

HE TOWED HER all the way up the drive and round into the old stable yard behind the house, and by the time he pulled up he'd got his temper back under control.

Not so the memories, but if he could just keep his mouth shut he might not say anything he'd regret.

Anything *else* he'd regret. Too late for what he'd already said today, and far too late for all the words they'd said nine years ago, the bitterness and acrimony and destruction they'd brought down on their relationship.

All this time later, he still couldn't see who'd been right or wrong, or even if there'd been a right or wrong at all. He just knew he missed her, he'd never stopped missing her, and all he'd done about it in those intervening years was to ignore it, shut it away in a cupboard marked 'No Entry'.

And she'd just ripped the door right off it. She and this damned house. Well, that would teach him to give in to sentiment. He should have let it rot and then he wouldn't have been here.

So who would have rescued them? No-one?

He sucked in a deep breath, got out of the car and detached the tow rope, flinging it back into the car on top of the shovel just in case there were any other lunatics out on the lane today, although he doubted it. He could hardly see his hand in front of his face for the snow now, and that was in the shelter of the stable yard.

Dammit, if this didn't let up soon he was going to be stuck with her for days, her and her two-year-old son, with fathoms-deep eyes that could break your heart. And that, more than anything, was what was getting to him. The child, and what might have happened to him if he'd not been there to help—

'Oh, man up, Corder,' he growled to himself, and slammed the tailgate.

'OK, little guy?'

She turned and looked at Josh over her shoulder, his face all eyes and doubt.

'Want G'annie and G'anpa.'

'I know, but we can't get there today because of the snow, so we're going to stay here tonight with Sebastian in his lovely house and have an adventure!'

She tried to smile, but it felt so false. She was dreading going inside with Sebastian into the house that contained so much of their past. It would trash all her happy memories, and the tense, awkward atmosphere, the unspoken recriminations, the hurt and pain and regret lurking just under the surface of her emotions would make this so difficult to cope with, but it wasn't his fault she was here and the least she could do was be a little gracious and accept his grudging hospitality.

She glanced round as her nemesis walked over to her car and opened the door.

'I'm sorry.'

They said it in unison, and he gave her a crooked smile that tore at her heart and stood back to let her out.

'Let's get you both in out of this. Can I give you a hand with anything?'

'Luggage? Realistically I'm not going anywhere to-night, am I?' She said it with a wry smile, and he let out a soft huff of laughter and started to pick up the luggage she was pulling from the boot.

He wondered how much one woman and a very small boy could possibly need for a single night. Baby stuff, he guessed, and slung a soft bag over his shoulder as he picked up another case and a long rectangular object she said was a travel cot.

'That should do for now. I might need to come back for something later.'

'OK.' He shut the tailgate as she opened the back door and reached in, emerging moments later with Josh.

Her son, he thought, and was shocked at the surge of jealousy at the thought of her carrying another man's child.

The grapevine had failed him, because he hadn't known she'd had a baby, but he'd known that her husband had died. A while ago now—a year, maybe two. While she was pregnant? The jealousy ebbed away, replaced by compassion. God, that must have been tough. Tough for all of them.

The boy looked at him solemnly for a moment with those huge, wary eyes that bored right through to his soul and found him wanting, and Sebastian turned away, swallowing a sudden lump in his throat, and led them in out of the cold.

'Oh!'

She stopped dead in the doorway and stared around her, her jaw sagging. He'd brought her into the old-est part of the house, through a lobby that acted as a boot room and into a warm and welcoming kitchen that could have stepped straight out of the pages of a glossy magazine.

His smile was wry. 'It's a bit different, isn't it?' he offered, and she gave a slight, disbelieving laugh.

The last time she'd seen it, it had been dark, gloomy and had birds nesting in it.

Not any more. Now, it was...

'Just a bit,' she said weakly. 'Wow.'

He watched her as she looked round the kitchen, her lips parted, her eyes wide. She was taking in every detail of the transformation, and he assessed her reaction, despising himself for caring what she thought and yet somehow, in some deep, dark place inside himself that he didn't want to analyse, needing her approval.

Ridiculous. He didn't need her approval for anything in his life. She'd given up the right to ask for that on the day she'd walked out, and he wasn't giving it back to her now, tacitly or otherwise.

He shrugged off his coat and hung it over the back of a chair by the Aga, then picked up the kettle.

'Tea?'

She dragged her eyes away from her cataloguing of the changes to the house and looked at him warily, nibbling her lip with even white teeth until he found himself longing to kiss away the tiny indentations she was leaving in its soft, pink plumpness—

'If you don't mind.'

But they'd already established that he did mind, in that tempestuous and savage exchange outside the gate, and he gave an uneven sigh and rammed a hand through his hair. It was wet with snow, dripping down his neck, and hers must be, too. Hating himself for that loss of temper and control, he got a tea towel out of the drawer and handed it to her, taking another one for himself.

'Here,' he said gruffly. 'Your hair's wet. Go and stand by the Aga and warm up.'

It wasn't an apology, but it could have been an olive branch and she accepted it as that. They were stuck with each other, there was nothing either of them could do about it, and Josh was cold and scared and hungry. And the snow was dripping off her hair and running down her face.

She propped herself up on the front of the Aga, Josh on her hip, and towelled her hair with her free hand while she tried not to study him. 'Tea would be lovely, please, and if you've got one Josh would probably like a biscuit.'

'No problem. I think we could probably withstand a siege—my entire family are here for Christmas from tomorrow so the cupboards are groaning. It's my first Christmas in the house and I offered to host it for my sins.'

'I expect they're looking forward to it. Your parents must be glad to have you close again.'

He gave a slightly bitter smile and turned away, giving her a perfect view of his broad shoulders as he got mugs out of a cupboard. 'Needs must. My mother's not well. She had a heart attack three years ago, and they gave her a by-pass at Easter.'

Ouch. She'd loved his mother, but his relationship with her had been a little rocky, although she'd never really been able to work out why. 'I'm sorry to hear that. I didn't know. I hope she's OK now.'

'She's getting over it—and why would you know? Unless you're keeping tabs on my family as well as me?' he said, his voice deceptively mild as he turned to look at her with those penetrating dark eyes.

She stared at him, taken aback by that. 'I'm not keeping tabs on you!'

'But you knew I was living here. When I answered the intercom, you knew it was me. There was no hesitation.'

As if she wouldn't have known his voice anywhere, she thought with a dull ache in her chest.

'I didn't know you'd moved in,' she told him honestly. 'That was just sheer luck under the circumstances, but the fact that you'd bought it was hardly a state secret. You were rescuing a listed house of historical importance on the verge of ruin, and people were talking about it. Bear in mind my husband was an estate agent.'

He frowned. That made sense. He contemplated saying something, but what? Sorry he'd died? Bit late to offer his condolences, and he hadn't felt able to at the time. Because it felt inappropriate? Probably. Or just keeping his distance from her, desperately trying to keep her in that cupboard she'd just ripped the door off. And now, in front of the child, wasn't the time to initiate that conversation.

So, after a pause in which he filled the kettle, he brought the subject back to the house. Safer, marginally, so long as he kept his memories under control.

'I didn't realise it had caused such a stir,' he said casually.

'Well, of course it did. It was on the at-risk register for years. I think everyone expected it to fall down before it was sold.'

'It wasn't that close. There wasn't much wrong with it that money couldn't solve, but the owner couldn't afford to do anything other than repair the roof and he hadn't wanted to sell it for development, so before he died he put a restrictive covenant on it to say it couldn't be di-

vided or turned into a hotel. And apparently nobody
wants a house like this any more. Too costly to repair,
too costly to run, too much red tape because of the list-
ing—it goes on and on, and so it just sat here waiting
while the executors tried to get the covenant lifted.'

'And then you rescued it.'

Because he hadn't been able to forget it. Or her.

'Yeah, well, we all make mistakes sometimes,' he
muttered, and lifting the hob cover, he put the kettle
on, getting another drift of her scent as he did so. He
moved away, making a production of finding biscuits
for Josh as he opened one cupboard after another, and
she watched him thoughtfully.

We all make mistakes sometimes.

Really? He thought it was a mistake? Why? Because it had been a money-sink? Or because of all the
memories—memories that were haunting her even
now, standing here with him in the house where they'd
fallen in love?

'Well, mistake or not,' she said softly, 'I'm really glad
you're here, because otherwise we'd still be out there in
the snow and it's not letting up. And you're right,' she
acknowledged. 'It could have ended quite differently.'

He met her eyes then, his brows tugging briefly together in a frown. He'd only been back here a couple
of days. And if he'd still been away—

'Yes. It could. Look, we'll see how it is tomorrow. If
the wind drops and the snow eases off, I might be able
to get you to your parents in the Range Rover, even if
you can't get your car there for now.'

She nodded. 'Thank you. That would be great. And
I really am sorry. I know I was a stroppy cow out there,
but I was just scared and I wanted to get home.'

His mouth flickered in a brief smile. 'Don't worry

about it. So—I take it you approve of what I've done in here?' he asked to change the subject, and then wanted to kick himself. Finally engaging his brain on the task of finding some biscuits, he opened the door of the pantry cupboard and stared at the shelves while he had another go at himself for fishing for her approval.

'Well, I do so far,' she said to his back. 'If this is representative of the rest of the house, you've done a lovely job of rescuing it.'

'Thanks.' He just stopped himself from offering her a guided tour, and grabbed a packet of amaretti biscuits and turned towards her. 'Are these OK?' he asked, and she nodded.

'Lovely. Thank you. He really likes those.'

Josh pointed at them and squirmed to get down. 'Biscuit,' he said, eyeing Sebastian as if he didn't quite trust him.

'Say please,' she prompted.

'P'ees.'

She put him on the floor and took off his coat, tugging the cuffs as he pulled his arms out, but then instead of coming over to get a biscuit from him, he stood there next to her, one arm round her leg, watching Sebastian with those wary eyes.

He opened the packet, then held it out.

'Here. Take them to Mummy, see if she wants one.'

He hesitated for a second then let go of her leg and took the packet, eyes wide, and ran back to her, tripping as he got there and scattering a few on the floor.

'Oops—three second rule,' she said with a grin that kicked him in the chest, and knelt down and gathered them up.

'Here,' he said, offering her a plate, and she put them on it and stood up with a rueful smile, just inches from him.

'Sorry about that.'

He backed away to a safe distance. 'Don't worry about it. It was my fault, I didn't think. He's only little.'

'Oh, he can do it. He's just a bit overawed by it all.'

And on the verge of tears now, hiding his face in his mother's legs and looking uncertain.

'Hey, I reckon we'd better eat these up, don't you, Josh?' Sebastian said encouragingly, and he took one of the slightly chipped biscuits from the plate, then glanced at Georgia. 'In case you're wondering, the floor's pristine. It was washed this morning.'

'No pets?'

He shook his head. 'No pets.'

'I thought a dog by the fire was part of the dream?' she said lightly, and then could have kicked herself, because his face shut down and he turned away.

'I gave up dreaming nine years ago,' he said flatly, and she let out a quiet sigh and gave Josh a biscuit.

'Sorry. Forget I said that. I'm on autopilot. In fact, do you think I could borrow your landline? I should call my mother—but I can't get a signal. She'll be wondering where we are.'

'Sure. There's one there.'

She nodded, picked it up and turned away, and he glanced down at the child.

Their eyes met, and Josh studied him briefly before pointing at the biscuits. 'More biscuit. And d'ink, Mummy.'

Georgia found a feeder cup and gave it to him to give Sebastian. 'What do you say?' she prompted from the other side of the kitchen.

'P'ees.'

'Good boy.' Sebastian smiled at him as he took the

cup, and the child smiled back shyly, making his heart squeeze.

Poor little tyke. He'd been expecting to go to his loving and welcoming grandparents, and he'd ended up with a grumpy recluse with a serious case of the sulks. Good job, Corder.

'Here, let's sit down,' he said, and sat on the floor, handed Josh his plastic feeder cup, and they tucked into the biscuits while he tried not to eavesdrop on Georgie's conversation.

She glanced over her shoulder, and saw Josh was on the floor with Sebastian. They seemed to be demolishing the entire plateful of biscuits, and she hid a smile.

He'd never eat all his supper, but frankly she didn't care. The fact that Josh wasn't still clinging to her leg was a minor miracle, and she let them get on with it while she soothed her mother.

'Mum, we're fine. The person who lives here is taking very good care of us, and he's been very kind and got my car off the road, so we're warm and safe and it's all good.'

'Are you sure? Because you can't be too careful.'

'Absolutely. It's just for tonight, and it'll be clear by tomorrow. They've got a Range Rover so he's going to give us a lift,' she said optimistically, crossing her fingers.

'Oh, well, that's all right, then,' her mother said with relief in her voice. 'I'm glad you're both safe, we were worried sick when you didn't ring, so do keep in touch. We'll see you tomorrow, and you stay safe. And give my love to Josh.'

'Will do. Bye, Mum.'

She cut the connection and put the phone back on

the charger, then turned and met his eyes. A brow flickered eloquently.

'They?' he murmured.

'Figure of speech.' And less of a red flag to her mother than 'he'...

He humphed slightly. 'You didn't tell her where you are.'

She blinked. 'Why would I?'

The brow flickered again. 'Lying by omission?'

She shrugged off her coat and draped it over a chair next to his at the huge table. 'It's not a lie, it's just an unnecessary fact that changes nothing material. And what she doesn't know...'

He didn't answer, just held her eyes for an endless moment before turning away. The kettle had boiled and he was making tea now while Josh cleaned up the last few crumbs on the plate, and she picked it up before he could break it.

'Here—your tea.' Sebastian put her cup down in the middle of the table out of Josh's reach and picked up his coat.

'Give me your keys. I'll put your car away in the coach-house. Is there anything else you need out of it?'

'Oh. There's a bag of Christmas presents. There are some things in there that don't really need to freeze. It's in the boot.'

'OK.' She passed him the keys and he went out, and she let the breath ease out of her lungs.

Just one night, she told herself. *You can do this. And at least you know he's not an axe murderer, so it could have been worse.*

'Mummy, finished.'

Josh handed her his cup and she found him a book in the changing bag and sat him on her lap. She was reading to him when Sebastian came back in a few minutes later, stamping snow off his boots and brushing it off his head and shoulders.

She put her tea down and stared at him in dismay. 'No sign of it stopping, then?'

He shook his head and held out her keys, and she reached out to take them, her fingers closing round his for a moment. They were freezing cold, wet with the snow, and she shivered slightly with the thought of what might have been. If he hadn't been here...

'Sebastian—thank you. For everything.'

His eyes searched hers, then flicked away. 'You're welcome.' He shrugged off his coat and hung it up again. 'I'll go and make sure your room's ready.'

'You don't need to do that just for one night! I can sleep on a sofa—'

He stared at her as if she'd sprouted another head. 'It's a ten-bedroomed house! Why on earth would you want to do that?'

'I just don't want you to go to any more trouble.'

'It's no trouble, the rooms are already made up. Where do you want these?'

'Ah.' She eyed the presents. 'Can you find somewhere for them that's not my room? Just to be on the safe side.'

'Sure. If you need the cloakroom it's at the end of the hall.'

He picked up all her bags and went out, and she let out her breath on another sigh. She hadn't realised she'd been holding it again, and the slackening of tension when he left the room was a huge relief.

She felt a tug on her sweater. 'Mummy, more biscuit.'

'No, Josh. You can't have any more. You won't eat your supper.'

'Supper at G'annie's house?' he said hopefully, and she shook her head, watching his face fall.

'No, darling, we're staying here. Grannie sends you her love and a great big kiss and she'll see you tomorrow, if it's stopped snowing.' Which it had better have done soon. She scooped him up and kissed him.

'I tell you what, why don't we play hide and seek?' she suggested, trying to inject some excitement into her voice, and he giggled and squirmed down. As she counted to ten he disappeared under the table, his little rump sticking out between the chair legs.

'I hiding! Mummy find me!'

'Oh! Where's he gone? Josh? Jo-osh, where are you?' she called softly, in a sing-song voice, and pretended to look. She opened the door Sebastian had got the biscuits from, and found a pantry cupboard laden with goodies. Heavens, he was right, they were ready for a siege! The shelves were groaning with expensive food from exclusive London shops like Fortnum's and Harrods, and the contents of the pantry were probably equal to her annual food budget.

She shut the door quickly and went back to her 'search' for the giggling child. 'Jo-osh! Where are you?'

She opened another cupboard, and found an enormous built-in fridge, then behind the next door a huge crockery cupboard. It was an exquisitely made hand-built painted kitchen, every piece custom made of solid wood and beautifully constructed, finished in a muted grey eggshell that went perfectly with the cream walls and the black slate floor. And rather than granite, the worktops were made of oiled wood—more traditional, softer than granite, warmer somehow.

The whole effect was classy and elegant at the same time as being homely and welcoming, and it was also well designed, an efficient working triangle. He'd done it properly—or someone had—

'Mummy! I here!'

'Josh? Goodness, I'm sure I can hear you, but I can't see you anywhere!'

'I under the table!'

'Under the table?'

She knelt down and peered through the legs of the chairs, bottom in the air, and of course that was how Sebastian found her when he came in a second later.

'Georgie?'

She closed her eyes briefly. *Marvellous*. She lifted her head and swiped her hair back out of her eyes as she sat back on her heels, her dignity in tatters. She could feel her cheeks flaming, and she swallowed hard. 'Hi,' she said, trying to smile. 'We're playing hide and seek.'

He gave a soft, rueful laugh. 'Nothing much changes, does it?' he murmured, and she felt heat sweep over her body.

They'd played hide and seek in the house often after that first time, and every time he'd found her, he'd kissed her.

She remembered it vividly, so vividly, and she could feel her cheeks burning up.

'Apparently not,' she said, and got hastily to her feet, brushing the non-existent dust from her jeans, ridiculously flustered. 'Um—I could probably do with changing his nappy. Where did you put our bags?'

'In your room. It's the one at the end of the landing on the right—do you want me to show you?'

'That might be an idea.'

Not because she needed showing, but because she didn't want to be tempted to stray into his room. He would have the master suite in the middle at the front, overlooking the carriage sweep, and the stairs came up right beside it.

Too tempting.

She called Josh, took his hand in hers and followed Sebastian up the elegant Georgian staircase and resolutely past the slightly open door of the bedroom where she'd given him her body—and her heart...

Why on earth had he brought up the past when she'd mentioned hide and seek?

Idiot, he chided himself. He'd already had to leave the kitchen on the pretext of putting the cars away when she'd taken her coat off and he'd seen the lush, feminine curves that motherhood had given her.

She'd always had curves, but they were rounder now, softer somehow, utterly unlike the scrawny beanpoles he normally came into contact with, and he ached to touch her, to mould the soft fullness, to cradle the smooth swell of her bottom in his hand and ease her closer.

Much closer.

So much closer that he'd had to get out of the kitchen and give himself a moment.

Now he realised it was going to take a miracle, not a moment, because when he'd run out of things to do he'd walked back in to the sight of that rounded bottom sticking up into the air as she played under the table with the baby, and then she'd straightened, her cheeks still pink from bending over, and he'd seen straight down the V neck of her sweater to the enticing valley between those soft, rounded breasts and lust had hit him like a sledgehammer.

'Here,' he said, pushing open the door of her room. 'It's got its own bathroom, but I haven't put up the travel cot, I'm afraid. I wouldn't know where to start—is that OK? Can you manage?'

'Oh. Yes. That's fine. Um—I don't suppose you've got a small blanket—a fleecy one or something? And a sheet? I don't have any bedding with me because my mother keeps some at hers.'

'I'm sure I can find something. I'll see you in the kitchen when you're done,' he said, and left them to it.

She looked around at the lovely room, beautifully furnished with antiques, and wondered who'd sourced everything. Him? It seemed unlikely. He'd probably paid an interior designer an obscene amount of money to do it, but that was fine, he had it.

He'd been outrageously successful, by all accounts, made a killing on the stock market in the early days and re-invested the money in other businesses. He had a reputation for being fair but firm, and companies that he'd taken over had been turned around and sold for vast amounts, or retained in his portfolio to earn him a nice little income.

Not that she'd been keeping tabs on him...

She sighed. 'Come here, Josh. Let's do your nappy.'

But Josh was exploring, investigating the utterly decadent bathroom with its free-standing white-enamelled bateau bath, the vintage loo with ornate high level cistern and gleaming brass downpipe, the vintage china basin set on an old marble-topped washstand painted the same soft grey as the kitchen and the outside of the bath. There was a rack piled high with sumptuous, fluffy white towels, and expensive toiletries stood on the side of the washstand.

Gorgeous. Utterly, utterly gorgeous. She eyed the bath longingly. Maybe later.

'Come on, tinker. Let's change you.'

But he ran off, giggling, and she had to chase him and catch him and pin him down, squirming like an eel and brimming with mischief. No wonder she didn't need the gym! Even if she had time, which she didn't. She hitched his trousers back up victoriously, mission accomplished, and grinned at him.

'Right, let's go back downstairs and have that tea, shall we?'

And see Sebastian again.

She bit her lip. He was being polite but distant, and she told herself it was what she wanted. Well, of course it was.

Except apparently her heart didn't think so, and a tiny corner of it was disappointed that he hadn't seemed pleased to see her. Well, what had she expected? She'd dumped him because he was too ambitious, too driven, too different from the boy she'd fallen in love with four years earlier, and he hadn't even tried to understand how she'd felt.

She obviously hadn't been that important to him then, and she certainly wouldn't be now, toting another man's child.

She rounded Josh up, took his hand and led him towards the stairs, but then he slipped out of her grasp and ran through a doorway.

The doorway to the master bedroom, she realised, and her heart sank.

'Josh? Come out. That's not our room.'

Silence.

Which left her no choice but to go in...

She pushed the door open and looked around, and the first thing she saw was the bed, huge, beautiful, piled high with snowy white linen and taking her breath away. To be fair, it would have been hard to miss even in such a large room, but it dominated the space, leaping out of her fantasies and taunting her with its perfection, and she felt her cheeks burn.

She dragged her eyes away from it and looked around.

There was no sign of Josh—but the cupboard was there in the corner, the cupboard where she'd hidden, where Sebastian had found her and kissed her the first time.

And there, in front of the fireplace, was where he'd spread the blanket covered in petals and—

'Mummy, find me!'

She pressed a hand to her chest and sucked in a slow, steadying breath. What on earth was she *doing*? Why was she there? She shouldn't be here, in this room, in this house, with this man!

With her memories running riot—

'Mummy!'

She let out her breath, drew it in again and pinned a smile on her face, because he could always tell if she was smiling.

'Ready or not, here I come,' she sang, and heard the words echo down the years, ringing in the empty corridors as she'd hidden in the cupboard and held back her innocent, girlish laughter.

And then he'd kissed her and everything had changed...

CHAPTER THREE

THEY WERE TAKING ages.

Maybe she'd decided to unpack, or bath Josh, or perhaps she was lost.

He gave a soft snort. As if. She knew the house like the back of her hand. More likely she was exploring, giving herself a guided tour. She'd always considered the house to be her own private property. The concept of trespass never seemed to occur to her.

He went to look for her, taking the soft woollen throw he'd found for Josh's bed, and saw his bedroom door standing wide open and voices coming from inside.

'Josh, now! Come out from under there this minute or I'm going downstairs without you.'

Irritated, he walked in and was greeted yet again by that delectable bottom sticking up in the air. Was she doing it on purpose? He dragged his eyes off it. 'Problems?' he asked crisply.

She jerked upright, her hand on her heart, and gave a little gasp. 'Oh—you startled me. I'm *so* sorry. The door was open and he ran in here and he's hiding under the middle of the bed and I can't reach him.'

She sounded exasperated and embarrassed, and he gave her the benefit of the doubt.

'Two-pronged attack?' he suggested with a slightly

strained smile, and went round to the other side of the bed and lay down. 'Hello, Josh. Time to come out, little man.'

Josh shook his head and wriggled towards the other side, and then shrieked and giggled as his mother's hand closed over his arm and tugged gently.

'Come on, or you won't have supper.'

'Want biscuits.'

Sebastian opened his mouth to offer them and caught the warning look she shot him under the bed, and winked. 'No biscuits,' he said firmly. 'Not unless you come straight out and eat all your supper first.'

He was out in seconds, and Georgie scooped him up and plonked him firmly on her hip. She was smiling apologetically, her hair wildly tangled and out of control, those teeth catching her lip again, and he wanted her so much he could hardly breathe.

The air was full of tension, and he wondered if she was remembering that he'd kissed her here for the first time. They'd been playing hide and seek, and she'd hidden in the cupboard beside the chimney breast. He'd found her easily, just followed the sound of her muted laughter and hauled the door open to find her there, hand over her mouth to hold in the giggles, eyes so like Josh's brimming with mischief and something else, something much, much older than either of them, as old as time, and he'd followed her into the cupboard, cradled her face in his hands and kissed her.

He thought he'd died and gone to heaven.

'You kept the cupboard,' she said, her eyes flicking to it briefly, and he knew she was remembering it. Remembering, too, when he'd spread a picnic blanket on the middle of the bedroom floor and scattered it with

the petals of the wisteria that still grew outside the bedroom window and laid her gently down—

'Yes. Well, it's useful,' he said gruffly, and dragged
in some much-needed air. 'I put the kettle on because
your tea was cold. It'll be boiling its head off.'

She seemed to draw herself back from the brink of
something momentous, and her eyes flicked to his and
away again, just as they had with the cupboard.

'Yes. Yes, it will. Come on, Josh, let's go and find
you some supper.' She spun on her heel and walked
swiftly out, the sound of her footsteps barely audible
on the soft, thick carpet, and he didn't breathe until he
heard her boot heels click hurriedly across the hall floor.

Then he let the air out in a rush and sat down heav-
ily on the edge of the huge four-poster bed his interior designer had sourced for him without consultation
and which haunted him every time he came in here.
He sucked in another breath, but her scent was in the
air and he closed his eyes, his hands fisting in the soft
woollen throw, and struggled with a tidal wave of need
and want and lust.

How was he going to survive this? The snow hadn't
let up at all, and the forecast was atrocious. With that
vicious wind blowing the snow straight off the field
and dumping it in the lane, there was no way they'd be
out of here in days, Range Rover or not. Nothing but a
snow plough could get past three foot drifts, and that's
what they'd been heading towards an hour ago.

Maybe the wind would drop overnight, he thought,
but it was a vain hope. He could hear it now, rattling the
windows in the front of the house, sweeping straight
across from Siberia like a solid wall.

He swore under his breath, hauled in another lungful of air, straightened his shoulders and headed down-stairs.

He'd keep out of her way. He could be polite but distant, give her the run of the kitchen and her bed-room and hide out in his study. Except he didn't want to, he discovered as he reached the hall and followed the sound of voices to the kitchen as if he'd been drawn by a magnet.

She turned with a wary smile as he walked in, and set a mug down on the table.

'I made you tea.'

'Thanks. What about Josh? What will he eat?'

'I don't know what you've got.'

He laughed softly and rolled his eyes. 'Everything. I gave my PA a guest list, a menu plan and a fairly loose brief. She used her initiative liberally.'

'I don't suppose she got any fish fingers?'

He felt himself recoil slightly. 'I doubt it. There's smoked salmon.'

She was suppressing a smile, and he could feel him-self responding. 'So—shall I just look?' she suggested, and he nodded and gestured at the kitchen.

'Help yourself. Clearly I would have no idea where to start.'

He dropped into a chair and watched her and the child as she foraged in the cupboards and came up tri-umphant.

'Pasta and pesto with cherry tomatoes, Josh?'

Josh nodded and ran to a chair, trying to pull it out.

'I have to cook it, darling. Five minutes. Why don't you sit and read your book?'

But reading the book was boring, apparently, and he came over to Sebastian and leaned against his legs and looked up at him hopefully. 'Hide and seek?' he asked, and Sebastian stared at Georgie a trifle desperately because the very *last* thing he wanted to play was hide and seek, with his memories running riot—

'Won't he get lost?'

'In here? Hardly.'

'Just in here? There's nowhere to hide.'

'Oh, you'd be surprised,' she said, her laugh like music to his ears. 'Go and hide, Josh. Sebastian will count to ten and look for you.' She met his eyes over the table, mischief dancing in them. 'It's simple. He "hides",' she explained with little air quotes, 'and you look for him. I'm sure you can remember how it works.'

Oh, yes. He could remember how it all worked, particularly the finding part. She'd never made that difficult after the first time...

He closed his eyes briefly, and when he opened them she'd looked away and was halving cherry tomatoes.

'Well, go on, then. Count!'

So he counted to ten, deluged with memories that refused to stay in their box, and then he got to his feet, ignoring the giggling child under the table, and said softly, 'Ready or not, here I come!'

Their eyes met, and he felt his heart bump against his ribs. The air seemed to be sucked out of the room, the tension palpable. And then she dropped the knife with a clatter, bent to pick it up and turned away, and he found he could breathe again.

'Has he settled?'

'Finally. I'm sorry it took so long.'

'Don't worry about it. It's a strange place. Will he be all right up there on his own?'

'Yes, he's gone out like a light now and I've got the baby monitor.'

He nodded. He was sprawled on a chair by the Aga, legs outstretched and crossed at the ankle, one arm resting on the dining table with a glass of wine held loosely in his fingers, watching the news.

He tilted his head towards the screen. 'The country seems to be gridlocked,' he said drily.

'Well, that's not a surprise. It always is if it snows.'

'Yeah. Well, there's over a foot already in the courtyard and the wind hasn't let up at all which doesn't bode well for the lane.'

'Which means you're stuck with us, then, doesn't it?' she said, her heart sinking, and swallowed. 'I'm so, so sorry. I should have left earlier, paid more attention to the weather forecast.' Gone the other way and stayed in the traffic jam, and she'd have been home by now instead of putting them both in this impossibly difficult situation.

He shook his head. 'They got it wrong. The wind picked up, a high pressure area shifted, and that was it. Not even you could cause this much havoc.'

But a wry smile softened his words, and he slid the bottle towards her. 'Try this. It's quite interesting. I've found some duck breasts. I thought it might go rather nicely.'

She poured a little into the clean glass that was waiting, and sipped. 'Mmm. Lovely. So—do you want me to cook for us?'

'No, I'll do it.'

She blinked. 'You can cook?'

'No,' he said drily. 'I have a resident housekeeper and if she's got a day off I get something delivered from the restaurant over the road—of course I can cook! I've been looking after myself for years. And anyway, my mother taught me.' He uncrossed his legs and stood up.

'So—how does pan-fried duck breast with a red wine and redcurrant *jus* on root-vegetable mash with tender-stem broccoli and julienne carrots sound?'

'Like a restaurant menu,' she said, trying not to laugh at him, but she had to bite her lips and he balled up a tea towel and threw it at her, his lips twitching.

'So is that yes or no?'

'Oh, yes—please. But only if you can manage it,' she added mischievously.

He rolled his eyes. 'Don't push your luck or you'll end up with beans on toast,' he warned, and rolled up his sleeves and started emptying the fridge onto the worktop.

'Can I help?'

'Yes. You can lay the table. I'll let you.'

'Big of you.'

'It is. Do it properly. The cutlery's in this drawer.'

She threw the tea towel back, catching him squarely in the middle of his chest, and he grabbed it and chuckled, and for a second the years seemed to melt away.

And then he turned, picking up a knife, and the moment was gone.

It was no hardship to watch him while he cooked.

She studied every nuance of his body, tracking the changes brought about in nine years. He'd only been twenty-one then, nearly twenty-two. Now, he was thirty-one, and a man in his prime.

Not that he'd been anything other than a man then, there'd been no doubt about that, but now his shoulders under the soft cotton shirt seemed broader, more solidly muscled, and he seemed a little taller. The skilfully cut trousers hugged the same neat hips, though, and hinted at the taut muscles of his legs. She'd always loved his legs, and every time he shifted, her body tightened in response.

And while she watched, greedily drinking in every movement of the frame she'd once known so well, he peeled and chopped and sliced, mashed and seasoned, deglazed the frying pan with a sizzle of the lovely red, stirred in a hefty dollop of port and redcurrant sauce and then arranged it all with mathematical precision on perfectly warmed plates.

'Voilà!'

He set the plates down on the places she'd laid, and she smiled. 'Very pretty.'

'We aim to please. Dig in.'

She dug, her mouth watering, and it was every bit as good as it looked and smelled.

'Oh, wow,' she mumbled, and he gave a wry huff of laughter.

'See? No faith in me. You never have had.'

Georgie shook her head. 'I've always had faith in you. I always knew you'd be a success, and you are.'

Even if she hadn't been able to live with him any more.

He shrugged. There was success, and then there was happiness. That still eluded him, chased out by a restless, fretful search for his identity, his fundamental self, and it had cost him Georgia and everything that went with her. Everything she'd then had with another man—and he really didn't want to think about that. He changed the subject. Sort of.

'Josh seems a nice little kid. I didn't know you'd had a child.'

She met his eyes, her fork suspended in mid-air. 'Why would you unless you were keeping tabs on me?'

A smile touched his eyes. 'Touché,' he murmured

softly, and the smile faded. 'I was sorry to hear about your husband. That must have been tough for you.'

Tough? He didn't know the half of it. 'It was,' she said quietly.

'What happened?'

She put her fork down. 'He had a heart attack. He was at work and I had a call to say he'd collapsed and died at his desk.'

He winced. 'Ouch. Wasn't he a bit young for that?'

'Thirty-nine. And we'd just moved and extended the mortgage, so things are a bit tight.'

'What about the life insurance? Surely that covered the mortgage?'

Her mouth twisted slightly. 'He'd cancelled it three months before.'

That shocked him. 'Cancelled it? Why would he cancel it?'

'Cash flow, I presume. Property wasn't selling, and because he'd cancelled the insurance of course they won't pay out, so I'm having to work full-time to pay the mortgage. And it's still not selling, so I can't shift the house, and I'm stuck.'

He rammed a hand through his hair. 'Oh, George. That's tough. I'm sorry.'

'Yeah, me, too, but there's nothing I can do. I just have to get on with it.'

He frowned, slowly turning his wine glass round and round by the stem with his thumb and forefinger. 'So what do you do with Josh while you're at work?'

'I have him with me. I work at home—mostly at night. He goes to nursery three mornings a week to give me a straight stretch of time, and it just about works.'

He topped up her glass and leaned back against the chair, his eyes searching her face. 'So what do you do?'

She smiled. 'I'm a virtual PA. My boss is very under-standing, and we get by, but I won't pretend it's easy.'

'No, I'm sure it's not.' For either of them. He thought of how he'd manage if he and Tash weren't in the same office, and then realised that they weren't for a lot of the time, but that was because he was the one out of the office, not her, and she was there in the thick of it and able to get him answers at the touch of a button.

The other way round—well, the mind boggled.

'How old was Josh when it happened?'

'Two months.'

Sebastian felt sick. 'He won't remember him at all,' he said, his voice sounding hollow to his ears. 'That's such a shame.'

'It is, it's a real shame. David was so proud of him. He would have adored him.'

'You will tell Josh all about him, won't you?'

'Of course I will. And he's got grandparents, too. David's parents live in Cambridge. Don't worry. He'll know all about his father, Sebastian. I won't let him grow up in a vacuum.'

He felt the tension leave him, but a wave of grief followed it. He hadn't grown up in a vacuum, but he'd been living a lie and he hadn't known it until he was eighteen. And then this void had opened up, a yawning hole where once had been certainty, and nothing had been the same since. Especially not since he'd been privy to the finer details. Not that there was anything fine about them, by any stretch of the imagination.

Had his father been proud of him? Had his mother? Had her voice softened when she talked about her little son, the way Georgie's did?

Who was he?

Endless questions, but no proper answers, even after

all this time, and realistically he knew now that there never would be. He sucked in a breath and turned his attention back to the food, but it tasted like sawdust.

'Hey—it's OK,' she said, frowning at him, her face concerned. 'We're doing all right. Life goes on.'

'Were you happy together, you and David?' he asked, wondering why he was beating himself up like this, but she didn't answer, and after a moment he looked up and met her eyes.

'He was a good man,' she said eventually. 'We lived in a nice house with good neighbours, we had some lovely friends—it was good.'

Good? What did that mean? Such an ineffectual word—or maybe not. Good was more than he had. 'And did you love him?'

Her eyes went blank. 'I don't think that's any of your business,' she said softly, and put her cutlery down, the food unfinished.

'I'll take that as a no, then,' he said, pushing it because he was angry about Josh, angry that she'd been playing happy families with someone else while he'd been alone—

'Take it as whatever you like, Sebastian. As I said, it's none of your business. If you don't mind, I think I'll go to bed now.'

'And if I mind?'

She stood up and looked at him expressionlessly. 'Then I'm still going to bed. Thank you for my meal and your hospitality,' she said politely. 'I'll see you tomorrow.'

He watched her go, and he swore softly and dropped his head into his hands. Why? Why hadn't he kept his mouth shut? Getting angry with her wouldn't change anything, any more than it had nine years ago.

He was reaching for the wine bottle when the lights on the baby monitor flashed, and he heard a sound that could have been a sigh or a sob or both.

'Why does he care, Josh? It's none of his business if I was happy with another man. *He* didn't make me happy in the long term, did he? He could have done, but he just didn't damn well care.'

Sebastian closed his eyes briefly, then picked up the baby monitor and took it upstairs, tapping lightly on her door and handing it to her silently when she opened it.

'Oh. Thanks.'

'You're welcome. And, for the record, I did care. I never stopped caring.'

She swallowed, and he could see the realisation that he'd heard everything she'd said register on her face. She coloured, but she didn't look away, just challenged him again, her voice soft so she didn't disturb the sleeping child.

'You didn't care enough to change for me, though, did you? You wouldn't even talk about it. You didn't even try to understand or explain why you never had time for me any more.'

No. He hadn't explained. He still couldn't. He wasn't sure he really knew himself, in some ways.

'I couldn't change,' he said, feeling exasperated and cornered. 'It wasn't possible. I had to do what I had to do to succeed, and I couldn't have changed that, not even for you.'

'No, Sebastian, you could have done. You just wouldn't.'

And she stepped back and closed the door quietly in his face.

He stared at the closed door, his thoughts reeling.

Was she right? Could he have changed the way he'd

done things, made it easier for her to live the life he'd had to live?

Not really. Not without giving up all he'd worked for, all he'd done to try and find out who he really was, deep down under all the layers that had been superimposed by his upbringing.

He was still no closer to knowing the answer, and maybe he never would be, but until then he couldn't stop striving to find out, to explore every avenue, every facet of himself, to push himself to the limit until he found out where those limits were.

And on the way, he'd discovered he could make money. Serious money. Enough to make a difference to the people who mattered? Maybe. He hoped so. The charities he supported seemed to think he was making a difference to the kids.

But Georgie mattered, too, and she was right, there hadn't been time for her in all of this.

OK, it had been tough—tough for both of them. He'd had a hectic life—working all day, networking every evening in one way or another. Dinner out with someone influential. Private views. Trade fairs, cocktails, fundraising dinners—a never-ending succession of opportunities to meet people and forge potentially beneficial links.

To do that had meant working eighteen-hour days, seven days a week. There'd been hardly any down time, and of course it had meant living in London, And that hadn't been compatible with her view of their relationship, or her need to follow her career—although there was no sign of that now.

She'd wanted to stay at university in Norwich, get her Biological Sciences degree and work in research, maybe do a PhD, but now it seemed she was a virtual PA with a 'very understanding' boss.

So much for her career plans, he thought bitterly.

Hell, she could have been his PA. She would have been amazing, and with him, by his side every minute of the day and night, and Josh would have been his child. That would have been a relationship worth having. Instead she'd chosen her career over him, and then gone on to live her dream with some other man who hadn't had the sense to keep his life insurance going to protect his family.

Great stuff. Good choice, Georgia.

Shaking his head in disgust, he turned away from the door and went downstairs to the kitchen. It was in uproar, the worktops covered with the wreckage of their meal and its preparation, but that was fine. He needed something to do, and it certainly needed doing, so he rolled up his sleeves and got stuck in.

The bath was wasted on her.

It should have been relaxing and wonderful, but instead she lay in the warm, scented water, utterly unable to relax, unable to shift the weight of guilt that was crushing her.

She got out, dried herself on what had to be the softest towel in the world and pulled on clean clothes. Not her night clothes—she wasn't that crazy—but jeans and a jumper and nice thick slipper socks, and picking up the baby monitor she padded softly downstairs to find him.

The kitchen door was ajar and she could hear him moving around in there—clearing up, probably, she thought with another stab of guilt. She shouldn't have stalked off like that, not without offering to help first, but he'd been so pushy, so—angry?

About David?

She opened the door and walked in, and he turned and met her eyes expressionlessly. 'I thought you'd gone to bed?'

She shook her head.

'I wasn't fair to you just now. I know you cared,' she said quietly, her voice suddenly choked.

He went very still, then turned away and picked up a cloth, wiping down the worktops even though they looked immaculate. 'So why say I didn't?'

'Because that was what it *felt* like. All you seemed to worry about was *your* career, *your* life, *your* plans for the future. There was never any time for *us*, just you, you, you. You and your brand new shiny friends and your meteoric rise to the top. You knew I wanted to finish my degree, but you just didn't seem to think that was important.'

He turned back, cloth in hand. 'Well, it doesn't seem important to you any longer, does it? You're doing a job you could easily have done in London, that's nothing to do with your degree or your PhD or anything else.'

'That's not by choice, though, and actually it's not true, I am still using my degree. I'm working for my old boss in Cambridge. I'd started my PhD and I was working there in research when I met David.'

'And then you had it all,' he said, his voice curiously bitter. 'Everything you'd always wanted. The career, the marriage, the baby—'

'No.' She stopped him with one word. 'No, I didn't have it all, Sebastian. I didn't have you. But you'd made it clear that you were going to take over the world, and I just hated everything about that lifestyle and what it had turned you into. You were never there, and when you were, we were hardly ever alone. I was just so unhappy. So lonely and isolated. I hated it.'

'Well, you made that pretty clear,' he said gruffly, and turned back to the pristine worktops, scrubbing them ferociously.

'It wasn't you, though. You weren't like that. You'd changed, turned into someone I'd never met, someone I didn't like. The people you mixed with, the parties you went to—'

'Networking, Georgia. Building bridges, making contacts. That's how it works.'

'But the people were *horrible*. They were so unfriendly to me. They made me feel really unwelcome, and I was like a fish out of water. And *so* much of the time you weren't even there. You were travelling all over the world, wheeling and dealing and counting your money—'

'It wasn't about money! It's never been about money.'

'Well what, then? Because it strikes me you aren't doing badly for someone who says it's not about money.'

She swept an arm around the room, pointing out the no-expense-spared, hand-built kitchen in the house that had cost him ridiculous amounts of money to restore on a foolish whim, and he sighed. 'That's just coincidence. I'm good at it. I can see how to turn companies around, how to make things work.'

'You couldn't make our relationship work.'

Her words fell like stones into the black pool of his emotions, and he felt the ripples reaching out into the depths of his lonely, aching soul, lapping against the wounds that just wouldn't heal.

'No. Apparently not.' He threw the cloth into the sink and braced his hands on the edge of the worktop, his head lowered. 'But then nor could you. It wasn't just me. It needs give and take.'

'And all you did was take.'

He turned then and met her eyes, and she saw raw pain and something that could have been regret in his face. 'I would have given you the world—'

'I didn't want the world! I wanted you, and you were never there. You were too busy looking over the horizon to even see what was right under your nose.'

'So you left me. Did it make you happy?'

She closed her eyes. 'No! Of course it didn't, not then, but gradually it stopped hurting quite so much, and then I moved to Cambridge and met David. I was looking for somewhere to live and I went into his office, and we got talking and he asked me out for a drink. He was kind and funny, and he thought that what I was doing was worthwhile, and we got on well, and it just grew from there. And he really *cared* about me, Sebastian. He made me feel that I mattered, that my opinion was valid.'

'That was all it took? Kind and funny?'

She gave him a steely glare. 'It was more than I got from you by the end.'

A muscle in his jaw flickered, but otherwise his face didn't move and he ignored her comment and moved on. 'So what happened to your PhD?'

'I found out I was pregnant, but he'd been moved to the Huntingdon office by then and I was commuting, which wasn't really satisfactory, and then the housing market collapsed. So I contacted my professor and he offered me this job, which kept us going, and then just after I had Josh, David died.'

'And do you miss him?' he asked. His voice was casual, but there was something strange going on in his eyes. Something curiously intense and disturbing. Jealousy? Of a dead man? 'Yes, of course I miss him,' she said softly. 'It's lonely in the house by myself, but life goes on, and I've got Josh, and I'm OK. He was a nice man, and I did love him, and he deserved more from me than I was ever able to give him, but I never felt the way I did with you, as if I couldn't breathe if he wasn't there. As if there was no colour, no music, no poetry. No sense to my life.'

His eyes burned into hers. 'And yet you walked away from me. From us.'

'Because it was *killing* me, Sebastian. *You* were killing me, the person you'd become. You never had any time for me, we never went anywhere or did anything that didn't serve another purpose. It was all about business, about making contacts that would make more money. I felt like an ornament, or a mistress, someone who should just be grateful for the crumbs that fell from your table. But I didn't want crumbs, I wanted you, I wanted what we'd had, but you shut me out, and you broke my heart, and I never want to let anyone that close to me ever again.

'So, no, I didn't feel for David the way I did for you. I didn't *want* to. He didn't give me what I'd thought I wanted when I was little more than a kid and everything was starry-eyed and rose-tinted, but he loved me, and he took care of me, and he made me happy.'

'And he cancelled the life insurance.'

Damn him! 'He had no choice! We were really struggling—'

'Did he tell you he was doing it? Did you discuss it? Or did he just do it and hope for the best? Because I would *never* have done that to you, Georgia,' he said passionately. 'I would never have left you so unprovided for. Would never have compromised your safety or security like that.'

'You have no idea what you would have done in those circumstances—'

'I know I'd starve before I did that—'

'You have no right to criticise him!'

'You were mine!' he said harshly. 'And you gave him all the things you'd promised me. Marriage. A child. Hearth and home and all of that—hell, George, we had so many dreams! How could you walk away? I loved you. You knew I loved you—'

His voice cracked on the last word, and her eyes flooded with tears; she closed them, unable to look at him any longer, unable to watch his face as he bared his soul to her. Because she *had* left him, and he *had* loved her, but she hadn't been mature enough or brave enough to cope with what he'd asked of her.

'I'm sorry,' she said, her heart aching with so many hurts and wrongs and losses she'd lost count. 'If it helps, I loved you, too, and it broke my heart to leave you.'

She heard him swear softly, then heard the sound of his footsteps as he walked up to her, his voice a soft sigh.

'Ahh, George, don't cry. No more tears. I'm sorry.'

She felt his hands on her shoulders, felt him ease her close against his chest, and with a ragged sigh she rested her cheek against his shirt and listened to the steady thudding of his heart. His arms closed around her, cradling her against his warmth and solidity, the mingled scent of his skin and the cologne he'd always used wrapping her in delicious, heart-wrenching familiarity.

She slid her arms around his waist, flattening her palms against the broad columns of muscle that bracketed his spine, and he held her without speaking, while their breathing steadied and their hearts slowed, until the tension left them.

But then another tension crept in, coiling tighter, pushing out everything else until it was the only thought, the only reason for breathing.

The only reason for being.

She felt his head shift, felt the warmth of his lips press tentatively against her forehead, and she tilted her head and met his blazing eyes.

CHAPTER FOUR

THE KISS WAS inevitable.

Slow, tender, fleeting, their lips brushing lightly, then gradually settling. Clinging. Melding into one, until she didn't know where she ended and he began.

She curled her fingers into his shirt, felt his fingers tunnel into her hair and steady her head as he plundered her mouth, taking, giving, duelling with her until abruptly, long before she was ready, he wrenched his head back and stepped away.

She pressed trembling fingers to her aching, tingling lips. They felt as if his had been ripped away from them, tearing them somehow, leaving them incomplete. Leaving her incomplete.

She looked up, and his eyes were black as night, his chest rising and falling unsteadily. She could hear the air sawing in and out of his lungs, see the muscle jumping in his jaw as he took another step away.

'I think you'd better go to bed,' he said gruffly, and handed her the baby monitor from the table.

She nodded, her heart thrashing, emotions tumbling one over the other as she turned and all but ran back to her room.

What had she been thinking of, to let him kiss her? After all that had happened, all the water under the bridge of their relationship, everything that had happened since—she must have been mad!

She'd finally found peace, after years of striving, of what had felt like settling for second best—which was so unfair on David, *so* unfair, but how could he compete with Sebastian? He couldn't. And, to be fair to him, she'd never asked him to. But still, it had felt like that, and it was only with Josh's birth and the bond that had formed between them after David's death that peace had finally come to her.

And now Sebastian had snatched it away, torn off the thin veneer of serenity and exposed the raw anguish in her heart. Because she still loved him. She'd always loved him, and now she was hurting all over again, her heart flayed raw by the knowledge of what she'd lost and what she'd done to him, but there was no way she could go back to that lifestyle, to the way he lived and the man he'd had to become.

She changed into her pyjamas and crawled into bed, lying there in a soft cloud of goose down and Egyptian cotton while her thoughts tumbled endlessly and went nowhere.

She heard him come upstairs to bed at something after midnight, but the sound didn't wake her because she was still lying awake, listening to the wind howling round the house, battering the windows with its unrelenting assault. There was no way she was getting out of there any time soon. The lane would be full to the top by now, the snow trapped against the crinkle-crankle wall with no escape, piling up endlessly as the wind drove it off the field.

Trapping her and Josh inside with Sebastian.

Oh, why had she let him kiss her?

Or had she kissed him? She wasn't sure, she only

knew it had been the most monumental mistake. It had broken down the barriers between them, ripped away her flimsy defences, opened the Pandora's box of their relationship, and try as they might, they'd never get the lid back on it in one piece.

She closed her eyes. She was *so* not looking forward to tomorrow...

He just couldn't sleep.

Well, there might have been a few minutes here and there, but mostly he just lay awake trying not to think about that kiss while he listened to the wind battering the house and blocking them in forever.

There was no way he was getting her out of here today. No way at all. Which was all made a whole sight more difficult by the fact that he'd let his guard down and weakened like that.

He should have kept his mouth shut, not dragged it all out again. And his voice cracking like that! What the hell was that about? He was *over* her...

Liar.

He sighed harshly. OK, so he wasn't over her, not totally, but he hadn't had to tell her that quite so graphically. He *certainly* hadn't needed to kiss her!

And now they were stuck here, forced together, with no prospect of escape for days. He rolled onto his front and folded his arms under his head, banging his forehead gently on them to knock some sense into himself.

Not working. So he lay there, fuming at his stupidity and resigning himself to a fraught and emotionally draining couple of days ahead.

It could have been worse. At least they had Josh there between them. They could hardly fight over his head, and he'd just have to make sure they were only together when he was around.

Although that was a problem in itself, because Josh, with his mother's eyes and engaging personality, was a vivid and living reminder of all he'd lost when she'd walked away. Josh could have been his son. *Should* have been his son. His first known living relative.

His family.

He swallowed hard, the ache in his chest making it hard to breathe.

It was no good. He'd never get to sleep again. He threw off the covers, tugged on his clothes and went downstairs. If nothing else, he could get some work done.

But he couldn't concentrate, and he ended up in the kitchen making yet more coffee at shortly before six in the morning. He put in some toast to blot it up a bit and give his stomach lining a rest, then sat at the table to eat it.

Not a good idea.

Little boys, he discovered, woke early, and he ended up with company.

Georgia, sleep-tousled, puffy-eyed and with a crease on one cheek, stumbled into the kitchen with Josh on her hip and came to an abrupt halt.

'Ah. Sorry.'

Not as sorry as he was. She was wearing pyjamas, but they were soft and stretchy and the child's weight on her hip had pulled the top askew and exposed an inviting expanse of soft, creamy flesh below her collar bone that drew his eyes like a magnet.

She followed the direction of his gaze and tugged it straight, colour flooding her cheeks, and he dragged his eyes away and jerked his head at the kettle.

'It's just boiled if you want tea?'

'Um—please. And do you have any spare milk? Josh usually has some when he wakes up.'

'Sure. I tell you what, why don't I get out of your way while you do whatever you want to do in here? Just help yourself to whatever you need.'

He left the room with almost indecent haste, and Georgie put Josh down on the floor and let her breath ease out of her lungs on a sigh of relief. She'd forgotten just how good he looked, how sexy, with his hair rumpled and his jaw roughened with stubble.

And tired. He'd looked tired, she thought, as if he'd been up all night. Because of the kiss? Or the wind, hammering against the house until she thought the windows were coming in? Between the kiss and the wind, they'd made sure she hadn't slept all night, and she'd only just crashed into oblivion when Josh had woken.

She hadn't realised it was so early until she saw the kitchen clock, because the snow made it lighter, the moon reflecting off it with an eerie, cold light that seemed to seep through the curtains for the sole purpose of reminding her of the mess she was in.

Why had she let him kiss her?

'Biscuit,' Josh said, and she sighed. They had this conversation every day, but he never gave up trying.

'No. You can have a drink of milk and a banana. There must be some bananas.'

She opened the pantry cupboard and found the fruit in a bowl. She pulled off a banana and peeled it and broke it into chunks for him, and left him kneeling up on a chair and eating it while she made some tea and warmed his milk in a little pan. She would have given it a couple of moments in the microwave, but she couldn't find one. She'd have to ask about that.

She sat down with her tea next to Josh, in the place where Sebastian had been. He'd left half a slice of toast on the plate, with a neat bite out of it, and she couldn't resist it. She should have finished her supper the night before instead of running out on him, and she was starving.

'Me toast,' Josh said, eyeing it hopefully, and she tore him off a chunk and ate the rest.

'More.'

'I'll make you some in a minute. Let's go and get dressed first.'

She took him upstairs, protesting all the way, and heard water running. Sebastian must be showering, she realised, and tried really, really hard not to think about that, about the times she'd joined him in the shower, getting in behind him and sliding her arms around his waist—

'Right. Let's get you dressed.'

'Then toast?'

'Then I have to get ready, and then you can have toast,' she promised, but she dragged out the dressing and teeth cleaning and face washing as long as possible, then sat Josh on the bed with a book while she washed and dressed herself and tidied the room.

The sound of running water from Sebastian's room had stopped, she realised as she tugged the bed straight. There was no sound at all, no drawers shutting or boards creaking. He must have finished in the shower and gone downstairs again. With any luck he was in the study, and if not, he could show her where the toaster was to save her scouring the kitchen for it.

She retrieved Josh from the bathroom where he was driving the nailbrush around on top of the washstand like a car.

'Toast?' she said, and he beamed and ran over to her, taking her outstretched hand. He chattered all the way down the stairs and into the kitchen, and she was suddenly really, really glad that he'd been with her in the car, that she hadn't been stuck here with Sebastian on her own.

Not with all the fizzing emotions in her chest—

She found the bread, but there wasn't a toaster and he wasn't around. She was still standing there with the bread in her hand and contemplating going to find him when Sebastian came back into the room.

She waved the bread at him. 'I can't find the toaster.'

'Ah. There's a mesh gadget for that in the slot on the left of the Aga. Just stick the bread in it and put it under the cover, and then flip it. It only takes a few seconds each side so keep an eye on it.'

He pulled the thing out and handed it to her, then headed into the boot room.

'I'm just going to check the lane,' he said. 'See how bad it is.'

'Really? It's almost dark still.'

Except it wasn't, of course, because of the eerie light from the snow and the fact that she'd dallied around for so long getting ready.

Even though she'd resisted putting make-up on...

The door shut behind him, and she put the bread between the two hinged flaps of mesh, laid it on the hotplate and put the cover down. Delicious smells wafted out in moments, and she flipped it and gave it another moment and then buttered the toast while the kettle boiled again.

It smelt so good she made a pile of it, unable to resist sinking her teeth into a bit while she worked, and all the time she wondered how he was getting on and what he'd found at the end of the drive.

Sheesh.

He stood inside the gates—well inside, as he couldn't actually get near them without a shovel and a few hours of solid graft—and stared in shock at the lane beyond.

He was already up to his knees in snow and it was getting deeper with every step. Beyond the gates, the snow reached to head height at either side of the entrance. It only dipped opposite the gates because the snow had had somewhere to go.

Straight across the entrance, through the bars of the gates and right up the drive.

There was at least a foot everywhere, but it wasn't smooth and level. It was sculpted, like sand in the Sahara, swirls and peaks and troughs in shades of brilliant white and cold bluey-purple in the light of dawn.

Beautiful, fascinating—and deadly. If he hadn't been here they could have been trapped inside the car, buried alive in the snow, slowly and gradually suffocating in the freezing temperatures—

He shut off that line of thought and concentrated on the here and now. It wasn't good.

In a freewheeling part of his brain that he hadn't even consulted he realised Georgie wouldn't even be able to get away if they landed a helicopter in the field opposite, despite the fact that it was virtually bare of snow now, because the snow in the lane was so deep they'd never cross it. Not that he'd really contemplated hiring a helicopter on Christmas Eve to take her and Josh away and bring his family back, but even if he had...

And the snow wasn't going anywhere soon. Although the wind had finally died away, it was cold. Bitterly, desperately cold, the change from the previous few days sudden and shocking, and he shrugged down inside his coat with a humourless laugh.

He hadn't needed a cold shower. He should have just come out here. Naked. That might have done the trick. The shower certainly hadn't.

He gave the lane one last disparaging look and waded back to the house, walking in to the smell of toast and the sound of laughter, and for a moment he felt his heart lift.

Crazy. Stupid. She left you.

But even so, he'd still have her there for another twenty-four hours at least. More, probably, and nobody was going to worry about this tiny little lane given that it was as bad elsewhere in the county as it was here. He'd already known it, he'd seen it on the news, and only wild optimism had sent him down the drive to check…

He swept the snow which had fallen in through the doorway back out into the courtyard, shut the door, stamped the snow off his boots and put them on the rack, hung up his coat and went back into the kitchen.

She'd made a pot of tea and was sitting at the table with Josh and a pile of hot buttered toast, playing peekabo behind a slice of toast. Josh, his face smeared with butter and crumbs, was giggling deliciously and Sebastian felt his heart squeeze.

'Smells good,' he said, rubbing his hands together to warm them, and Georgie looked up and searched his face.

'And the answer is?' she asked, the laughter fading in her eyes, and he shook his head.

'We're going nowhere. The lane's full to head height.'

'Head height?' she gasped, and her eyes looked

shocked. As if she was imagining being out there with Josh, trapped in the car, seeing what he'd seen in his mind's eye?

'Hey, it's all right, I was here,' he said softly, reading her mind, and she looked up at him again and their eyes locked.

'But what if...?'

'No what ifs. Don't go there, George.' He certainly wasn't going there again. Once was enough. He took a mug out of the cupboard. 'Any more tea in the pot?'

'Mmm. And I made you more toast. I wasn't sure if you'd want it but I made it anyway because we interrupted your breakfast.'

He dropped into the chair opposite her and reached for a slice. 'That's fine, I could do with more,' he said, and sank his teeth into it, suddenly hungry.

Hungry for all sorts of things.

Her warmth. Her laughter.

Her little boy, so like her, so mischievous and delightful, a part of her. What did that feel like? To have someone to love, someone who was part of you?

He looked quickly away and turned on the television to give himself something to do.

So much for his defences. They were in tatters, strewn around him like an old timber barn after a hurricane, and she and her child had walked straight through them as if they'd never even existed.

Maybe they hadn't. Maybe they'd just never been tested before, but they were being tested now, with bells on.

Jingle bells.

She was watching the screen, looking at the pictures of snow sent in by viewers of the local breakfast news programme. Not just them, then—not by a long way. And tomorrow was Christmas Day.

'There's no chance we'll be out of here by tomorrow, is there?' she said flatly.

Had she read his mind? Probably, as easily as he'd read hers. They'd always been good at it. Except at the end—

'I think it's very unlikely. I'm sorry. Your parents will be disappointed.' She nodded. Josh was playing on the floor now, driving a piece of toast around like a car, and she met Sebastian's eyes, worrying her lip again in that way of hers.

'They will be disappointed,' she said softly, lowering her voice. 'So will yours. Was it just them coming?'

'No. My brothers were coming up from London— well, Surrey. I expect they'll spend it together now. They live pretty close to each other. What about your family? Was it just your parents, or was Jack going to be there?'

'No, just them. Jack's got his own family now.' She sighed. 'I really wanted this Christmas to be special. Josh was too small to understand his first Christmas, and last year—well, it just didn't happen really, without David. It seemed wrong, and he was still too young to understand it, so we just spent it very quietly with my parents. But this year...'

'This year he's old enough, and you've moved on,' he murmured.

She nodded. 'Yes. Yes, I have, and he is, and it was going to be so lovely—'

She broke off and swallowed her disappointment, and he couldn't leave her like that. Her, or a little boy who'd lost his father. He had no idea how his own first Christmases had been spent. He didn't even know the religion of his real parents, their nationality, their age. Nothing. Just a void. And he couldn't bear the thought that Josh would have a void where Christmas should have been. He'd make sure that didn't happen if it killed him.

He took a deep breath, buried his misgivings and smiled at her.

'Well, we'll just have to make sure it *is* lovely,' he said. 'Heaven knows we've got enough food, and I've got all the decorations and there's a tree outside waiting to come in, if I can find it under the snow. And we can't do anything else. My family aren't going to be able to get here, and you can't get away, so why don't we just go for it? Give Josh a Christmas to remember.'

She stared at him, taking in his words, registering just what it must be costing him to make the offer— although she might have known he would. The old Sebastian, the one she loved, wouldn't have hesitated. The new one—well, she was beginning to realise she didn't know him at all, but he might not be as bad as she'd feared.

'That would be lovely,' she said softly, her eyes welling. 'Thank you. I know you don't—'

He lifted his hand, silencing her. 'Let it go, George. Let's just take it at face value, have a bit of fun and give Josh his Christmas—no strings, no harking on the past, no recriminations. And no repeats of last night. Can we do that?'

Could they? She wasn't sure, but she wanted to try.

She felt the tears welling faster now, and pressed her lips together as she smiled at him. 'Yes. Yes, we can do that. Thank you.'

He returned her smile a little wryly, and got to his feet.

'So—want to help me decorate the house?'

* * *

He gave them a guided tour of the ground floor.

Josh loved it. There were so many places to hide, so much to explore. And Georgie—well, she loved it in a different way, a bitter-sweet, this-could-have-been-ours way that made her heart ache.

No what ifs.

His words echoed in her head, and she put the thoughts out of her mind and concentrated on what he'd done to the house.

A lot.

'Oh, wow!' she said, laughing in surprise when they went into the dining room. 'That's a pretty big table.'

'It extends, too,' he said, his mouth twitching, and she felt her eyes widen.

'Really?' She went to the far end and sat down. 'Can you hear me?'

His smile was wry with old memories. 'Just about. Probably not with the extra leaves in.'

Their eyes held for just a beat too long, and she felt a whole whirlpool of emotions swirling in her chest. She got up and came towards him, running her fingers slowly over the gleaming wood, avoiding his eyes while she got herself back under control. 'Did you get the grand piano for the music room?' she asked lightly, and looked up in time to catch a flicker of something strange in his eyes.

He shook his head. 'No. It seemed pointless. I don't play the piano, but I do listen to music in there sometimes. It's my study now. I prefer it to the library, the view's better. Come and see the sitting room—the old one, in the Tudor part. I think it's probably where I'll put the tree.'

'Not in the hall?'

He shrugged. 'What's the point? I'm never in the hall, I just walk through it. And I thought, over Christmas, we might want to sit somewhere warm and cosy and less like a barn than the drawing room. It's huge, if you remember, and a bit unfriendly. It'll be better in the summer.'

She nodded. It *was* huge, but it was stunningly elegant and ornate in a restrained way, and it had a long sash window that slid up inside the wall so you could walk out through it onto the terrace. She'd loved it, but she could see his point.

In winter, the little sitting room—which was still twice the size of her main reception room—would be much more appropriate. Next to the kitchen in the same area of the house, it was beamed and somehow much less formal than its Georgian counterpart, and it had a ginormous inglenook fireplace big enough to stand inside.

He pushed open the door, and she went in and sighed longingly.

'Oh, this looks really cosy.' Huge, squashy sofas bracketed the inglenook, and there were logs in the old iron dog grate waiting to be lit. She could just imagine curling up there in the corner of a sofa with a book, with a dog leaning on her knees and Josh driving his toy cars around on the floor.

Dreaming again.

'Where are you going to put the tree?'

'In this corner. There's a power socket for the lights, and it's out of the way.'

'How big is it?'

He shrugged. 'I don't know. Eight foot?'

Her eyes widened. 'Will it fit under the beams?'

He grinned and shrugged again. 'Probably. I can always trim it. Only one way to find out.'

'Finding out' turned out to be a bit of a mission. It was in the courtyard, close to the coach house, but the snow was deep except by the back door where it had all fallen in earlier.

'A shovel would make this a lot easier,' he said, standing at the door in his boots and eyeing the snow with disgust.

'I thought you had a shovel in the car?'

'I do. Look at the coach-house.'

'Ah.' Snow was banked up in front of the doors, and digging it out without a shovel wasn't really practical.

'I should have thought of that last night,' he said, but of course he hadn't, and nor had she, because they'd had quite enough to think about already.

She didn't want to think about last night.

She picked Josh up and stood in the kitchen watching through the window as Sebastian ploughed his way through the snow to a huge, shapeless lump in the corner by the coach-house door. He plunged his arm into the snow, grabbed something and shook, and a conical shape gradually appeared.

'Mummy, what 'Bastian doing?'

'He's finding the Christmas tree. It's buried under the snow—look, there it is!'

'Oh..!' He watched, spellbound, as the tree emerged from its snowy shroud and Sebastian hauled it out of the corner and hoisted it into the air.

She went to the boot room door.

'Can I help you get it in?'

'I doubt it. I should stand back, this is going to be wet and messy.'

She moved out of the way, and he dragged it through

the doorway, shedding snow and needles and other debris all over the place. Then he emerged from underneath it, propped it in the corner and grinned at them both.

'Well, that's the easy bit done,' he said. There was a leaf in his hair, in amongst the sprinkles of snow, and she had to stuff her hand in her pocket to stop from reaching out and picking it off.

'What's the hard bit?' she said, trying to concentrate.

'Getting it to stay upright in the stand, and finding the right side.'

She chuckled, still eyeing the leaf. 'I can remember one year my mother cut so much off the tree trying to even it up she threw it out onto the compost heap and bought an artificial one.'

He laughed and turned his back on the tree and met her eyes with a smile. 'Well, that won't happen here. There's no way I can find the secateurs, and the compost heap's far too far away.'

'Well, let's hope it's a good tree, then,' she said drily. 'How about coffee while it drip-dries? And then, talking of my mother, I really should phone her and tell her what's happening.'

'Do that now, although I expect she's worked it out. The news is full of it. The entire country's ground to a halt, so at least we're not alone. And at least you're both safe. There are plenty of people who've been stuck on the motorways overnight.'

'Really?'

'Oh, yeah. It's bad. Go on, ring her, and I'll make the coffee,' he offered, so she picked up the phone and dialled the number, and the moment she said, 'Hi, Mum,' Josh was clamouring for the phone.

'Want G'annie! Me phone!'

'Oh, Mum, just have a quick word with him, can you, and then I'll fill you in.'

'Are you stuck there? We thought you must be. It's dreadful here.'

'Oh, yes. Well and truly—OK, Josh, you can talk to Grannie now.'

She handed over the phone to the pleading child, and he beamed and started chatting. And because he was two, he just said the things that mattered to him.

'G'annie, 'Bastian got a big tree!'

Oh, no! Why hadn't she thought of that? She held out her hand for the phone. 'OK, darling, let Mummy have the phone now. You've said hello to Grannie.'

But he was having none of it, and ran off. 'We got snow, and we stuck,' he went on, oblivious. 'And we having a 'venture, and 'Bastian got biscuits—'

Biscuits. That was the way forward.

She grabbed the packet off the table and waved them at him. 'Come and sit down and give me the phone and you can have biscuits,' she said, and wrestled the receiver off him.

'Hi. Sorry about that. He's a bit excited. Anyway, Mum, I'm really just ringing to say we're stuck here for the foreseeable. The lane is head high, apparently, and there's just no way out, so we aren't going to be able to get to you until it's cleared, and I very much doubt it'll be today—'

'Did he say Sebastian?'

Oh, rats. Trust her to cut to the chase. 'Uh—yeah. He did.'

'As in Sebastian Corder? At Easton Court? Is that where you are?'

'Uh—yeah.' Her brain dried up, and she ground to a

halt, but it didn't matter because her mother had plenty to say and no hesitation in saying it.

'I can't believe you didn't tell me last night! Are you all right? Of all the places to be stuck—is he OK with you? And you said "they"—is there someone else there? His family? A woman? Not a woman—oh, darling, do be careful—'

'Mum, it's fine—'

'How can it be fine? Georgia, he broke your heart!'

'I think it was pretty mutual,' she said softly. 'Look, Mum, I know it's not what you want to hear, but we're OK, and we're alive, which is the main thing, and he's being really generous and it's fine. And there's nobody else here, just us. His family were coming today. Don't stress. Nothing's going to happen.'

Nothing more than the kiss they'd already exchanged, but they'd promised each other no repeats...

'You can't just tell me not to stress, I'm your mother. That's what we do! And he's—' Her mother broke off and floundered for a moment, lost for a definition.

'What?' Georgie prompted softly. 'An old friend? And at least we know he's not a serial killer.'

'He doesn't need to be. There's more than one way to hurt someone.'

And didn't she know that. 'Mum, it's fine. I'm a big girl now. I can manage. Look, I have to go, he's made coffee for us and then we're going to decorate the tree. I'll give you a ring as soon as I know what's happening with the snow, OK? And give Dad a hug from us and tell him we'll see him soon. I'll ring you tomorrow.'

She hung up before her mother could say any more, and turned to find Sebastian watching her thoughtfully across the table.

'I take it she's not impressed.'

She rolled her eyes. 'You'd think you were holding us hostage, the fuss she's making.'

'She's your mother. She's bound to stress.'

'That's exactly what she said.' She sat down at the table with a plonk and gave a frustrated little laugh. 'I'm so sorry.'

'About your mother, who you have no control over, or the weather, for which ditto?' He smiled wryly and pushed the biscuits towards her.

'Here, have one of these before your son finishes them all, and let's go and tackle this tree.'

CHAPTER FIVE

EASIER SAID THAN done.

It took the best part of an hour to wrestle the tree into the room and get it in the right position, and by the end of it he was hot, cross and had a nice bruise on his finger from pinching it in the clamp.

'Look on the bright side,' Georgie said, standing back to study it critically. 'At least it's a nice soft fir and not a prickly old spruce. And it fitted under the beam.'

He stuck his head out from underneath it and gave her a look. 'Just don't tell me to turn it round again,' he growled, and she smiled sweetly and widened her eyes.

'As if. It looks good. It's even vertical. That's a miracle in itself. So, where are the decorations?'

He worked his way out from under the tree and stood up, brushing bits of vegetation off his cashmere sweater. Probably not the best choice of garment for the task in hand, but with Georgia in the house he didn't seem to be able to think clearly. 'In my study. Come and have a look.'

She followed him to the room that they'd christened the music room, under her bedroom. There was a desk in there positioned to take advantage of the views over the garden, and apart from the laptop on the desk, there was nothing to give away that it was an office. She wondered how much work he did here, or was planning to, or if it was just a weekend cottage.

Some cottage, she thought drily.

There was a stack of boxes beside the desk, and he pulled one of the boxes off the pile and opened it on the desk. 'I'm not convinced they're child-friendly.'

Probably not, she thought, eyeing the expensive packaging. The decorations were all immaculately boxed, individually wrapped in tissue paper and made of glass. Beautiful though they were, she wasn't in a hurry to put them in reach of Josh.

'Not good?' he asked, and she shrugged.

'They're lovely. Beautiful, but they aren't really safe within his reach. He's a bit small to understand about cutting his fingers off.'

Sebastian winced. 'We could put them higher up, out of his reach.'

'We could. And we could decorate the lower part with other things. And they aren't all glass. Look, these ones are traditional pâpier maché, it says. They'll be all right, and I can make gingerbread stars and trees, and decorate them with icing—have you got icing sugar and colourings?'

He raised his hands palm-up and pulled a face. 'How would I know?'

'You put the stuff away in your kitchen?'

He shook his head. 'My mother put a lot of the food away. She was here when it arrived. I was still in London.'

'Ah. Well, in that case we'll have to go and look or be imaginative. There are fir trees in the grounds. We can find fir cones and berries and things—'

'May I remind you that everything in the garden is submerged under a foot of snow?' he said drily, and she smiled.

'I'm sure you'll manage. Coloured paper? Glue? Sticky tape?'

He had a horrible feeling the tree was going to end up looking like a refugee from a craft programme on the television, but then Josh crawled through the knee-hole of the desk pushing his stapler along the floor and making 'vroom vroom' noises, and he suddenly didn't care what the tree looked like. He just wanted Josh to be safe, and happy, and together they could have fun making stuff for the tree.

Well, Josh could. He wasn't sure he'd be so thrilled by it, but hey. Josh was just a kid, and Sebastian wasn't going to put his own feelings before the child's. No way.

'Let's put this lot on the top half,' he suggested, 'and I'll go and see what I can find in the garden while you make the biscuits. I'm sure I've got ribbon and sticky tape and coloured wrapping paper left from the presents.'

She smiled, her whole face softening. 'Thanks. That would be great. OK, Josh, let's go and make the tree pretty, shall we?'

'Lights first,' Sebastian said, picking up the box.

'Do they flash?'

'No they don't,' he said, appalled. 'Nor are they blue. Christmas tree lights should be white, like stars.'

'Stars twinkle,' she pointed out, and started singing 'Twinkle, twinkle, little star', but he'd had enough. Laughing in exasperation, he turned her shoulders, gave her a little push towards the door and followed her back to the sitting room, trying really, really hard not to breathe in the scent of her perfume.

'Your mother rang.'

He paused in the act of tugging off his boots and met her eyes. 'Ah. I sent her a text earlier saying the lane was impassable and Christmas wasn't going to happen tomorrow. What did you say to her?'

She rolled her eyes at him. 'Nothing. I'm not that stupid. She rang the house first, and I heard the answerphone cut in, and then she rang your mobile. It came up on the screen.'

'Right. OK. I'll go and call her.'

'So did you find fir cones and berries?'

'Fir cones. Not berries. The birds were all over them, and I thought their need was greater, but I've got some greenery. I've left it all out here to drip for a bit. Something smells good.'

'That's the biscuits.'

'Mmm. They probably need testing. Did you make spares?' he asked hopefully.

She shook her head, then relented and smiled at him when he pulled a disappointed face. 'I'm sure there'll be breakages.'

He felt his mouth twitch. 'I'm sure it can be arranged even if there aren't. Stick the kettle on, I'm starving and I could do with a drink. I'll go and call my mother and then we can have lunch.'

He went into the study and picked up the phone, listened to the message and rang her. 'So how is it? Are you cut off, too?'

'Yes, and your brothers aren't here, either. They were coming up last night but of course they watched the news and thought better of it. They're spending Christmas together, though, so they'll be fine.'

'So you'll be alone?'

'Well, we hope not. We were still hoping you might be able to get out with your Range Rover to collect us.'

'No chance. It's head high in the lane and I don't see it thawing with the weather so cold and clear. We're going to have to postpone Christmas for days, I'm afraid. It could be ages before they get through here with a snow plough.'

'Oh, darling, I'm so sorry, how disappointing. And I can't bear to think of you spending your first Christmas there on your own.'

Except, of course, he wouldn't be, but there was no way he was telling her that. 'I'm more worried for you,' he said, hastily moving the subject on. 'I don't know what you're going to eat, I've got all the food here at this end.'

'Well, don't try and keep it. Just have it and enjoy it and we'll worry about restocking later. At least it's only us, and I'm sure I've got things in the freezer. We'll be fine, but be careful with all that food at yours and freeze anything you can't use in time. You don't want to get food poisoning eating it past its use-by date—'

'Mum,' he said warningly, and she sighed.

'Sorry, but you can't stop me worrying about you. Big as you are, you're still my son.'

If only that was true, he thought with a pang, but he didn't go there because he knew that in every way that mattered, he was. Well, his heart knew that, and now, after all these years, he was finally able to accept it. His head, though—that still wanted answers—

He heard a noise and realised that Josh had followed him into the study and was crawling around on the floor with the stapler vrooming again, and he swivelled the chair round and watched him out of the corner of his eye while he listened to his mother making alternative plans and telling him how they were going to get together with the neighbours and it would all be fine, and they'd see him soon.

And then Josh stood up under the desk and banged his head, and started to cry.

'Hang on.' He dropped the phone and scooped Josh up into his arms, cross with himself for not anticipating it so that now Josh was hurt, and cross with Georgia for letting him out of her sight so that it could happen in the first place.

And he was hurt. Real tears were welling in his eyes, and without thinking Sebastian sat back in his chair, cuddled him close and kissed his head better, murmuring reassurance. Josh snuggled into him, sniffing a little, and from the phone on the desk he could hear his mother's tinny voice saying, 'Sebastian? Sebastian, whose child is that?'

Why hadn't he just hung up? But he hadn't, and there was no way round this. He picked up the receiver with a sigh and prepared himself for an earbashing.

'It's Georgia Becket's little boy—'

'Georgie's? I didn't know you were seeing her! How long's this been going on?'

'It's not. It isn't,' he told her hastily. 'She was on her way home for Christmas yesterday afternoon and the other road was blocked so she tried the short cut and got stuck outside the gates. And it was almost dark, so the obvious thing to do was let them stay. I was going to take her home today, but the weather rather messed that up so we're just making the best of it, really.'

Shut up! Too much information. Stop talking!

But then of course his mother started again.

'Oh, Sebastian! Well, thank goodness you were there! Who knows what would have happened if you hadn't been—it doesn't bear thinking about, her and her little boy—'

'Well, I was here, so it's fine, and it's only till the snow clears so don't get excited.'

'I'm not excited. I'm just concerned for her. How is she? That poor girl's been through so much—'

'She's fine,' he said shortly, and then added, 'She's making gingerbread decorations for the tree at the moment.'

Why? Why had he told her that? It sounded so cosy and domesticated and just plain happy families, and his mother latched onto it like a terrier.

'Oh, how lovely! She always was a clever girl. She was so good for you—I never did understand why you let her go, but you were behaving so oddly then, I expect you just drove her away. I don't suppose you ever talked to her, explained anything?'

He said nothing. He didn't need to. His mother was on a roll.

'No, of course you didn't. You weren't talking to anyone at that time, least of all us.' She sighed. 'I wish we'd told you sooner. We should have done.'

'You should.'

His voice was harsh, and he heard her suck in her breath. 'Well, whatever, you be nice to her. Don't you dare hurt her again, Sebastian, she doesn't deserve it. And—try talking to her. Tell her what was going on then, how you were feeling about the adoption and everything. How you still feel. I'm sure she'll understand. She's a lovely girl and it would be wonderful if you got back together. I'd love to see you happy, and that poor little boy of hers...'

He swallowed hard, pressing his lips briefly to Josh's dark, glossy hair. 'Well, you can put all that out of your head. It's over. It was over years ago, and it's just not going to happen. Look, I'll give you a call when I know more, but in the meantime you take care and don't let Dad overdo it shovelling snow. I know what he's like about clearing the drive.'

'I'll pass it on, but I can't guarantee he'll listen. And I'm sorry we aren't going to be with you, but I'm really glad Georgie is. And her little boy. You'll have so much fun together. How old is he?'

'Two. He's two—well, two and a bit.' *The same age I was...*

His mother sucked in a breath. 'Oh, Sebastian! He's going to love it! I remember your first Christmas with us—'

'Mum, I've got to go. I'm expecting a call. I'll ring you tomorrow.'

He ended the call abruptly and put the phone down, and then swivelled the chair to find Georgie standing there watching him thoughtfully.

'What's not going to happen?'

'Us,' he said shortly, and put Josh back on his feet. 'What can I do for you?'

She could think of a million things, none of which he'd want to hear and all of them disastrous for her emotional security. 'Nothing. I was looking for Josh and I heard him crying. What happened?'

'He stood up under the desk. He's fine now, aren't you, little guy?'

Josh nodded, and she held out her hand to him. 'Lunch is ready when you are,' she told Sebastian. 'Come on, Josh. Let's go and have something to eat.' And she left him to follow them in his own time.

Great. His mother must have heard Josh cry and asked who he was, which would have opened a whole can of worms.

She'd have to apologise for that because it was her fault, of course, for letting Josh run off like that, but she'd been busy rescuing the biscuits from the Aga and one minute he was there and the next he was gone.

Interestingly, though, it sounded as if his mother, unlike hers, wanted them back together. Well, as he'd said, it just wasn't going to happen. It was *so* not going to happen! Been there, done that, and had the scars to prove it.

And so did he, and from the sound of his voice he wasn't any more keen than she was. He'd certainly cut his mother off short when she started asking questions about Josh.

She towed him back to the kitchen and shut the door to keep him there so he didn't cause any more havoc, and sat him down at the table. She'd made cheese and caramelised onion chutney sandwiches, a big pile of them, and there were little golden brown trees and stars cooling on a wire rack on the worktop.

There were even a few failures. Sebastian would be pleased. Or he would have been. Now, with his mother sticking her oar in and putting him on the defensive, things might not be so jolly. She sucked in a deep breath when she heard the door open and forced herself to smile.

'You got lucky,' she told him. 'Some of the ginger-bread trees were cracked so we can't use them for decorations. And I found some packets of stock cubes which would make perfect tree ornaments if I wrapped them up. Can you spare them for a few days?'

'Probably. You could take some out just in case we need them, but no, that's fine, go for it.' And dropping into a chair, he picked up a sandwich and bit into it. 'Nice bread.'

She raised an eyebrow at him. 'Well, don't look at me, I just raided the kitchen. It was entirely your PA's choice. I suggest you give her a substantial bonus.'

'I already did.'

She laughed and shook her head, then put the kettle on again to make tea and sat down opposite him. 'I'm sorry I let Josh give me the slip. It must have been— awkward with your mother.'

He rolled his eyes. 'You know what she's like.'

'I do. She loves you, though, even though you fight with her all the time. You do know that?'

'Of course I know that.' He frowned and pushed back his chair. 'Look, I've got work to do, so I might just take a pile of sandwiches and disappear into my study. I'll see you later.'

Oh, great, she'd driven him out. It wasn't hard. All she had to do was mention his mother and it was enough to send him running. She felt her shoulders drop as he left the room, and let out a long, slow breath.

They'd agreed to spend Christmas together and ignore the past for Josh's sake, but the past just kept getting in the way, one way or the other, and tainting the atmosphere, as if it was determined to have its say.

She looked out of the window, but the snow was still there, and it was even snowing again lightly, just tiny bits of dust in the air. Was it ever going to thaw so they could escape?

Not nearly soon enough. She cleared the table, gave it a wipe and smiled at her son.

'Are you going to help me ice the decorations for the tree?' she asked, but he was more interested in eating them, so she gave him a pile of little bits to keep him occupied and piped white 'snow' onto the trees and the stars through the snipped-off corner of a sandwich bag, which seemed to work all right until it split and splodged icing on the last one.

She saved it for Sebastian and took it in to him with a cup of tea, knocking on the open door before she went in.

He didn't seem to be working. He was sitting with his feet on the corner of the desk, his fingers linked and lying loosely on his board-flat abdomen, and he glanced at her and frowned.

'Sorry. My mother just got to me.'

'Don't apologise. It was my fault for not keeping a closer eye on Josh. Here. I messed up one of the biscuits. I thought you might like it, and I've brought you a cup of tea.'

'Thanks.'

He dropped his feet to the floor and sighed. 'I wish this damn snow would clear,' he muttered, and she gave a short laugh.

'I don't think there's any chance. I think it's got it in for us. It was snowing again a moment ago.'

'I noticed.' He looked around. 'Where's Josh?'

'Eating broken biscuits.'

'I thought they were mine?'

'You walked out, Sebastian.'

'Well, it makes a change for it to be me.'

She sucked in a breath, took a step back and turned on her heel and walked away. She got all the way to the door before she stopped and turned back.

'I didn't walk out,' she reminded him. 'You drove me out. There's a difference. And if you had the slightest chance, you'd do it again, right now. But don't worry. The moment the snow clears, I'll be out of here, and you'll never have to see me again.'

'Wait.'

His voice stopped her in the doorway, and she heard the creak of his chair as he got up and crossed the room to her.

She could feel him behind her, just inches away, unmoving. After a moment his hands cupped her shoulders, but he still didn't move, didn't say anything, just stood there and held her, as if he didn't quite know what to say or do but wanted to do something.

She turned and looked up into his eyes, and they were troubled. Hers probably were, too. Goodness knows there was enough to trouble them. She let her breath out on a long, quiet sigh, and lifted her hand and touched his cheek, making contact.

Even though he'd shaved that morning she could feel the tantalising rasp of stubble against her palm, and under her fingers his jaw clenched, the muscle twitching.

'I'm sorry,' he murmured. 'I know it wasn't just you. I know I wasn't easy to live with. I'm not. But—we have to do Christmas for Josh, and I really want to do it right, and I know I said we wouldn't talk about it and I just broke the rule. Can we start again?'

She dropped her hand. 'Start what again?'

He was silent for long moments, then his mouth flickered into a smile filled with remorse and tenderness and pain. 'Christmas. Nothing else. I know you don't want more than that.'

Didn't she? Suddenly she wasn't so sure, but then it wasn't what he was offering, so she nodded and stepped back a little and tried to smile.

'OK. No more snide remarks, no more cheap shots, no more bickering. And maybe a bit more respect for who we are and where we are now?'

He nodded slowly. 'Sounds good to me,' he said

gruffly, and he smiled again, that same sad smile that brought a lump to her throat and made her hurt inside.

How long they would have stood there she had no idea, but there was a crash from the kitchen and she fled, her heart in her mouth.

She found Josh on the floor looking stunned, a biscuit in his hand, the wire rack teetering on the edge of the worktop and a chair lying on its side, and guilt flooded her yet again.

'Is he all right?'

'I think so.' She gathered him up, and he clung to her like a little monkey, arms and legs wrapping round her as he burrowed into her shoulder and sobbed. 'I think he's probably just frightened himself.'

And her. And Sebastian, judging by the look on his face.

He reached out a hand and laid it gently on Josh's back. 'Are you OK, little guy? You're really in the wars today, aren't you?'

'I've told him so many times not to climb on chairs.'

'He's a boy. They climb. I was covered in bruises from falling off or out of things until I was about seventeen. Then I started driving.'

She gave him a dry look. 'Thanks. It's really good to know what's in store.'

He smiled at her over her son's head, and this time it was a real smile. His soft chuckle filled the kitchen, warming her, and she sat down on the righted chair and hugged Josh and examined him for bumps and bruises and odd-shaped limbs.

Just a fright, she concluded, and a little egg on the side of his head, but that could have been from standing up under the desk.

'Tea?' Sebastian offered, and she nodded.

'Tea sounds like a good idea. Thank you.'

'Universal panacea, isn't it? When all else fails, make tea.'

He put the kettle on and went back to his study to bring his mug and the uneaten biscuit, pausing for a moment to take a few deep breaths and slow his heart rate. He'd had no idea what they'd find, and the relief that Josh seemed to be OK was enormous.

Crazily enormous. Hell, the little kid was getting right under his skin—

He strode briskly back to the kitchen, stood his mug on the side of the Aga so it didn't cool any more and made her a fresh mug.

'How is he?'

'He's fine, aren't you, Josh? It's probably time he had a nap. I usually put him down after lunch for a little while. I might go up with him and read for a bit while he sleeps.'

He frowned as he analysed an unfamiliar emotion. *Disappointment? Really? What was the matter with him?*

'Good idea. I'll get on with my work, and then we'll decorate the tree later.'

'Mistletoe?'

He'd cut mistletoe, of all the things! Like that was *really* going to help—

'I know, I know,' he sighed shortly, 'but it is Christmassy, and everything else was out of reach or too tough, and I could cut it with scissors, and I have no idea where the secateurs might be. I made sure it didn't have berries on, either, in case Josh should try and eat them, because they're poisonous. But there is one bit of holly—for the Christmas pudding.'

She tipped her head on one side and eyed him in disbelief, trying not to laugh. 'The Christmas pudding?'

'Absolutely. You have to have a bit of holly on fire in the middle of the Christmas pudding when it's brought to the table. It's the law.'

She suppressed a splutter of laughter. 'Is that the same law that says that lights must be white? My, aren't we traditional?' she teased, but he just folded his arms and quirked a brow.

'Absolutely. Christmas is Christmas. It has to be done properly. Have you got a problem with that?'

She smiled slowly. 'Do you know what? You've got a good heart, Sebastian Corder, for all you're as prickly as a hedgehog. And no, I don't have a problem with that. Not at all.'

He cleared his throat. 'Good. Right. So, what's next?' he asked, avoiding her eyes and fluffing up his prickles.

Still smiling, she handed him the boxes of stock cubes and a few other little things she'd found that could be wrapped, and they sat down at the table, gave Josh a piece of paper and a pencil to do a drawing, and made little parcels for the tree.

She'd snapped off some twigs from a shrub outside the sitting room window, and once the other parcels were done they made them into little bundles to dangle on the tree.

'Finger,' he demanded, and she put her finger on the knot and he tugged the gold ribbon tight, and made a loop to hang it by.

'You're good at this. You might have found your vocation.'

'I have a vocation.'

'What, making money?'

He sighed and put the little bundle of sticks down on the growing pile.

'George—'

She raised her hands. 'It's OK, I'm sorry, cheap shot.'

'Yes, it was. And I don't just spend it all on myself. I employ a lot of people, and I support various charities and organisations—and I really don't need to explain myself to you.'

She searched his eyes. 'Maybe you do,' she said softly. 'Maybe you always did, instead of just rushing off and doing.'

'Yeah, well, there's been a lot of water under the bridge since then, and as you were kind enough to point out to me when I was asking about David, it's actually none of your business. Now, are we going to finish this tree or not?'

He got to his feet, scooping the little parcels up in his big hands and heading out of the door. She grabbed the fir cones, ribbon and scissors and stood up. He was never going to change, never going to compromise. The word wasn't even in his vocabulary.

'Josh, come on, we're going to decorate the tree,' she told her son, and he wriggled down off the chair and followed her into the sitting room.

CHAPTER SIX

'IT LOOKS GOOD.'

She put the baby monitor on the coffee table, sat down at the other end of the sofa and studied the tree with satisfaction.

Not exactly elegant, with its slightly squiffy little parcels and random bunches of twigs and soggy fir cones—well, the top half wasn't so bad, although there were a few odd bits up there just to link it in so it didn't look like a game of Consequences—but it looked like a proper, family Christmas tree.

And that brought a huge lump to her throat.

Josh had had so much fun putting all their home-made bits and pieces on there, and Sebastian hadn't turned a hair when he'd pulled too hard and the whole tree had wobbled. He'd just got a bit of string and tied it to a hook on the beam above so it couldn't fall.

'It does look good,' she said softly. 'It looks lovely. Thank you.'

Sebastian turned his head and frowned slightly at her. 'Why are you thanking me? You've helped me decorate my tree.'

'And we've done it for my son, which has meant not being able to use all your lovely decorations and smothering the bottom of it in all sorts of weird home-made bits and pieces, which I'm perfectly sure wasn't your intention, so—yes, thank *you*.'

The frown deepened for a moment, then cleared as he shook his head and looked back at the tree.

'Actually, I rather like all the home-made things,' he said after a moment, and she had to swallow the lump in her throat.

'Especially the gingerbread trees and stars,' she said, trying to lighten the moment. 'And don't think I haven't noticed that every time you "accidentally" bump into the tree another one breaks so you get to eat it. Between you and Josh there are hardly any left.'

He grinned. 'I don't know what you mean. And if we're running out, it's your fault. I told you to make plenty.'

She rolled her eyes and rested her head back against the sofa cushions with a lazy groan. 'This is really comfortable,' she mumbled.

'It is. I love this room. I think it's probably my favourite room in the whole house.'

Because they'd never made any plans for it? Maybe, she thought, considering it. Or had they? Hadn't there been some mention of it being a playroom for all the hordes of children? But they hadn't spent any *significant* time in it. Not like the bedroom. Maybe that made the difference.

Or maybe he just liked it.

She rolled her head towards him and changed the subject.

'So, what's the programme for tomorrow? Since you have such strong opinions on how it should be done...'

Another grin flashed across his face. 'Cheeky.' He hitched his leg up, resting his arm on the back of the sofa and propping his head on his hand so he was facing her, thoughtful now.

'I think that probably depends on you and Josh. What are you going to do about presents for him? Are you going to wait until you're with your parents?'

'I don't know. I don't think so. He was really excited about the tree and he knows there will be presents under it because they had them at nursery, so I think there probably should be something for him to find tomorrow, otherwise it might be a bit of an anti-climax.'

'You don't think it will anyway, with just us and a few presents instead of a big family affair? Wouldn't you rather wait?'

'Do you think I should?'

He shrugged. 'I don't know. It's up to you, but it makes me feel a bit awkward because there isn't one from me, and it'll look as if I don't care and I'd hate him to think that, but obviously I haven't got anything to give him. Either of you.'

She stared at him, unbearably touched that he should feel so strongly about it—and so wrongly. She reached out a hand to him, grasping his and squeezing it.

'Oh, Sebastian. You're giving us Christmas! How much more could we possibly ask? You've opened your home to us, let us create absolute havoc in it, we've taken it over completely so you haven't even been able to work, and—well, frankly, without you we might not even be alive for it, so I really don't think you need to worry about some gaudy plastic toy wrapped up and stuck under the tree! In the grand scheme of things, what you've given him—given us—is immeasurable, and whatever else is going on between us, I'll never forget that.'

Sebastian frowned again—he was doing that a lot—and turned away, his jaw working.

'He's just a kid, George,' he said gruffly.

'I know,' she said softly. 'And for some reason that really seems to get to you.'

He shrugged and eased his hand away, as if the contact made him uncomfortable. 'I don't like to think of kids being unhappy at Christmas. Or ever. Any time. And as I've said, I've got nothing else to do and nowhere else to be. So—presents, or not presents?'

She thought about it for a moment. Her parents had spoiled him on his birthday just four weeks ago, and he'd had so many presents he hadn't really known what to play with first. And there was nothing here in the house, really, that he could play with safely.

And then she had an idea that would solve it all. 'I think—presents? Or some of them, at least. I've got him a wooden train set, and it comes in two boxes. There's the main set, and there are some little people and a bench and trees and things in another box. You could give him that, if you're really worried about him having something from you under the tree.'

'Don't you mind?'

She laughed. 'Why should I mind? He's still getting the toy, and it would give him something constructive to play with while we're stuck here. And I've got a little stocking for him from Father Christmas. That ought to go up tonight because he's bound to get up early.'

'Does he even know who Father Christmas is?'

She smiled ruefully. 'I don't know. We went to see him, but I'm not sure he was that impressed. He looked a bit worried, to be honest, but it might make him like the old guy a bit better if he brings him chocolate.'

They shared a smiled, and he nodded.

'You could hang it from the beam over the fire.'

'I could. We might need to let the fire go out first, though, so the chocolate buttons don't melt.'

'Ah. Yes, of course. Good plan. Well, if we let it die down now, it should be all right by the end of the evening. It can go at the side, out of the direct heat. And, yes, please, if I can put my name on the other box of train stuff, that would be good. But you must let me pay you for it.'

She just laughed at that, it was so outrageous. 'You have to be kidding! The amount you're spending on us already? I'll have you know I eat a lot on Christmas Day.'

'Good. Have you seen the size of the goose?'

'We have goose?' she said, her jaw dropping open in delight. 'Oh, wow, I love goose! What stuffing?'

'Prune and apple and Armagnac,' he told her, and she sighed with contentment and slumped back onto the sofa cushions, grinning.

'Oh, joy. Deep, deep joy. Bring it on...'

He laughed and stood up, slapping her leg lightly in passing. 'That's your job. I have no idea how to cook a goose, especially not in an Aga, so I was hoping you'd do it. Shall I get the presents?'

'I'll come. I only want a few. Where did you put them?'

'In my room.'

Ah.

Was her face so transparent? Because he took one look at her and smiled and shook his head.

'You're perfectly safe, George. I'm not going to do anything crazy.'

No. And wishing she wouldn't be quite so perfectly

safe was crazy. Utterly crazy. Good job one of them was thinking clearly.

She nodded slowly and stood up. 'OK. We'll just get the train set boxes and the stocking and leave the rest for when I'm with my parents. Then I can just put the whole bag in the car when I leave.'

He didn't want her to leave.

It dawned on him suddenly, with a dip in his stomach, as they went upstairs to the bedroom, walking up side by side as if they were going to bed.

And he needed to stop thinking about that right there before he embarrassed them both.

He pushed the door open and flicked on the light. 'They're in here,' he said, and let her through the communicating door into his dressing room. It had been cut in half, the half with the window becoming the bathroom, this half now lined out with wardrobes fitted with racks and shelves and hanging space.

He'd dumped the bag of presents inside one of the practically empty cupboards, and he pulled it out and turned to find her looking around, studying the wardrobes minutely.

'Useful. Really useful. What sensible storage. They're great.'

'They are. How anybody managed with that little cupboard in the bedroom I have no idea.'

'Maybe they didn't have as many clothes. Or maybe they just used it to play hide and seek?' she said lightly.

She was bending over the presents as he held them, and he stared down at the top of her head and tried to work out what was going on in there. Why had she said that? Why chuck something so contentious into the mix?

Although it was him that had raised the subject of the cupboard in the first place...

He had to get out of there. Now.

'Right, why don't I leave you to sort out what you want to bring down, and I'll go and get on. I've got a few loose ends to tie up before tomorrow. Just stick them back in the cupboard when you're done.'

And he handed her the bag and left. Swiftly, before he gave in to the temptation to grab her by the shoulders, haul her up straight and kiss her senseless.

'Here. This is the train set stuff. Did you want to wrap yours in different paper?'

She put the boxes down on the kitchen table and he studied them thoughtfully. 'Does it matter if they're the same?'

'Not necessarily.'

He gave a slight smile. 'I'll do whatever, but I have to say my wrapping paper doesn't really compete with little trains being driven by Santas.'

She smiled back. 'Probably not. And he won't think about the fact that they're the same. He'll just want to unwrap them. He knows what presents are now, having just had a birthday.'

'When was his birthday?'

'Three days after yours.'

His eyebrows crunched briefly together again in another little frown, and she wondered what she'd said this time. Was it because she remembered his birthday? Unlikely. She'd always remembered everyone's birthdays. That was what she did. Remembered stuff. It was her forte, just as his was making money.

She gave up trying to work him out.

'So, lunch tomorrow or whenever we're having it.

Are we going for lunchtime, or mid-afternoon, or evening, or what?'

He turned his hands palm up and shrugged. 'Look, this is all for Josh. I don't care what time we eat, so long as we eat. I'm sure we'll manage whenever it is. Just do whatever you think will suit him best.'

'Lunch, probably, if that's OK? What veg do you have? And actually, where is the goose? It's not in the fridge so I hope it's not still frozen.'

'It's in the larder.'

'Larder?' The kitchen had been so derelict she hadn't even realised it'd had a larder. Or maybe he'd created one?

He walked across to what she'd assumed was a broom cupboard or something, and opened the door. A light came on automatically, illuminating the small room, and she saw stone shelves laden with food. So much food.

'Wow. And this was just for you and your family?'

He gave a wry smile. 'I told you my PA had gone mad.'

Not that mad, she thought, studying the shelves. Yes, there was a lot of food, but much of it would keep and it was only the goose and the fresh vegetables that might struggle.

She shivered. 'It's chilly in here. Ideal storage. I didn't even know it existed. Was it here?'

'Yes. It had one slate shelf and I had the others put in, and it's got a vent to the outside and faces north, which keeps it cool.'

'Which is why it feels like a fridge.'

He smiled. 'Indeed. Perfect for the days when fridges didn't exist. So—there you are. Feel free to indulge us with anything you can find.'

'Oh, I will.'

She ran her eye over it all again, mentally planning the menu, then shut the door behind them and sat back down at the table to write a list.

'Do you really want Brussels sprouts?'

'Definitely. Christmas isn't Christmas without sprouts.'

'And burnt holly.'

'And burnt holly,' he said with a grin.

She bit down on the smile and added sprouts to the list, then looked up as he set a glass of wine down on the table in front of her.

'Here, Cookie. To get you into the festive spirit.'

'Thank you. And talking of Cookie, are you about to cook, by any chance, or was that a hint for me?'

'I've done it. There's a pizza in the oven and some salad, and we could have fruit or icecream to follow. I thought I'd let you off the hook, seeing as you'll be doing quite enough tomorrow.'

'How noble of you.' She sipped her wine and glanced at her list. 'Is the goose stuffed already?'

'So I was told. Ready to go straight in the oven. It says four hours.'

'I thought you didn't know how to cook it?' she asked drily, and he smiled, his eyes dancing with mischief.

'I didn't want to do you out of the pleasure—and this way you get all the glory.'

'What glory?'

'The glory of basking in my adoration,' he murmured, and she wasn't sure but there seemed to be a mildly flirtatious tone in his voice.

She held his eyes for a startled moment, then gave a slightly strained little laugh and looked away. 'Always assuming I don't burn it.'

'You won't. I'll make sure of that. Right, let's label that present with a new tag, and you go and stick them under the tree and I'll dish up.'

But what to write? His pen hovered for a moment over the tag he'd found. Did it matter? The child couldn't read.

'To Josh from Sebastian' would do.

But he put *love* in there, just because it seemed right. Weirdly right.

'OK, that's done, we need to eat or the pizza will be ruined.'

He slid the box across the table to her, pushed back his chair and made himself busy. So busy he didn't have time to think about what he'd written.

Or why.

She put the presents under the tree while he dished up, and then after they'd eaten and cleared away they peeled sprouts and potatoes and parsnips and carrots, until finally he called a halt.

'Enough,' he said firmly, took the knife out of her hand, replaced it with her wine glass and ushered her through to the sitting room.

The fire was low, the embers glowing, and they sat there with just the faint glow of the fairy lights and the occasional spark from the fire, his arm stretched out along the back of the sofa, his head turned towards her as they talked about the timetable for tomorrow.

If he moved his fingers just a millimetre—

'Tell me about the renovations,' she said then, and shifted, settling further into the corner, and he reached for his glass and pulled his arm back a little, out of temptation, and as he told her about the house and what he'd had done to it, he watched her and wondered just how much he was going to miss her when she left...

* * *

Josh woke early.

He always did, but she'd sat up with Sebastian talking about the house and the building work and what his plans were for the gardens until the fire had died away to ash and her eyes were drooping.

He'd hung the little stocking up on the beam, off to one side so the chocolate didn't melt, and then he'd taken himself off to his study while she'd come up to bed.

She'd heard him come up later, but not much later, and she'd turned on her side then and fallen sound asleep until Josh's cheerful chatter had woken her.

Bless his darling heart, she loved him so much but she could have done with another half hour. She prised open her eyes and he beamed at her and stood up in the travel cot, holding up his arms.

'Happy Christmas, Josh,' she said softly, gathering him up and hugging him tight. He gave her a big, sloppy kiss, and she laughed and kissed him back and tickled him, then she changed his nappy and took him down to the kitchen.

To her amazement the lights were blazing, the kettle was on and there was a wonderful smell of baking.

And it was after seven! How did that happen?

'Biscuit, Mummy,' Josh said, just as Sebastian came back into the kitchen.

He was wearing checked pyjama trousers and a jumper, his hair was rumpled and he definitely hadn't shaved, but he'd never looked so good, and her heart squeezed.

No! Don't fall in love with him again!

But then Josh ran over to him and he scooped him up and hugged him, tolerated the sloppy kiss with amazing grace and even kissed him back. 'Happy Christmas, Tiger,' he said, ruffling his hair, and Josh growled at him and made him laugh.

He growled back, and Josh giggled and squirmed down and ran back to her. 'Biscuit, Mummy! Bastian want biscuit too.'

'Ah. Sebastian's actually cooking croissants and pain au chocolat,' he confessed, his eyes flicking to hers in apology.

She smiled. 'It's Christmas. And they smell amazing.'

'They are. And they'll be burnt if I don't take them out. Coffee or tea?'

'Both. Tea first. I'll make it. What do you want?'

'Same. Tea, then coffee. I'll put a jug on for later.'

How domesticated, she thought, getting out the mugs and making the tea while he rescued the pastries and found plates and butter and jam, and she poured the tea and he sat Josh down and pulled up his pyjama sleeves so he didn't get plastered in butter.

We're like an old married couple, she thought, *just getting breakfast together on Christmas morning, and in a minute we'll go through to the sitting room and open Josh's presents and play with him, and the goose will cook and...*

She cut herself off.

This was a one-off. They weren't married. They were never getting married. And she needed to stop dreaming.

The train set was a hit.

They moved a table out of the way, and Sebastian got down on the floor with Josh and helped him set up the track, and she sat with her feet tucked up under her bottom, still in her pyjamas, cradling a cup of coffee and watching them.

Josh had opened his stocking, with the little cars and a packet of chocolate buttons and a satsuma she'd taken from the fruit bowl, and Sebastian had lit the fire and thrown the peel on it and it smelled Christmassy and wonderful.

So wonderful.

Her eyes filled. What had happened to him to make him change so much, to become so driven, so remote, so focused on something she couldn't understand that their love had withered and died?

He wasn't like that now. Or not today, at least. He'd been pretty crabby out in the lane in the snow, but since then he'd made a real effort.

Or maybe it was just because of Josh, to make him happy. That seemed really important to him, but was there more to it than that?

He'd written 'love from Sebastian' on the gift tag.

Just a figure of speech, the thing everyone always writes? Or because he meant it?

She had no idea, she just knew, watching him, listening to the two of them talking, that he'd really taken her little boy to his heart, and she found it unbearably touching.

'Right. Time to put the goose in,' he said, and she yanked herself out of her thoughts and put the cup down. 'I'll do it.'

'No. It's heavy. I'll put it in. You can do the tricky stuff later.'

He went out, taking their mugs, and came back a few minutes later with a refill and a handful of satsumas.

'Is that an attempt to compensate for the croissants?' she said drily, and he chuckled and lobbed one over to her, dropping down onto the other sofa and turning so he could watch Josh over the back.

'He chatters away, doesn't he?'

'Oh, yes. He didn't talk very early, but boys don't, I don't think. And they stop talking again in their teens, of course, and just start grunting.'

He frowned again, looking thoughtful for a moment. 'I'm sure I didn't grunt. Nor did my brothers, as far as I'm aware.'

'My brother did. He was monosyllabic for years. It made a refreshing change from all the arguments.'

'How is he? We lost touch when—well, then.'

She ignored his hesitation. 'Fine. He's working in Norwich. He's a surveyor. He's stopped grunting now and he's quite civilised. He's married with two children and a dog.'

He looked away. 'Lucky Jack.'

'He is. He's very happy.'

'I'm glad. Give him my regards.'

'I will. How are your brothers?'

'Better now they've grown up. They both work for me. Andy's an accountant, and Matt's a sales director.'

'Don't they mind answering to you?'

He laughed softly. 'It makes for interesting board meetings sometimes,' he confessed, and she laughed too.

'I'm sure. Talking of families, I ought to ring my parents. They'll want to say Happy Christmas to Josh.'

'How about doing it from my computer with the web-cam, so they can see you?'

'Can we? That would be brilliant!'

'Well, since they know you're here, you might as well. Do it in my study.'

She looked down at herself, suddenly aware of what

she was wearing. 'I might get dressed first. Just so they don't think we're hanging out all day in PJs.'

And then she looked up, and his eyes were on her, filled with a dark emotion she didn't want to try to understand, and she took Josh upstairs, protesting all the way, and washed and dressed him.

She needed a shower, really, and her hair washed, but she didn't like to let Josh run riot and she could hear water running in Sebastian's room, so she told him to stay there and look at a book, shot into the bathroom and showered and came out to find the door open and no sign of him.

'Josh? Josh, where are you?'

She ran out onto the landing, clutching the towel together, and slammed straight into Sebastian's chest. His bare, wet chest. His hands came up and steadied her, and she stared, mesmerised, as a dribble of water ran down through the light scatter of hair across his pecs and disappeared into the towel at his hips.

'If you're looking for Josh, he's in my room.'

His voice, low and gravelly, cut through her thoughts and she sucked in a breath. *What was she doing?*

He let go of her shoulders and stepped back, and she hitched her towel up and blushed. 'He is?'

'Yes. Don't worry. He came to find me. You take your time, we're fine.'

'Are you sure? Because I really need to—' She waved a hand vaguely at her towel, and his eyes tracked over it and he smiled slightly.

'Yes. You do.'

She glanced down, and saw it was gaping. Dear God, could it get any worse?

Blushing furiously and clutching it together, she went back into her room and closed the door, leant back against it and shut her eyes, humiliation washing over her. How could she have gone out there with her towel flapping open and revealing—well, everything, pretty much!

Not that he'd been exactly covered. Had he always looked that good naked?

Yes. Always. He was more solid now, but he'd always looked good. Tall, broad, muscular, without an ounce of spare flesh on him.

And she really, really didn't need to be thinking about that now! She pushed away from the door, dried herself quickly and wrestled her still-damp body into jeans and a jumper.

Her hair needed careful combing and drying, but it wasn't going to get it.

Or was it? There was a knock on the door and it opened a crack.

'There's a hairdryer in the top drawer of the bed-side table. I'm taking Josh downstairs. There's no rush. We're going to play with the train set.'

She sat down on the edge of the bed and sighed. Well, it would give her time to dry her hair properly and put on some make-up. And gather herself together a little. Her composure was scattered in all directions, and she was ready to die of humiliation.

Too right she'd take her time. She was in no hurry to face him again!

Her towel had slipped.

Not far enough. Just enough to taunt him, not enough to see anything. He'd gone back into his room, found Josh under the bed giggling and got dressed before Georgie had time to come looking for him again and caused another incident.

And Josh was more than happy to come downstairs and play with his trains. So was Sebastian. Only too happy, because it reminded him of all the reasons why getting involved with Georgie again would be such a mistake.

She'd walked out on him once, but they'd been the only ones who could get hurt in that situation, and he knew he'd been at least partly responsible. OK, maybe largely responsible, but not solely. He wasn't taking all the blame for her lack of sticking power.

But this time, Josh would be involved. And he was so open, so trusting, so vulnerable. Two was a bad time for your world to fall apart. He knew that, in some deep, inaccessible but intrinsic part of him that still ached with loss.

Wounds that deep never really healed. And that was another reason to keep his distance.

So he played with Josh until she came down, and then he went into the kitchen and started putting the lunch together.

She followed him, Josh in tow. 'You said I could hook up with my parents,' she reminded him, and he nodded, put the timer on for the potatoes and took her to the study, connected her up and left them to it. Five minutes later they were back.

'I thought I was supposed to be cooking?' she said, but he shook his head.

'Don't worry about it. It actually looks pretty straightforward and the instructions are idiot-proof.'

'Are you sure? I thought that was the deal?'

'There's no deal,' he said shortly. 'Go and play with your son. It's Christmas. He needs you, not me. I'll do this.'

In fact there wasn't that much to do, to his regret.

He parboiled the potatoes and parsnips, put them in a roasting pan with some of the goose fat and put them in the oven, moving the goose to the bottom oven to continue cooking slowly.

And then there was nothing to do for an hour.

Well, he had two choices. He could spend his Christmas Day sitting alone in the kitchen, or he could go back into the sitting room with Georgie and Josh and try not to remember what he'd seen under her towel…

The sitting room won, hands down.

CHAPTER SEVEN

GEORGIE SAT BACK and sighed happily.

'Sebastian, for someone who claims not to know how to cook a goose, that was an amazing lunch. Thank you so much.'

His shoulders twitched in that little shrug of his that she was getting so used to. 'Good ingredients. I can't take any credit.'

That was rubbish and they both knew it, but he'd always been modest about his achievements. For such a high achiever, it was a strange trait, and rather endearing. She smiled at him.

'Nevertheless, it was delicious and I'm washing up.'

'No. The dishwasher's washing up. And the sun's out and it's warmer, so let's not waste the day in here. Has Josh got anything he can wear outside?'

'Yes. Wellies and overalls, in the car, and I brought my wellies, too—hey, we could make snow angels!'

He chuckled. 'I think you'll find if we put him down in the snow, he'll vanish without trace, unless we can find a bit where it's not so deep. Right, let's go!'

So they abandoned the devastated kitchen, wrapped themselves up and headed out into the garden. Sebastian hoisted Josh up onto his shoulders and the little boy anchored his chubby fingers into Sebastian's hair, his happy grin almost splitting his face in half.

'Wait, let me take a photo,' she said, and pulled out her phone. They posed dutifully, and she carried on, snapping off several shots of them as he turned and walked through the archway into the sunlit garden.

And it was glorious. He was right, it would have been criminal to miss it. The wind had died away completely and the sun shone with real warmth, sparkling on the snow and blinding them with its brilliance.

She scooped up a handful of snow and let Josh touch it, probing it with his finger. He was wary, but fascinated, and Sebastian lifted him down on the grass in the little orchard where the snow wasn't so deep and lowered him carefully into it, and Josh watched his feet disappear and giggled.

Then Sebastian turned and looked at her, and she knew what was coming.

She saw it in his eyes, saw the way he carefully gathered up a great big handful of snow and showed Josh how to squash it into a snowball.

'No. Sebastian, no! I mean it—!'

It got her right in the middle of the chest.

'Oh, you rat!' she squealed indignantly, and he just picked up her giggling son and laughed, his head tilted back, his mouth open, his face tipped up to the sun as Josh laughed with him, and if she could have bottled it, she would.

Instead she whipped out her phone and took a photo, the instant before he set Josh back in the snow.

Then she filed her phone safely in her pocket, because this was war and she wasn't taking any prisoners.

Sebastian's eyes were alight with mischief, and she scraped up a handful and hurled it back, missing him by miles. The next one got him, though, but not before his got her, and they ended up chasing each other through the snow, Sebastian carrying Josh in his arms, until he cornered her in one of the recesses of the crinkle-crankle wall and trapped her.

'Got that snowball, Josh?' he asked, advancing on her with a wicked smile that made her heart race for a whole lot of reasons, and he held her still, pinning her against the wall with his body while Josh put snow down her neck and made her shriek.

'Oh, that was so mean! Just you wait, Corder!'

'Oh, I'm so scared.' He grinned cockily, turning away, and she took her chance and pelted him right on the back of his neck.

'Like that, is it?' he said softly, and she felt her heart flip against her ribs.

But he did nothing, because they found a clear bit of snow where it wasn't too deep, and one by one they fell over backwards and made snow angels.

Josh's angel was a bit crooked, but Sebastian's was brilliant, huge and crisp and clean. How he stood up without damaging it she had no idea, but he did, and she looked down at it next to Josh's little angel and then hers, and felt something huge swelling in her chest.

And then she got a handful of snow shoved down the back of her neck, which would teach her to turn her back on Sebastian, and it jerked her out of her sentimental daze.

'Thought you'd got away with it, didn't you?' he teased, his mischievous grin taunting her, and she chased him through the orchard, dodging round the trees with Josh running after them and giggling hysterically.

Then he stopped, and she cannoned into him just as

he turned so that she ended up plastered against him, his arms locking reflexively round her to steady her.

And then he glanced up. She followed his gaze and saw the mistletoe, but it was too late. Too late to move or object or do anything except stand there transfixed, her heart pounding, while he smiled slowly and cupped her chilly, glowing face in his frozen hands and kissed her.

His lips were warm, their touch gentle, and the years seemed to melt away until she was eighteen again, and he was just twenty, and they were in love.

She'd forgotten.

She, who remembered everything about everything, had forgotten that all those Christmases ago he'd brought her here, to the orchard where that summer they'd made love in the dappled shade under the gnarled old apple trees, and kissed her.

Under this very mistletoe?

Possibly. It seemed very familiar, although the kiss was completely different.

That kiss had been wonderfully romantic and passionate. This one was utterly spontaneous and playful; tender, filled with nostalgia, it rocked her composure as passion never would have done. Passion she could have dismissed. This…

She backed away, her hand over her mouth, and spun round in the snow to look for Josh.

He was busy squashing more snow up, pressing his hands into it and laughing, and she waded over to him and picked him up, holding him against her like a shield.

'Oh, Josh, your hands are freezing! Come on, darling, time to go back inside.' And without waiting to see what Sebastian was doing, she carried Josh back to the relative safety of the house.

As she pulled off their snowy clothes in the boot

room, she noticed the little heap of mistletoe on the floor. It was still lying in the corner where he'd left it yesterday, and she'd forgotten all about it. Had he? Or had he taken her to the orchard deliberately, so he could kiss her right there underneath the tree where it had been growing for all these years? Where he'd kissed her all those Christmases ago?

If so, it had been a mistake. No kisses, she'd said, and he'd promised. They both had. And it had lasted a whole twenty-four hours.

Great. Fantastic. What a result...

Sebastian watched her go, kicking himself for that crazy, unnecessary lapse in common sense.

He hadn't even put up the mistletoe in the house because in the end it had seemed like such a bad idea, and then he'd brought her out here and they'd played in the snow just as they had eleven years ago, right under that great hanging bunch of mistletoe.

And he'd kissed her under it.

In front of Josh.

Of all the stupid, stupid things...

'Oh, you *idiot*.'

Shaking his head in disbelief, he made his way back inside and found she'd hung up their wet coats in front of the Aga to dry. Josh was playing on the floor with one of the cars out of his stocking, and she was pulling up her sleeves and getting stuck into the clearing up.

'I've put the kettle on,' she said. 'I thought we could do with a hot drink.'

'Good idea,' he said, but he noticed that she didn't look at him, and he only noticed that out of the corner of his eye because he was so busy not looking at her.

No repeats.

That had been the deal. He'd give Josh Christmas, and there'd be no recriminations, no harking back to their breakup, and no repeats of that kiss.

So far, it seemed, they were failing on all fronts.

Idiot! he repeated in his head, and pushing up his own sleeves, he tackled what was left.

'I'm sorry.'

The words were weary, and Georgie searched his eyes.

She'd put Josh to bed, waited until he was asleep and then forced herself to come downstairs. She'd hoped he'd be in the study, but he wasn't, he was in the kitchen making sandwiches with the left-over goose and cranberry sauce, and now she was here, too. Having walked in, there was no way of walking out without appearing appallingly rude, and then he'd turned to her and apologised.

And it had really only been a lighthearted, playful little kiss, she told herself, but she knew that she was lying.

'It's OK,' she said, although it wasn't, because it had affected her much more than she was letting on. She gave a little shrug. 'It was nothing really.'

'Well, I'll have to do better next time, then,' he said softly, and her eyes flew back to his.

'There won't be a next time. You promised.'

'I know. It was a joke.'

'Well, it wasn't funny.'

He sighed and rammed his hand through his hair, the smile leaving his eyes. 'We're not doing well, are we?'

'You're not. It was you that raised the walking out issue, you that kissed me. So far I think I've pretty much stuck to my side of the bargain.'

'Apart from running around in a scanty little towel that didn't quite meet.'

She felt hot colour run up her cheeks, and turned away. 'That was an accident. I was worried about Josh. And you didn't have a lot on, either.'

'No.' He sighed again. 'I have to say, as apologies go, this isn't going very well, is it?'

She gave a soft, exasperated laugh and turned back to him, meeting the wry smile in his eyes and relenting.

'Not really. Why don't we just draw a line under it and start again? As you said, it was warmer today. It'll thaw soon. We just have to get through the next day or two. I'm sure we can manage that.'

'I'm sure we can. I thought you might be hungry, so I threw something together.' He cut the sandwiches in quarters as he spoke, stacked them on a plate and put them on a tray. Glasses, side plates, cheese, a slab of fruit cake and the remains of lunchtime's bottle of Rioja followed, and he picked the tray up and walked towards her. 'Open the door?'

She opened it, followed him to the sitting room and sat down. This was so awkward. All of it, everything, was so awkward, pretending that it was all OK and being civilised when all they really wanted to do was yell at each other.

Or make love.

'George, don't.'

'Don't what?'

He sat down on the other sofa, opposite her, and held her eyes with his. 'Don't look like that. I know it's difficult. I'm sorry, I'm an idiot, I've just made it more uncomfortable, but—we were good friends once, Georgie—'

'We were lovers,' she said bluntly, and he smiled sadly.

'We were friends, too. We should be able to talk to each other in a civilised manner. We managed last night.'

'That was before you kissed me again.'

He sighed and rammed his hand through his hair, and she began to feel sorry for it.

'The kiss was nothing,' he said shortly, 'you know that, you said so yourself. And I'm sorry it upset you. It just seemed—right. Natural. The obvious thing to do. We were playing, and then there you were, right under the mistletoe, and—well, I just acted on impulse. It really, really won't happen again. I promise.'

She didn't challenge him on that. He'd promised to love her forever, and he'd driven her away. She knew about his promises. And hers weren't a lot better, because she'd promised to love him, too, and she'd left him.

What a mess. *Please, please thaw so we can get away from him...*

She reached for a sandwich and bit into it, and he sat forward, pouring the wine and sliding a glass towards her.

'You didn't tell me what you thought of this wine at lunch.'

'Is it important?'

He shrugged. 'In a way. I've got shares in the bodega. It's a good vintage. I just wondered if you liked it.'

'Yes, it's lovely.' She sipped, giving it thought. 'It goes well with the goose and the cranberries. It is nice—really nice, although if it's fiendishly expensive it's wasted on me. I could talk a lot of rubbish about it being packed with plump, luscious fruit and dark chocolate with a long, slow finish because I watch the television, but I wouldn't really know what I was talking about. But it is nice. I like it.'

He laughed. 'You don't need to know anything else. You just need to know what you like and what you don't like, and I like my wines soft. Rounded. Full of plump, luscious fruit,' he said, and there was something in his eyes that made her catch her breath and remember the gaping towel.

She looked hastily away, grabbing another sandwich and making a production of eating it, and he sat back and worked his way down a little pile of them, and for a while there was silence.

'So,' he said, breaking it at last, 'what's the plan for your house? You say you can't sell it at the moment, but what will you do when you have? Buy another? Rent?'

'Move back home.'

'Home? As in, come back and live with your parents?'

'Yes. I'll have childcare on tap, they'll get to see lots of Josh and I can work for my boss as easily here as I can in Huntingdon.'

He nodded, but there was a little crease between his eyebrows, the beginnings of a frown. 'Wouldn't you rather have your independence?'

She put down the shredded crusts of her sandwich and sighed. 'Well, of course, and I've tried that, but it doesn't feel like independence, really, not with Josh. It's just difficult. Every day's an uphill struggle to get everything done, hence watching the television when I'm too tired to work any more. There's no adult to talk to, I'm alone all day and all night except for the company of a two-year-old, and after he's in bed it's just lonely.'

The frown was back. 'He's very good company though when he is around. He's a great little kid.'

'He is, but his conversation is a wee bit lacking.'

Sebastian chuckled and reached for his wine. 'We don't seem to be doing so well, either.'

'So what do you want to talk about? Politics? The economy? Biogenetics? I can tell you all about that.'

'Is that what you do?'

'A bit. I don't really do anything any more. I just collate stuff for them and check for research trials and see if I can validate them. Some are a bit sketchy. It's an interesting field, genetic engineering, and it's going to be increasingly useful in medicine and agriculture in the future.'

'Tell me.'

So she talked about her work, about what her professor was doing at the moment, what they'd done, and what she'd been studying for her PhD before she'd had to abandon it.

'Would you like to finish it?' he asked, and she rolled her eyes.

'Of course! But I can't. I've got Josh now. I have other priorities.'

'But later?'

She shrugged. 'Later might be too late. Things move on, and what I was researching won't be relevant any longer. Things move so fast in genetics, so that what wasn't possible yesterday will be commonplace tomorrow. Take the use of DNA tests, for example. It's got all sorts of forensic and familial implications that simply couldn't have been imagined not that long ago, and now it's just accepted.'

His heart thumped.

'Familial implications? Things like tracing members of your family?' he suggested, keeping his voice carefully neutral.

'Yes. Yes, absolutely. It can be used to prove that people are or aren't related, it can tell you where in the world you've come from, where your distant ancestors came from—using mitochondrial DNA, which our bodies are absolutely rammed with, most Europeans can be traced back down the female line to one of a handful of women if you go back enough thousands of years. It's incredible.'

But not infallible. Not if you didn't know enough to start with. And not clever enough to give a match to someone who'd never been tested or had their DNA stored on a relevant database. He knew all about that and its frustrations.

Tell her.

'So, tell me about this bodega,' she said, settling back with a slab of fruitcake and a chunk of cheese, and he let the tension ease out of him at the change of subject.

'The bodega?'

'Mmm. I've decided it's a rather nice wine. I might have some more when I've finished eating. I'm not sure it'd go with cake and cheese.'

'I'm not sure cake and cheese go together in the first place.'

'You are joking?' She stared at him, her mouth slightly open. 'You're not joking. Try it.'

She held out the piece of cake with the cheese perched on top, the marks made by her even teeth clear at the edge of the bite, and he leant in and bit off the part her mouth had touched.

He felt something kick in his gut, but then the flavour burst through and he sat back and tried to concentrate on the cake and cheese combo and not the fact that he felt as if he'd indirectly kissed her.

'Wow. That is actually rather nice.'

She rolled her eyes again. 'You are so sceptical. It's like ham and pineapple, and lamb and redcurrant jelly.'

'Chalk and cheese.'

'Now you're just being silly. I thought you liked it?'

'I do.' He cut himself a chunk of both and put them together, mostly so he didn't have to watch her bite off the bit his own teeth had touched.

Hell. How could it be so ridiculously erotic?

'So—the bodega?'

'Um. Yeah.' He groped for his brain and got it into gear again, more or less, and told her all about it—about how he'd been driving along a quiet country road and he'd broken down and a man had stopped to help him.

'He turned out to be the owner of the bodega. He took me back there and contacted the local garage, and while we waited we got talking, and to cut a long story short I ended up bailing them out.'

'That was a good day's business for them.'

He chuckled. 'It wasn't a bad one for me. I stumbled on it by accident, I now own thirty per cent, and they're doing well. They've had three good vintages on the trot, I get a regular supply of wine I can trust, and we're all happy.'

'And if it's a bad year?'

'Then we've got the financial resilience to weather it.'

Or he had, she thought. They'd been lucky to find him.

'Where is it?' she asked. 'Does Rioja have to come from a very specific region?'

'Yes. It's in northern Spain. They grow a variety of

grapes—it's a region rather than a grape variety, and they use mostly Tempranillo which gives it that lovely softness.'

He opened another bottle, a different vintage, and as he told her about it, about how they made it, the barrels they used, the effect of the climate, he stopped thinking about her mouth and what it would be like to kiss her again, and began to relax and just enjoy her company.

He didn't normally spend much time like this, and certainly not with anyone as interesting and restful to be with as Georgie. Not nearly enough, he realised. He was too busy, too harassed, too driven by the workload to take time out. And that was a mistake.

Hence why he'd turned off his mobile phone and ignored it for the last twenty-four hours. It was Christmas. He was allowed a day off, and he intended to take advantage of every minute of it. Tomorrow would come soon enough.

He peeled a satsuma from the bowl and threw it to her, and peeled himself another one, then they cracked some nuts and threw the shells in the fire and watched it die down slowly.

It seemed as if neither of them wanted to move, to call it a night, to do anything to disturb the fragile truce, and so they sat there, staring into the fire and talking about safe subjects.

Uncontroversial ones, with no bones of contention, no trigger points, no sore spots, as if by mutual agreement. They talked about his mother's heart attack, her father's retirement plans, his plans for the restoration of the walled garden, and gradually the fire died away to ash and it grew chilly in the room.

'I ought to go up and make sure Josh is all right,' she said, although the baby monitor was there on the table and hadn't done more than blink a couple of times, just enough so they knew it was working.

But he didn't argue, because they were running out of safe topics and it was better to quit while they were winning and before he did something stupid like kiss her.

He got to his feet, gathered up their glasses and put them on the tray with the plates, made sure the fire guard was secure and carried the tray through to the kitchen.

She was getting herself a glass of water, and he put the tray down beside the sink and turned towards her.

'Got everything you need?'

No, she thought. She needed him, but he wasn't good for her, and she certainly hadn't been good for him. Not in the long term. 'Yes, I'm fine,' she said, and then hesitated.

His eyes were unreadable, but the air was thick with tension. It would have been so natural, so easy to lean in and kiss him goodnight.

So dangerous.

So tempting…

She paused in the doorway and looked back, and he was watching her, his face shuttered.

'Thank you for today,' she said quietly. 'It's been really lovely. Really lovely. Josh has had a brilliant time, and so've I.'

'Even the kiss?'

She laughed softly. 'There was never any doubt about your kisses, Sebastian. None at all.'

'Wrong place, wrong time?' he suggested, and she shook her head.

'Wrong time.'

'And the place?'

'You can never go back,' she said simply, and with a sad smile, she closed the door and left him standing there in what should have been their kitchen, gazing after the woman he still loved but knew he'd lost forever.

'Damn,' he said softly.

It was a fine time to discover that he still wanted her, that he still loved her, that he should have done more to stop her leaving. But his head had been in the wrong place then, and hers was now.

You should have told her.

He should. But he hadn't, and now wasn't the time. It was too late. She'd moved on, and so had he.

Hadn't he?

He poured himself another glass of wine and left the kitchen, retreating into his study and the thing that kept him sane. Work. Always work. The one constant in his life.

He turned his phone on, and it beeped at him furiously as the emails and messages came pouring in. Even on Christmas Day. He was obviously not the only workaholic, he thought drily, and then he opened them.

Greetings. Christmas greetings from family, friends, work colleagues.

And he'd meant to contact all of them, and so far had only rung his immediate family.

He'd do it now. He had nothing better to do, either, and it beat lying in bed next to Georgie's room and listening to the sounds of her getting ready for bed. Although even in his study he could hear her, because she was immediately overhead.

He listened to the sound of water running, the creak of the boards as she crossed the room to the bed. A different creak as she climbed into it and lay down.

He tried to tune it out, but it was impossible, so he put

the radio on quietly. Carols from King's College, Cambridge, flooded the room and drowned out the sound of her movements.

Pity they couldn't drown out his thoughts...

CHAPTER EIGHT

'Mummy! Mummy, wake up!'

She prised her eyes open. Light was leaking round the edges of the curtains, and it looked—astonishingly—like sunlight. She propped herself up on one elbow and scraped her hair back out of her eyes.

'Hello, Mummy!'

He was beaming at her, and she felt her heart melt. 'Hello, darling. Are you all right? Did you sleep well?'

He nodded vigorously. He was standing in the cot, bobbing up and down with unchannelled energy, and he looked bright-eyed and bushy-tailed.

'Want Bastian,' he said. 'Play in snow.'

The cot rocked wildly, and she sat up and grabbed the edge to steady it. 'Let's get up first, shall we? Nappy, drink, clothes on? Then we'll see.'

He nodded and held up his arms, and she lifted him out. He was warm and he smelled of sleepy baby, and she breathed him in and snuggled him close for a moment, but he wasn't having any of it. There was snow outside with his name on it, and he wanted out.

Now.

She changed his nappy, hesitated for a moment and pulled on his clothes, then dressed herself quickly, just in case Sebastian was around. That almost-kiss last night was still tormenting her as it had been all night so she wasn't going to tempt fate, but Josh was starving and in a hurry.

Teeth and a quick wash could wait till after breakfast, she decided, and opened the bedroom door to the wonderful smell of bacon cooking. And toast, the aromas wafting up the stairs and making her mouth water.

He turned as she went in, frying pan in hand, and smiled at them. 'You're up bright and early.'

'Well, someone is,' she said drily, as Josh ran over to Sebastian and put his arms round his legs, tilting his head back and looking up pleadingly.

'Want snow,' he said, and Sebastian gave a slightly stunned laugh.

'Whoa, little fella, it's a bit early for that. How about some nice breakfast first?' He looked across at Georgie. 'Does he like bacon sandwiches?'

She laughed. 'Probably. He's never had one, but he likes bacon and he eats sandwiches. And I certainly do.'

His smile was a little twisted, his voice soft. 'I know.'

Of course he did. They'd had bacon sandwiches for breakfast every Sunday morning when they'd been together, either at home or in a café. And he hadn't forgotten, apparently, any more than she had.

Those dangerous emotions swirled in the air for a moment, carried, like the memories, on the smell of frying bacon, and she pulled herself together with an effort.

'Can I do anything?' she asked briskly. 'Make tea? Coffee?'

'Tea. I've had coffee. I've been up a couple of hours.'

'Really?'

She glanced at the old school-style clock on the wall and did a mild double-take.

'It's after eight! When did that happen?'

'While you were sleeping?' he said, his eyes gently mocking. 'I was about to come up and open the bedroom door when I heard Josh chatting. I knew you wouldn't be long if I let the smell of bacon in.'

'Like one of Pavlov's dogs?'

'If the cap fits...'

'You are so rude.' She stared at the worktop blankly. 'What was I doing?'

'Making tea?' he offered, his mouth twitching, and she threw the tea towel at him and put the kettle on while he moved the bacon to the slower burner and sliced some bread.

In the time it took her to make the tea and give Josh a drink of milk, he'd flipped the bacon out onto kitchen paper to drain, cracked some eggs into a pan and scrambled them while the toast cooked, sliced some tomatoes, split the toast and made a stack of club sandwiches.

'He might be happier with bread,' she said, but Josh reached out, his little hand opening and closing frantically. 'Me have Bastian sandwich,' he said.

He was getting a serious and rather worrying case of hero worship, she realised with a sigh, but she shrugged and cut him off a chunk. She didn't think he'd eat it, but he did, and demanded more.

'I'm not sure I'm going to give him any more, this is soooo good,' she mumbled through a mouthful, and Sebastian just laughed and handed Josh the rest of his own.

Just like a father would.

She blinked, sucked in a quiet breath and gave herself a mental shake. He was *not* Josh's father, and he wasn't going to be his stepfather, or surrogate father, or even a best uncle! He was nobody to Josh except an old friend of hers who'd rescued them one Christmas, and that was the way it had to stay if she didn't want to risk him getting hurt. Hero worship notwithstanding.

Frankly, he'd lost enough already. And so had she.

'Right, I'm going out to clear the drive. The snow's beginning to soften slightly. It didn't freeze last night, and with the sun on it the drive might thaw if I can get most of the snow off it. I wouldn't be surprised if they don't clear the lane tomorrow.'

'Not today?' she asked, sort of hopefully, although a part of her definitely didn't want it cleared yet.

'Not on Boxing Day,' he said. 'It's unlikely. They'll be clearing the main roads still, making sure the urban areas are safe for the majority of the population. This lane is incredibly small potatoes in comparison. It's probably not even on their to-do list so it might be a local farmer.'

She nodded slowly. That made sense, and if the farmer had stock, he might be too busy with them to worry about the lane for days.

And she wasn't at all sure how that made her feel.

Yes, she was!

She had to get out of here before—well, before it got any worse. Before Josh's idolisation of Sebastian got out of proportion. And before one or other of them cracked big-time and gave into the magnetic tug of attraction that time didn't seem to have done anything to weaken. And that meant being able to get the car out.

'If you've got another shovel, can I give you a hand?'

'I haven't, but you can come out and cheerlead if you like. I'm sure Josh'll have fun out there playing in the snow, won't you, Josh? There aren't any roses or anything lurking under the snow to hurt him, not near the drive, so he can't come to any harm.'

'Me snow!' he begged, bouncing up and down beside her, his eyes pleading, and she gave up the unequal struggle. They didn't have to stay out there for long.

'Teeth first, and then we'll go outside. OK?'

'OK!'

He ran off, heading towards the stairs, with Georgie in hot pursuit, and as they left the kitchen Sebastian found himself smiling.

Why?

Because he was happy?

Because they were coming outside to help him clear the drive, and he'd get to play with Josh again?

Not to mention Georgie...

Stop it!

They could make a snowman, he thought, dragging his mind back to the child, and he tracked down a carrot for his nose and two Brussels sprouts for eyes, then wrapped up warm and went outside to get started.

The snow wasn't quite as deep as it had been, but there was still quite enough of it and the first thing he did was cut a path through to the gates and clear around the bottom of them so they had room to swing open.

Assuming the mechanism wasn't frozen solid. It had better not be, he'd paid enough for them to be restored and the electric openers to be fitted.

He wouldn't test them. Not yct, not until the sun had time to get on them and warm them up a little, but he could clear the rest of the snow from in front of them.

He'd hardly started when Georgie and Josh arrived. He'd heard them coming, Josh's excited chatter reaching him long before Georgie's mellow tones.

'How are you doing?'

'OK. It's slow.'

'Is it OK if we build a snowman?' she asked.

He straightened up and turned to look at them. Josh

was busy making a snowball, crouched down with his little bottom stuck out and perched on the snow, and Georgie, bundled up in her coat and gloves, looked so like she had all those years ago when they'd played in the orchard right here that his heart tugged.

He pulled out the carrot and sprouts. 'Great minds think alike,' he said with a smile, and handed them to her.

'What's that?' Josh asked, peering at them, the snowball forgotten.

'His nose and eyes,' he said, and got a sceptical look, but Georgie just laughed, the sound rippling through him like a shock wave.

'You'll see, Josh. Now, where shall we build him?'

'Over there?' Sebastian suggested, pointing at a piece of ground he knew was firm and flat, so they went over to it, and she started rolling up a ball to make the body while he carried on shovelling the drive.

'Gosh, it's heavy!'

He turned to watch her. She was shoving it with both hands, and after a moment her feet slipped and she faceplanted into the snow.

He had to laugh.

He couldn't help it, and nor could Josh, the laughter bubbling up inside them irresistibly, but then he relented and went over and held out a hand, hauling her to her feet.

Her eyes were laughing, even though she was pretending to be cross with them, and she brushed herself off and straightened, just inches from him. There was a trickle of melting snow on her cheek, and he wiped it gently away with his thumb.

Their eyes met and locked, and for a moment time

seemed suspended. Then Josh floundered over to them, and the spell was broken, and he breathed again.

'Need a hand with your snowman?' he asked.

'I never turn down muscle when it's offered,' she said, and he chuckled.

'I take it that's a yes,' he said and, abandoning the shovel, he joined in the fun.

'There!'

He'd rolled up a smaller ball for the head, heaved it on top of the body and set it in a little hollow so it didn't rock off, and she'd pushed in the carrot and sprouts to make his face and found a stick for a pipe.

They were standing back to admire their handiwork, and Georgie frowned.

'He needs a scarf,' she said, and he shrugged and unravelled the scarf from round his neck.

She blinked. 'I can't use that,' she said, sounding scandalised. 'It's a really nice one. It feels like cashmere.'

He shrugged again. 'It's fine.'

It meant he wouldn't have one until the snow went, but that didn't matter. He could rescue it then, and it could be washed. Even if it got ruined, which it probably would, he realised he didn't care.

Didn't care at all, because Josh was giggling and having a brilliant time, and that was all that mattered.

But then the brilliant time came to an end. His fingers were cold, his nose was bright red and he was hungry, and Georgie took him back inside, leaving Sebastian to his shovelling.

He studied the drive, assessing the task.

Monumental, really. He would be there all day, but

it needed doing, and the hard physical exertion was a distraction from his thoughts.

It worked well, until he had to stop for a while, straightening up with a groan and shoving his hands in the small of his back and arching it out straight.

'Ouch.' Clearly not as fit as he imagined he was.

He turned to look at the snowman, and found himself smiling.

His eyes weren't on the same level, his nose was bent, his head wasn't quite in the middle, but the scarf looked good.

He gave a wry huff of laughter. So it should, but it had been worth it just to see the little boy's face. And Georgie's.

He felt a wash of emotion that he didn't really want to analyse. It felt curiously like happy families, and it felt good, and that wasn't a great idea. Not at all.

Damn. It's not going to happen. Don't go there.

He went back to the shovelling, working until the burning in his back muscles forced him to stop. He creaked up straight, studied the drive again and shrugged.

The gates had opened when he'd tested them, and the area beyond the gates was cleared, as was the drive for the first thirty or so feet. His car would get through the uncleared bit if he took it steady. All he needed now was for the farmer to come and clear the lane, and he was home free.

Or, rather, she would be.

He ignored the stab of something that he didn't want to think about, and headed inside into the warm. Not that his body was cold, but his nose and ears were a bit chilly and his hands were cold where the gloves had got soaked making the snowman.

With any luck, he thought as he kicked off his boots, Georgie and Josh would be in the little sitting room and he could go straight into his study and distract himself in there.

They weren't. They were in the kitchen, Josh playing on the floor with a little car, and the air was full of the aroma of freshly brewed coffee.

She walked over to the boot room door and leant on the frame with a smile. 'You've saved me a journey,' she said. 'I was just about to bring you a drink.'

'I'm done. My back aches and I've cleared enough.'

She tsked under her breath. 'I knew you'd do too much. Where does it hurt? Do you want me to rub it for you?'

He gave her an incredulous look. 'I don't think that's a good idea.'

'But you're hurting.'

He sighed softly and met her eyes, his dark with all manner of nameless emotions that made her heart lurch in her chest. 'Let me put it in words of one syllable,' he said slowly. 'I am trying-'

'That's two,' she said, trying to lighten the stifling atmosphere.

He rolled his eyes. 'OK,' he said, his voice ultrasoft so Josh wouldn't hear. 'I. Need. To. Keep. My. Hands. Off. You. And. If. You. Touch. Me. That. Will. Not. Help!'

And without waiting for her to make some sassy reply, he cupped her shoulders in his hands, moved her out of his way and forced himself to walk away from temptation.

Georgie closed her eyes and blew out her breath slowly.

What an idiot she was! Of course he didn't want her

touching him! It was hard enough as it was. Throw any more fuel on the fire between them and it would rage out of control like a bushfire. And neither of them needed that.

Yes...!

No! No, no, no, no, NO!

She poured a coffee for him, told Josh she would only be a moment and followed him to his study, her heart pounding.

She knew he was there because the music was on and she could hear it from the kitchen doorway. She tapped, pushed the door open and went in, leaving the door open for safety.

'Coffee,' she said, setting it down on the mat on his desk, and he turned his head and looked up at her.

'George—I'm sorry. It's just...'

'I know. It's my fault. I wasn't thinking. I'll see you later for lunch. Half an hour OK?'

He nodded. 'That would be great. Thanks.'

She took herself back to the kitchen, poured a coffee for herself and took Josh back into the little sitting room to play with the train set for a few minutes. It was nearer to Sebastian, but they weren't making a lot of noise and she didn't think they'd disturb him, especially not over the music.

But then the door opened and he came in, cup in hand, and joined them.

Why?

Because he couldn't stay away?

'I've just spoken to the local farmer. He's going to clear the lane. He'll make a start today, but it might be tomorrow before he gets to the gate.'

'Oh. Right.' She forced a smile. 'Well, that's good to know. I'll tell my mother to expect us.'

'So—shall I get lunch?'

'Goose sandwiches?' she teased, but he shook his head.

'We had sandwiches for breakfast and for supper. It might be time for something more imaginative. We have a whole groaning larder to choose from.'

They did.

She made a winter salad tossed in a honey and mustard dressing to go with the goose which he shredded and crisped in the oven, and Josh had a little of it with some pasta and pesto and a handful of cherry tomatoes.

'That was nice and healthy,' she said, and he laughed and got out the Christmas cake.

'It was. And I'm starving. You can be too healthy. Want cheese with it?'

'Mmm. And tea.'

She cubed some cheese for Josh, gave him a sliver of the cake without icing and then cut them both a chunk.

Sebastian was munching his way through a slab the size of his hand when he glanced up and frowned.

'It's raining!'

'What?'

She turned and looked out of the window.

Rain. Only light rain, but rain, not snow. And that meant a sudden thaw.

'It could flood tomorrow,' she said.

'It could, if it keeps on. In the meantime, I guess my activities on the drive are over.'

'Well, it won't be necessary anyway if it's going to rain hard. It's a pity, though. I was hoping I could take Josh outside again for a bit more running around.'

Sebastian shrugged. 'There's plenty of room in the house. He can run around in here, can't you, Josh?'

'Well, that's true,' she said. 'If he just tears up and down the hall he'll wear himself out in half an hour.'

'Play hide and seek?' Josh said hopefully, and Sebastian smiled indulgently at him.

'Sure. Heaven knows there are plenty of places to hide,' he said drily, his eyes flicking up to Georgie's.

There were. More than enough. And she'd hidden in all of them, and he'd found her.

And kissed her.

She looked hastily away.

'I think we could stick to the ground floor.'

'Or the attic?'

'The attic? Have you done anything with it?'

'Not much. It's been cleaned out and repaired when the roof was sorted, but it's pretty much as it was. I thought the house was big enough for me with just two floors.'

'What's a tick?' Josh asked, looking puzzled, and Georgie suppressed a smile.

'Not a tick, an attic. It's—well, we'll show you, shall we? It's just the very, very, very upstairs.'

'Oh.'

Sebastian chuckled softly. 'I can hear the cogs turning.'

'Oh, yeah. Watching him learn is amazing. Let's go and show him.'

He opened the door at the top of the stairs, and Georgie followed him and looked around, her eyes wide.

'Gosh. It looks enormous now you can see it all. It used to be full of cobwebs and birds' nests and clutter.'

'It was—especially the clutter. We lost count of the number of skips it took to take it all away.'

'Was there anything interesting?'

'There was, but most of the stuff was damaged because the birds had got in. I've got some of the things that were rescued downstairs, but most of it was beyond saving. And there was a lot of rubbish. You know what people are like. They put stuff away and leave it "just in case", and then forget it.'

She walked slowly through the rooms, Josh's hand firmly in hers, and checked that it was safe. It was. There was nothing that could harm him, and so she let go of his hand.

'Right. Are we going to play hide and seek?'

'Yay! Hide and seek! Yay!'

Josh was bouncing on the spot, and she put her hands over her eyes and peeped through her fingers.

'You peeping!' he said, and she laughed.

'I'm going to count. Josh, Sebastian, go and hide!'

He grabbed Josh by the hand and grinned. 'Come on. I know a good place.'

He did. It was under the eaves, behind the chimney, and he pulled Josh in there and held him close.

'Ready or not, here I come!'

He could hear her footsteps coming, and Josh started to giggle.

'Shh,' he whispered. 'Don't make a sound.'

He could hear her footsteps coming, going into another room, then coming closer, closer...

Like the walls, closing in on him, the small boy leaning on his leg, a voice saying 'Shh,' the sound almost inaudible in the silence.

Silence broken only by the sound of footsteps...

A sudden wave of panic came out of nowhere, and he tried to swallow it, but it wouldn't subside, and with a sudden rush he straightened and burst out of the tight space and into the light.

'Sebastian?'

She was right there, staring at him curiously, her mouth moving, but he could hardly hear her through the pounding of his heart. It was running like an express train, deafening him, and he made some vague excuse about having something to do and walked swiftly away on legs like overcooked spaghetti.

Georgia stared after him.

Busy? It was Boxing Day, all businesses except retail outlets were closed.

No. It was just an excuse not to be with her and Josh. Maybe he felt she was just sucking him in again?

But it had seemed like more than that. Much more. There had been something in his eyes...

No matter. He'd left, claiming pressure of work, and so she left him to it and played with Josh for a while, hiding in easy to find places, making enough noise to give him a clue, and they giggled and hugged and had fun.

And all the time, in the back of her mind, was Sebastian. And she was troubled, for some reason.

'Right, that's enough of hide and seek. It's very dirty up here. Shall we go and play with your train again?'

'Bastian play with me?'

'No, darling, he's busy, but I will. Of course I will.'

But first, she had to find Sebastian. She sorted Josh out, settled him down with the train set and went to find him.

He was in the study, of course, doing something on his computer, and he glanced up at her and carried on.

'OK, what's going on?'

'Nothing. I'm fine. I'm just busy.'

'No, you aren't. Sebastian, talk to me. What's the matter? What happened back there?'

'Nothing. I just don't like being shut in. You know that. It's why I never go in a lift.'

'I know, but—'

'But nothing. It's fine.'

'It's not fine. You ought to see someone about that,' she told him softly. 'They can do things about claustrophobia.'

'I take the stairs. It's good for me.'

'But—'

'Georgia, leave it.'

Georgia. Not George, not Georgie.

She hesitated a moment, then gave a defeated little shrug and walked away. He was shutting her out again, shutting her out as he always did.

Well, she was tired of fighting him. With any luck the rain which she'd heard gurgling in the gutters was washing away the snow on the roads, and first thing in the morning, as soon as the lane was clear, she was off, because she just couldn't do this any more.

He didn't appear again that day. She cooked supper for Josh, then took him up and bathed him and put him to bed, and when she came down she could see that Sebastian had helped himself to something.

A goose sandwich, ironically, she thought from the evidence left scattered about on the worktop. And carefully timed for when she was out of the way.

She shrugged. Oh, well, if he didn't want her company, she wasn't going to force it on him. And even though she didn't really need another sandwich, she made herself one and ate it at the table. Just in case he was in the little sitting room.

He wasn't.

She realised that after she'd finished her sandwich and cleared up the kitchen. She'd made a cup of tea, and picking up the baby monitor she went out into the hall. It was dimly lit, and she could see light coming under the study door, but the door to the little sitting room was open and it was dark inside.

Fair enough. She'd sit in there, watch the television and start packing up Josh's toys.

Once the lane was cleared, she didn't want to be here a minute longer than necessary. They'd clearly outstayed their welcome, and she felt emotionally exhausted.

So exhausted, in fact, that she went up to bed as soon as she'd dismantled the little train set. Josh didn't stir when she went in, and she turned off the monitor, put it down on the bedside table and got ready for bed in the bathroom.

She would have liked to read, but her book was in the car and anyway she doubted she'd be able to concentrate. She lay down, closed her eyes and tried not to think about him, but it was impossible.

Her mind was full of images—him playing in the snow with Josh, shovelling snow, laughing at her as she fell on her face, kissing her under the mistletoe—and coming out from behind the chimney in the attic as if the hounds of hell were after him. He'd always been claustrophobic, but it had looked like more than that.

No. He'd never liked being shut in. He never went in lifts, as he'd reminded her, and he'd never hidden anywhere cramped when they'd been playing hide and seek.

He'd been rubbish at hiding. Good at finding, but rubbish at hiding. And he'd been hiding with Josh, in behind the chimney. It was tight in there, tight and dark, and although she'd never been afraid of it, she could see why he might have been.

Well, it had been his idea to go in the attic, and a bit of claustrophobia wasn't going to have kept him holed up in his study for the rest of the day.

No, he was sick of them being there, interrupting his routine, cluttering up his house and his life and just generally taking over. Well, just a few more hours and she'd be gone. She'd looked out of the bathroom window and the snow was patchy already. By the morning, it would be clear and she could get away.

And she wouldn't need to see him again.

The noise woke her.

Not a scream, more of a muffled shout, a cry of pain. Sebastian.

She grabbed the baby monitor and tiptoed out of the room, closing the door behind her. His door was never completely closed, but as she opened it further she could hear him breathing fast, muttering in his sleep, wordless sounds of distress.

The dream again. 'Sebastian?'

She switched on the bedside light and reached for him, shaking his shoulder gently.

'Sebastian? Wake up. It's a dream. It's just a dream.'

His eyes flew open and locked on hers, and then he turned away, throwing his arm up over his eyes, his chest heaving.

He looked awful. His face was ashen, his eyes wary, and he was breathing hard, as if he'd been running, and it shocked her.

'Sebastian?'

She reached out a hand and touched him tentatively,

and he dropped his arm and dragged a hand down over his face.

'I'm all right. I didn't mean to disturb you. Go back to bed.'

'You had the dream again, didn't you?'

He swallowed hard.

'I'm fine.'

'No, you're not. Do you want a cup of tea?'

He shook his head. 'No. You need to be with Josh.'

But he was shaking all over, his skin grey, and she turned on the baby monitor and put it on the bedside cabinet, then got into bed beside him and pulled him into her arms.

'It's OK,' she said, murmuring to him as she would to Josh. 'It's OK. I've got you.'

He shuddered, and then slumped his head against her shoulder, letting the tension out of his body in a rush. 'I'm sorry.'

'Don't be. I wish you'd talk to me.'

'No. I don't want to talk about it.'

But he needed her, and she was there, just there, in his bed, in his arms, and he gave up fighting. His hand came up and cradled her face, his fingers still shaking, and then his mouth was on hers, her body under his, her hands running over him as she made desperate little pleading noises.

He lifted his head and she followed him, her mouth searching for his, her lips clinging, and he followed her back down to the pillow and let go of the last shred of his self-control.

CHAPTER NINE

WHEN HE WOKE in the morning, he was alone.

Had he dreamed it?

Dreamed it all, not just *the dream*—hell, he hadn't had it for ages, but last night—and then afterwards...

Had she come to him?

No.

Or had she? It had seemed so real...

He rolled his face into the pillow and breathed in, and the faint, lingering scent of her perfume dragged him right back to the dream.

No. Not the dream. The thing that wasn't a dream. The thing that had been a really, really bad idea.

Damn.

He rolled onto his back and stared at the ceiling. It was dark outside, and he could hear the rain falling, but his watch had beeped ages ago which meant it was long after six.

He peered at the hands. Six forty-eight. Nearly seven.

He threw back the bedclothes and hit the shower, standing under the pounding blast and letting it wash away the fog of fear and confusion that lingered in the corners of his mind.

And with the washing away of the fog came clarity, and with it, the realisation of just what he'd done.

He must have been crazy! How could he have let himself do that? Of all the stupid, stupid things—

He turned off the water and stepped out, burying his face in the towel for a long moment before towelling himself roughly dry.

He heard something—machinery?—and strode to the window, yanking the curtain out of the way.

There were lights on the lane; a tractor, clearing the snow in the almost-dark. The drive looked almost completely free of snow.

Which meant Georgie could leave.

Good. That was good, he told himself, but it didn't feel good, and just underlined how big a mistake he'd made last night. Well, never again. He was done with breaking his heart over Georgia Beckett.

He was up.

She could hear him moving around in his room, hear the water running. Josh was playing on the floor, and she'd showered and dressed and she was packing their things.

His cot, with the bedding Sebastian had lent her. All their wash things. Random toys and bits and pieces scattered about all over the room by Josh.

She checked under the bed and found the nappy cream she'd lost last night, and put it in the changing bag. Time he was potty trained, anyway. She'd do that as soon as she was home, but she hadn't wanted to do anything when he was out of routine. Not a good time to set yourself up for a fall.

And talking of doing that, what had she been thinking about last night? Why get into bed with him? *On* the bed, maybe, but *in* it?

Asking for trouble, and she'd got it, with bells on.

He needed you.

And you needed him, every bit as much.

'Josh, come on, let's take these things downstairs and we can go and have breakfast with Grannie and Grandpa!'

'Now?'

She nodded, dredging up a bright smile from somewhere. 'Yes. Look. The farmer's cleared all the snow from the lane. We can get out now, and go to Grannie's house.'

'Bastian come?'

Oh, here we go. 'No, darling. Sebastian lives here.'

'Us live here.'

'No. We can't, Josh. It's not our house, and anyway, we've got a house already.'

He stuck his chin out. 'Want Bastian.'

So did she, but it wasn't going to happen in this lifetime.

She picked up the travel cot, slung the changing bag over her shoulder and pulled up the handle on her case. 'Come on, downstairs, please.'

She trundled the case to the top of the stairs, then picked it up and struggled down the first few steps.

Then a firm hand on her shoulder stopped her, the case was removed from her grasp, the travel cot removed from the other hand and Sebastian carried them down to the kitchen without a word.

'Anything else up there?'

He met her eyes, but warily, and she felt hers skitter away. 'No. That's everything. There's just the train set. I packed it up last night. Oh, and the bag of presents in your room.'

He nodded, went and got everything and returned, putting the train set boxes on the big kitchen table where

they seemed to have shared so many important moments in the last few days.

Josh was trailing him, talking to him non-stop, asking if they could live there, if he was coming for breakfast with Grannie, if they were coming back.

He either didn't understand Josh, which was possible, or didn't want to understand, which was much
more likely.

'Josh, leave Sebastian alone, we can't stay here and
he's not coming with us,' she said softly, and he started
to cry.

'Hey. Don't cry, little guy,' Sebastian said, finally
relenting and crouching down to Josh's level. 'Mummy's right. You can't stay here, you have to go home to
your house, and I can't come with you because I have
to stay here in mine.'

'Me stay here,' he said, and he wrapped his arms
tightly round Sebastian's neck and hung on.

A pained expression crossed his face for a fleeting
second, and he hugged him briefly, but then he gently
but firmly disentangled the little boy's arms and prised
him away, setting him down on the floor and standing up. 'Come on, Josh, don't cry. You're going to see
your Grannie.'

But Josh's arms were wrapped round his legs now,
and Georgie unwrapped them and picked him up, sob-
bing piteously, and Sebastian pushed past her and pulled
on his coat and sloshed across to the coach-house to
get her car out.

He was gone longer than she expected, but then she
heard the car pull up. 'The traction seems fine, the slush
is really wet,' he said as he came back in, leaving the
car running just by the door. 'The drive's fine and the

lane's clear. I just drove down to have a look. You should be OK.'

OK? She doubted it, but she nodded and pulled her coat on, one arm at a time with Josh still in her arms, and then while Sebastian put their luggage in the car, she sat down on a chair to put Josh's coat on.

He wasn't having any of it.

'Come on, Josh,' she pleaded, but he just made it even harder, burrowing into her and hiding his hands, so she carried him out to the car as he was and strapped him in.

'Will he be all right without it?'

'He'll be fine,' she said crisply. 'Look, I think I've got everything but it's really hard with Josh, he carts stuff about all over the place. If you find anything, maybe you could pile it all up and my father could come and collect it.'

He nodded. 'Or I can post it to you.'

'They can do that,' she said, reluctant to give him her address. She really, really didn't need any more scenes like this one.

And then there was nothing more to say but good-bye, and thank you.

For what?

For opening his home to her, but not his heart?

For making love to her one last time, so she could treasure it in the cold, lonely hours of the nights to come?

For saving her son's life?

'I'll miss you,' he said gruffly. 'Both of you.'

Her eyes flooded with tears, and she nodded. She couldn't speak. Couldn't move. Couldn't do anything except stand there mutely and blink away the stupid, stupid tears—

His thumbs were gentle as he wiped them away.

'Don't cry, George. We're no good for each other.'

But they had been. All this time, the last few days, they'd got on really, really well. Except for the times they hadn't.

She tried to smile, but it was a shaky effort.

'Goodbye, Sebastian. And thank you. For everything.'

Going up on tiptoe, she pressed a gentle, rather wistful kiss to his lips, and then turned and walked out of the door, her head bowed against the rain, her eyes flooding with tears as she left the man she'd never stopped loving standing on the step behind her.

She didn't look back.

He was glad. If she had, he might have weakened, said something.

Like what? Begging her to stay?

He opened the gates remotely from the hall, watched on the security camera as her car turned out of the drive and headed left, the direction the farmer had cleared already.

The car slithered a little, and he frowned. He had his coat on. His keys were in his pocket. He had to make sure she was safe.

He followed her, staying well behind out of sight, and ten minutes later he cruised by the end of her parents' drive.

Her car was there, and her father was carrying her things in, her mother was holding Josh and Georgie was lifting the bag of presents out of the front of the car.

She was safe. Home, and safe.

Duty discharged.

He went home, turned into the drive and saw the

soggy remains of the snowman wilting gently on the lawn beside the drive. His nose had fallen out, and one of his eyes, and the scarf had definitely seen better days.

He left it there. It seemed wrong to take it off until the snowman had gone completely, and anyway, it was already ruined.

Everything, he discovered, seemed wrong.

The house, which until Monday had seemed calm and peaceful and a haven, was silent and empty.

The kitchen echoed to his footsteps. The boot room had a little coat, a snuggly jacket and two pairs of wellies missing from it. And under the table was a toy car.

He picked it up, tossing it pensively in his hand. It was a toy Josh might never have played with, if things had been different. If he hadn't been here. If the snow had come a little earlier, or she'd stopped a little later.

If nothing else, Josh and his mother were still alive, they still had each other and they could move on with their lives. And so could he.

Even if the house echoed with every sound he made.

He made some toast and coffee, took it through to the study and paused en route to check the little sitting room.

And saw the Christmas tree, festooned with all the little toys and sticks and fir cones Georgie had made at the kitchen table and Josh had put on the tree.

There were no gingerbread trees or stars left.

Or at least, only one. High up, out of Josh's reach.

He left it there, left it all there and went into the study and phoned his mother.

'Hi. The lane's clear. When do you want to come?'

'Oh. That was quick. Are you all right?'

'Of course I'm all right. Why wouldn't I be?'

'You tell me, darling,' his mother said softly. 'How's Georgie?'

'She's fine. Look, I don't want to talk about this. Are you coming over, or not?'

'Oh, we're coming, whenever you're ready for us. Andrew and Matthew are here, too. Shall we come now?'

'That would be fine. Come as soon as you like.'

'Do you have anything left to eat, or do you want us to get something on the way?'

He gave a slightly strangled laugh. 'There's plenty here. I've got a joint of beef. We can have it for dinner tonight.'

And maybe having a full house would drown out the echoes…

'I knew it.'

'Knew what?'

'That you'd be upset.'

Georgie put the tea towel down on the worktop and rolled her eyes. 'Mum, don't start—'

'Sorry. I'm sorry, but you look so—'

'Mum…'

'OK. Point taken. I'll back off. So—how was your Christmas?'

Wonderful. Heartbreakingly wonderful.

'I don't really want to talk about it,' she said. 'He did us a huge favour, he made a real effort to be nice to Josh who's completely idolised him as you might have guessed, and it's over now and I'd rather just forget it. How was yours?'

'Oh, quiet. We missed you. We were on our own, of course, so I put the turkey in the freezer, but I've got a chicken in the fridge so we could have it for supper or even a late lunch. We've still got most of the trimmings. We could still make it a proper Christmas dinner.'

She forced a smile. She wasn't really hungry, but she owed her mother the courtesy of good manners. 'That would be lovely. Thank you. Want me to peel some potatoes?'

'If you like. It would be nice to have your company, and Josh seems happy enough for now with his Grandpa and the train set.'

Except for the word 'Bastian' that seemed to crop up in every conversation...

He went back to London as soon as his parents and brothers went.

He hadn't intended to, but the empty house was driving him insane, so he loaded up the car with a ton of fresh food out of the pantry and took it to the refuge. He was never going to get through it, so there was no point in wasting it.

He also took back a lot for the office staff, things his PA had over-supplied in her enthusiasm but that would keep until the office reopened and yet more for the refuge. Tash had really overdone it.

And then he went back to work.

He hadn't intended to do that, either, but he was there before the office reopened, sitting at his desk filling his time and his mind with anything rather than Georgie and her apparently rather lovable little boy. Not that there was a lot to do until everyone was back, so in the end he gave up and just walked the streets and went to the theatre and the odd art exhibition, watched the fireworks on New Year's Eve from the window in his apartment and wondered what the New Year would bring.

Nothing he was about to get excited about.

Then he went back into the office at the crack of dawn on the second of January, champing at the bit and ready to get on. Anything rather than this agonising limbo he seemed to be in.

Tash sashayed into his office, humming softly to herself, and stopped dead. 'Hey, boss, what are you doing back? I thought you'd be there till next week. I wasn't expecting you in till Monday.'

He looked up and met his PA's astonished eyes. Her hair was pink this week. Last week it had been orange—or was it the week before? 'It's a bit quiet in the country.'

She frowned, and perched on the edge of his desk, twisting her hair up and anchoring it with a pencil out of the pot.

'Really? I thought you liked that.'

'I do.' He did. He had. Until Georgie came.

'So how was the food? Did you get through it all?'

He laughed. 'Not really. I've brought a lot in for everyone—I thought we could have a sort of random buffet to welcome everyone back.'

He'd got more, too, in the back of the car, but he'd drop that off later at the refuge, to kick the New Year off.

Pity he couldn't seem to kick his year off. Off a cliff, maybe.

'So how was your Christmas?' he asked belatedly.

She gurgled with laughter. Positively gurgled, and flashed a ring under his nose.

He grabbed her hand and held it still, studying the ring in astonishment. 'He did it?'

'He did. In style. Took me to a posh restaurant and went down on one knee and everything.'

He chuckled, and stood up and hugged her. 'I'm really pleased for you, Tash. That's great news.'

Her smile faltered and she pulled a face. 'Yeah. That's the good news.'

'And the bad?' he said, with a sense of impending doom.

'He's got a job offer. He's moving to America for a year—to Chicago—and he wants me to go with him.'

He sat down again, propping his ankle on his knee, his foot jiggling. This was not good news—well, not for him. 'When?'

'As soon as you can replace me.'

He shook his head slowly. 'I'll never be able to replace you, Tash, but you can go as soon as it's right for you. I'll manage.'

'How?'

He grazed his knuckles lightly over her cheek. 'You're not indispensable,' he said gently. 'But I will miss you and there'll always be a place for you here if you want to come back.'

'Oh, Sebastian, I'll miss you, too,' she said, and flung her arms around his neck. 'I wish you could be happy. I hate it that you're so sad.'

'I'm not sad,' he protested, but she gave him a sceptical look.

'Yes, you are. You've been sad ever since I've known you. You don't even realise it. I don't know who she was, but I'm guessing you've seen her over Christmas, because your eyes look even sadder today.'

He looked away, uncomfortable with her all too accurate analysis.

'Since when were you a psychotherapist?' he asked brusquely, but it didn't put her off. Nothing put Tash off, not when she felt she was on the scent. Maybe it was just as well she was leaving—

'Is she married?'

He gave up. 'No. Not any more.'

'Well, there you are, then. Do you love her? No, don't answer that, it's obvious. Does she love you?'

Did she?

'Yes. But we're not right for each other. Sometimes love's just not enough.'

'Rubbish. It's always enough. Talk to her, Sebastian. I know you. You never talk about anything that matters to you, not really. The only thing you get really worked up about is the refuge, and you never talk about why.'

'It's a good cause.'

She rolled her eyes and pulled the pencil out, shaking her hair down around her shoulders in a shower of shocking pink.

'Go and see her,' she said, stabbing him repeatedly in the chest with the end of the pencil to punctuate every word. 'And talk. *Properly.*'

She dropped the pencil on the desk and swished out of the door. 'Want a coffee before you go?' she asked over her shoulder.

Go? 'Who said anything about going?' he yelled after her, but she ignored him, so he sat down again and stared out of the window at the river.

It was brown with silt from all the run-off after the thaw, and it looked bleak and uninviting.

Like his house.

Was Tash right? Was he sad all the time?

He swallowed hard. Maybe. He hadn't always been. Not while he was with Georgie. She'd taken away the ache, made him feel whole again. And this Christmas, with Josh—he'd been happy.

'Forget the coffee,' he said, snagging his coat off the hook in Tash's office on the way past. 'Don't forget the food. It's in the board room. Share it out. And tell Craig he's a lucky man.'

'Break a leg,' she yelled after him, and he gave a little huff of laughter.

He wasn't really sure what he was doing, and he was far less sure that it would work, but he had to do something, and dithering around for another nine years wasn't going to achieve anything.

It was time to talk to Georgie. Time to tell her the truth in all its ugly glory.

He went home first.

Not to his flat, but to the house.

He'd dropped off the extravagant goodies at the refuge on the way, and wished them all a happy New Year, and then he drove back up to Suffolk and let himself in.

He needed the files, so he could show her. And the test results. Everything.

And then he just had to convince her parents to give him her address in Huntingdon.

It wasn't easy. Her mother was like a Rottweiler, and she wasn't going to give in without a fight.

'Why do you want to see her?'

'I need to talk to her. There are things I need to tell her.'

'You've hurt her.'

He opened his mouth to point out that she'd left him, and shut it. 'I know,' he said after a pause. 'But I want to put it right.'

'How?'

'That's between me and Georgie, Mrs Becket. But

I don't want to hurt her, and I especially don't want to hurt Josh.'

'But you will. If you go there, you will.'

'Not if I don't go when he's awake.'

She seemed to consider that for a moment, but then her husband appeared behind her shoulder and frowned at him.

'I don't know whether to shake your hand for saving their lives or punch your lights out,' he growled, and Sebastian sighed.

'Look, this is nothing to do with Christmas. This is about me, and things about me that she doesn't know. Things I should have told her years ago.'

'So why didn't you?' his mother asked.

He shrugged, swallowing hard. 'Because it's not easy.'

She said nothing for a long moment, then gave a shaky sigh.

'It never is easy, making yourself vulnerable. 42 Wincanton Close.'

'Thank you.' He let his breath out slowly, then sucked it in again. 'Don't tell her I'm coming. I don't want her to do anything silly like go out. I'll ring her when I'm there, tell her I want to talk to her, ask if she'll see me. I won't just rock up on the doorstep. Not if she doesn't want me to.'

Her mother nodded. 'Good. Don't hurt her again, Sebastian. Whatever you do, don't hurt her again.'

'Don't worry, Mrs Becket. I won't hurt her. Not intentionally. I love her. I've always loved her.'

'I know that. If I didn't, I wouldn't have given you her address.'

And taking him completely by surprise, she leant forwards and kissed his cheek. 'Good luck.'

He swallowed. 'Thank you. I have a feeling I'll need it.'

'I don't think so. It's been too long coming, but she'll hear you out. She's always been fair.'

He nodded, shook her father's proffered hand and got back in the car. On the seat beside him were a handful of Josh's toys. The car he'd found under the kitchen table. A train carriage, a piece of track, a little wooden tree. And George's shampoo out of the corner of the shower cubicle in her room.

He'd nearly kept it, just in case she kicked him out, because the smell of it reminded him so much of her.

42 Wincanton Close, Huntingdon. He punched it into the satellite navigation system in the car, reversed carefully off their drive and hit the road.

No rush.

He had well over an hour before Josh was in bed, maybe more. Plenty of time to work out what he was going to say.

He laughed at himself.

He'd had years. Nine, for the worst bits. Thirteen for the rest, all the time he'd known her. If he didn't know what to say now, he never would.

'Oh, man up, Corder. She can only kick you out.'

His gut clenched, and he shut his eyes briefly. He didn't need to think about failure. Not now.

He just needed to see her. Everything else would follow.

CHAPTER TEN

HE FOUND THE house easily. It was the one with the 'For Sale' board outside, and the lights were on.

He slowed down to a crawl with a sigh of relief, and looked around.

She was right, it was in a nice neighbourhood. Tree lined roads, pleasant modern detached houses in different styles each with their own garage, arranged at different angles to soften the lines.

Respectable, decent. Safe.

He was glad she was safe. Safe was important.

He drove past, turned round and pulled up not quite opposite the house, where he could see it and she could see him, and spent a moment gathering his thoughts.

Hell, it was hard. His heart was pounding, his mouth felt dry and his gut was so tight it almost hurt.

It was time.

He pulled the phone out of his pocket and dialled her number.

She didn't answer the first time he rang, so he rang again. He knew it was her phone number, because he'd found her phone lying around and she'd got the number stored under 'me'.

He smiled. Predictable George, to keep the same number. All she had to do was pick up.

She didn't, so he sent her a text, and sat and waited.

The text just said, 'Call me' and gave his number, just in case her phone didn't come up with it. Unlikely, but he wasn't giving her any excuses. Not at this point. There was too much riding on it.

And then she rang him, just when he thought she wouldn't.

'Sebastian? What is it? I've had two missed calls from you and a text. What's going on?'

'I need to see you. We need to talk.' He paused, then went on, his voice gruff. 'There are things you should know. Things I should have told you years ago. Well, one thing, really, the only one that really matters.'

There was a second of shocked silence. 'Can you wait an hour? Just until I've fed Josh and got him to bed? We've been out and I'm on the drag.'

He nodded, although she couldn't see him. 'It's kept for thirteen years. It'll keep another hour.'

'I'll call you.'

'Don't bother. I'm outside, in the car. Just flash the porch lights and I'll come over.'

He saw the curtain twitch, and heard her swift intake of breath. 'OK. I'll see you later.'

He was here.

She couldn't believe it. Her heart was thrashing, and yet there was something dawning that could have been hope.

'Josh, do you really want any more of that?' she asked, and he pushed the plate away and shook his head.

'Can I play trains?'

'No. You can have a bath, and I'll read you a story and you can go to sleep. You've got nursery in the morning and it's late.'

'Want trains,' he said, but he trailed upstairs anyway and sat on the loo on his toddler seat while she ran the bath.

She washed his hair because he'd managed to get ketchup in it, and then she dried him and dressed him in his night nappy and pyjamas, curled up with him on the chair in his room and read him a story, and then snuggled him into his cot.

His eyes were wilting, and before she was out of the door he was asleep.

She gave it five minutes, though, because she didn't want him waking up and interrupting what she instinctively knew was probably the most pivotal conversation of her life.

Cripes.

She went into her bedroom, turned on the bathroom light and studied her face.

She'd been out, and she'd put on a light touch of make-up. Nothing fancy, nothing elaborate, just a touch of eyeshadow and a flick of mascara.

She combed her hair, though, wrestling out the tangles, and eyed her clothes critically. Jeans, a nice jumper, socks.

Hardly dressed to kill, but if he'd wanted that he would have given her notice. And it really, really didn't matter. Not now. There were far bigger fish to fry.

Her heart in her mouth, she went downstairs and flashed the porch light.

Game on.

He got out of the car, ran a finger round his collar and crossed the road, locking the car as he walked.

The door swung open, and he stopped on the step.

'Are you OK with this?'

She searched his eyes, and nodded. 'Come in. Just don't talk too loudly. He's only just gone down.'

Talk too loudly? Now he was here, he didn't want to talk at all, but that had always been his problem.

She led him into the sitting room, closing the door behind them, and he looked around.

'Nice house.'

'Thank you. Can I get you a drink?'

He was dying of thirst. His mouth felt like the desert. 'Mineral water?'

She nodded and went out, returning a moment later with a bottle and two glasses. She set them down on the coffee table, filled the glasses and then perched on the edge of the sofa, waving her hand at the other end of it.

'Sit down, Sebastian. You're cluttering the place up.'

He sat, clearing his throat, sipping the water.

Wondering where to start...

He's nervous, she realised. It surprised her, and it was somehow comforting. Working on the principle that nature abhorred a vacuum, she didn't speak, supressing the urge to fill the silence in the hope that he would.

He did. He gave a short and utterly humourless laugh, and lifted his head.

'I don't know where to start.'

She shifted closer and took his hand, squeezing it gently, her heart pounding. 'So why don't you start with saying it straight out, whatever it is, like, I'm gay, or I've got cancer, or whatever? And then explain.'

He gave a hollow laugh and his fingers tightened in hers. 'OK. Well, for a start I'm definitely not gay, and as far as I know I don't have cancer. I just—I don't know who I am.'

'What?' She searched his eyes, trying to read them,

but they were bleak and empty. Lost. And that scared her. She gripped his hand tighter. 'Sebastian, talk to me.'

He hesitated, then sucked in a breath and said the words that had been dammed up inside him for so long.

'I'm adopted.'

She stared at him. 'You're *what?* When did you find out?'

'When I was seventeen, nearly eighteen. I had no idea until I wanted to get a driving license. We'd never been abroad, I'd never needed a passport, but I wanted to learn to drive, and my parents procrastinated, and then they had to tell me, because I needed my birth certificate and—well, basically it's a fabrication.'

She frowned. 'A fabrication? How?'

He let out a shaky sigh, and his fingers tightened on hers, as if this was the hard bit. 'Because nobody knew anything about me. I was found,' he said carefully. 'In a cubicle, of all places, in the Ladies' room in a department store.'

'Oh, Sebastian! That's so sad. Did they never find your mother? Had she given birth to you in the loos?'

'No, she hadn't just given birth to me. I wasn't a baby. And I was with my mother. She was dead,' he said, his voice hollow. 'Dead, and pregnant, and she'd been beaten up. The cleaner found us in the morning, when the department store opened.'

She pressed a hand to her mouth, the shock rippling through her like an explosion. 'You'd been there *all night*?'

He swallowed, looked away, then looked back at her, and she could see an echo of the horror lurking in the back of his eyes.

He nodded. 'I must have been. I was two, or there-abouts.'

'Josh's age,' she whispered, feeling sick.

He nodded again. 'They didn't know exactly, of course, but they gave me a birth date based on my calculated developmental age, and the place of birth is the town where I was found. They never managed to identify my mother. No woman answering her description was ever reported missing, and nobody's looked for her since. She had no ID of any sort on her, no handbag, no wallet. Nothing.'

She didn't know what to say. Shock held her rigid, and it was long seconds before she started to breathe again, short, shaky breaths of horror. She rested her head on his shoulder, and his other hand came up and cradled it tight. She could feel the tremors running through him, the shaking of his hand, the jerky breaths.

What on earth had he gone through in those long, dark hours? She thought of her baby, her precious, darling baby, trapped alone with her dead body in a public toilet cubicle, and silent tears cascaded down her cheeks. She lifted her free hand and found his jaw, cradled it in her palm, turned her head and kissed him.

His tears mingled with hers, and for a long time they sat there holding each other, cheek to cheek, just letting the shockwaves die away. Then he eased away from her and scrubbed his face with his hands, swiping away the tears and sucking in much-needed air.

'My parents didn't tell me that all at once. They just told me I was adopted, that I'd been found and nobody knew who my mother was. I assumed she'd abandoned me, so I spent three years hating her, and three years hating my parents for not telling me, for letting me think I was theirs. And then I found out the truth. The whole, ugly, sordid truth, and other things started to make sense. The dreams I'd had all my life. The claustrophobia, the fear of being in a tight space in the dark.'

'Which is why you freaked out when you were in the attic with Josh.'

He nodded. 'I heard your footsteps coming, and I said to Josh, "Shh, don't make a sound," and we held our breath, and suddenly I had this rush of—I don't know. Memory? Or just an overworked imagination? But it suddenly seemed so real, as if I recognised the words. And I hear it in my dreams, someone telling me to hush, and the footsteps, and hidden in there with his tiny body next to mine—I just had to get the hell out. Was he all right?'

'Yes, he was fine, but I wondered what on earth had happened. I knew about your claustrophobia, but it looked—I don't know. Worse. You looked awful, but you wouldn't talk to me.'

'I couldn't. I'm sorry. I find it really hard to talk about. And I couldn't talk then, apparently. I didn't talk until I was nearly three—or what they'd decided was nearly three, although apparently I might have been younger. They kept a growth chart and you're supposed to be half your adult height at two, and I wasn't half my current height until I was supposedly two and five months, so I was probably younger than they thought when I was found.'

'So maybe not even talking at that point.'

'No. But I was silent, George. It wasn't just that I didn't talk, I didn't cry, or laugh, or babble. I didn't make a sound—and telling Josh to shush—did she tell me not to make a sound? My mother? Probably, because shut in there with Josh it all felt terrifyingly familiar, so maybe I was just too afraid to speak in case something else bad happened.'

Poor, poor little boy. She shook her head slowly, rubbing the back of his hand with her thumb, slowly, rhythmically, her heart aching for him. Oh, Sebastian...

'So what happened to you, after you were found? Where did you go?'

'My parents fostered me. I was put with them straight away, and they moved heaven and earth to adopt me, and gradually I grew more confident and turned into a normal, healthy child, but they never told me. All those years I thought I was theirs, all those birthday parties that weren't my birthday at all, and then this huge hole opened up underneath me, this void where I'd had security and certainty and a sense of history, of belonging. And it was all a lie. It was only later I learned there had been even more lies, covering up the bits of the truth that even then they didn't feel they could tell me.'

Her fingers tightened on his. 'They weren't lying to you, Sebastian. They were protecting you. Doing what they felt was best.'

'I know. I know that, and I know they love me, and don't get me wrong, I love them, too, and I'm deeply grateful for everything they've done for me, but—I'm not theirs, and I thought I was, and that really hurts. If they'd told me the truth, right from the beginning, that my mother was dead and that they didn't know who she was, then it wouldn't have been such a shock when I heard it.'

'So when did you find out about your mother? Was that when you changed, when you went so funny on me? You said three years after you first realised you were adopted, so you would have been—what? Twenty? Nearly twenty-one?'

He nodded. 'Yes. And I just retreated into myself.'

'Why didn't you tell me?' she asked, desolate now that he'd carried this all alone for so long. 'Oh, Sebastian, why didn't you tell me? You should have trusted me. I would have understood.'

'Because I didn't want anything to change. I felt that you were the only person who loved me for myself. You weren't hiding a guilty secret from me, you had no obligation to me, and I was afraid to tell you in case it changed things. That's why I bought the house, because the time I spent there with you was the happiest time of my life.'

He looked down at her, his eyes tender. 'I fell in love with you there, on our first date, when you took me there and showed it to me.'

'That wasn't a date!'

'Yes, it was. I knew Jack wasn't going to be around, and you'd always been friendly towards me. I'd just found out I was adopted, and I needed to get out, give myself time for it all to sink in. And there you were, in a skimpy little top and shorts, your skin kissed by the sun, and when you suggested we went out for the bike ride I thought all my Christmases had come at once.'

'It *was* just a bike ride.'

'No. It was you showing me your secret hideaway, letting me into your dreams, sharing your fantasies, and we made fantasies of our own. I was still reeling from the news that I was adopted, and it was an escape from it, a different reality. In the next few weeks it became our own world, somewhere safe that I could go. And suddenly it all seemed plausible. If I could get rich enough, so I could afford it, we could buy the house and live there and found our dynasty, yours and mine, and I would have a real family, my own flesh and blood.'

She touched his cheek, wiping away the last trace of their tears. 'You should have told me, Sebastian.'

He looked away, his face bleak, and she let her hand fall.

'I know, but I didn't want to change things. You knew who you were. You look like your parents. You're part of them, they're part of you. And I don't have that. My brothers do—they aren't adopted. Nature seemed to have sorted itself out for my parents by that point, and there's no question that Matt and Andy are theirs, but not me. For me, my identity, my origins, even my nationality will always be a mystery. I'm a cuckoo in the nest, Georgie, and I never forget how much I owe them, but they should have told me.'

'They had their reasons. Maybe they thought it would hurt you more? It must have been really traumatic—you were hardly more than a baby, but much more aware than a baby would have been. The impact must have been horrific, and they would have wanted to protect you.'

'I know. Logically, I know, but I didn't feel logical. Suddenly I didn't belong, and that was so shocking to me. It rocked me to my foundations. And when I found out the rest, when I saw my adoption file and the police file, and it was so sordid and harsh, it was even worse. How could I tell you that? I didn't want to distress or disgust you-'

'Disgust me? It wouldn't have disgusted me!'

'I didn't know that. I still don't know that. She could have been anyone, George. She could have been a prostitute or a drug addict, a murderer, even-'

'She was somebody's *daughter*,' she said, appalled that he could think that she was so shallow that his mother's plight would put her off him. 'However she ended up there, she was just a girl—how old was she?'

He shrugged. 'Early twenties, they thought, maybe younger?'

Her eyes flooded again. 'Poor, poor girl. She must have been so terrified. And she must have loved you— she tried to protect you, shut you away in a public place where a man couldn't get to you without drawing attention to himself, and it cost her her life.'

He nodded slowly. 'Yes, it did. And I'd spent three years hating her for something she hadn't done. I didn't realise how much it had changed me, thinking I'd been abandoned, that she hadn't loved me enough to keep me. Why not? What kind of vile child had I been that I wasn't I lovable? But then I heard the truth, and I just needed to find out all I could about her, but there's nothing. I still don't know who she was, and nobody's launched any kind of official search for anyone answering her description in all this time.'

'What about DNA?' she asked, finally on solid ground. 'I know it can't tell you much, but it can tell you something about where you're from.'

'Northern Europe, probably England. No more than that. And if nobody's looked, then the trail's lost and I'll never know who she was, or who I am. And that's the worst thing. I have no idea who I really am. My name, my place and date of birth—not even what nationality I am. Just speculation, all of it.'

'No! You *know* who you are,' she said fiercely. 'And *I* know who you are. I've always known. It wouldn't have made any difference to me where you'd come from, what you were called, what date you were born. You were you, and you've always been you, and it's you I loved. You should have *told* me, Sebastian. You should have trusted me.'

He turned his head slowly and looked at her, his eyes bleak. 'But I did trust you. And you left me.'

She opened her mouth to argue, but then shut it again, because it was true. She had left him. She'd walked away and left him, when she'd promised to love him forever.

Well, that hadn't been a lie. She loved him still, but she'd left him when he'd needed her the most, and it tore her apart.

'I'm so sorry,' she said brokenly. 'I had no idea what you were going through. I wish you'd told me, shared it with me. I would never have left you if I'd known. I loved you so much, I've always loved you. You're a good man, and you always have been, and you must never doubt that—look what you did for Josh and me over Christmas—but still you didn't let us into your heart. You gave us so much, and you didn't need to do that, but you held yourself back like you always do, because everyone you've ever loved has let you down, haven't they, one way or another? No wonder you don't trust your feelings or give your heart to anyone, least of all me.'

'I gave my heart to you,' he said quietly. 'I gave it to you thirteen years ago, and you still have it. That offer stands.'

She shook her head. 'But I left you. I don't deserve it.'

'Yes, you do. I was a nightmare. I know that. But I needed you, and I loved you, and I still do, Georgia. And I know you love me. What I don't know is if you can forgive me, or if you can live with a man from nowhere.'

'Oh, Sebastian. Of course I can forgive you. And whether or not I can live with you is nothing to do with where you've come from so much as where you're going and how. That was what changed. That was the problem, the thing I couldn't live with.'

'I know. I'm sorry. But there was a reason I was so driven.'

'A reason you didn't share with me!'

'I know. I should have.'

'You should. I could have helped you with the DNA research. It's my field, Sebastian. I might have been able to find out more.'

'I doubt it. I've paid a fortune for the best advice-'

'The best isn't necessarily commercially available. And I'm on the inside. Don't overlook that.'

He nodded. 'I won't. But it can't alter the way I was then, how driven I was—still am. After I found out what had actually happened to my mother, the emphasis changed. I needed to make more money—much more, not for me, but to make sure it couldn't happen again, that there'd be somewhere safe for women to go. I support various charities, for women and children who are victims of domestic violence, and I set up a refuge which I fund and maintain. I had to, to stay sane. I couldn't just let it go, and it was eating me up, but now I'm doing something, and making a difference, and I feel I've got my priorities right.'

'You have. You've settled down.'

'Grown up?' he said drily, and she laughed.

'Probably. I prefer to think you've developed a more mature and balanced perspective. And I have, too, so before you start worrying, I'm sure I can live with you now even if I couldn't then.'

'You can?'

'Of course I can—and I could have done then if you'd shared this with me. I think it's a fabulous cause, and I would have supported you and worked with you on it, but you never gave me a chance.'

His eyes were filled with shadows. 'I know. I'm sorry. I just didn't know how to say it, and the longer it went on, the harder it got. And after you went I was so hurt and angry that you'd left me, there was no way I was going to tell you. Then I heard you were married, and I thought you'd moved on.'

'No. I'll never move on from loving you. I've loved you for thirteen years—I fell in love with you on that first date, too, and I promised to love you forever. That hasn't changed, even though I couldn't stay with you then. I still love you. I've never stopped loving you.'

'Even though you were married to David?'

She shrugged. 'He was a nice man, and we were both lonely. You wouldn't let me in, you'd done nothing but shut me out for months. Years later, you still hadn't contacted me again and I had no reason to suppose you ever would. And if we hadn't been snowed in together this Christmas, I don't know that that would have ever changed.'

'No. Maybe not. As I said, I just assumed you'd moved on.'

'Only in a way. Not in my heart. It was a compromise, a rationalisation, and I can't regret it because it's given me Josh, but it was only ever a way of finding a measure of happiness. You were my first love, my only true love, but I was never going to have you, and I didn't want to be alone, and if David hadn't died, we would have been together forever. But he did die, and we're talking, at last, and maybe finally sorting out what we should have sorted out years ago.'

She reached up and cradled his cheek in her hand. 'I

love you, Sebastian. And if you're asking me to marry you, the answer's yes.'

'I asked you years ago.'

'No, you didn't. You promised me we'd be together forever, and we talked about being married, but I don't believe you ever asked me.'

He gave a soft laugh, and eased off the sofa, landing on one knee at her feet. He took her hand in his and stared up into her eyes with a wry smile.

'Georgia Becket Pullman, I love you now as much as I've ever loved you, more than life itself. Without you I'm nothing. With you, I can conquer the world. Marry me. Have my children, to keep your little Josh company and give him a whole host of brothers and sisters. Our dynasty. My very own, real family.'

His smile faded, and his eyes grew bright.

'Marry me, George? Please?'

Her eyes filled. 'Oh, Sebastian—of course I'll marry you! I've already said yes.'

'You made me ask you,' he accused.

'Only because I wanted to hear you say it,' she laughed, but the laugh hiccupped into a sob, and she slid off the sofa onto her knees and went into his arms, hugging him tight to her heart, aching for the little boy he'd been and the strong, courageous man he'd become.

He shifted onto the sofa, lifting her easily onto his lap and cradling her close. 'It's a pity you've got a job,' he said.

She tilted her head and peered at him. 'Why? It might be useful to you in the future, trying to track your family. I've got all the right contacts.'

A week ago, that would have made his heart race faster. Now, he found he didn't care, because he had the only thing that could ever matter this much to him.

"I could still use your skill and expertise now,' he said. 'Why?'

He smiled. 'Because my PA's leaving. She's getting married and moving to Chicago, and I'll need someone to fill in until I can replace her. But that's only short term. Long term, of course, we've got a dynasty to work on. Maybe you'd better warn your boss.'

She laughed and rested her head on his shoulder. 'Yes, I better had. The first little Corder is due on the nineteenth of September.'

He went utterly still, and then he gave a shaky, incredulous laugh and hugged her tight. 'Really? You're having my baby?'

'It would seem so. I did the test this morning. It was very faint, but it was positive.'

'Wow.' He laughed again. 'I didn't even think—that night, when I had the dream?'

'When else? There was only the once.'

'And you're sure? The test can't be wrong?'

'No. You can have a false negative, but never a false positive. I deliberately got a very sensitive test kit.'

'Have you told your mother?'

She shook her head. 'No. Not before you. I was trying to work out how to tell you, but I knew you'd go all Neanderthal and insist on marrying me, so I really wanted to talk to you first and get you to open up to me so I'd know you wanted it for the right reasons.'

'And I came to you. You'd better thank Tash for that. She said she wished I wasn't always sad. I said I wasn't. She pointed out that I was. I am. I have been for years, and the only time I'm not sad is when I'm with you.

'It's like you said to me once, when you were talking about David. He was a nice man, and you loved him, but you didn't feel as if you couldn't breathe if he wasn't there. As if there was no colour, no music, no poetry. No sense to your life. That's how I feel when I'm with you. As if my life has colour and music and poetry, and it all makes sense, and after you'd gone everything was grey and empty and silent. It took Tash to point it out to me.'

'You *really* owe her a bonus now.'

He laughed and hugged her closer. 'I tell you what, they're going to have a cracker of a wedding present.'

'Good. I hope we get invited to the wedding. I want to thank her.'

'That's easy.' He pulled his phone out of his pocket, hit a speed dial number and smiled. 'Tash? My fiancée would like a word with you.'

EPILOGUE

'HAPPY CHRISTMAS, Mrs Corder?'

His arms slid round her from behind, his chin resting on her shoulder. She felt his lips nuzzle her ear, and she laughed and leaned back into him.

'*Very* Happy Christmas, Mr Corder.' She turned in his arms with a smile, and found it reflected in his eyes. 'Where's Evie?'

'Sleeping. On my mother.'

'Not mine, then.'

'For a change, not,' he said with a lazy smile. 'Come and sit down. You've done enough in the kitchen today.'

'I've hardly done anything,' she protested as he towed her down the hall. 'You wouldn't let me.'

'You're a nursing mother.'

'Yes. Not an invalid.'

He smiled indulgently. 'Humour me. I like looking after you. I've got a lot of years to catch up on. So, how do you think it's going?'

'Christmas? Brilliantly. Nobody's had a fight yet, everyone's enjoyed the food-'

'I should hope so. I let Tash loose on the ordering again, remember.'

She chuckled. 'Yes. She's good at it. Impeccable taste.'

'She just knows what I like.'

'So modest.'

He gave a soft huff of laughter and hugged her closer to his side. From down the hall they could hear the hubbub of conversation, interspersed with laughter and the occasional raised voice as someone tried to put their point.

The family were all gathered in the drawing room in front of a roaring fire, playing silly games and getting over the monumental feast that had been Christmas lunch. There wasn't room in the smaller sitting room for all of them, and even the enormous dining table had been filled to capacity.

The house was straining at the seams, all ten bedrooms occupied. Both sets of parents had come to share the celebrations, together with her brother Jack and his wife and two children, Sebastian's brothers Andy and Matt and their girlfriends, and Tash and Craig, who were honorary family members. Including them and Josh and Evie, that made eighteen—nineteen if you counted Tash's burgeoning bump. Twenty-one if you counted the dog and cat.

Not bad for a start at family life, she thought contentedly.

He pulled her to a halt in the hall, next to the Christmas tree. It was decorated with last year's stock cube parcels and bundles of twigs, fresh gingerbread trees and stars and little home-made angels that dangled around the lower branches.

The sophisticated glass baubles were safely near the top of the tree, glinting in the light from the enormous crystal chandelier that hung above it, and it looked wonderful.

She sighed happily. 'What a lovely tree.'

'Isn't it?'

He glanced up, and there overhead, dangling from the landing bannisters above, was a sprig of mistletoe.

'Well, now, would you look at that?' he murmured, his eyes twinkling with mischief, and threading his hands into her hair, he lowered his head and kissed her...

* * * * *

STRANDED WITH
THE TYCOON

SOPHIE PEMBROKE

For Holly.
I'm proud of you all the way to the moon, too.

Sophie Pembroke has been reading and writing romance ever since she read her first Mills & Boon romance at university, so getting to write them for a living is a dream come true! Sophie lives in a little Hertfordshire market town in the UK, with her scientist husband and her incredibly imaginative six-year-old daughter. She writes stories about friends, family and falling in love—usually while drinking too much tea and eating homemade cakes. She also keeps a blog at sophiepembroke.com.

CHAPTER ONE

LUCINDA MYLES WASN'T the sort of woman to panic, usually. But the prospect of being without a bed for the night five days before Christmas, in the midst of the coldest December the north-west of England had seen in decades, was decidedly unappealing. The city of Chester was booked solid by Christmas shoppers and by the other unfortunate academics attending the badly timed *Bringing History to the Future* conference. If the Royal Court Hotel didn't find her booking…well, she was going to need a new plan. But first she'd try dogged persistence. It had always worked for her grandfather.

'I understand that you're fully booked,' Luce said, in her most patient and forbearing voice. The one she usually saved for her brother Tom, when he was being particularly obtuse. 'But one of those room bookings should be for me. Dr Lucinda Myles.' She leant across the reception desk to try to see the girl's computer screen. 'M-Y-L-E-S.'

The blonde behind the desk angled the screen away from her. 'I'm afraid there is no booking at this hotel under that name for tonight. Or any other night, for that matter.'

Luce gritted her teeth. This was what she got for letting the conference staff take charge of her hotel booking. She really should have known better. *Take responsibility.*

Take control. Words to live by, her grandfather had always said. Shame she was the only one in the family to listen.

As if to echo the thought, her phone buzzed in her pocket. Luce sighed as she reached in to dig it out, knowing without looking that it would be Tom. 'And there are absolutely no free rooms in the hotel tonight?' she asked the blonde, figuring it was worth one more shot. 'Even the suites are booked?' She could make the university reimburse her. They wanted her here at the conference— the least they could do was give her a decent room for the night.

'Everything. Every room is booked. It's Christmas, in case you hadn't noticed. And now, if I can't be of any further assistance…' The blonde looked over Luce's shoulder.

Glancing back herself, Luce saw a growing queue of people waiting to check in. Well, they were just going to have to wait. She wasn't going to be intimidated by this fancy hotel with its marble floors, elegant golden Christmas tree, chandeliers and impatient businessmen. She'd had one hell of a day, and she was taking responsibility for making it better. 'Actually, perhaps you could check if any of the other local hotels have a free room. Since you've lost my reservation.'

'We haven't—' the blonde started, but Luce cut her off with a look. She sighed. 'I'll just check.'

While the blonde motioned to her colleague to come and assist with the check-in queue, Luce slid a finger across the touch screen of her phone to check her messages. Three texts and a voicemail. All in the last twenty minutes, while she'd been arguing with the receptionist. A light day, really.

She scrolled to the first text while the disgruntled businessman behind her checked in at the next computer. It was from Tom, of course.

Has Mum spoken to you about Christmas Eve? Can you do it?

Christmas Eve? Luce frowned. That meant the voicemail was probably from her mother, changing their festive plans for the sixth time that month.

The next text was from her sister Dolly.

Looking forward to Xmas Eve—especially chocolate pots!

That didn't bode well. Christmas Day was planned and sorted and all due for delivery from the local supermarket on the twenty-third—apart from the turkey, which was safely stored in her freezer. Christmas Eve, however—that was a whole different proposition.

The final text was Tom again.

Mum says we have a go! Fantastic. See you then.

Luce sighed. Whatever Mum's new plan was, apparently it was a done deal. *'You're the responsible one, Lucinda,'* her grandfather had always said. *'The rest of them couldn't take care of themselves for a minute out there in the real world. You and I know that. Which is why you're going to have to do it for them.'*

Apparently they needed looking after again. With a Christmas Eve dinner. And chocolate puddings. Presumably in addition to the three-course dinner she'd be expected to produce the following day. Perfect.

Luce clicked the phone off as the blonde came back. The voicemail from her mother, hopefully explaining everything, could wait until Luce had a bed for the night.

'I'm sorry,' the blonde said, without a hint of apology

in her voice. 'There's some history conference in town, and with all the Christmas shoppers as well I'm afraid the local accommodation has been booked up for months.'

Of course it has, Luce wanted to say. *I'm here for the damn conference. I booked my room months ago. I've just spent all morning discussing how to bring history into the future. I deserve a room.*

But instead she clenched her jaw while she thought her way out of the problem.

'Right, then,' she said after a moment. 'I'm going to go and sit over there and try calling some places myself.' She motioned to the bar at the side of the lobby, where discreet twinkling fairy lights beckoned. This day would definitely be better with a gin and tonic. 'In the meantime, if you have any cancellations, I'd appreciate it if you'd book the room under my name.'

'Of course.' The blonde nodded, but her tone said, *You'll be lucky.*

Sighing, Luce turned away from the desk, only to find her path to a G&T barred by a broad chest in an expensive shirt. A nice chest. A wide, warm chest. The sort of chest you could bury your face in and forget about your day and let the owner of the chest solve your problems instead.

Not that she needed a man to fix her problems, of course. She was perfectly capable of doing that herself, thank you.

But it would be nice if one offered, just once.

Raising her gaze, she saw that the chest was topped by an almost unbelievably good-looking face. Dark hair brushed back from tanned skin. Golden-brown eyes that glowed above an amused mouth. A small scar marring his left eyebrow.

Hang on. That scar was familiar. She knew this man. And she should probably stop staring.

'Is there a problem with your reservation, madam?' he asked, and Luce blinked.

'Um, only that it doesn't seem to exist.' She glanced back at the reception desk to discover that the blonde, rather than assisting the next guest in the queue, was practically hanging over the counter to get in on their conversation.

'Daisy?' The man raised his scarred eyebrow at the blonde.

Luce definitely recognised that expression. But from where? A conference? A lecture? Somebody's ex? Hell, maybe even from TV? One of those reality shows about real life in a hotel? Except Luce didn't usually have time to watch such programmes. But the subconscious was a funny thing. Maybe his image had been imprinted on her brain, somehow, in eerie preparation for this moment.

'There's no reservation in her name, sir, and the hotel's fully booked tonight. I tried the usual places, of course, but everyone's booked out.'

For the first time Daisy sounded helpful and efficient. Obviously this guy was someone who mattered. Or Daisy had a huge crush on him. Or, most likely, both. After all, Luce could tell from the way he stood—feet apart, just enough to anchor him firmly to the earth—that this was a man used to the world bending around him rather than the other way round. And really, even with the scar—especially with the scar, actually—what young, healthy, straight woman wouldn't feel a certain *ping* of attraction to him?

Except Luce, of course. She had too many bigger things to worry about to waste time on attraction. Like where she was going to sleep that night. And who the hell he was.

Luce frowned. So annoying. Normally she was good at this stuff. Of course the man hadn't given any indication that he recognised *her*, so maybe she was wrong. Or just less memorable than he was.

Suddenly Luce was rather glad she couldn't put her finger on his identity. How much more embarrassing would it be to have to explain to him how he knew her while he stared at her blankly? Much better to get this whole interaction over with quickly. She'd probably figure out where she knew him from when she was on the train back to Cardiff on Thursday morning, by which time it wouldn't matter anyway.

'What about the King James Suite?' he asked.

Luce was amused to see Daisy actually blush.

'Well, I didn't think… I mean…' she stammered.

Luce, seeing her chance, jumped in. 'You thought I couldn't afford it?' she guessed. 'Firstly, you really shouldn't make such assumptions about your guests. Secondly, since you lost my reservation I'd expect that a free upgrade would be the least you could do. So I'm very interested to hear your response to the gentleman's question.'

Arms folded across her chest, just like her grandfather used to do when he was disappointed in her, Luce stared Daisy down and waited for an answer. This was it, she was sure. The moment her luck turned for the day and she got to spend the night in the best luxury the Royal Court Hotel had to offer. Never mind the gin and tonic—she was having champagne in the bathtub at this rate.

Daisy, redder and more flustered than ever, turned wide blue eyes on her boss. 'But, Mr Hampton, sir…I didn't offer her the King James Suite because *you're* staying there.'

Mr Hampton. Ben Hampton. The memory fell into place just as Daisy's words registered.

Luce winced. Apparently her day wasn't improving after all.

* * *

Ben Hampton couldn't keep from smirking when he saw his potential suite-mate roll her eyes to heaven and turn folded arms and an accusing stare on him. This was going to be fun.

Five minutes earlier he'd been about to head out for the evening when he'd seen the brunette holding up the reservations queue in the lobby. His first instinct had been to intervene, to get things moving again. Being one half of the 'sons' in the Hampton & Sons hotel chain meant that he fixed things wherever he saw them. He kept the guests happy, the staff working hard and the hotel ticking over, wherever he happened to be staying at the time. That was his job: keep things moving. Including himself. But of course staff evaluation was also important, his brother Seb would have said, and this had looked like the perfect opportunity to observe how the Royal Court's reception staff dealt with a difficult guest.

So he'd stayed back, trying not to look as if he was loitering behind the ostentatious golden Christmas tree in the lobby, and watched. He'd heard the woman give her name as Lucinda Myles and a jolt of recognition had stabbed through him. Lucinda Myles. *Luce.* They'd teased her about that, hadn't they? Such an absurd nickname for someone so uptight. Ben knew from six months of dating her university roommate that Luce Myles had been the twenty-year-old most likely to be doing extra course reading on a Friday night, while the rest of them were in the pub. And he'd been able to tell from three metres away that she was still the most tightly wound person he'd ever met.

Luce had vibrated with irritation and impatience, just as she had whenever he and the girlfriend had emerged from their bed at noon on a weekday. Ben frowned. What had her name been, anyway? The girlfriend? Molly? Mandy?

Hell, it *had* been eight years ago—even if six months was something of a relationship record for him. Was he supposed to remember the name of every girl he'd ever dated? But Luce Myles...that wholly inaccurate name had stuck with him down the years.

Casually, he'd turned his head to get a better look at her. Dark hair, clipped at the back of her head, had revealed the creamy curve of her neck down to her collarbone, shoulders, tense under her sweater. The heel of her boot had been tapping against the marble as she waited for Daisy to finish calling around for a room Ben knew wouldn't exist. She'd been knotted so tight she might have snapped at any moment, and he'd wondered why—passing acquaintance aside—he was even vaguely interested in her. Yes, he liked a woman who knew what she wanted, but usually she wanted a good time—and him. Lucinda Myles didn't look as if she'd gained any conception of what a good time was in the last decade, let alone a desire to have one.

In fact, he'd realised with a jolt, he knew exactly what she looked like. That permanent frown etched in her forehead, the frustration around her eyes—they were familiar. He'd seen them on his mother's face often enough.

But that hadn't explained his sudden interest. He'd studied her closer and eventually decided it was her clothes. Despite the 'stay away' vibes her demeanour gave out, her clothes were just begging to be touched. Straight velvet skirt in the darkest plum, a navy sweater that looked so soft it had to be cashmere. Even her sensible brown boots were suede. She certainly hadn't dressed like that at university. Ben appreciated fine fabrics, and the sight had made his fingers itch to touch them.

He'd wondered what she had on underneath.

A woman couldn't wear clothes that strokeable if she didn't have something of a sensual nature under them.

Even if she didn't know it was there yet. Maybe Lucinda Myles had an inner sensuality just begging to be let out after all these years. Ben had thought he might like to help her with that. For old times' sake.

Daisy had returned to report on the utter lack of available hotel rooms in the local area, and Luce had moved away—which simply didn't fit in with Ben's plans. So he'd stepped forward and suggested the King James Suite, which had had the added bonus of enabling him to watch Luce's face when she realised who she'd be sharing with.

Except her reaction wasn't quite what he'd been expecting.

There'd been no sign that she recognised him, for a start, which was a bit of a blow to the ego. He liked to think he was a fairly memorable guy. But then, he'd grown up in eight years. Changed just as she had. Would he have recognised her without hearing her name? Probably not. So he could forgive her that. No, the cutting part was that instead of flushing red or widening her eyes, like Daisy did, or even giving him a glimpse through her armour of tension and irritation like any other woman would have, Lucinda Myles had winced.

Winced. At the prospect of spending the night with him.

Daisy's eyes grew wider than ever and Ben decided it might be better for his reputation—and ego—if they moved this conversation elsewhere.

'Before you get entirely the wrong idea about my intentions,' he said, angling an arm behind Luce to guide her towards the bar, 'I should point out that I'm the owner of this hotel rather than an opportunistic guest. Ben Hampton, by the way.' A slow blink from Luce. Recognition? Ben pressed on anyway. 'And you should also know that the King James Suite has two very finely appointed bedrooms.'

Luce pursed her lips and eyed him speculatively before giving a sharp nod. 'Buy me a gin and tonic and you can explain exactly what you *did* mean by propositioning me in that manner while I try and find somewhere else to stay tonight.'

It wasn't entirely what he'd intended, but it would do. It would give her time to remember him, or for him to introduce himself all over again. And getting her even more tightly wound than usual would only make it more glorious when she fell apart under his touch.

CHAPTER TWO

LUCE SMIRKED AT Ben Hampton's retreating back and wondered what on earth had possessed the owner of a luxury hotel like the Royal Court to offer to share his suite with a complete stranger. Unless, of course, he remembered her, too. In which case, why hadn't he just said so? She was pretty sure Ben Hampton had never suffered from the sort of crippling embarrassment that sometimes held her back even now. He certainly hadn't when he was twenty.

Ben Hampton. Of course it was. She remembered that same scarred eyebrow raised at her over the breakfast table—a subtle mocking of the fact that while he and Mandy had been out having fun she'd been in studying. Again. They'd never been friends, never had any real meaningful conversations. Not even that last night, at another of his dad's swanky hotels for Ben's twenty-first birthday. She hadn't known him and she'd never cared to. The little she'd observed of him had told her his entire personality, and from what she'd seen today he hadn't changed. He still expected the world to bend to him and women to fall at his feet, just as he always had. And she still refused to do either. They were worlds apart—maybe even more so now than they had been at university.

So why offer her his room? For old times' sake?

Not that she'd be taking him up on the offer, of course. Especially if he didn't know who she was. Still, she had no reservations about acquiring a free drink from the exchange, while she worked on finding alternative accommodation.

Pulling out her phone again, Luce saw she had another message. Great. She dialled her voicemail and prepared to decipher her mother's rambling.

'Lucinda? Are you there, darling? No? Are you sure?'

A pause while Tabitha Myles waited to see if her eldest daughter was simply pretending to be an answering machine. Listening, Luce closed her eyes and shook her head a little.

'Well, in that case, I suppose I should...maybe I should call back later? Except Tom did ask... You see, the thing is, darling, Tom's decided he should spend Christmas Day with his new girlfriend. Vanessa. Did he tell you about her? She sounds delightful. She has two children, I understand, and you know how Tom loves children... Anyway, since he won't be with us on Christmas Day we thought it might be nice to have a family dinner at the house on Christmas Eve so we can all meet Vanessa! Won't that be lovely? I think this could be a real step forward for him... after everything. And you always say the house still belongs to all of us, really. Dolly says she'll come too, as long as you're making your special chocolate puddings. I told her of course you would. And you can invite that lovely man of yours along. Been ages since we saw Dennis. Anyway, so that's that sorted. Friday evening, yes? See you then, darling. Lovely to talk to you. Bye!'

Fantastic. It was Monday afternoon and she was stuck in Chester at the conference until Thursday morning, assuming she found somewhere to stay. What the hell was she supposed to cook that was worthy of Tom's tentative first steps out of depression and into the world of love *and* went with chocolate pots for Dolly? Maybe she could amend her supermarket order if she could get online. Which just left getting the house in a state Tabitha could tolerate, explaining once again that Dennis was not her boyfriend and writing her conference report. Not to mention the completed draft she'd promised her publisher of her first book. The university did like its lecturers to publish.

'Looks like I'll be working on the train,' she muttered to herself, tugging her organiser from her bag to start a new 'To Do' list. She saved Tabitha's message and her voicemail moved swiftly onto a harried conference organiser, apologising profusely for a 'slight confusion' with the hotel booking arrangements. Luce could hear the poor girl's boss yelling in the background.

Sighing, Luce deleted the message. So, still homeless. Maybe she should call it quits and head back to Cardiff. She'd already given her lecture. And, interesting as the rest of the conference looked, it wasn't worth going without a bed for. Except her ticket was non-refundable, and the walk-up price would be astronomical. But if it meant she could just go home it might be worth it.

Her phone buzzed in her hand and Luce automatically swept a finger across the screen to open the e-mail. The cheery informality of Dennis's words set her teeth on edge from the first line.

Dr Luce! Bet you're living it up in Chester. Don't forget my summary on tomorrow's lecture, will you? D.

See? Things could be worse. Dennis could have come to Chester with her. Fortunately he was far too important and busy to spend time away from the university. That was why he sent Luce instead. Of course now she had to attend a really dull lecture on his behalf and take notes, but that was a price worth paying for his absence.

Tossing her phone onto the table, Luce scanned the bar to see where Ben had got to with her drink. She needed to formulate a plan to get through the next week, and that would definitely be easier with an icy G&T in her hand. Except it didn't look as if she'd be getting it any time soon.

At the bar, Ben Hampton had his phone clamped to his ear and was smiling at the redhead in the short skirt who'd claimed the barstool next to him. Typical. What did she expect from a man who offered to share his suite with a woman he barely knew? As if she needed further evidence that he hadn't changed since university. His sort never did. Luce remembered well enough Mandy stomping into the flat at two in the morning, more than once, wailing about how she'd caught Ben out with another woman. Remembered the one time he'd ever shown any interest in *her* at all, when Mandy hadn't been looking. Did he? she wondered. He'd been pretty drunk.

Luce narrowed her eyes as she observed him. But then he turned, leaning against the bar behind him, and raised that scarred eyebrow at Luce instead of at the redhead. A shiver ran across her shoulders and she glanced away. She really didn't have time for the sort of distractions Ben's smile promised. She had responsibilities, after all. And she knew far, far better than to get involved with men like Ben Hampton. Whatever game he was playing.

Take responsibility. Take control. She had to remember that.

Without looking up again, Luce grabbed her organiser and started planning how to get through her week.

Ben ignored his brother's voice in his ear and studied Luce instead. She was staring at her diary, where it rested on her crossed legs, and brushed an escaped strand of hair out of her eyes. Her pen was poised over the paper, but she wasn't writing anything. She looked like a woman trying to save the world one 'To Do' list at a time. His initial impression had definitely been right, even if he hadn't seen her in nearly a decade. This was a woman who needed saving from herself.

Not my responsibility, though, he reminded himself. *Not my fix this time.*

'So, what do you think?' Sebastian asked down the phone. 'Is it worth saving?'

'Definitely,' Ben answered, before realising that Seb was talking about the Royal Court Hotel, not Lucinda Myles. 'I mean, yes—I think it's worth working with.' The Royal Court was a relatively new acquisition, and Ben's job for the week was to find out how it ticked and how to make it work the Hampton & Sons way. 'You stayed here, right? Before we bought it? I mean, you must have done.'

'Dad did,' Seb said, his voice suddenly darker. 'I have his report, but...'

It was hard to ask questions about the room service and the bathroom refits when the old man was six feet under, Ben supposed. 'Right—sure. And there were concerns?'

'Perhaps.' Seb sounded exactly as their father had, whenever *he* hadn't said something that mattered. Keeping information from his youngest son because he didn't trust him to step up and do his job. To take responsibility for making things right.

Ben had hoped Seb knew him better than their father had. Apparently not.

Perhaps that was just what happened when you spent your childhood in different boarding schools. With five years between them, Ben had always been too far behind to catch up with his talented older brother. He'd always wondered what life had been like for Seb before he came along.

'Fine. I'll type up a new evaluation tonight and get it

over to you. Okay?' It wouldn't take long—especially if he could get the original report e-mailed over from head office. But work responsibilities could wait until later. First he had plans. Like finding out just how strokeable *Dr* Lucinda Myles really was under those clothes. Because *of course* she'd gone on to get her PhD. The woman was born for academia.

'That'd be great,' Seb said.

He sounded tired, and Ben could imagine him sitting behind Dad's big oak desk, rubbing a hand over his forehead. Because now it wasn't years and schools keeping them apart, it was the burden of responsibility.

Working together, especially since their father had died, had enabled Ben to get to know his brother better than ever before. They were close, he supposed, in their way. Possibly because neither of them really had anyone else.

And Seb was his brother before he was his boss. He had to remember that.

A stab of guilt at the thought made Ben ask, 'Is there anything else you need me to do?'

The pause at the other end of the line suggested that there was, but whatever it was Seb obviously didn't trust him to do it. 'Nah, don't worry about it. Enjoy your week in Chester. Take in a Roman relic or something. Or—no, you were planning on heading off to your cottage, weren't you?'

'I thought I might,' Ben said cautiously. God, after the last twelve months all he wanted was to hole up in the middle of nowhere with a good bottle of whisky, some really great music and some old movies. 'But if you need me back in the office—'

'No. You haven't had a holiday in nearly a year.' *Since before Dad died,* went unspoken. 'You deserve a break.'

Not as much as Seb did. The idea of persuading his ultra-responsible older brother to take time off was frankly laughable, but apparently Ben wasn't nearly as essential to the well-being of Hampton & Sons. Something he might as well take advantage of, he supposed. 'Well, you know where I am if you need me.'

'In bed with a hot blonde?' his brother joked, a hint of the old, relaxed Seb coming out.

Relief seeped through Ben at the sound of it. 'Brunette, hopefully.' Ben eyed Luce again. Still ignoring him. If she remembered him at all she probably felt exactly the same way about him as his father had—that he was still the same man she'd known him to be at twenty, incapable of growing up. Well, maybe he'd have a chance tonight to show her exactly what sort of man he'd grown into.

Seb's laugh lacked any real humour. 'Then I wish you luck. I'm sure you'll have her begging you for more in no time.'

'That's the plan.'

'And then you'll just have to figure out how to get rid of her when she inevitably loses her head over you.'

Quite aside from the fact that Ben found it impossible to imagine Lucinda Myles losing her head over anyone, something in Seb's words rankled.

'Hey, be fair. I'm always honest with them. They know exactly what to expect. No commitment, no strings, no future, and—'

'No more than one night together in a row,' Seb finished for him. 'I know. But they always think they'll be the one to change you.'

Ben shrugged, even though Seb couldn't see him. 'Not my responsibility. I don't do long-term.'

'Just the short-term fix.' Seb chuckled. 'Well, if that's all you want enjoy yourself. I'll see you back in London on Friday.' He hung up.

Ben put his brother's mocking out of his head. As if Seb was any better, anyway. Ben couldn't remember the last time he'd even seen him with a date.

Life was all about priorities, their father had always said. And just because Ben had never shared David Hampton's priorities when he was alive, and didn't intend to start now, that didn't make the sentiment any less valid.

His priorities weren't love and marriage. And his priority for the night certainly wasn't Seb and the business. It was Luce Myles. Grabbing two gin and tonics from the bartender, Ben was pretty sure he knew exactly how to get under her skin.

Luce's 'To Do' list was stretching to several pages by the time Ben finally returned with their drinks.

'Queue at the bar?' she asked, raising her eyebrows as he placed the glasses on the table. A girl couldn't be expected to deal with so many demands on her without a drink.

'Phone call from the office,' he countered with an apologetic smile.

She supposed that running a hotel chain did require some level of responsibility, hard though it was to imagine from Ben Hampton. On the other hand, he had described it as the 'Hampton & Sons' chain, so maybe he was just the heir apparent, running errands for Daddy, and the phone call was about him maxing out his company credit card. That would explain a lot, actually.

He folded himself into the low bucket chair, his long legs stretched out in front of him, and Luce allowed herself to be distracted from how the man made a living. A more interesting question was how did he manage to look so comfortable, so relaxed, in a chair so clearly not designed for someone of his height or size? Luce couldn't manage it, and the chair might have been made for her.

'You look like you kept yourself occupied, anyway.' He motioned at her list, and she winced.

'Busy week. Time of the year.' She started to close the cover of her organiser, but Ben's hand slipped between the pages and pushed it open again.

'Let's see what's keeping Dr Lucinda Myles so busy.'

Tugging the diary towards him, he flashed her a grin that made her middle glow a little, against her better judgement. She didn't remember him being this damn attractive. His behaviour was unacceptably intrusive, an invasion of her privacy, and her 'To Do' list was absolutely none of his business. And yet she didn't stop him. All because he had a wickedly attractive smile. Clearly she was losing her edge.

I need some time off. The thought was a familiar one, but Luce knew from past experience that nothing would come of it. Yes, some time to recharge her batteries—hell, even some time to focus on her book—would be beneficial. But when on earth would she ever find the time to make it happen?

Ben flipped through the list and gave a low whistle. 'Conference, followed by what I imagine to be a long and tedious conference report, family dinner party on Christmas Eve, Christmas Day entertaining, house repairs, cat-sitting for your neighbour, university New Year's Eve event, student evaluations, your actual day job. When were you planning on sleeping?'

'I wasn't.' Luce took a long sip of her gin and tonic. 'Especially since I still don't have a bed for the night.'

'I believe I offered you a solution to that particular problem.' Ben slammed her organiser shut, but kept his hand on it. 'In fact, after seeing your "To Do" list, I have an even better proposition.'

'So you *are* propositioning me, then?' Luce said, trying to sound accusing rather than amused. Or aroused. This was unacceptable behaviour—especially from the owner of a hotel. And she was not the sort of woman who had one-night stands in hotels just to get a bed for the night. However attractive the man. But part of her couldn't help wondering if he'd be doing this if he didn't remember her. Or, perhaps more likely, he'd never be doing this at all if he knew who she really was. *Which is it?*

Ben just smiled a lazy, seductive grin. 'Were you ever really in any doubt? Now, do you want to hear this proposition or not?'

She shouldn't. But her curious nature was what had led her into academia, into history, in the first place. She wanted to know what had happened, when and why. She couldn't help but remember all those long, dull evenings staying in to study, until Ben and Mandy stumbled into the flat, ready to tell her everything she'd missed, their eyes pitying. She needed to know what it was Ben Hampton saw in her *now* to make him waste his time trying to seduce her. 'Go on, then.'

'Take the night off.'

Luce blinked. 'That's it?'

Folding his arms behind his head, Ben smirked. 'It's elegant in its simplicity.'

'It's not possible.' Luce reached for her organiser, shaking her head. 'I need to type up my notes from today, I need to talk to my brother about this dinner, and I need to—'

'You need to slow down.' Peeling her fingers from the cover of her diary, Ben picked it up and slipped it into the pocket of his jacket.

Luce lunged across the table to try to grab it, but she was too slow. 'I need that. You can't just—'

'Trust me, it's for the best.' Luce glared at him, and

he sighed. 'Okay—tell you what. You listen to the rest of my plan, and if you honestly don't think it sounds like a good idea I'll give you your stupid planner back and you can go wander the streets of Chester looking for a hotel. All right?'

Even Luce had to admit that her options were a little limited. 'All right. What's the plan?'

'A night off. With me. You put on your best party dress, let me take you out to dinner. You talk about yourself—not the things you're supposed to be doing. You let me take responsibility for showing you a good time. You relax. We have a nightcap in my suite, and then you get a good night's sleep.'

'In my own room?' Luce stamped down on the corner of her mind that was happily imagining what might happen if they were both in *his* room.

Ben's smile grew a little wolfish. 'Well, now...that's up to you.'

'Really?' Luce said flatly.

'Of course.' Ben looked mildly offended. 'I'm not saying I won't give it my best shot. You're a beautiful woman, and I enjoy the company of beautiful women. But at the end of the night *you* get the choice of my bed or the spare room. Either way you have a bed for the night.'

Luce found her gaze caught on his. He thought she was beautiful? Ben Hampton actually wanted her? Sober, all grown-up, not obviously crazy...and he wanted her. She could have dinner with him, flirt, kiss...more. All she had to do was say yes.

She tore her gaze away.

'And tomorrow?' she asked.

Ben's smile slipped. 'Tomorrow I'm leaving town. Look, whichever way tonight goes, it's nothing sordid. Nothing to be ashamed of. We can enjoy each other's company then

go our separate ways. I'm not asking you for anything beyond tonight.'

'So romantic,' Luce muttered. She hated how unworldly
he made her feel. His matter-of-fact proposition of a one-
night stand was miles away from any date she'd been on
in the last ten year. And also the reason she couldn't give
in to it. She wanted more from a night of passion than a
kiss on the cheek at the end of it and never seeing each
other again.

'This isn't romance,' Ben said. 'It's much more fun than
that. And, either way, I bet you feel better in the morning.'

And she would. Sex aside, she'd get a stress-free evening, with no need to entertain since Ben was clearly capable of making his own fun. She could just relax and let
someone else take charge for a few hours. Could she even
do that? She wasn't sure she ever had before.

'Admit it—you're tempted.'

Ben leant across the table, that scarred eyebrow raised,
and Luce knew that she was. In more ways than one.

'By dinner,' she told him firmly. 'Nothing else.'

Ben gave her a lazy smile. 'As you like.'

It might be the worst idea she'd ever had. But at least
she'd have somewhere to sleep for the night, and the whole
week ahead would look more manageable after a relaxing
evening and a solid eight hours' rest. And maybe tomorrow morning she could tell him who she was and watch
his amused composure slip as he realised he'd tried to
seduce Loser Luce. Again. That would almost make it
worth it in itself.

I shouldn't. I have responsibilities.

But even Grandad Myles, duty and responsibility's biggest advocate, would have wanted her to take a night off
once in a while. Wouldn't he? She was stressed, overwhelmed and exhausted—and utterly useless to anybody

in such a state. A night off to regroup would enable her to better help others and get things done more efficiently. Nothing at all to do with wanting to find out what she'd been missing on all those university nights out.

Besides, hadn't she fantasised about a night in the Royal Court's best suite?

'On one condition,' she said.

Ben grinned. 'Anything.'

'I want to take advantage of your hopefully plush and expensive bathroom first.' With bubbles. And maybe champagne.

Ben's grin grew wider. 'Deal.'

'Then give me my organiser back.' She was already starting to feel a bit jittery without it. Maybe she could review her lists in the bath. Multi-tasking—that was the key to a productive life.

But Ben shook his head. 'First thing tomorrow it's all yours. Not one moment before.'

'But I need—'

'Trust me,' Ben said, taking her hand in his across the table. 'Tonight I'll be in charge of meeting all your needs.'

A red-hot flush ran across Luce's skin. Perhaps this wasn't such a good idea after all.

CHAPTER THREE

LUCE HAD NEVER seen such a magnificent bathroom.

The size of the rolltop tub almost helped her forget the sight of Ben locking her beloved crimson leather organiser in the suite's mini-safe. And the glass of champagne he'd poured her before she'd absconded to the bathroom more than made up for the way she'd blushed when he'd asked if she was sure she didn't want him to help scrub her back.

Tearing her eyes away from the bath, Luce checked the door, then turned the lock. She'd told him as clearly as she could that the only part of his offer she was interested in was dinner and the spare bed. No point giving him the wrong idea now.

Of course she wasn't entirely sure what the right idea was. Accepting an offer of a night out with a gorgeous man—whatever the terms and conditions—wasn't exactly typical Luce behaviour. She hadn't even made a pros and cons list, for a start.

But the decision was made now. She might as well make the most of it.

Turning on the taps, Luce rifled through the tiny bottles of complimentary lotions and potions, settling on something that claimed to be a 'relaxing and soothing' bath foam. Sounded perfect. After a moment's consideration she tipped the whole bottle into the running water. She was in need of all the relaxation she could get. That was the point of this whole night, wasn't it? And, since it was the only one she was likely to get for a while, she really should make the most of it.

Luce took a swig of her champagne, stripped off her clothes and climbed into the heavenly scented hot water.

Relaxation. How hard could it be?

It would be a whole lot easier, she decided after a few moments of remaining tense, if Ben Hampton wasn't waiting outside for her.

Tipping her head back against the edge of the bath, Luce tried to conjure up the image of the last time she'd seen him. After so many years of trying to forget she'd thought it would be harder to remember. But the sounds, scents, sights were all as fresh in her mind as they'd been eight years ago, at the swanky Palace Hotel, London, for Ben's twenty-first birthday party.

It had been a stupid idea to go in the first place. But Mandy had wanted someone to travel down on the train with and Ben had raised his eyebrows in surprise and said, 'Well, sure you can come. If you really want to.' And Luce *had* wanted to—just a bit. Just to see what birthdays looked like for the rich and privileged.

Much as she'd expected, it turned out. Too much champagne. Too many people laughing too loudly. Bright lights and dancing and shimmery expensive dresses. In her green cotton frock, and with her hair long and loose instead of pinned back in one of the intricate styles the other girls had seemed to favour, Luce had felt just as out of place as she'd predicted.

So she'd hidden in another room—some sort of sitting area decked out like a gentleman's library. Books never made her feel inadequate, after all. She could sit and read until Mandy was ready to head back to their tiny shared hotel room. Not a Hampton hotel, but a cheap, probably infested place three tube stops away. It had been the perfect plan—until Ben had found her.

'You've got the right idea,' he'd said, lurching into the chair next to her.

Luce, who'd already watched him down glass after glass of champagne that evening, had inched further away. 'Not enjoying your party?' she'd asked.

Ben had shrugged. 'It's a party. Hard not to enjoy a party.' His eyes had narrowed as he'd studied her. 'Although you seem to be managing it.'

Looking away, Luce had fiddled with the hem of her dress. 'It's not really my kind of party.'

'It's not really mine either,' Ben had said.

When Luce had glanced across at him he'd been staring at the door. But then his attention had jerked back to her, and a wide, not entirely believable grin had been on his face. 'It's just my dad showing off, really. There are more of his business associates here than my friends.'

'And yet you invited me?'

He'd laughed at that. 'We're friends, aren't we?'

'Not really.' They'd had nothing in common besides proximity to Mandy until that moment, right then, when Luce had felt his gaze meeting hers, connecting them—until she'd realised she was leaning forward, into him, waiting for his answer.

'We could be.'

He'd inched closer too, leaning over the arm of his chair until Luce had been able to smell the champagne on his breath.

'You're a hell of a lot of a nicer person than Mandy.'

'Mandy's my friend,' Luce had said, trying to find the energy to defend her. But all she'd been able to see was

Ben's eyes, pupils black and wide. 'Your girlfriend.' She couldn't think with him so close.

'Mandy's out there flirting with a forty-something businessman she knows will never leave his wife but might buy her some nice jewellery.'

Luce had winced. He was probably right. For a moment she'd felt her first ever pang of sympathy for Ben Hampton.

But then he'd leant in further, his hand coming up to rest against her cheek, and Luce had known she should pull away, run away, get away from Ben Hampton for good.

His lips had been soft, gentle against hers, she remembered. But only for a brief moment. One insane lapse in judgement. Before she jerked back, leaving him bent over the space where she'd been. She'd upped and run—just as she should have done the moment she'd arrived at the party and seen how much she didn't fit in.

Luce sighed and let the memory go. Much more pleasant to focus on the hot water and scented bubbles of her bath than on Ben's face as she'd turned back at the doorway. Or the humiliation she'd felt, her cheeks burning, as she'd run out, his laughter echoing in her ears, and dragged Mandy away from her businessman and back to that flea-ridden hotel.

He probably didn't remember. He'd been drunk and young and stupid. He'd certainly never have done it sober. Why else would he have laughed? The whole incident was ridiculous. Luce was a grown woman now, with bigger concerns than what Ben Hampton thought of her.

Except he was waiting outside the bathroom door, ready to take her out for dinner. And afterwards…

Luce shut her eyes and dunked her head under the water.

What the hell was she doing in there?

Ben checked his watch, then poured himself another

glass of champagne. It was coming up to three quarters of an hour since he'd heard the lock turn, and since then there had been only the occasional splash. Apparently she was taking the whole relaxing thing seriously. He should have remembered earlier how his ex-girlfriend had complained about Luce disappearing into the bathroom with her history texts and using up all the hot water on ridiculously indulgent baths. At the time he'd just found it comforting to know that the woman had some weaknesses. Now it was seriously holding up his evening.

But at least it gave him the opportunity to do some research. Unlocking the safe, he pulled out Luce's organiser again and sank into the armchair by the window to read. Really, the woman was the epitome of over-scheduled. And almost none of the things written into the tiny diary spaces in neat block capitals seemed like things she'd be doing for herself. Christmas dinners—plural—for family, attending lectures for colleagues, looking after someone else's cat... And then, on a Sunday near the end of January, the words 'BOOK DRAFT DEADLINE' in red capitals. Interesting. Definitely something to talk about over dinner.

She baffled him. That was why he wanted to know more. On the one hand, he was pretty sure he could predict her entire life story leading from university to here. On the other, however...there was something else there. Something he hadn't seen or noticed when they were younger. Something that hooked him in even if he wasn't ready to admit why. Yes, she was attractive. That on its own was nothing new. But this self-sacrificing mentality—was it a martyr complex? A bullying mother? Luce hadn't ever seemed weak, so why was she doing everything for other people?

Particularly her family, it seemed. Flicking through the pages, Ben tried to remember if he'd ever met them at university, but if he had they hadn't made much of an impression. Now he thought about it, he did remember Luce disappearing home to Cardiff every few weeks to visit them.

Obviously a sign of things to come.

Leaning back in his chair, Ben closed the organiser and tried to resist the memories pressing against his brain. But they were too strong. Another dark-haired woman, just as tired, just as self-sacrificing—until the day she broke.

'I'm sorry, Benji,' she'd said. 'Mummy has to go.'

And it didn't matter that he'd tried everything, done anything he could think of to be good enough to make her stay. He hadn't been able to fix things for her.

Maybe he could for Luce.

Laughing at himself, he sat up, shaking the memories away. Luce wasn't his mother. She wasn't tied by marriage or children. She could make her own choices far more freely. And what could he do in one night, anyway? Other than help her relax. Maybe that would be enough. Maybe all she needed was to realise that she had needs, too. And Ben was very good at assessing women's needs.

A repetitive beeping noise interrupted his thoughts, and it took him a moment to register it as a ringtone. As he looked up, his gaze caught on Luce's rich purple coat, slung across the sofa on the other side of the glass coffee table. She'd taken her suitcase and handbag into the bathroom with her—obvious paranoia in Ben's view—but he'd seen her drop her phone into her coat pocket before they left the bar.

Interesting.

He should feel guilty, he supposed, but really it was all for the woman's own good. She needed saving from herself. She needed his help.

The noise had stopped before he could retrieve the

phone from the pocket of her coat, and Ben stared at the flashing screen for a moment, wondering how one woman could have so many people needing to contact her. In addition to a missed call from her mother, her notifications screen told him straight off that she had three texts from a guy called Tom, an e-mail from a man named Dennis and another missed call from an improbably named 'Dolly'. All in the hour since they'd left the bar.

Scanning over the snippets on the screen told him all he really needed to know—every person who'd contacted her wanted something from her. Dropping the phone back into her pocket, Ben considered the evening ahead.

His plan, ill thought out to start with, had been to have a fun evening and hopefully a fun night. To show Luce a good time, then remind her who he was so they could have a laugh about it. Or *he* could, anyway. But now…he was invested.

Who *was* Lucinda Myles these days?

The last time he'd seen her must have been the night of his spectacularly disastrous twenty-first birthday party. He remembered spotting her sloping out of the hotel ballroom towards one of the drawing rooms, but after that far too much champagne had blurred the evening until the following morning and a headbangingly loud lecture from his father about appropriate behaviour and responsibility to the family reputation. Friends had helpfully filled him in on the more humorous of his antics that night, but no one had mentioned Luce.

Then the ex had broken up with him for humiliating her and 'possibly ruining her future', whatever that meant, and he'd had no reason to see Luce again. Who knew how much she'd changed in the intervening years?

Ben paused in his thoughts. She couldn't have changed

that much, given what he'd seen so far that day. In which case...

Grabbing the phone from the table next to him, he called down to Reception.

'Daisy? Can you cancel my booking at The Edge tonight?' Trendy, stainless-steel, cutting-edge fusion restaurants just weren't Luce's style, no matter who the concierge had needed to bribe to get him a table there that night. 'No, don't worry. I'll sort out an alternative myself.'

Something more Luce. More fun too, probably.

One more quick phone call ascertained that the restaurant he was thinking of still existed. Perfect. Hanging up, Ben glanced at the bathroom door and then at his watch again. He'd given Luce long enough. Time to move on to the next stage of their evening.

Pausing first to replace the diary in the safe, he gave the bathroom door a quick rap with his knuckles and then said, loud enough to be sure he could be heard through it, 'You've got five more minutes in there before I start trying to guess the pass code for your phone.'

To his surprise, the lock turned and the door opened almost instantly. Eyebrows raised, Luce stared at him and said, 'Threats aren't traditionally very relaxing, you know.'

But baths clearly were. Especially for Dr Lucinda Myles.

She'd changed out of those clothes he'd been longing to run his hands over, but since she'd replaced them with a slippery, silky purple dress he really wasn't complaining. Her hair was pinned up off her neck, with a few damp tendrils curling behind her ears and across her forehead. She smiled at him, her deep red lips curving in amusement. 'I didn't think you were the sort of man to do speechless. I like it.'

A rush of lavender hit his lungs as she swept past him,

reminding him of the château in summer, and he realised he still hadn't spoken. 'If I'd known you were using your time so well I'd have been much more patient,' he said, finding his voice at last.

Luce slipped her arms into her coat, her fingers reaching into the pocket for her phone. Time for another distraction. Ben offered her his arm and she took it, forestalling her return to the world of technology and messages from people who wanted far less fun things from her than he did. 'Now, if you're ready, won't you let me escort you to dinner?'

She still looked suspicious as she nodded, but she left the room beside him, steady on higher heels than he'd have expected her to be comfortable wearing. Ben smiled. This was going to be a good evening. He was sure of it. The hotel and the business were fine, and he had the company of a beautiful and intriguing woman for the night—one he might be able to help a little. And then he'd get to decamp to the cottage for the rest of the week, feeling good about himself.

Life was great.

There should be laws against men looking quite that good in a suit. Men she was determined to resist, anyway. If Dennis had ever looked even half as good maybe they would have managed more than a few coffees and the occasional fake date when he needed a partner for a university dinner or she needed someone for a family event.

Actually, no, they wouldn't. Quite aside from the fact that Dennis became intensely irritating after more than a couple of hours in his company, she'd never felt that... *spark*—that connection she needed to take the risk of building an actual relationship. To her surprise, Ben Hampton had a spark. Not a relationship one, of course, but maybe something more intense. Something that definitely hadn't been there the last time they met. Which was just as well, as he'd been dating her roommate at the time. But there was definitely something.

It was almost a shame she didn't have the time, energy or courage to take him up on his offer to find out exactly what.

Her phone buzzed in her pocket and her fingers itched to reach for it. She hadn't called her mother back, and she'd only worry if she didn't hear from her. Well, actually, she probably wouldn't. Tabitha saved her concern for Tom and Dolly, safe in the knowledge that Luce could take care of herself far better than the rest of them.

Still, she'd get annoyed, which was even worse, and pull a guilt trip on Luce next time they spoke.

She really should call her back. But Ben's arm held her hand trapped against his body, and she could feel the warmth of him even through his coat and suit jacket. Was that intentional? Trying to cut her off from her real life and keep her in this surreal bubble of a night he'd created?

Ben Hampton had invaded her life and her personal space since she'd bumped into him again, only a couple of hours ago, and she'd let him. Sat back and let him take charge, point out the problems in her life, rearrange all her plans for the evening. What had happened to taking responsibility and control?

Okay, she needed a new plan for the night. Something to wrest back control. At the very least she needed to know if he remembered her…

She shivered as they left the hotel lobby, the bitter night air stinging her face and her lungs. Icicle Christmas lights dangled above the cobbled streets, twinkling in the night like the real thing. Ben tugged her a little closer, and she wondered how it was he stayed so warm despite the winter chill.

'Where are we going?' she asked, belatedly realising he hadn't even told her where he was taking her. Some fancy restaurant, probably, she'd figured when pulling out the dress she'd packed for the conference gala dinner. But that wasn't the point. No one knew where she was—least of all her. It was madness. She was out in a strange city at night with a man she barely knew. A little surreptitious internet searching in the bar while he'd been fetching the drinks had told her the bare bones of his professional career since university—which mostly seemed to be doing whatever his father needed him to do—but it hadn't told her what sort of a man he was. She hadn't seen him in eight years, and she hadn't known him all that well back then. He certainly hadn't been the kind of guy the twenty-year-old Luce had willingly spent time with. This was foolishness beyond compare. Dennis would be horrified.

Of course her mother would probably be relieved. Tabitha had always been a little afraid that her daughter had inherited none of her more flighty attributes at all.

'A little French restaurant I know,' Ben said, answering the question she'd almost forgotten she'd asked. 'It's up past the Cross, on the Rows. You okay to walk in those shoes?'

'Of course.' Luce spoke the words automatically, even though the balls of her feet had started to smart as she struggled over the cobbles. *Show no weakness.* That was another of her grandad's rules to live by. If she couldn't keep the other one tonight, she might as well try to hang on to something.

'You never used to wear shoes like that.'

Luce couldn't tell if the warm feeling that settled over her shoulders at Ben's words was relief or confusion. 'You do remember me, then?' she blurted out before she could stop herself. 'I wasn't sure.'

'You think I invite strange women up to my suite all the time?'

Luce shrugged. 'University was a long time ago. I have no idea what kind of man you are now. And, actually…'

'Yeah, yeah.' Ben rolled his eyes. 'Eight years ago I'd have invited *all* women up to my room.'

'I hope you've grown up a little since then.' A hitch in Ben's step made her glance up. 'What?'

He shook his head. 'Nothing. Just depends who you ask.'

Picking up speed again, Ben led them up the very steep steps onto the medieval Rows, a second layer of shops and restaurants above the street-level ones. The historian in Luce was fascinated by the structure—the timber fronts, the overhanging storey above making a covered walkway. There was no other example in the world—the Chester Rows were unique. She should be savouring every detail.

And instead all she could think was, *He remembers me.* Well, at least she knew now. Except…just because he remembered her, that didn't mean he remembered the last time they'd seen each other.

Maybe he'd forgotten it entirely. And maybe that meant she could, too.

It was too cold for much more conversation. They made their way along the Rows, Luce tucked tightly into Ben's body for warmth, until he said, 'Here we are,' and Luce's whole body relaxed at the sight of a cosy little restaurant tucked away behind a few closed shops with sparkling Christmas window displays.

'Thank God for that,' she said, smiling up at Ben. 'I'm freezing.'

CHAPTER FOUR

SMILING UP AT HIM, complaining about the cold, Luce seemed relaxed for the first time. As if this was any usual date, not a peculiar arrangement to help an uptight woman cut loose. And she remembered him. That was a start. He wasn't sure he could have made it all through dinner without knowing.

Ben pushed open the door to La Cuillère d'Argent and let Luce walk into the warmth first. Her face brightened in the candlelit restaurant, and she glanced back at him with surprise on her face.

'I'm overdressed,' she said, taking in the rustic wooden tables and chairs. There weren't many other people eating there, but those who were wore mostly casual clothes.

'You look perfect.' He smiled at the waiter approaching. 'Table for two, please?'

Seated at a candlelit table in the window, looking out at the people hurrying past, Luce stripped off her coat and asked, 'How did you know about this place?'

'Not what you were expecting?'

She shook her head, and Ben knew what she was thinking. She'd expected somewhere impressive, somewhere fancy and expensive—somewhere that would make her feel kindly towards him when he paid, possibly impressed enough to take him to bed when they got back to the hotel.

Somewhere like The Edge. Somewhere that said, *I'm Ben Hampton and I've just inherited half of a multi-million-pound hotel chain, and I still have time to flatter and treat you. Aren't you impressed?*

But that would have defeated the object of the evening. He wanted Luce to relax, and he knew she wasn't the sort to be impressed by or enjoy over-priced, over-fiddly food. Too practical for that, with her epic 'To Do' lists and her martyr complex. She'd probably feel guilty the whole time, which wouldn't help his cause at all.

No, he needed somewhere cosy and intimate, somewhere he could actually talk to her, learn about her life since uni, find out what made her tick. This place was perfect for that. Ben blinked in the candlelight as he realised, belatedly, that he *wanted* to know her. Not just seduce her or entertain her. He wanted to know the truth of Luce Myles.

Of course seducing her was still firmly part of the plan. He just didn't mind a little small talk first.

'Have you been here before?' Luce asked, scanning the wine list. 'Do you live in Chester?'

Ben shook his head. 'Just visiting to check on the hotel. But I came here with my mother years ago. She was born in France, you see. Knew every great French restaurant in the country.' It must have been fifteen years ago or more, he realised. 'I checked while you were in the bath to make sure it was still here, actually. It really has been a while.'

'What does it mean?' Luce asked, staring at the front of the menu, where the restaurant name curled across the card. '"La Cuillère d'Argent",' she read slowly.

'The Silver Spoon,' Ben translated, tapping a finger against the picture under the words—an ornate piece of silverware not unlike the ones on the table for their use.

'I like it,' Luce announced, smiling at him over the menu.

Ben's shoulders dropped as a tension he hadn't realised he was feeling left him. That was wrong. She was the one who was supposed to be relaxing. He was always relaxed. That was who he was.

'Good,' he said, a little unnerved, and motioned a waiter over to order a carafe of white wine to start. He rather thought he might need it tonight.

They made polite conversation about the menu options, and the freshly baked bread with olive tapenade the waiter brought them, before Luce asked, 'So, if you're just visiting, where is home these days?'

Ben shrugged. Home wasn't exactly something he associated with his stark and minimalist penthouse suite. And since he hadn't been to the cottage in Wales for over a year, and the château in France for far longer, he was pretty sure they didn't count.

'I'm based out of London, but mostly I'm on the road. Wherever there's a Hampton & Sons hotel I've got a bed for the night, so I do okay.'

Across the table Luce's eyes widened with what Ben recognised as pity. 'That must be hard. Not having anywhere to call home.'

Must it? 'I'm used to it, I guess. Even growing up, I lived in the hotels.' A different one every time he came home from boarding school, after his mother left. 'I've got a penthouse suite in one of the London hotels to crash in, if I want. Fully serviced and maintained.'

'Thus neatly getting out of one of the joys of home ownership,' Luce said wryly.

Ben remembered the 'House Repairs' entry on her 'To Do' list.

'Your house takes some upkeep, then?'

'It's falling apart,' Luce said, her voice blunt, and reached for her wine. 'But it was my grandfather's house, and I grew up there. I could never sell it even if I found someone willing to take it on.'

'Still, sounds like a lot of work on top of all your other commitments.' Was this something else she was doing for her family? For the sake of others? 'Are you sure you wouldn't be happier in a cosy little flat near the university?'

He was mostly joking, so the force of her reply surprised him. *'Never.'*

'Okay.'

Dropping her eyes to the table, Luce shook her head a little before smiling up at him. 'Sorry. It's just…I worry about it a lot. But one day I'll finish fixing the place up and it'll be the perfect family home. It's just getting there that's proving trying.'

Ben shrugged. 'I guess I don't really get it. I mean, I own properties and such. I've even renovated one of them. But they're just bricks and mortar to me. If I had to sell them, or if getting rid of them gave me another opportunity—well, it wouldn't worry me.'

'You don't get attached, huh?' She gave him a lopsided smile. 'Probably a good choice if you're always moving around.'

'Exactly. Don't get tied down. It's one of my rules for life.'

'Yeah? What are the others?'

Ben couldn't tell if she was honestly interested or mocking him. 'Most importantly: enjoy life. And avoid responsibility, of course.'

'Of course,' she echoed with a smile, reaching for the bread basket. 'You never were big on that.'

There was an awkward silence while Ben imagined Luce rerunning every stupid moment he'd had at university in her head. Time to change the subject.

'So, you're in Chester for some conference thing?' he asked.

Luce nodded, swallowing the bread she was chewing. '*"Bringing History to the Future"*.' Ben smiled at the sarcasm in her voice.

'You're not a fan?'

'It's not that,' Luce replied with a shrug. 'It's just… there's so much important preservation and research to be done, and finding a way to make the importance of our history fit into a series of thirty-minute television programmes with accompanying books does tend to interfere a bit.'

'But if it's not important to the bulk of the populace…?'

'Then we lose funding and the chance to study important sites and documents. I know, I know…'

From the way she waved her hands in a dismissive manner Ben gathered this wasn't the first time she'd heard the argument. 'You have this debate a lot?'

Luce gave him a lopsided smile. 'Mostly with myself. I understand the need, but sometimes I'd rather be holed up in a secluded library somewhere, doing real research, real work, not worrying about who was going to read and dissect it without understanding the background.'

'This is your book?' Ben tore himself another piece of bread and smeared it with tapenade, but kept his gaze on her.

Luce pulled a face. 'My book is somewhere between the two. "Popular history for armchair historians," my editor calls it. Or it will be if I ever finish it.'

'What's it about?'

'An obscure Welsh princess who became the mistress of Henry I, and whose rape caused the end of the truce between the Normans and the Welsh.' The words sounded rote, as if she'd been telling people the same line for a long time without making any progress.

Ben scoured his vague memory of 'A' Level history, but they hadn't covered much Welsh history in his very English boarding schools. 'You're still based in Wales, then?' he asked.

Luce nodded. 'Cardiff. But not just for the history. It's where I grew up. Where my family lives. It's home. And when Grandad left me the house I knew it was where I was meant to stay.'

'That's nice,' Ben said absently, thinking again of the overgrown château that was his heritage from his maternal grandmother. He should probably check in on it some time soon.

The waiter brought their meals, and the conversation moved on to discussing the dishes in front of them.

'So,' he said, when they'd both agreed their food was delicious, and Luce had stolen a bite of his rabbit with mustard sauce, 'tell me more about this Welsh princess of yours.'

Her eyebrows jumped up in surprise. 'You're interested?'

'I have a cottage in Wales,' he explained. 'Down in the Brecons. It's where I'm headed tomorrow, actually. A good story might get me in the right mood for my rural retreat.'

'What do you want to know?'

Ben shrugged. 'Everything.'

The surprised look stayed, but Luce obliged all the same.

'Um…Princess Nest. She was the daughter of the King of Deheubarth, in South West Wales, and she gave Henry I a son before he married her off to his steward in Wales.'

'Nice of him,' Ben murmured.

'How things worked then. Anyway, the reason she's remembered, really, is her abduction.'

'She was kidnapped?' Letting his fork drop to his plate, Ben started paying real attention. Against the odds, this was actually interesting.

Luce nodded. 'Owain ap Cadwgan, the head of the Welsh resistance, fell in love with her. He and his men stole into Cilgerran Castle and took her.'

Ben blinked. 'What happened next?'

'A lot of things.' Luce smiled. 'A whole book's worth, in fact. Some people say she fell in love with Owain, too. But really, if you want to know the whole story, you'll have to read my book.'

'I will,' Ben promised. If she ever finished writing it, of course.

Okay, she had to give Ben Hampton this much—he was a better judge of restaurants than she'd expected. And a better conversationalist than she remembered. He'd actually sounded interested when she'd talked about Princess Nest and her book, which was more than anyone in her family had ever managed. Of course he was only doing it to get her into bed—she wasn't stupid, and he'd all but told her as much—but she had no qualms at all about turning him down at the bedroom door. She couldn't imagine for a moment that someone with the charm and self-confidence of Ben Hampton would have any trouble shaking off that kind of rejection.

She, on the other hand, had absolutely no desire to be the one being ushered out of the bedroom before breakfast the next morning, when he'd got what he wanted and lost interest in her.

The waiter cleared away their dessert plates and deposited the coffees they'd ordered in front of them, along with two oversized liqueur glasses with a small amount of thick amber liquid pooled at the base.

'Calvados,' Ben explained, lifting his glass to his lips. 'Apple brandy. It's a traditional Normandy *digestif*.'

Luce followed suit. The brandy taste she remembered from occasional late nights with her grandfather during university holidays was deepened by the hint of fruit. 'It's good.'

Ben shrugged. 'I like it.'

While she was drinking it he paid the bill. She realised too late to insist on paying her half. 'Let me give you something for my—'

'Absolutely not.'

Ben clamped a hand down over hers as she reached for her purse, and she felt the thrill of a shiver running up her wrist to her shoulder. It must be the brandy, she decided, affecting her judgement. Because, however attractive Ben Hampton was, and however intense his focus on her and her conversation made her feel, she was not going to sleep with him tonight.

She couldn't help but wonder, though, how all that concentration on the moment would feel if he was focusing it on her body. Her pleasure.

Luce shook her head. Too much Calvados. Some fresh air would sort that out.

Ben slipped her coat over her shoulders, and that same frisson ran through her as he stood close behind her. Luce wondered whether her room in the suite had a lock on its door. For keeping him out or her in, she wasn't entirely sure.

The cold night air bit into the exposed skin of her face and hands. Luce glanced at her watch: nearly midnight. She needed to get some sleep if she was going to make that lecture for Dennis in the morning. She huddled into her coat and felt Ben's arm settle on her shoulders, holding her close against him again.

'So, feeling any more relaxed?' he asked.

'Lots,' Luce answered honestly. 'But that might just be the alcohol.'

'True.'

They walked a few more steps, and Luce almost thought he might drop the subject.

Then he asked, 'So, what do you think might relax you a little more?'

Truly great sex, Luce thought, but didn't say. The sort that made you forget your own name, just for a little while. The sort that let you sleep so deeply you woke refreshed and energised, however much of the night you'd spent exploring each other's bodies.

Not that she'd ever actually *had* sex like that herself, of course. But Dolly was adamant that it existed.

'Um…handing in my book draft on time?' she said finally, when she realised he was still waiting for an answer.

'And how do you plan to do that when your "To Do" list is full of stuff you need to do for other people?'

It was a question she'd asked herself often enough, but hearing it in Ben's relaxed, carefree voice made her bristle. 'What do you care? If you're so against helping others, why do you care if I get my book in or not?'

Ben shrugged. 'Well, I've listened to Nest's life story this evening. I'm invested now. I told you—I want to read the damn thing when you finish it.'

'Oh.' Luce tried to hide her astonishment.

'Besides, I didn't say I was against helping others. I'm here in Chester because I'm doing a favour for my brother.'

Apparently he wasn't going to stop surprising her any time soon.

'What favour?'

'The person who was supposed to be checking out the hotel this week got sick, so I offered to swing by on my way to a week off.'

Ben smiled down at her, and Luce felt it in her cold bones.

'So, you see, it's not helping out others I object to.'

'Then what is it?' Luce asked, remembering that she was supposed to be annoyed.

'I object to you giving up your whole life to serve others. I think you need to put your own wants and needs first for a while.'

It sounded so reasonable when he said it. So tempting. But then Luce remembered the pages of 'To Do' lists filling her stolen organiser. 'And how, exactly, do you suggest I do that?'

'Well, actually,' Ben said, grinning, 'I do have one idea.'

They were nearly back at the hotel now. Luce stopped walking and raised her eyebrows. 'Are you really trying to tell me that sleeping with you would solve all my problems?'

Ben chuckled. 'No. But it would be a good start.'

Luce closed her eyes and laughed. 'You are incorrigible.'

'Come on,' he said, tugging her forward again. 'Let's get inside.'

CHAPTER FIVE

THE SUITE WAS almost too hot after the bite of the December night air. Ben stripped off his coat and jacket, rolling up his shirtsleeves as he made his way across to the bar area. 'What can I get you? More brandy?'

'Um…peppermint tea?' Luce asked.

He couldn't help but smile at her. 'Is that to help you resist my charms?' he asked.

'To help me get up for this lecture in the morning.'

Luce sprawled into the chair he'd been sitting in earlier, and Ben admired the way her slim calves stretched out in front of her. She'd kicked her shoes off the moment they'd got into the room, and she pointed her toes as she flexed her feet.

There was absolutely no reason at all for that to be sexy. And yet…

Flicking on the kettle, he said, 'I wanted to talk to you about that, actually.' If she wasn't going to let him help her relax the way he knew best, maybe he could at least draw her attention to some of the unnecessary things that were stressing her out.

Luce raised her eyebrows at him and waited for him to continue.

'What is it, exactly, that you'll get out of attending this lecture for a colleague?'

'It's a favour,' Luce said. 'I'm not expecting to get anything out of it.'

'So this guy won't do the same for you at a later date? It's not somehow tangentially related to your own research and might prove helpful one day? The university won't look fondly on your actions and bear it in mind in the future when it comes to promotions and such?' He was watching carefully, so he saw her squirm a little in her seat. Had she never considered how little she got back from all she gave out?

'Well, no. Not really.' She shifted again, looking down at her hands. 'Dennis doesn't like leaving the university much, and I can't imagine he'll let on to anyone at the university that I went for him in the first place. Plus the topic's pretty dull.'

The kettle boiled and Ben poured hot water onto a tea bag in one of the fine china mugs. Then he poured himself a large brandy while it brewed. 'In that case, I can only assume that this man is important to you in some way. Are you dating?'

'No!'

The answer was so quick and so vehement that Ben suspected he wasn't the first person to suspect it. But maybe it wouldn't bother her so much if it wasn't him asking. He could hope, anyway.

'Then why are you doing it?'

'Because he asked,' Luce said, sounding miserable.

'And you can't say no?'

Her glare was scathing. 'I said no to you, didn't I?'

Ben took her the tea before he replied. 'You told me you wouldn't stay here tonight, and now you are.'

'I told you I wouldn't sleep with you. I'm holding firm on that one.'

He chuckled, and saw her frown grow deeper. Had she

always been this much fun to tease? How had he not noticed? 'We'll see. Anyway, the point is you do all these
things for other people and you get nothing back. You need
to think about what you want for yourself.'

Luce sighed into her cup of tea. 'I know.'

She sounded defeated, which wasn't quite what Ben had
been going for. She hadn't stopped fighting him since they
met in the lobby. He kind of liked that about her.

'But there's just never any time. If I don't take care of
things for Tom, or Dolly, or Mum, it'll just cause a bigger mess further along the line that I'll have to clear up.'

'Tom and Dolly—your brother and sister?' He didn't
remember her even talking about her family at university.
Not that they'd ever really had any long, meaningful talks
about their lives, of course. But he was starting to wish
they had. Maybe then Luce would make more sense to him.

Luce nodded. 'They…they're not very good at getting
by on their own. Neither is Mum. It was different when
Grandad was still alive. But now…'

'They all rely on you.' Ben slouched down in his chair,
stretching his foot out to nudge against hers. 'Sounds to
me like you need someone you can rely on for a change.'

Her head jerked up in surprise. 'You cannot possibly
be suggesting that person is you.'

'Good God, no!' Ben shuddered at the very thought.
'Good for one night only. I have a rule.'

'Of course you do. Every girl's dream.'

Ben gave her a wry smile. 'You'd be surprised.' There
were always enough women looking for exactly that.

'So, what are you suggesting?' Luce asked.

The hint of desperation in her voice, the pleading in her
eyes, told him she was really hoping he had an answer.
She was in so deep she didn't even know how to get out.

'Stay here tonight with me, like we planned. And tomorrow, first thing, head back to Cardiff. Screw your colleague and his lecture. Forget about your family for a couple of days. You're supposed to be in Chester until Thursday, right? So no one will know you're home. You can knuckle down, sort out your book, and then spend Christmas relaxing instead of stressing out about all the work you should be doing.'

Luce's gaze darted away. 'I'm not sure I even remember how to relax.'

Ben smiled. 'Spend the night with me and I'll remind you.'

Oh, it was so, so tempting. Not just the sex—although that was bad enough. But the thought of three whole days with nothing to do except work on her book. No one asking her for anything.

Luce bit her lip. 'What about the lecture? Or my conference report? Or the Christmas Eve dinner?'

'Screw them,' Ben said, raising his glass to her. 'Decide, right here and now, that *you* are more important than what other people want from you. Decide that your book is what matters most to you at this moment in time and focus on that for the week. Make your family help you for a change. Get some priorities for once.'

He was right. The world might stop turning on its axis because of it, but he, Ben Hampton, was actually right. Maybe he'd been wrong every time he'd called her boring or obsessed at university—or maybe he hadn't been. But now he was right. She needed priorities. And maybe, if nothing else, three days alone would help her figure out what they were.

'Maybe I can get my ticket refunded. Or changed to tomorrow,' she mused. The conference organisers had bought the original ticket, but after the fiasco with her hotel room she didn't feel inclined to trust them to re-arrange her travel home. She'd head down to the station in the morning—see what they could do.

'I'll buy you a ticket,' Ben said carelessly. 'First-class. You can work on the train.'

Luce raised her eyebrows at him. 'What? As payment for services rendered? I'm not sleeping with you, remember?'

'As an apology.' Sitting up straighter, Ben fixed his gaze onto her own, and she found it impossible to look away. 'From Hampton & Sons. For losing your booking. I don't pay for sex.'

He looked more than insulted. He looked hurt. Luce's gaze darted away. 'Sorry. I didn't mean…'

'Yes, you did.' Ben sighed. 'Look. You're pretty much out of options here, Luce. I'm leaving tomorrow, and I have no doubt that this suite will be booked up for the rest of the week. You can try and find somewhere else in the city with a cancellation, or you can go home. And once you're there it's your choice whether you let anyone else know you're back.'

'Why are you doing this?' Luce asked. 'Trying to help me, I mean?' Could he possibly be so determined to get her to sleep with him that he'd try to fix her whole life to achieve it? Surely even Ben Hampton couldn't be that single-minded.

More to the point, how the hell was she meant to keep on resisting him if he was?

But Ben just shrugged. 'Because I can. Because fixing things is what I do for a living. Because it's so blatantly obvious what you need.' His words were casual, thrown away without thinking. But there was a tightness around his eyes that suggested something more.

Did he remember that night in the library? Was that what he was trying to make up for by helping her?

And, really, did it really matter? It was eight years ago. But she might never see the man again after tomorrow, and she knew the curiosity alone would drive her insane. 'Do you remember the night of your twenty-first birthday?'

Ben didn't even blink at the change of subject. 'Barely. Mostly I remember the hangover the next day. That kind of misery stays with you.'

He didn't remember. And if he didn't remember, it was as if it had never happened. She could forget it, too. Let the past go.

'I do know that I got dumped because of my actions that night.' Ben raised an eyebrow at her. 'Care to fill in the missing memories?'

Luce smiled. 'Maybe one day.' Except there wouldn't be another day, would there? Tomorrow she'd take the train home and forget all about Ben Hampton.

She tried to remind herself that this was a good thing.

Ben drained the last of his brandy and got to his feet. 'Well, I guess I'd better let you sleep on your decision. Unless...' He gave her a hopeful look.

'I am not sleeping with you.' Whatever her rebellious body was hoping. She could feel a tightness growing in her belly just thinking about it.

He laughed, far more cheerful than she'd expected him to be about being turned down. 'In that case, if you'll excuse me, I have a long drive ahead of me tomorrow.'

Bending down, he brushed a kiss against her cheek. His lips were softer than she'd imagined. Not that she'd been thinking of them.

'Goodnight, Luce.'

She watched him place his glass on the counter and

saunter into the bedroom, closing the door firmly behind him. And yet she was still staring at the door.

Her fingers brushed her cheek, as if she could trace the kiss his lips had left.

Damn him. Somehow she knew that all she'd dream about that night was what might have happened if she'd said yes.

Ben was not naturally an early riser, but his father had been, and Seb had inherited the trait, so he'd had to learn to function well before seven-thirty. And, given the motivation of breakfast with Luce before he packed her off to her new and improved existence in Cardiff, he was awake, showered and dressed before the sun was fully up the next morning. Which wasn't as impressive in December as it would have been in July, but Ben still felt a little pleased with himself as he knocked on Luce's door.

At least he was until she answered it moments later, already dressed in some sort of knitted jumper dress and those incredibly enticing boots.

He'd spent a lot of the previous evening thinking about those boots. And what Luce might be wearing under that dress. It hadn't been his most restful night's sleep ever, but his mind had at least been happily occupied.

'You're up at last, then,' Luce said, eyebrows raised.

'Were you always so smug in the mornings?' he asked as Luce wheeled her already packed suitcase into the living area. He had Seb for smugness. He really didn't need any more *smug* in his life. At least not unless he was getting to feel it for once.

'Probably.' Luce flashed him a superior smile. 'But you were mostly sleeping in while I was up working. You might not have noticed.'

Taking her suitcase and resting it against the wall by

the door, Ben decided it was time to change the subject. 'So, have you decided what you're doing today?'

Luce bit her lip. 'Heading back to Cardiff, if that offer of a train ticket still stands?'

Ben nodded. 'Of course. And when you get there?'

'I finish my book. In secret.'

A sense of relief washed over him. 'Good.' He'd done it. He might not have been able to bring his mother back from the brink before she jumped ship, but he'd fixed this. He'd fixed that little bit of Luce's life that he could influence and now he could move on, forget all about her.

That, right there, was one good day's work.

'I've ordered us breakfast,' he said, just as a knock on the door indicated its arrival.

'If nothing else, the Hampton & Sons hotel chain has certainly fed me well during my stay,' Luce said, taking a seat at the table in the dining area. 'I should write to the management.'

'I'll pass on a message.' Ben let in the room service staff member and took his own seat as platters of food were laid on the table. Eggs, bacon, toast, pastries—and plenty of hot coffee. Should keep him going on his drive through Wales, and it would make sure Luce had one more good meal before she lost herself in research and writing for the rest of the week.

'Shall I open the curtains, sir?' the room service guy asked, and Ben nodded.

Helping himself to eggs as Luce poured the coffee, Ben couldn't help but think how domestic this was. Far more couply than he'd ever managed, even with women he'd actually slept with. It was a good job she was leaving today, or she'd be straightening his tie and calling him 'honey' in no time. She was that sort.

'I'll call the station when we've eaten,' he said as light

flooded into the room from the opened curtains. 'See what times your trains are.'

But Luce wasn't listening to him. Instead she stared out of the window, coffee cup halfway to her mouth. Ben followed her gaze.

Outside, rooftops and roads were coated in a thick layer of snow, gleaming white and icy. Heavy flakes fell lazily from the sky, adding to the perfect Christmas scene.

'Huh!' Ben said, watching it fall. 'When did *that* happen?'

'I should never have gone out for dinner,' Luce muttered to herself as she waited on hold for the station. If she hadn't gone out for dinner with Ben Hampton she'd have had to try to find somewhere else to stay. When that had inevitably failed she'd have had no option but to get a train home. She'd be warm and cosy in Cardiff, watching the snow fall as she worked on her book.

Except, if she was honest with herself, she knew she wouldn't be. She'd have called her mother as soon as she got back to sort out the Christmas Eve dinner, and then she'd have been caught up in the responsibility net again. She'd be at her family's beck and call, sorting out their problems and organising their Christmas season. The book wouldn't have got a look-in.

Of course she would still have had a roof over her head, which was more than she'd have right now if the trains weren't running.

The hotel room door slammed open and shut and Ben walked back in, his hair damp with snowflakes. 'It's really not stopping out there,' he said, shrugging out of his coat. 'I spoke to Reception—apparently all trains are subject to significant delays, and a lot simply aren't running.'

Luce pressed the 'end call' button and dropped her

phone onto the sofa before perching on the arm herself. 'Fantastic.'

'You're thinking this is all my fault somehow, aren't you?'

'Yes.' What the hell did she do now?

Ben pulled up a chair and sat opposite her. 'Okay, well, let's see what we can do to fix this.'

Luce rolled her eyes. 'I know you pride yourself on being able to solve problems in hotels, but I think the British railway network might be beyond even your capabilities.'

Ben ignored her. 'Daisy on Reception says this room's booked out for tonight, and the guest has just called to confirm they'll still be coming, despite the snow. So that's out. We might possibly be able to find you another room if we get some cancellations, but there's no guarantee. Or...'

'Or?' Luce sat up a little straighter. Another option was exactly what she needed right now. Unless, of course, this was another Ben Hampton plan to seduce her.

'I'm driving south today anyway. Headed to my cottage down in the Brecons. Apparently it's not so bad further south just yet, and I'm confident my four-by-four can handle it.' He shrugged. 'Wouldn't be too far out of my way to take you on down to Cardiff. I can always stop for the night in one of our hotels there if the snow worsens.'

Blinking at him, Luce considered. It would mean hours in a car with Ben, on bad roads, but somehow she felt he was a surer bet than the trains. And not even he would try to seduce her in a snowdrift, right? 'You'd do that?'

'I still owe you for the room mix-up, remember? And this is cheaper than a first-class train ticket, anyway.'

He made it sound like nothing, but Luce knew better. He was fixing her life again. But if it got her home and her book finished maybe she should just let him. Accept help for once.

Grandad hadn't had a saying to cover that one, but Luce thought there might be potential in it all the same.

'Okay, then,' she said, grabbing her phone and standing up. 'Let's go.'

CHAPTER SIX

SOMEWHERE AROUND WELSHPOOL Ben finally admitted to himself that this might not have been the best idea he'd ever had.

The integral sat nav in the car had wanted him to cross over the border and drive south through England, before nipping back into Wales just before Cardiff. But Ben had done the drive south through Wales to the Brecons and the cottage enough times to feel confident in his route, and he didn't need advice for the uninitiated. Besides, the travel news had reported a pile-up on the A49 that would make things incredibly tedious, so really a drive through the hills had been the only option.

Right now, though, he'd take a three-hour traffic jam over these roads.

Daisy on the front desk had assured him that the snow was worst in the north. What she hadn't mentioned was that it was heading south. Every mile of their journey had been undertaken with snow clouds hovering above, keeping pace, and dumping more of the white stuff in their path as they drove.

Ben's arms ached from gripping the steering wheel tightly enough to yank the car back under control as the road twisted and slipped under them. His eyes felt gritty from staring into the falling snow, trying to see the path ahead. And Luce was not helping at all.

To start with she'd just looked tense. Then her hands had balled up against her thighs. Then she'd grabbed onto the seat, knuckles white. Ben had stopped looking over at her as the road grew more treacherous, but he'd bet money that she had a look of terror on her face now.

'Are you sure this is the best way to go?' Luce asked, her voice a little faint.

'Yes.' At least at this point it was pretty much the only option.

'Do you think…? Is the snow getting heavier?'

'No.' Except it was. Any idiot could see that. But the last thing Ben needed was Luce freaking out on him in the middle of a snowstorm.

'Are you just saying that to make me feel better?'

That sounded more like the Luce he'd had dinner with last night. Sharp and insightful.

'Yes.'

'Thought so.' She took a breath and released her death grip on the seat. 'Okay. What do you need me to do?'

'Keep quiet and don't freak out.' Ben ground the words out. Distraction was dangerous.

'Okay. I can do that.'

He wasn't sure if she was reassuring herself or him, but she did seem to relax a little. At least until they hit the Brecon Beacons National Park.

As the car climbed the hills the skies darkened even further, looking more like night than afternoon. The falling flakes doubled in size, until his windscreen wipers couldn't keep up, and the slow progress he'd been making dropped to a crawl. The road ahead had disappeared into a mist of white and the hills were blending into the sky.

They were never going to make it to Cardiff tonight.

'Okay. New plan.' Running through the road systems in his head, Ben prodded a couple of buttons on the sat nav and decided that maybe, just this once, he'd take its advice. Anything that got him off these roads, out of this car and somewhere warm. Preferably with a large drink.

'What? Where are we going?' Luce peered at the sat nav, which was insistently telling him to turn right. 'We need to get to Cardiff!'

'We're never going to make Cardiff in this.' Ben swung the car slowly to the right and hoped he'd hit an actual road. 'We need to get somewhere safe until this passes.'

'Like where?' Luce asked, her tone rising in incredulity.

'My cottage,' Ben reminded her. 'It's a damn sight closer than Cardiff, and a lot safer than these roads.'

There was silence from the passenger seat. When Ben finally risked a glance over, Luce was staring at him. 'What?'

'You planned this,' she said, her words firm and full of conviction. 'This was the plan all along.'

'Getting stuck in a snowstorm? I know I'm a powerful man, Luce, but the weather's up there with the rail network on the list of things I can't control.'

'That's why we came this way. You *knew* the snow would be bad, so you planned to kidnap me and take me to your cottage. You're still mad I wouldn't sleep with you last night.'

Was the woman actually insane?

'Trust me—sleeping with you is the last thing on my mind right now. I'm more concerned with us—oh, I don't know—not dying.'

'I should have taken the train.' The words were muffled as Luce buried her mouth into the long fluffy scarf wrapped around her neck.

'Next time I'll let you,' Ben promised, relief seeping

through him as he made out enough letters on the next road sign to reassure him they were nearly at the village nearest his cottage. Two more turns and they'd be there. Once they got onto the last rocky upward track. 'Hold on,' he warned her. Then he took a breath and turned the wheel.

Luce had never liked rollercoasters. Or fairground rides. Or ferries, actually. And the journey through the hills with Ben had felt far too much like all three for her liking. Rising and falling, rocking, swaying in the wind... She could feel breakfast threatening to rise up in her throat as they bumped over the rocky track Ben had just violently swerved up.

All she wanted was to be at home. Warm, safe and merrily lost in the Middle Ages. Was that so much to ask?

But instead she was...*where*, exactly? Somewhere in the Brecon Beacons, she supposed. Risking her life on an unsafe track to get to Ben's love-nest in the hills. Somewhere to wait out the storm and focus very hard on reasons not to indulge in a one-night stand with Ben.

Suddenly Cardiff felt a very long way away.

The car jerked to a halt and Luce rubbed at her collarbone where the seatbelt dug in.

'We're here.' Ben threw open the door and jumped out into the snow, as if any amount of cold were better than being stuck in the car with her.

He was still mad about her suspicions, then. And, yes, okay—rationally she knew he probably hadn't intended this to happen and couldn't actually control the snow.

But it was still all a little too convenient and willpower-testing for her liking.

Unfastening her seatbelt, Luce followed, stepping gingerly into the soft piles of snow and wishing she'd packed more practical boots. Peering through the snow, she followed Ben's tracks up what she presumed must be a path under all the white and saw, at last, Ben's cottage.

Luce wasn't sure what she'd expected, exactly. Maybe a collection of holiday chalets attached to a hotel. Or an ostentatious, look-how-rich-I-am manor house sort of thing that could only be called a cottage ironically. Whatever it was, it wasn't this. An actual, honest-to-God stone cottage in the hills.

It was perfect.

'Come on,' Ben said, and she realised the front door was open. 'If you freeze to death you'll never forgive me.'

'True,' Luce said, and hurried in after him.

With the door closed fast behind them, the wild winds and swirling snow seemed suddenly miles away. It wasn't hot in the cottage, by any means, but it was warm at least. Ben turned his attention immediately to the stone fireplace that dominated the lounge, stacking sticks and paper with practised ease.

Luce stared around her, taking in the unexpected surroundings. It certainly wasn't the sort of space she'd imagined Ben feeling comfortable in. Yes, it had a modern open-plan layout, but there were none of the bright white surfaces and stainless-steel accessories she'd expected, even after seeing the rustic outlook of the place. Instead the large main room was decorated in earthy colours— warming, welcoming reds and browns and greens. The battered leather sofas had tawny throw blankets and cushions on them—perfect for curling up in front of the fire. And the sheepskin rug before the fireplace made even the grey stone floor more warming.

Not Ben. Not at all.

'When did you buy this place?' she asked, stripping off her coat and scarf and hanging them over the back of a kitchen chair before removing her boots.

'A couple of years ago. I wanted somewhere separate. Somewhere that was mine.'

Luce thought she could understand that. Of course she encouraged her family to treat her house as theirs, but technically it belonged to her. That mattered.

'Did you get someone in to decorate?' Because this was the perfect rustic-cottage look. The sort of thing that either happened naturally or cost thousands via an interior designer. She didn't see Ben as the naturally rustic type.

'I did it,' Ben said, without looking up from the tiny flame he was coaxing.

Luce tried to hide her surprise. 'Well, it's gorgeous,' she said after a moment. Because it was—even more so, somehow, now she knew it was his own work. It wasn't beautiful, or tasteful, or on trend. It was warm and cosy and she loved it.

As the fire caught Ben flashed her a smile—the first she'd seen since they left Chester.

'So glad you approve.'

In that moment the cottage itself ceased to be the most attractive thing in the vicinity. Luce swallowed, looked away and said, 'Um…so, how long do you think we'll be stuck here?'

Standing up, Ben straightened, brushing his hands off on his jeans. 'Until the snow stops, at least. Don't think we'll be going anywhere until tomorrow.'

Tomorrow. Which meant spending another night in close proximity to Ben Hampton. Another night of not throwing caution to the wind and saying, *Seduce me.* Just to find out, after eight years of wondering, what it would be like.

The look he gave her suggested that he'd read her mind—but imperfectly. 'Don't fret. There's a spare room. It even has a key to lock it from the inside, if you're still worried that this is some great master plan to get into your knickers.'

Heat flushed in Luce's cheeks. She should probably apologise for that at some point. But since he was the one who'd point-blank propositioned her the night before maybe sorry could wait. Besides, just as the night before, she was more concerned that she'd need the lock to keep herself in, rather than him out.

Not thinking about it.

'What do we do until then?' she asked.

Ben shrugged. 'Up to you. Work, if you like. Personally, I'm going to make myself an Irish coffee and warm up by the fire. Then, once this snow slows down, I'm going to walk down into the village and see if the Eight Bells is serving dinner. I'd invite you to join me, but I'd hate for you to get the wrong idea about my intentions.'

'I do still need to eat,' Luce pointed out. 'And besides, Hampton & Sons have once again failed to make good on their promise—I was supposed to be in Cardiff by now. The way I figure it, you owe me another dinner.'

Ben raised an eyebrow. 'Really? Seems to me that you relying on me for a bed for the night—without, I might add, any of the activities that usually make such a thing worthwhile—is becoming a bit of a habit. So, is that dinner *instead* of a night's free accommodation in a charmingly rustic cottage?'

Luce considered. 'Maybe we could go halves on dinner?'

'Good plan.' Ben moved into the kitchen area and pulled a bag of coffee from the cupboard. 'So, do you want the grand tour?'

Luce spun round to smile at him and nodded. 'Yes, please.'

'Right, then.' Waving an arm expansively around the

living, dining and kitchen space, he said, 'This is the main room. Bathroom's over there. That's my room. That's yours.' He pointed at the relevant doors in turn. 'Back door leads out to the mountain. Front door leads to the car and a lot of snow. That's about it. Now, how Irish do you want your coffee?'

She should take advantage of the afternoon to work, really. But her laptop was still in the car, and she was cold and tired and stuck with Ben Hampton for another night. She deserved a warming drink and a sit by the fire, didn't she?

Luce perched on a kitchen stool and watched him fill the coffee maker. 'Make sure it's at least got a decent accent.'

Ben grinned at her. 'Will do.'

Ben had been more concerned with getting in and getting warm than studying Luce's expression when they arrived at the cottage. But now, watching her sink into the sofa, coffee in hand and feet stretched out towards the fire, he smiled to see her looking so at home there.

It wasn't an impressive cottage. He knew that. None of the homes in a ten-mile radius had more than three bedrooms; anything bigger would have been ostentatious. Ben wanted to fit in here. So when he'd bought the tumbledown stone building he hadn't extended it, just rebuilt it as it would have been. And it wasn't the most expensive of his properties—not by a long stretch. But it was his favourite. Not least because it was the only one that was really *his*. Bought with his own money, chosen by himself, decorated by himself. The penthouse in London, impressive as it was, belonged to the company and had been decorated by their interior designer. And the château... That still had his grandmother's favourite rose print wallpaper all over it. He really needed to get out there and start sorting that place out.

But not now. This was his week off. His week of relaxation in his favourite place. Albeit with an unexpected, suspicious and snappish guest, and the prospect of a round trip to Cardiff in the snow tomorrow.

Sipping his own coffee, Ben let the warmth of the cottage flood his bones, relax his muscles, the way it always did when he came home.

Home. Luce had asked him where it was and he'd said he didn't have one. He hadn't explained that he didn't want one. He'd had a home once, only to lose it when his father's obsession with work drove his mother away.

He didn't need a home that could be taken from him. He just needed a bolthole to hide out and recharge. Could be anywhere. Right now it just happened to be here, that was all.

I need to spend more time here.

Once he'd deposited Luce home he'd come back and look at his work schedule for the next twelve months. Figure out where there might be a break long enough to get back to Wales again. Maybe even over to France.

Luce drained her coffee and said, 'So, this pub you mentioned?'

'The Eight Bells. Best pint and best pies this side of the border.' They'd missed lunch in the snow. She was probably as starving as he was.

'Sounds promising,' Luce said, but she didn't sound convinced.

Ben decided to put her out of her misery. 'And, for you townies, there's a pretty decent wine list, too.'

'Oh, thank God.' Her face brightened.

Ben chuckled. 'Less than a day with me and you're already desperate for a drink? What? The coffee not Irish enough for you?'

'It's lovely,' Luce said. 'But after this day I'm ready for a hearty meal and a large glass of wine.'

Ben enjoyed one more moment of warmth by the fire, then got to his feet. 'In that case, I guess we'd better prepare to face the elements again. You ready?'

Luce grinned and took his hand to let him pull her up. 'As I'll ever be.'

CHAPTER SEVEN

AFTER A SNOWY, freezing and downright treacherous walk into the village, Luce stamped the snow off her boots, unwound her scarf and let Ben go and find menus and drinks while she settled into a chair at the rustic wood table by an inglenook fireplace. The Eight Bells was certainly a lot nicer than she'd expected in a local village pub, but then, she supposed they were in the heart of tourist Wales around here. Made sense to cater to the townies.

Not that there were many of them around tonight. Only a handful of tables were occupied, and those were by locals discussing the weather and when the roads would be cleared.

She shouldn't have been surprised that Ben would find a cottage near fine dining and local shops that delivered organic produce, she supposed. That was just who he was. How had she forgotten that?

It was the cottage, she decided. It was so homely. Somewhere she could imagine actually living herself. Nothing like the fancy hotel he'd been living in when she and Mandy had visited from university. Not even anything like the suite at the Royal Court in Chester. And yet it was his. Maybe there were nuances to Ben Hampton she was missing after all.

'Check out the pie list.' Ben dropped a couple of menus

on the table, then placed a glass of white wine in front of her. Wrapping her fingers round the stem, she took a long sip. Ben was right; this place had really good wine.

'You recommend the pies, then?' she asked, scanning the menu.

'I recommend everything on the menu.' He wasn't even looking at it, she realised.

'You come here often?'

'As often as I can.' He sipped his pint. 'The owner's an old friend of mine.'

That was one constant. Ben had always had a lot of friends around. When Mandy had started dating him Luce had assumed that his hangers-on were after his money, or the parties he could get them into. But over time it had become clear that they genuinely enjoyed his company. Ben was one of those people with a talent for making people like him.

Not a talent Luce had ever claimed to possess.

'I'll try the chicken pie, then,' she said, closing the menu. Ben nodded, and went to place their order. Watching him go, Luce studied the width of his shoulders, the confidence of his stride. Apart from a little extra muscle and size, how much had he really changed in the last eight years? Was he still the same boy who had kissed her in the hotel library?

Would he try again?

He was back before she had anything approaching an answer to that question.

'So,' he said, settling himself into his chair with practised ease, 'Old Joe over there tells me the snow should be over for now, but we might get another load tomorrow night. Hopefully the roads will be clear enough tomorrow to make a break for Cardiff before it hits. A few of the locals plan to take the tractors out in the morning and clear them.'

'That's good.' Getting home tomorrow would still give her a day and a half to work, at the least.

'Until then I'm afraid you're stuck with me. So, in the meantime, I believe this is the part where we make small talk. What topic do you want? Politics? Religion?'

'Tell me what you've been doing since university.' He looked surprised, so she added, 'I bored you about Nest last night. Now it's your turn.'

She needed to know where he'd been, what he'd done, so she could understand who he was now. For some reason it seemed vitally important that she make sense of him before they headed back to the cottage and their separate beds. Luce very carefully ignored the small part of her brain that murmured, *And if I understand him, if I know him, I'll know if it's safe to ask him to kiss me tonight.*

But Ben just shrugged and said, 'Pretty much as expected. Graduated and went to work for the family business…'

'It seems to be doing well enough.'

His smile was a trifle smug. 'Doubled the profits in my first five years. On track to triple them in the next two.'

That Ben was familiar. The one who thought money was the most important thing in the world. 'Your father must be very proud,' she said, thinking of the stern grey-haired man she'd met that one fateful day she'd spent in Ben's world. She didn't mean it to sound so dry, so sarcastic, but it came out that way regardless.

'He died about a year ago.' Ben's eyes were on his glass rather than her as he spoke, and a sharp spike of sympathy pierced Luce's chest.

'I'm so sorry.' She knew how that felt. That hole—the

space where a person should be. Trying to find a way to live without someone who'd defined you all your life.

But Ben rolled his shoulders back and gave her a strange half-smile. 'I wouldn't be. To be honest, I've barely noticed the difference. Just means that now it's my brother Seb checking up on my methods instead.'

There he was. The boy who'd had so little regard for the things that mattered—family, friends, responsibility, doing the right thing—had grown up exactly as she'd expected. Into a man who still had no respect for the things that mattered to her. A man she couldn't consider sleeping with even if she was sure it would be magnificent. *And* a sure way to find that relaxation he promised.

Except there was something in his eyes. Something else. 'You must miss him, though?'

'He wasn't really the sort of father you missed.'

She wanted to ask more, to try to understand how his father's death could have had so little impact on him. But before she could find the right question the waitress brought their food and Ben had switched the conversation to pies and homemade chips.

In fact, Luce realised as she tucked into her truly delicious meal, he seemed almost too keen to keep the conversation light and inconsequential. As he started another story about a hotel somewhere in Scotland that had served compulsory haggis to its guests for breakfast every Sunday Luce smiled politely, nodded in the right places and tried to think of a way to get him to open up. He was hiding something, she was sure, and her incurable curiosity was determined to find out what it was before she had to return to Cardiff.

'Let's have another drink before we head home,' she suggested, when he paused in regaling her with his tales.

Home. Oh, God, she'd just called the cottage 'home'. If

ever anything was guaranteed to send a man running in the opposite direction, laying claim to his house as your own before you'd even really been on a proper date was probably it. But Ben hadn't flinched or reacted. Maybe he hadn't noticed. Maybe Luce really could be that lucky.

'Sure. But I warn you now: I'm not carrying you back in that snow.'

'I think I can manage.'

Ben studied her carefully, as if he suspected an ulterior motive, but at least he didn't seem terrified at her presumption. Luce tried not to shift under his gaze and pretended very hard that she'd said nothing of consequence at all.

'Okay, then.' Ben got to his feet. 'You have a look at the pudding menu while I get the drinks.'

Now, *that* was a mission Luce could get stuck into. Then all she had to do was figure out a way to get Ben to open up to her.

Ben rested his weight against the bar, waiting for their drinks, and watched Luce from the corner of his eye. Not that she'd notice. She seemed completely absorbed by the dessert menu, and he wondered if she'd go for the chocolate mousse or the sticky toffee pudding. She didn't seem like a fruit salad girl. It was one of the things he liked about her.

That was a surprise in itself. The Lucinda he'd known so many years ago hadn't been someone you liked. She hadn't let anyone close enough to find out any of her likable qualities. Locked up in her room studying, running off to the library or covering the tiny kitchen table in the flat with papers and textbooks. That was how he remembered her. The way she'd always run off to her room when he and Mandy had arrived home. Apart from a few hastily eaten dinners together, when Mandy insisted on them 'getting to know each other', that was all he'd known of her. He'd never been able to understand how someone as outgoing and fun-loving as Mandy could even be friends with her. Hadn't believed her when she'd said that Luce could be fun sometimes.

He could see it now, though. She was the sort of woman who grew into herself. Her confidence and self-possession had let her beauty, humour and personality shine out at last. And she'd grown into her body, too. Had she grown into her sexuality in the same way?

It bothered him how much he wanted to find out.

And now the weather had given him the perfect chance to do just that. It might not have been a plan in the way Luce had accused him, but it certainly was an opportunity to take advantage of.

One night in a secluded cottage was even more perfect than one night in a luxury hotel. As long as it was just one night and the snow didn't strand them there any longer. Two nights in a row and women started to get ideas, Ben had found. Which was why he'd committed to his one-night rule.

And Luce was up to something; that much was clear. Given another glass of wine, he was pretty sure he could figure out what, and how it might affect his seduction plans.

The barmaid handed over their drinks and Ben took them with a wide, friendly smile before heading back to Luce. He had hopes for what was going on here, and if he was right the evening could be set for a much better ending than he'd dared to assume the night before.

'So, what are you fancying?' Ben put the drinks down on the table and tried not to smirk when Luce looked up, eyes wide and face flustered.

'Um…' Her gaze flicked back down to the menu. 'The sticky toffee pudding?'

'Good choice.' Dropping into his chair, Ben reached his arms out across the back and felt his muscles stretch. 'Tracy says she'll be over to take our order in a moment.'

'Great.' Placing the menu back on the table, Luce folded her hands over it.

Ben braced himself for whatever line of questioning was coming next.

'So, what do you do when you're not working?'

To his horror, Ben actually had to think about an answer. When had he become so obsessed with work? That was Seb and Dad. Not him.

'Oh, you know. The usual. Fine dining. Trips abroad.' That sounded obnoxious. She already thought he was obnoxious. He really shouldn't make it any worse. 'I have a château in France—well, my grandmother did. She left it to me. I'm renovating it.' Or he should be. He *would* be. As soon as he found the time.

Luce raised her eyebrows and Ben cast his gaze over to the bar to see where the hell Tracy the barmaid had got to.

'You're interested in property development? First the cottage, now the château?'

'Yes,' Ben lied. It had nothing to do with making money. He'd done up the cottage so he had somewhere to escape to. And he wanted to do the château because...well, he couldn't just leave it there to crumble, now, could he?

'So what's next?' Luce asked, then glanced up and said, 'Oh, the sticky toffee pudding for me, please.'

It took Ben a moment to catch up, to realise that Tracy was standing patiently behind him with her notebook. 'Same for me, please.' He gave her a smile and watched her walk back to the bar. Maybe Luce would get cross enough at him paying attention to another woman that she'd stop asking questions he didn't want to answer.

No such luck.

'So?' she repeated. 'What comes after the château?'

'No idea,' Ben said with a shrug. 'You know me—I'm a take-one-day-at-a-time kind of guy.'

Except he wasn't any more. Not really. He couldn't be— not when Seb was relying on him so much these days. He knew exactly what would be next. More visits to more hotels. More reports on what was working and what wasn't. Long, long meetings with Seb and his team about where the company was going. More spot inspections on long-standing members of the Hampton & Sons chain. More firing old managers and putting in their own people. More budget meetings where the accountants told them they should get the hotels to improve drastically without giving them any money to do it.

Business was business, after all.

'Still?' Luce asked. 'I suppose I shouldn't be surprised. People don't really change at heart, do they?'

Ben looked at her, sipping her wine across the table, her gaze too knowing, and for once he wanted to tell someone the truth. That sometimes he was sick of all the rules he'd set for himself. That sometimes he did want to stop. To stay in one place for a while.

Downing the rest of his pint, he said, 'I need another drink,' and headed to the bar before the urge became too strong.

CHAPTER EIGHT

BEN RETURNED WITH another pint for himself and another glass of wine for Luce. She hadn't drunk more than half of the glass she already had, but she accepted it gracefully anyway. She had a feeling that he wasn't so much trying to get her drunk to take advantage of her, more to distract her.

Clearly he'd never experienced the Myles curiosity in full flow before.

'So, you left university, joined the family business, and you're still there?' She tipped her head sideways to look at him. 'So either you really have changed a little bit, or there's something about your job you truly love. Because the Ben Hampton I knew couldn't stick at anything for more than six months.' Which had, incidentally, been the exact length of his relationship with Mandy before the kiss in the library. Not that she'd counted.

Ben's hand was already on his pint. 'It's a job. It pays me very, very well and I don't have to sit in an office all day.'

Now, *that* sounded like the Ben she'd known. But it still felt wrong, somehow. And Luce had drunk enough wine to tell him so. 'That doesn't sound like it makes you happy.'

'Are jobs supposed to make you happy?' Ben asked, eyebrow raised.

'Mine does,' Luce said, in an immediate unconsidered response.

'Really?'

'Of course.' At least as long as she didn't think too much about the particulars. A lecturing position at the university and the opportunity to do her own research into areas of history that fascinated her. That was all she'd ever wanted.

It was just that day-to-day, dealing with the academic system, the obscure rules and regulations of academia, funding, and other colleagues…well, it could be a little… frustrating.

'So, which part do you love the most?' Ben asked. 'Attending dull lectures your colleagues can't be bothered to go to? Grading unoriginal essays? Applying for funding all the time just to actually do your job?'

Which was just a bit too close to her own thoughts for Luce's comfort. 'I'm not saying there aren't downsides, or days that aren't particularly joyous. But at the heart of it I love discovering the past. I love finding out about the lives of women long dead and how they influenced the world around them. That's what matters to me.'

Ben's gaze was curious now. How had this got turned around? Wasn't *she* supposed to be questioning *him*?

'In that case,' he asked, 'why aren't you spending all your time on your book? Looking at a linked lecture tour or even a TV programme? Why are you wasting time writing reports for your lazy colleague?'

'This is just how it works,' Luce said, reaching for her glass as an excuse not to look at him. 'It can't be all fun, all the time. There has to be responsibility, too.'

'And that's why I'm still working for the family business,' Ben said. 'Told you I could be responsible sometimes. Ah, look—pudding.'

Tracy put their bowls on the table with a curious glance between them. How many women had he brought here? Luce wondered. Was she the latest in a long line? Did she not fit the usual stereotype? Was that why everyone kept looking at her tonight?

She couldn't think about that now. What did it matter, anyway? Tomorrow she'd be back in Cardiff. She'd probably never think of Ben Hampton again.

Liar.

'Okay, then,' she said, reaching for her spoon. 'What would you be doing if you weren't working for the illustrious Hampton & Sons?'

Ben's spoon paused halfway to his mouth. 'Honestly? I have no idea.' He looked as if the concept had never even occurred to him. As if he'd never thought about what he'd actually *like* to do. He'd just fallen into his job and kept going.

Which was so entirely out of keeping with what Luce had thought she knew about his character that she forgot about pudding entirely.

'Well, what do you love doing?' she asked. 'Renovating properties?'

'I suppose.' He put his spoon back in his bowl and looked at her. 'Look, you seem to have the wrong impression here. I am very good at my job, and it serves the purpose I want it to serve—namely paying me more than enough to enjoy my life. Doing my job well keeps my brother and the investors happy. And I get to live my life my way. I never wanted my job to be my life, so this arrangement suits me pretty much perfectly.'

Explanation over, he dug back into his sticky toffee pudding and ignored Luce completely.

Which was fine by her. No need for him to see the utter confusion she was sure was painted across her face.

She just couldn't get a handle on this man. Every time she thought she understood something—that he'd changed, that he hadn't—he pulled the rug out again. Just when she was sure that he was a man stuck in a job he hated, searching for something to fulfil him, he turned round and told her that was the last thing he wanted.

She just didn't understand.

'You're looking baffled,' Ben said.

Luce glanced up to see him smiling in amusement. 'Just...trying to understand.'

His mouth took a sympathetic downturn, but his eyes were still laughing. 'I know. It's always hard for overachievers to understand that work isn't everything.'

'That's not... There are plenty of things in my life besides work.'

'Oh, of course. Like running around after your family and friends, making their lives run smoothly.'

'Aren't you doing the same for your brother?'

Ben shook his head. 'Not at all. My job is my job, and I am compensated very handsomely for it, thank you.'

'There isn't a price you can put on love.'

'No,' Ben said, his voice suddenly, shockingly hard. 'There isn't. But what you do for them? That isn't love. That's pandering.'

Luce's emotions swung back again. No, he hadn't changed. Not at all. He still thought that he and his thoughts, his wants, his opinions, were the only things in the world that mattered. Couldn't begin to imagine that he might be wrong. That it might be different for other people.

'No—listen to me.'

Ben reached out and grabbed her hand with his own as he spoke, and Luce looked up into unexpectedly serious eyes.

'What do you want more than anything in the world?'

His skin against hers. His attention firmly placed on her. Those were the only reasons she felt a jolt of lust through her body at his question. The only reason her mind answered, *You.*

Luce pulled her hand away. *Note to self: I do not want to sleep with this man. It would be disastrous.*

'I want my family to be happy. Settled.' Because, she admitted, to herself if not out loud, if they were—if they didn't need her so damn much—maybe she could go out and find what made *her* happy.

'Because that would set you free?' Ben said.

Luce's gaze shot to his in surprise.

'Because if they were happy you wouldn't have to worry about them. But, Luce, they're never going to be happy and settled without you as long as you're still there bailing them out at every turn. You'll give and give until there's nothing of you left. And then you'll crack. My mother—' He stopped, looked away. 'I've seen it before. You can't give up your own life for your family.'

Luce swallowed. 'You have no idea what you're talking about.'

'I think I do.' The words were bitter.

But he didn't. And Luce couldn't tell him. How could she explain a grandfather who'd worked hard all his life for the little he had to a man who'd been born with everything? How could she explain the importance of doing the best job she could, giving it everything she had so she could be proud of herself at the end of the day? His job meant nothing to Ben, was just a means to an end. It was all about the money. So how could she explain the passion she felt when she uncovered a hidden bit of women's history? When she brought untold stories to light?

'You don't. My grandfather's last words to me… He made me promise to take care of my family. I'm the only one, you see. My mother's a wonderful woman, but she's lost in her own world most of the time. And my brother and sister inherited that. They don't see the real world. None of them do. That's why they need me.'

'They're not your responsibility.'

Ben's voice was gentle, but the words still stung.

'And maybe it's time for a change. For them to learn to look after themselves.'

Luce shook her head. 'I told you. They are what they are. They're not going to change now.'

'Not if you don't give them the chance.'

That wasn't fair. 'People don't change. Not really.'

'Not even you?' Ben asked, eyebrow raised.

Luce laughed. 'Especially not me. I'm exactly the same Lucinda Myles you remember from university, right?'

Ben's gaze trailed slowly across her face, down her body, and Luce felt her blood warm.

'Not exactly the same.'

'That's not the point. My family are my responsibility, whatever you think.' Because they were all she had, too. And wasn't that a sad thing, at twenty-eight, to have nothing else but a family that needed you? Luce drained the last of her wine. 'I think it's time to go home,' she said, and Ben nodded.

They were halfway to the cottage before she realised she'd called it 'home' again.

They walked back to the cottage in silence. The snow had stopped, at last, but the paths were still slippery underfoot. The air stung Ben's lungs as they climbed the path, making it too painful to talk even if he'd had any idea of what to say.

Why was she so entrenched in solving things for her family? Because she'd promised her grandfather? That didn't seem enough. There had to be something else, but he was damned if he could figure out what. When would she learn? You couldn't fix everything for anyone. So you did what you could and you moved on. You couldn't let other people pull you down.

Had she been like this at university? He couldn't remember. She must have gone home a lot, though, since he and Mandy had often taken advantage of the flat being empty at weekends. A sliver of self-loathing jarred into him. Of course *that* was what he remembered. Why hadn't he paid more attention to Luce then?

Or perhaps the better question was, why was he paying so much attention to her now?

Finally they reached the cottage and Ben dug in his pockets for the keys. Luce waited silently at his side for the door to open. Inside, the under-floor heating was doing its job admirably, which was just as well as the fire had all but burnt out. They both stripped off their outer layers, and Ben took the coats and hung them by the back door. When he turned round Luce still stood where he'd left her, looking at him, her eyes huge and sad.

'Do you really believe that your family aren't your responsibility?'

She looked distraught at the idea that anyone could believe such a thing. *She should have spent some time with my old man.*

He wanted to say the right thing. Words that would make her smile again, as she had over dinner. But he wasn't going to lie to her.

'I think that your family need to learn to manage without you for a while. You can't mortgage your own life, your own happiness, for theirs.'

Luce just shook her head. 'We really haven't changed at all, have we?'

Despite her assertions that people didn't change, she sounded so forlorn at the idea that Ben moved closer, his body determined to comfort her even if his mind knew it was a bad idea. His hands settled at her waist as she spoke again.

'We're exactly the same people we were at university.'

'No.' Even to his own ears his voice sounded harsh. 'We're not.'

Luce looked up at him. She was so close that he could see the uncertainty in her eyes.

'Aren't we? I may not wear jeans and baggy jumpers every day, but I'd still rather be working than in the pub. Tonight notwithstanding,' she added, a small smile on her lips.

'You came to the pub, though. That's new.'

'Maybe. And what about you? Back then…'

'I spent every night in the pub and didn't care about work,' Ben finished for her. 'I promise you that tonight is not representative of my adult life.'

'Back then,' Luce repeated, 'you cared about yourself first. Your own happiness was most important, and you didn't want the responsibility of anyone else's on your shoulders.'

A memory struck him—something long forgotten and hidden. A book-lined room and a dark-haired girl in the moonlight, a plain dress draped over her body, fear and confusion in her eyes as he moved closer. Had that really been him? No wonder Mandy had ditched him. He hadn't cared about Luce's happiness then, had he? Or the responsibility he had to his girlfriend. *Hell.* Did Luce remember? She must. That was why she'd asked. No wonder she needed to know if he'd changed.

'I care enough about you to try and help you finish your book. Reclaim your life.' He was grasping at straws, he knew. Trying to find something to show her he *had* changed.

Luce tipped her head to the side. 'Do you? Or are you just trying to get me into bed?'

'I can't do both?' Ben joked, but Luce's face was serious. He sighed. 'Trust me, I wouldn't do all of this just for sex.' He pulled away, but her hand brushed his arm, a silent request to stay close, and despite the desperate urge to leave this conversation behind and retreat to his room with a bottle of whisky, Ben found he couldn't move.

'I have to know. Do you really not remember your twenty-first? Are you sure you're not trying to make up for that night?'

Ben shook his head automatically. It hadn't even occurred to him that he should.

'Or finish what you started?'

'I didn't even remember until just now. I…I knew I hadn't been kind to you back then. Maybe that was why I took you to dinner last night. Gave you somewhere to stay. This is something entirely different.'

Her teeth sank into her lower lip as she stepped forward, closer than before, so close that he could feel her breath through the cotton of his shirt. She looked up, her eyes bright, and Ben felt his breath catch in his chest.

'Then the only thing I can think is that you wanted me here so you could hear me beg you to seduce me.'

God, yes. Heat flooded through his body at her words, fierce and unchecked. Her lashes fluttered shut over her eyes and Ben knew this was his chance. This was the closest she'd let herself get to asking for what she wanted. This was the moment he should sweep her up in his arms and off to bed, like Owain kidnapping Nest.

And he couldn't.

He couldn't be what she remembered—alcohol on his breath as he pushed a kiss on her, whether she wanted it or not. He was a different man now, and she needed to know that. People really did change.

Stepping back caused him physical pain. His muscles were aching to stay with her, to pull her against his chest and hold her close.

'Not like this,' he said, his voice hoarse.

And then he walked away.

CHAPTER NINE

LUCE WOKE UP on Wednesday morning determined not to spend one more sleepless night on Ben Hampton.

She was through. From nights spent waiting for him and Mandy to kick everyone else out of the flat and go to bed at university, to the long, long night after she ran away from him in the hotel library, to that night in Chester, to last night, spent wondering and wondering. It was enough.

It didn't matter if he'd changed his mind about seducing her. In fact it was a good thing that he hadn't. Because the very last thing Luce needed at the moment was someone else needing her to take care of their lives. She had a book to write, after all, and Ben Hampton's life was a mess— even if he was too busy trying to fix hers to notice it.

Actually, she told herself, staring up at the uneven ceiling of the cottage, it was probably all for the best. She'd made a decision eight years ago not to get involved with this man. A decision she'd renewed and confirmed in Chester, and again yesterday when he brought her to the cottage. She might have nearly broken that resolution because of too much wine and conversation, or because of a brief, misguided hope that people really could change, but that wasn't enough. She should thank Ben, really, for *not* taking advantage of her vulnerable position and letting her stick to her beliefs.

Not that she was going to, of course.

Shifting under the sheet, Luce turned over with a sigh. The problem was that she wanted him. She might not be the most obviously sexual person in the world—but she was an academic, not a nun. Although they might as well be the same thing at the moment. Too much time working, researching, writing, lecturing… It didn't leave a lot of time for romance. Or even just a fun encounter with a gorgeous guy.

But Luce wasn't supposed to want that, was she? It wasn't the way she was made. Wasn't in her history. No, she was supposed to study, to learn, to improve herself. Sex didn't improve anything in her admittedly limited experience. Hell, even Nest, in her restricted, disapproving time, had managed to have more sex with considerably more guys than Luce had.

Her head flopped back against the pillow and she finally admitted the truth to herself. She'd wanted Ben Hampton last night. And, more than that, she'd wanted him to make the first move—to take her—so that she could rationalise away her desire this morning. She'd wanted to be able to say it was a weak moment, that it was the wine and the romantic snowbound cottage. She'd wanted to be able to move on and forget it without admitting that sex with him was something she really wanted.

Craved. Needed.

Well, she was just going to have to get used to going without. Because there was no way she could ask him for it now. Humiliation really wasn't her colour, and she wouldn't risk him turning her down again.

Damn it.

With a deep breath, Luce sat up. 'Time to move on,' she said softly.

Her room—the spare room—had a desk, a king-sized

bed and an *en suite* bathroom. If you had to be stranded in the middle of nowhere, Luce figured this was the sort of place you wanted to be stuck. It wasn't a particularly feminine room, but then, Luce wouldn't have expected it to be. Ben had decorated it, after all. The huge bed was draped in a wine-red quilt, soft and cosy, with cushions and pillows piled up at the head. Beside the bed stood a chenille-covered armchair, perfect for curling up with a book. And under the window was the desk—sturdy, probably antique, and exactly what she needed. Slipping out of bed, Luce ran a hand across its scarred wooden surface and for the first time could imagine herself finishing her book. Telling Nest's story to the world, finally, the way she wanted it to be known.

Might as well make the best of a bad situation. She was stuck there at least until Ben woke up. She'd retrieved her laptop from the car before their trip to the pub, so she could at least get some work done.

Luce listened for movement outside her door and, hearing nothing, risked slipping out long enough to make a pot of tea and some toast and sneak it back into her room. Then, wrapped up in her pyjamas, socks and an old jumper she'd found in one of the drawers, she settled down at her desk.

Ben Hampton didn't matter any more. All that did matter was telling Nest's story the right way.

There was no sign of Luce when Ben emerged from his room the next morning. Which was probably for the best. His surge of nobility, admittedly spurred on by a determination to prove that he *had* changed in the last eight years, might not have lasted in the face of Luce in pyjamas. Or a nightdress. Or maybe nothing at all…

After a night of contemplating the possibilities, and

imagining what might have happened if he'd just kissed her properly and carried her off to bed, those images were firmly burned onto his brain. God only knew what it was going to take to get them out again. And knowing she was just metres away, probably still in bed, really wasn't helping.

Ben eyed the closed bedroom door, grabbed his keys and headed out. Fresh air and distance was what he needed. And he could check out the state of the roads while he was at it.

Ben took the drive into the village slowly. The snow showed no sign of melting, but the roads were clearer than he'd expected—obviously some of the local farm vehicles had already been out. Ben parked up outside the Eight Bells and decided he deserved a warming cup of something, and maybe some of Tracy's homemade cake, before he hit the village store for supplies and a weather forecast.

Johnny, the landlord, raised his eyebrows from behind the pumps at the sight of him. 'Didn't expect to see you out of bed so early.'

'It's gone ten,' Ben pointed out, leaning against the bar.

'Exactly.' Johnny reached behind him to flick the coffee machine on. 'Tracy said it looked like you and your new friend were planning to hit the sheets for the rest of the week when you left here last night.'

'Well, Tracy was wrong,' Ben said, trying not to think about how close to right she might have been. 'Besides, Luce is an old friend—not a new one. We were at university together.' No need to get into the details.

'Hmm.' The corners of Johnny's mouth dipped down for a moment, as if to say, *Okay, then. If you say so,* as he handed over a cup of coffee.

'What?'

'Just… You do realise she's the first person—male or female—you've ever brought to my pub?'

'So?'

'Is she the first person you've taken up to your cottage at all?'

An uncomfortable feeling crept up Ben's back. 'Yeah. We were driving to Cardiff when the snow got heavy, so we stopped off here.'

'That explains it, then, I guess. We just figured she must be someone important.' He didn't sound pleased at the explanation. 'So. Old friend?'

'Yeah, you know. Nice to catch up and stuff.' Ben picked up his coffee, and motioned to one of the tables by the window. 'Anyway, I'd better drink up and get back to her. Lousy host, really.'

'I can imagine,' Johnny said.

But the frown line between his eyebrows told Ben he was still a little disappointed by the set-up.

Why? he wondered as he made his way over to the table. Was it so inconceivable that he'd bring a friend to visit? Just because he hadn't done it in the last few years? Why *hadn't* he, actually? He supposed it hadn't occurred to him. The women he spent time with all preferred a night at one of the hotels, the swankier the better, and since Hampton & Sons didn't have anything under five stars except their newest acquisitions—in this case, the Royal Court, which had a measly four—it was easier just to check into the nearest one. And if he was meeting friends it was the local pub or the curry house. No need for them to trek all the way to the middle of nowhere in Wales. Besides, the cottage was *his* place. It was where he went when he needed to escape from the real world. There'd never been much point in bringing the real world with him.

Luce wasn't the real world. This brief sojourn in the

snow had nothing to do with reality. Once he'd taken her back to Cardiff the brief time bubble would be over and he'd forget all about her for another eight years, while he got on with his life and she refused to. Easy.

His phone rang as soon as he sat down. 'Hampton.'

'Other Hampton.'

Seb's dry voice sounded out of place as Ben sat staring across at the Welsh mountains. Seb was urban and urbane. He was the city, and the company, and the polished wood of his office.

He'd definitely never invited Seb up to the cottage. Maybe he should.

'What can I do for you today, oh, fearless leader?'

'Stop calling me that, for a start.'

On the other end of the line Ben heard his brother shuffling papers before he continued.

'I just got through reading your report from Chester.'

'And?'

A pause. Never good.

Then Seb said, 'When are you back in London?'

'Tomorrow night was the plan. Might make it Friday—snow dependent.'

'Can you stop by and see me on Friday? I know it's Christmas Eve, and you're supposed to be off the rest of the week…'

'I can,' Ben said. 'But if there's a problem with my report I'd rather you just tell me now.'

Another pause.

'It's not a problem, exactly.'

Seb didn't sound annoyed, or let down, which Ben was pretty sure their father would have done. That was something.

'Just an idea I want to talk through with you.'

Now, *that* was new. For the last six months Seb had

been making the decisions and Ben had been making them happen. That was how they operated, and it worked well. But if Seb was willing to let him in, loosen his grip on the reins... *Maybe he won't turn into Dad after all.*

'Okay. So, how's London coping without me?'

'Never mind London,' Seb said. 'Tell me about this brunette from Chester. Did you actually take her to your cottage? The forbidden inner sanctum?'

It felt wrong to hear Luce described that way, and Ben regretted ever mentioning her to Seb. He clamped down on the surge of anger filling his chest, reminding himself that Seb was only talking about her the way Ben himself had, last time they'd spoken.

'It's not... She's an old friend,' Ben said, repeating the line he'd used with Johnny and wondering why it felt like such a lie. Because they'd never really *been* friends, he supposed. 'I was driving her back to Cardiff and we detoured to the cottage because of the snow.'

'Wow. You *did* actually take her to your fabled cottage? I was kidding about that part. She must be pretty important.'

'More that I didn't want to die in a snowy crash,' Ben assured him. 'Her train was cancelled, I was headed this way anyway, so I drove her. That's all.'

'Hmm.'

Ben didn't think Seb needed to sound quite so disbelieving. 'Yeah, well, I should get back to my host duties,' he said, draining his coffee. 'I'll see you on Friday.'

It didn't matter what Seb thought about Luce, he reminded himself as he stood and put on his coat. Because after today she'd be out of his life again.

Which was a good thing. Right?

Except if he wasn't going to see her again... The thought of not having her, just once, burned at his heart.

He needed to touch her, to feel her—hell, even just to hold her. The memory of her swaying into his arms the night before wasn't fading. How could he *not* experience more than that?

But after turning her down the night before...? Ben wasn't stupid. She wasn't going to ask again. He'd head back to the cottage, they'd pack up the car and drive to Cardiff, and that would be it. He'd blown the only chance he'd get with Luce Myles.

But as he left the Eight Bells a leaflet in the rack for tourists caught his eye, and Ben realised that maybe there was one more thing he could give Luce before they parted ways. Something for her to remember these strange, snowy few days by.

Pocketing the leaflet, he headed over to the village shop, his mood suddenly a whole lot lighter.

It hadn't been Luce's most productive morning ever.

She'd started well—up with the lark and at the desk with her computer cursor blinking at her. Outside, the snow looked as if it might be starting to clear, which gave her hope that they might make it to Cardiff today. She'd heard the front door slam after she'd been working a couple of hours, and reasoned that Ben had probably gone to check on the conditions. She'd have to wait until he got back to face him. Heat had flooded to her cheeks at the very thought. Really no hurry on that one. Then they'd be on their way and it would all be over. She'd be home again.

In the meantime, the book wouldn't write itself.

The first couple of pages of the section dealing with Nest's life at Cilgerran Castle, before her abduction, had come in an inspired burst, leaving her feeling buoyant and excited. And then...nothing.

After another half an hour of staring at the screen and

adjusting punctuation, Luce had given up and indulged in a long soak in the bath instead. Hot water and bubbles were almost guaranteed to help inspiration strike, surely?

Except when she settled back down at the desk, fully dressed in a long knitted skirt and wine-red sweater, she still had nothing.

'Going well?'

Luce spun round to see Ben leaning against the door-frame, arms folded over his chest and his eyebrow raised. He betrayed no sign of his rejection the night before—which was a small point in his favour, Luce supposed.

'I think I'm getting some really useful stuff,' she lied, and hoped he hadn't heard the bath water draining out.

Ben held up a bakery bag. 'Well, brunch will help. I brought ham and cheese croissants.'

Luce's stomach rumbled at the very mention.

As they sat down together at the small kitchen table Luce asked, 'What are the roads like? Can we make Cardiff today?'

Ben nodded, already chewing. 'More snow due tonight, but we should be able to beat it.'

She should be relieved. Thrilled that she was heading home. So what was with the strange, sad part of her that was already missing the cottage before they'd even left?

And not just the cottage. The company.

Luce stared down at her plate. Definitely time to go.

'I should go and get packed up, then,' she said, even though the only things she'd really unpacked were her laptop and notes.

'Actually...'

Ben paused and she looked up at him. Was he going to ask her to stay? No. That was ridiculous.

'There's somewhere I'd like to take you. Before you go. It's not exactly on our way, but I think it'll be worth it.'

Luce frowned. 'How out of our way? Where is it?'

'It's a surprise.' Ben's smile was slow and teasing. 'But I promise you you'll like it.'

The problem with that, Luce reflected, was that what she liked and wanted wasn't always good for her. But if this was her last ever day with Ben, how could she turn down the chance to spend a few more hours with him?

'Finish your croissant first,' he said, and she obeyed.

Twenty minutes later they were all packed up. Pulling on her thick coat and boots, Luce followed Ben out to the car, her eyes drawn to the way his upper body filled out his coat. He really had grown into his size over the last eight years. How was she supposed to forget how good it had felt to be held against that chest the night before when he was just *there*, looking gorgeous?

Of course after today he wouldn't be.

Sighing, she got into the car, fastening her seatbelt without looking at him again. Instead, she looked back at the cottage as they drove away, and wondered if there was any chance she'd ever see it again.

'You okay?' Ben asked as they reached the main road out of the village.

'Fine.' She flashed him a quick smile, then glanced away. So much pretty countryside to look at, all white and sparkling. Why should she look at him anyway? 'Are you really not going to tell me where we're going?'

'I told you. It's a surprise.'

Luce didn't know the area well enough to be able to guess where they were headed, and by the time they hit the bigger roads she was too absorbed in her own thoughts and the snow-capped hills and frosted trees around her to pay attention to road signs. What would this countryside have looked like in Nest's time? Would she have ridden through these hills? How had it felt when she'd had to leave this landscape behind and move to England?

What would Ben do if she kissed him?

Luce closed her eyes. *No.* Back to what mattered. Nest. Her book. Not her sex drive.

Although Nest had obviously had enough of one, given the number of men she'd been connected to and the number of children she'd borne.

Not the point. Okay. Enough about Nest the woman. Focus on the book itself. The structure. Should she break Chapter Seven into two parts? Should she ask Ben in for dinner when they got to Cardiff? Or more…

Oh, God, this was hopeless.

'We're here,' Ben said, his voice amused, and Luce realised belatedly that the car had stopped moving.

Fumbling with the handle, Luce threw the door open and stepped out into the snow. She smoothed down her skirt with one hand, aware that Ben was walking around the car towards her.

'Figured out where we are yet?' he asked.

He was standing too close for her to think straight. She could feel the warmth of his breath on her neck, a wonderful contrast to the wintry chill.

She stepped away quickly and looked up. 'Oh!'

The twin round towers of Cilgerran Castle loomed overhead, grey and dark against the sky, snow capping them, and Luce's breath caught in her throat. She'd have known where she was in an instant, even without the information board at the edge of the car park. This place mattered. This was history made real, right before her. 'This is it. This is—'

'Cilgerran Castle. Where they say Nest was abducted from.'

Ben moved behind her and she could feel his warmth through her coat.

'Good idea?'

She nodded, her head jerking up and down hard to show him just what a fantastic idea she thought it was. This was what she needed. To get close to Nest physically as well as intellectually. She needed to stand where she had stood, needed to feel the stone walls around her. Needed to understand how Nest had felt so many years ago.

Why hadn't she come here before? Oh, she had, she supposed, back when she was studying for her Masters and Nest had been just a passing interest in half a module of her course. But never since. After all, she'd done it already. Why waste the day getting there and back to Cardiff again when there was so much else she needed to do?

But she'd never felt then what she felt now. The feeling that all of history was coming together in one place, just to help her understand.

'I hadn't realised it was so close,' she murmured, and felt Ben shrug behind her. He was so close, too.

'A couple of hours. You were daydreaming on the way here.'

Had it really been that long? They could have got to Cardiff and back already. 'I was thinking about Nest.' Mostly.

'I saw a leaflet for it in the Eight Bells rack earlier. Thought it looked like your sort of thing. And when I remembered how you told me Nest had lived here, was taken from here, I had to bring you.'

Luce spun round, finding herself nose to chest with him. How had she forgotten he was so close? His hand settled on her waist to steady her when she stumbled on the uneven ground and heat radiated through Luce's body. Raising her gaze to meet his, she said, 'Thank you.'

'You're welcome.'

The words were simple, but the emotions they evoked were anything but. His lips were just inches away. If she went up on tiptoes she could kiss him so easily. It would be a thank-you kiss, nothing more, but she'd get to feel his mouth against hers. And, oh, how she wanted to...

She bit down on her own lip to try to curb the temptation. But Ben's fingers still pressed against her waist. Then he glanced away, hands dropping from her body, and she saw his Adam's apple bob as he swallowed.

'Shall we go in?' he asked.

Luce stepped back and nodded again. Nest—that was why she was here. And then she was leaving. She really had to try to remember that.

CHAPTER TEN

BEN WATCHED LUCE'S rear move enticingly under that touchable flowing skirt as she gripped the handrail of the bridge over the moat, struggling to keep her footing on the icy wood as she made her way into the castle. It had seemed like such a good, obvious idea to bring her when he'd seen the leaflet. Killing two birds with one big hunk of tumbledown rock. Lots of Brownie points for him for thinking of it, meaning she'd be thinking kindly of him again as they drove to Cardiff. Maybe even enough to say yes if he asked her to dinner again. He could spend the night in Cardiff, head straight to London in the morning. Because this wasn't over yet. It couldn't be.

Memories of his twenty-first birthday flashed through his mind again. He'd wanted to seduce this woman eight years ago, before he'd even really known her. And now that feeling was a thousand times stronger.

He was pretty sure she'd go along with it this time, if he did. Last night's awkward resolution notwithstanding, he'd seen the signs. The way her body swayed into his whenever he got close, the way her eyes widened when her gaze caught his. And the way her teeth had pressed down into her lip, displaying just how plump and kissable it was. Her resistance was definitely crumbling.

He had to stop thinking about this. He had to wait. Oth-

erwise he'd be seducing her up against a very cold stone
castle keep.

Inside the castle walls Ben found a bench near an information board, brushed off the snow as best he could and
sat down to watch the show. Cilgerran was a nice enough
castle, he supposed, but not exactly his main area of interest. That, right now, would be Luce.

The castle had free entry until the end of March, but no
one else was taking advantage of it. Clearly the weather had
scared them off, but they were missing out, Ben thought.
Luce flitted from wall to wall, from snow-covered step to
window, from arch to arrow-hole, the breeze keeping her
skirt plastered against her curves under her short jacket,
her colour high and eyes bright. From time to time she'd
call out to him, telling him about what she was looking at,
what had happened here. The wind whisked away every
other word, but it didn't matter. Ben didn't care about the
castle. He was too entranced by her.

She was beautiful.

It wasn't as if he hadn't noticed before, of course. But
it had always been a pale, reserved beauty. The sort you
could look at but not touch. Hell, she'd practically had
'Keep Out' signs plastered all over her. But here...here she
was radiant. She was real. And how he wanted to touch her.

He couldn't have said how long it was before she jumped
down from the low remains of an interior wall, sending a
puff of snow flying up. Time seemed to pass differently
when he was absorbed in watching her.

Her cheeks were pink and flushed as she flung herself
onto the patch of bench he'd cleared beside him. 'This
place is fantastic,' she said, sounding slightly out of breath
from hopping around the castle walls.

'I'm glad you like it.' The urge to lean back against the
bench, stretch an arm around her shoulders and pull her

into him was almost overpowering. In an attempt to resist, Ben leant forward instead, resting his forearms along his thighs. 'It must have been pretty impressive back in the day.'

'It's impressive now.'

Luce's voice held a tone of reverence, and he knew she saw something here that he never could—something beyond his world. It didn't matter. He was content to enjoy it through her, to see her eyes light up at the history she saw here. He'd bring her back every week if he could. Just to see that sparkle, that life in her face.

Except maybe it would wear off over time. Maybe they'd have to tour all the castles in Wales. And the rest of Britain. And overseas. *I wonder how she feels about French châteaux?*

Or maybe he'd take her back to Cardiff and never see her again, as planned.

That thought made the winter air colder, the clouds overhead more threatening. Ben squinted up at the sky. The reports said no more snow until that night, but those skies just screamed bad weather. They should get going or they might not make it to Cardiff. Again.

But he didn't want to leave. Not yet. He wanted a little more time with this Luce first. Excited, vibrant, castle Luce. Was that so much to ask?

'So, where do you think Nest was taken from?' Ben got to his feet as he spoke, reaching a hand out to pull Luce up again.

She rolled her eyes as she stood. 'The castle would have looked completely different then. Most of what you see today was probably built in the thirteenth century—a hundred years or more after Owain took Nest.'

'Okay, so tell me what it would have looked like then.'

'Earth and timber building, probably. We can't really

be sure.' Luce gazed around her again and Ben realised he was staring at her the same way she looked at the castle. He didn't stop.

Luce carried on talking, almost as if to herself. 'It doesn't matter that it looks different now. The landscape's the same. The feeling. She was here, and now I am. And I feel… It's ridiculous.' She dropped her head.

'Go on,' Ben said, trying to resist the desperate temptation to move closer to her.

Luce reached out to place a hand against the stone of the castle wall, palm flat, as if she were connecting herself to the site. 'I feel like I can understand her better here. Make more sense of her life and what happened to her. There's so few facts that we can be sure about. But here they come together better.'

'So it's helped?'

She looked up, her eyes wide and shining, and smiled at him. Ben felt the moment he lost himself as a dull ache in his chest.

'It's helped a lot,' she said. 'Thank you.'

It was too late, now, he realised. He'd been hers since the moment he saw her again in Chester. Maybe longer. Maybe since that night in the library. It didn't matter. None of it mattered any more. He just had to have her.

Stepping forward, he raised his hands to her cold face, his body moving into her space as she fell back to rest against the castle wall.

'We should get going.'

Sharp white teeth bit down on her lip again after she spoke, and Ben almost groaned at the sight.

'I know.' But he didn't move away.

'Kiss me,' she said, anyway, and he lowered his mouth to hers, the wind whipping round them, cold and icy and utterly unimportant in the moment.

Her lips were soft and sweet under his as he teased them open, drinking in the taste and the feel of her. Luce's arms wrapped around his waist, her hands firm against his back, pulling him in deeper, closer, even as he pressed his body against hers, the softness of her curves driving him wild.

As the first cold drops hit the back of his neck, Ben pulled his mouth away, his hands tugging her body into the warmth and safety of his arms. Luce rubbed her cheek against his coat and he kissed the top of her head.

'We need to get out of here,' he said, and she moved away, leaving him cold and bereft.

She blinked up at him and snowflakes landed on her lashes. 'It's snowing again.'

'And it's going to get heavier. But, more importantly, I need to get you somewhere more private than a ruined public castle.' He took a breath. 'So—Cardiff or the cottage?'

Luce's lips quirked up in a naughty smile, and the expression was so utterly unexpected that Ben bit back a laugh.

'Whichever is closer,' she said, and he grabbed her hand as they ran for the exit.

Finally, Ben thought, as the car doors slammed behind them and he set a course back to the cottage. Finally something was looking up.

The journey back to the cottage seemed to take twice as long as the trip to the castle had done, and that was only due in part to the increasingly heavy snowfall. It seemed worse even than the drive from Chester had been. Cardiff would have to wait another day, apparently, but somehow the thought bothered her far less now. She couldn't have left without having this, having *him*, just once.

Ben drove steadily through the worsening weather, taking bends and dips in his stride. Luce kept her hands clenched against her knees, more to stop herself touching him than from fear of the drive.

'You okay?' he asked finally, just as the sky went from grey to black and Luce made out a sign welcoming them to the Brecon Beacons National Park through the falling snow.

'I'm fine,' she said

'Really?'

No. I want you to pull over so I can ravish you in the back seat. Luce felt her eyes widen at the very thought. Not a very Dr Lucinda Myles type desire at all.

'You're not over-thinking this?'

She looked up at Ben as he spoke. His eyes were still firmly on the road, his arms braced tight to the wheel. He looked as if every muscle in his body was taut. Was that because of the weather? Or because he was resisting a similar urge to hers?

Luce gave herself one moment to believe it was the latter, then realised she still hadn't answered his question. With a soft laugh she said, 'Honestly, Ben, I'm barely thinking at all right now.'

She was watching, so she saw him blow out a long breath, saw his shoulders sink, his body start to relax. Had he really been that worried about her?

'I'm not going to fall apart because you kissed me, you know,' she said, forehead furrowed with the effort of trying to figure out what he was thinking.

His mouth slipped into a half-smile. 'Yeah, but I might if I don't get to do it again soon.'

The heat that pooled in her belly seemed hotter, more desperate at his words than it had been even in the castle. Back there she'd told herself it was the location, the romanticism of the castle and its history. But here, when he should be focused on the road, he was still thinking about kissing her.

'Are we nearly there yet?' She could hear the wanting in her own voice, and Ben obviously did, too. He glanced over at her, just for a moment, surprise on his face.

'Nearly,' he answered, his voice low and full of promise.

Luce was almost certain that the rest of the journey took considerably less time than it should have done. But he had to slow down again as they reached the twisting path up to the cottage itself, and Luce gripped the edge of her seat as the car slipped and slid over the still falling snow. *Not going to be fun trying to get back through this to Cardiff, even tomorrow.*

The thought was too depressing to dwell on. Instead, Luce focused on thinking about what might happen when they got inside the cottage and bit her lip.

'Okay, this is as close as we're getting,' Ben said eventually, wrestling the car onto the side of the road and pulling on the handbrake. They hadn't even made it to the parking spot they'd managed the day before. This snowstorm was making yesterday's look like a mere sprinkling. 'Think you can walk from here?'

Luce nodded because, honestly, she could do anything if it meant Ben was going to kiss her again soon.

He trudged round to the other side of the car, helping her out into the snow, and pulled her arm through his so he held her tight against the side of his body. Together, heads down against the snow flurries, they made their slow way up the last of the hill to the cottage, with Ben yanking her upright whenever her boots slipped.

And then, just when Luce had started to fear they were never going to make it, the cottage appeared through the snow, and warmth burst through her despite the weather.

Ben fumbled the door open and in moments had slammed

it shut behind them and pressed her up against it, his hands cold as they found their way under her coat and jumper to bare skin. His lips were hot, though, warm and demanding, and Luce let her head fall back against the wood and surrendered herself to his kiss.

Then he wrenched himself away again and Luce's body ached with the loss.

'This is what you want?' he asked.

Luce nodded furiously. 'Of course—'

'For *you*,' he interrupted. His eyes were dark with want, but his face was serious. 'Not because someone else wants you to, or because it's what you should do, or even because you're trying to be something you weren't in university. Because you want it.'

'Yes.'

'And you know…you know what this is?'

At last Luce realised what he really wanted, and even though she'd promised herself she wouldn't give it to him, the need that burned through her body meant she couldn't stop the words even if she wanted to.

'I want you, Ben. Me. I want your hands and your mouth and your body on me. Just for tonight. Just one night.'

His hands tightened around her waist as she spoke and Luce swallowed at the heat in his eyes. Then she said the words she knew he was waiting for.

'Seduce me.'

That was all Ben needed to hear. With a growl of satisfaction he captured her lips again, even as his hands pushed her coat from her shoulders.

'You're wearing far too many clothes,' he murmured, working his kisses down her throat.

She bent her neck enticingly, to give him better access, and he allowed himself a moment to admire the pale skin there, and the line of her throat to her shoulders. How had he never noticed how beautiful she was when they were younger? Maybe she was more confident now, better dressed, more aware of her own attraction. But her beauty had always lain in the essence of her, the bones and the lines, and he just hadn't been looking carefully enough.

Except for that one night, drunk and stupid. Then he'd seen it.

'It was cold in the castle,' Luce said, and Ben had to concentrate to remember what they'd even been talking about. He was past words already.

God, how had she bewitched him so completely, so quickly? Taken charge of his senses so that all that mattered was getting her in his bed as quickly as possible? Hell, he didn't even care about the bed. He was on the verge of taking her right here against the door.

He needed to regain some control. He needed to be able to walk away from this tomorrow. The wild, blood-boiling feeling that had taken over had stripped away what he knew of himself. He needed this to be back on his terms.

With more effort than he would have liked, he pulled her away from the door. 'Bedroom,' he said, sentences still beyond him.

Luce glanced around as though she'd forgotten entirely where she was, hadn't even noticed the splintered door at her back. At least he wasn't the only one losing control.

She followed him without argument as he tugged her towards his bedroom and kicked the door shut behind them. He'd worried that she might be spooked when they were finally there, that once it became too real she'd change her mind. But instead she melted into his arms as he stripped off her clothes, her fingers already dragging his jumper up over his head.

Skin to skin, touch to touch, Ben laid her back on the

bed, covering her with his own body. She was so smooth under his hands, and every touch made her arch and moan and mew, responsive in a way he could never have imagined. And he responded in turn, his fingers and his mouth reaching deeper, more demanding, until finally, *finally*, he slid home into her and felt her moan against his shoulder.

'Okay?' He kissed her ear as they stilled for a moment, letting her adjust.

'More than,' she whispered back, and then Ben couldn't help but move and move, until she was falling apart under him, and his whole world narrowed to the feel of her, to a pinpoint of sensation that made his body tense until it might break...

Afterwards, once enough of his brain had returned to his body, Ben rolled onto his side, pulling Luce with him so she was tucked safe in his arms. Her breathing was the only sound, deep and even, as if she were trying to bring her body back under her own control. It was too late, though. He'd already seen the wildness at the centre of her, the free parts she kept locked up tight. The hidden side of her that wanted, wanted—wanted so much.

He couldn't let her lock that up again.

CHAPTER ELEVEN

THE ROOM LAY under a strange hush, as if nothing existed beyond the bed in which they lay. Luce supposed it was the snow, blanketing the world outside and deadening the sounds. But maybe it was the sex as well. After all, such a moment deserved a reverential silence, surely?

Because it wasn't just sex. Luce felt a stab in her chest at the realisation, and she must have flinched, because Ben's arm tightened around her, pulling her closer into that magnificent chest. She felt his mouth brush against her hair, soothing, comforting. As if he was trying not to startle her.

'Freaking out?' he asked, his voice a murmur. But the grip on her body told her he wasn't letting go even if she was.

'A little,' she admitted, and cursed herself even as she spoke. The last thing she needed Ben to know was that sex had reduced her to a gibbering wreck.

Except it wasn't the sex. The sex had been phenomenal, taking her everywhere she'd needed to go and then some. Her whole body was thanking her for the sex in its own languid, melted way. No, the sex was just fine.

It was the feelings that went along with it that caused the problems.

She wasn't deluded enough to think that Ben would break his one-night rule for her. But, lying in his arms, it was hard to imagine how she would tear herself away the next morning.

But she had to. Because Ben wasn't a man looking for responsibility, family, a wife. And she knew herself. She wasn't Nest, for all that she'd been taken from Cilgerran Castle and bedded tonight. She had a family she had to take care of, and Ben would never be able to bear to have anything take affections away from him. If she were to fall in love, to find someone to make a life with, it had to be someone who supported her, helped her, understood that she had other responsibilities.

Ben Hampton was not that man. Ben was so far from being that man it was almost funny. Or hugely depressing.

The best she could hope for with Ben was an occasional night together when he happened to be in town and it suited him—and even then never more than one night in a row. And that wasn't enough for her. He wanted her to think about her own needs? Well, she needed more than that from a relationship.

'What can I do to help you relax?' he asked, his voice soft and seductive.

Luce felt her body reacting even though every muscle in it was already exhausted.

'I'm never going to be able to sleep if you keep thinking so loud. Normally a woman is more relaxed after I finish my work.' He sounded faintly put out at that.

Luce bit her lip. She had to leave tomorrow morning. She knew that. But that didn't mean she couldn't make the most of her one night.

Shifting in his arms so she was facing him, Luce let him pull her flush against him, her breasts brushing against the hairs on his chest, his right leg pressing between her thighs.

'Maybe you haven't finished work for the night, then,' she said, and watched his eyes darken as he smiled.

Yes, if she only got one night with Ben Hampton, Luce was going to make sure every moment counted.

According to the clock on the bedside table, it was late morning when Ben awoke, but the room remained dim and close. *Guess it hasn't stopped snowing, then.* He supposed he could get up and look, see what they were dealing with. But the bed was so warm, and when he shifted Luce snuggled closer into his arms.

Yeah, he wasn't going anywhere in a hurry.

And neither, he realised, was she. Not if the snow was as heavy as it had looked before they'd retired to the bedroom for the night. If he hadn't been able to get the car all the way up to the cottage yesterday afternoon, they'd be lucky even to get back to it this morning. No point even trying.

Not, of course, that logic meant she wouldn't need some convincing of that fact. Ben smiled. Given how responsive she'd been to his 'convincing' the night before, he didn't see it being a particularly arduous task.

'Are you awake?' Luce asked, her voice fuzzy with sleep.

'Yeah,' he murmured, and she turned over in his arms to face him.

'Has it stopped snowing?'

She was blinking up at him, her hair falling into her eyes, her face pink and sleepy, and Ben thought she looked more beautiful than he'd ever seen her.

'Don't know.'

Wriggling out of his embrace, she wrapped the extra blanket from the bottom of the bed around her and padded to the window, ducking under the curtain to look out.

Then she swore. Ben didn't think he'd ever heard her do that before. He hadn't even been sure she knew such words.

Flinging the curtains open, she turned to him with an

accusing glare. 'Look at it! It's piled up halfway to the window! We're never going to get back to Cardiff in this!'

Shuffling into a seated position, lounging against the headboard, Ben shrugged. 'So we spend another day here. Is that so bad?'

'Yes!' Luce ran a hand through her tangled hair and almost lost her grip on the blanket. 'It's Christmas Eve *tomorrow*, Ben. I have to get home. Never mind the book. I've got to get things ready for my family. I haven't even *thought* about dinner for tomorrow.' She yanked the blanket up again, covering all but a hint of her cleavage. 'This is all your fault.'

'I thought we'd established that I can't control the weather?' Ben said mildly.

'Maybe not. But you said it wouldn't snow again until last night. And you didn't tell me it would be heavy enough to drift!'

Ben winced. That much was, in fact, true. He'd known how bad the snow would be and still brought her back here, instead of taking her home. 'I gave you a choice: the cottage or Cardiff. You chose here.'

'Because I didn't have all the information! You *trapped* me here.'

She looked so anguished Ben almost felt sorry for her. Except that she was trying to blame him for her decisions and accusing him of imaginary plots. Again. As if he hadn't done all he could to help her for the last three days. As if what they'd shared was nothing more than an attempt to get her into bed. Well, if that was what she thought— fine. Let her believe him to be exactly the sort of man she'd always thought. She'd never believe he'd changed, anyway. So why should he change? What had he been thinking to believe for even a moment that this could be more than a one-night stand? They were as different now as they'd ever been.

'Trapped you here?' Ben raised his eyebrows in deliberate disbelief. 'Why would I do that? You know my one-night rule. Trust me—I'm as ready to get back to civilisation as you are.'

He wished he could take back the words the moment he'd spoken them. Not least because he knew he'd put an end to any chance of spending another day—and night—in bed with Luce. But mostly because of the way her face froze, eyes wide, mouth slightly open, fingers wrapped in the blanket as she held it tight to her chest.

The moment lasted too long—a cold chill between them as the silence of the snow pressed in. Then Luce broke. She took a step back, towards the door, and shook her head just a little. 'Of course. If we're stuck here I need to work. Tell me when it clears enough for us to leave.'

She didn't even slam the door behind her. Instead she closed it carefully, letting the latch click quietly into place. And Ben fell back down onto the bed and wished he'd never heard of Cilgerran Castle.

Luce fumbled her way into her clothes with chilly fingers, trying to convince herself that it was only the cold making her shake. But the anger still bubbling up in her chest told her different.

She was furious. With Ben, naturally, for being exactly what she'd always known he was. And she was even more angry with herself.

Dropping to sit on the bed as she yanked on thick socks over her woolly tights, Luce tried to calm down. She'd never get any work done like this.

How could she have been so stupid? She knew beyond a doubt exactly what sort of a man Ben was. Hell, he'd told her himself! His ridiculous one-night rule was a prime example. As if only spending one night together could make falling in love less likely.

Not that she was in love with Ben Hampton. Not even *she* was that idiotic.

She'd brought this on herself. *Take responsibility. Take control.* Well, she'd take the responsibility, anyway. Control seemed to be entirely out of her hands.

This was her punishment for taking what she wanted for a change—for forgetting about her obligations, about her family. Would the snow clear for them to get through? The thought of spending another night in the cottage, even in her own room, made her shiver. And what if she didn't make it home for Christmas Eve and Tom's dinner? Or, worse, Christmas Day itself?

If giving in to her foolish desire to sleep with Ben Hampton ruined Christmas for her family they'd never forgive her. Hell, she'd never forgive herself.

In a flurry of movement Luce crossed the room and settled into the chair, flipping open her laptop and tapping her fingers against the wood of the desk as she waited for it to bring up her manuscript. Work. That was what she needed. Something to distract her and give her purpose. Except...

How am I supposed to concentrate on ancient history when my own past and present is naked in the next room?

No, she needed to focus. Nest. What happened after Owain took her from Cilgerran? Henry I intervened. So, how to frame it? Consider how one woman, a Welsh princess, caused uproar in the English court? Or tell the more personal story of her ex-lover coming to the rescue of her reputation?

Her lips tightened. God only knew what her grandfather would make of *her* reputation right now if he were still alive.

Nest had it easy. One quick kidnapping and she was set.

With a sigh, Luce turned her attention to the document in front of her and pushed all thoughts of Ben, the night before and what the hell happened next out of her head. The only thing she could fix right now was her book.

Ben was still cursing himself for an idiot two hours later when, as he waited for the kettle to boil for an apologetic cup of peppermint tea, the lights went out. Cursing, he flipped a few switches on and off, then stalked off towards the fuse box. Chances were it was a power cut, given the snow, but his luck had to turn some time. Maybe it was a tripped switch.

It wasn't. And by the time he returned to the kitchen Luce stood in front of the fire, arms crossed over her chest, glaring at him. 'What the hell's happened *now*?'

'Power cut,' Ben said. 'At least best I can tell. Might be a line down somewhere.'

'So what do we do?' Luce asked, a snap in her voice. 'Don't you have an emergency generator or something?'

At least she was talking to him. He supposed he should be grateful for that. 'No generator. Now we build up the fire, keep warm and survive on whatever in the fridge doesn't need cooking.' Maybe he had some marshmallows they could toast somewhere at the back of a cupboard.

Luce glared out of the window and he followed her gaze to where the snow was still fluttering to the ground. 'I'm thinking very fondly of the Eight Bells right now.'

'We'd never get down the path,' Ben said.

'Just as long as it clears enough for us to get to Cardiff. I'm not staying another day here with you.' Luce's tone was firm, as if daring the weather to disagree with her again. But, given the way the snow had started to drift, driving anywhere in the next few days would be a really stupid idea.

Of course getting snowed in at his cottage, during a power cut, with a furious Lucinda Myles was also kind of idiotic. Apparently there was something about her that made him lose his mind.

'Are you hungry?' he asked, checking his watch in the firelight. He wasn't sure what meal they were on, but it had been a while since either of them had eaten.

'That depends on what's in your fridge.' Luce eyed him with suspicion, as if he might be about to add poisoning to his list of crimes.

'I picked up some bits from the village shop yesterday. There should be enough to tide us over.' Just about. He'd only planned on having to feed himself, after all.

'Fine. But the power had better come back on before my laptop battery runs out.' Turning on her heel, Luce stalked back towards her room. 'Call me when the food's ready.'

Ben sighed and watched her go. Apparently any sort of reconciliation was still a way off.

There wasn't much to prepare. Ben arranged cheeses and bread on plates, adding some cold meats he'd picked up, then carried them over to the low table in front of the fire. Then, as an afterthought, he grabbed a bottle of red wine and two glasses. Wine always made things more of a feast.

'Grub's up,' he called, and moments later Luce appeared. She'd added another jumper on top of her outfit from earlier. With the electric under-floor heating out of commission the cottage was becoming very chilly, very quickly. 'Sorry it's not much.'

Luce took the glass of wine he'd poured for her and sat at the end of the sofa nearest the fire. 'Better than nothing.

At least it's warm in here.' Her words were short, terse. And she still wasn't looking at him.

With a deep breath, Ben sat down beside her, reaching for his own wine. 'That's not all I'm sorry for.'

Slowly she turned to look at him, without speaking. It wasn't much, but Ben took it as a sign she was at least willing to listen. 'I'm sorry about what I said. About…'

'Your one-night rule?'

'Yeah.'

'Fine.'

She'd turned her attention back to her plate again, picking at the bread. Ben watched her, waiting for something more, but it wasn't forthcoming.

'Not feeling inclined to apologise for accusing me of trapping you in this cottage purely to seduce you?'

'Not really.' She reached for her wine glass. 'Apart from anything else, you *did* seduce me.'

She had a point there. And somehow Ben knew that saying, *You asked me to* wasn't going to make anything any better.

'How does it even work, anyway?' she asked, after a long moment's silence in the flickering firelight. 'Your stupid rule? What? You just live your life going from one-night stand to one-night stand?'

'No.' Ben rubbed a hand across his forehead. *Now* she wanted to talk about this? There was a reason he usually had this talk before he hit the sheets. 'Of course not.'

'Then what?' Putting down her plate, Luce turned her body to face his, all attention on him. 'Come on. I want to know.'

For a moment she thought he wasn't going to answer. But, Luce rationalised, as a victim of his stupid rule, at the very least she deserved to understand it.

Finally Ben spoke. 'I date women. Same as anyone. I just make a point not to spend more than one night with them at a time.'

'Because twenty-four hours is too much like commitment?' Luce said, rolling her eyes. Men. What were they so damn scared of?

Ben sighed. 'Because if one night becomes two nights then it's all too easy for it to be three nights. A week. A month. More. And suddenly she's expecting a ring and a life. Something I can't give her.'

'You've tried, then?' Luce folded her legs up under her, twisting so her feet were closer to the hearth. With just the flickering fire to light the room it felt smaller, cosier. As if the world were only just big enough to encircle the two of them and their shadows.

'I don't have to. I've seen it before.' The way he said it, Luce knew that whatever he'd witnessed it had been up close and far too personal.

Frowning, she made an educated guess. 'Your parents?'

'Yeah.' Ben topped up their wine glasses, even though neither of them had drunk very much. 'Dad...his life was the business. Everything came second to Hampton & Sons. Even the sons.'

How must that have felt? Knowing he was less important than a building? Luce couldn't imagine. Her family might expect a lot from her, but at least she always knew they needed her.

'And your mum?' she asked.

Ben blew out a long breath. 'Mum would follow him around from business opportunity to networking dinner, smiling when he wanted her to smile, wearing what he wanted her to wear. She gave up her whole life to satisfy him, until finally she realised she'd given up herself.'

'She left?'

'When I was eight.' Ben stared into the fire. 'She just…
she couldn't do it any more. We didn't see her much after
that. And then she died two years later.'

Luce swallowed, her heart heavy in her chest. 'I'm
sorry. I never knew.' She could almost imagine him, ten
years old, perfectly turned out in a suit at his mother's
graveside. His heart must have broken. Was that when
he'd given up on family?

Ben shrugged. 'No reason you should. Anyway, that's
why. My life—it's all about fixing things and moving on.
Just like Dad. And I won't subject a wife or a child to that.'

'So you just don't let anyone get close enough to want
it?' Couldn't he see how bleak that existence was?

'Seems easiest.' He drained his wine and poured himself another glass. 'So, what about you? What is it that
makes *you* believe that bricks and mortar are important?
I mean, I'm all for lucrative property opportunities. But
your house is more than that to you, isn't it?'

'It's home,' Luce agreed. 'It always will be.'

'So tell me. What makes it home?'

Luce glanced over and saw that Ben's eyes were closed,
as if by not being able to see her he was distancing himself from the question he was asking. But if he wanted to
understand what made a house a home, she wasn't going
to deny him.

'It was my grandfather's house, originally. I told you
that, right?' She trailed her finger around the stem of her
glass, trying to find the words to explain what the house
meant to her. 'He bought it after he moved to Cardiff with
Grandma and made a little money, back in the fifties. It's
not in a great area, but it's still more than I could afford
to buy today. And it's close to the university.'

'He left it to you?'

Luce nodded. 'When he died, yeah. We grew up there,

you see. My father left when Dolly was a baby, and my Mum…that's when she retreated to her own bubble. Grandad moved us in, helped bring us up. Grandma had been dead for years, and the house was too big for just him, he always said.'

'You were his favourite, though,' Ben said. 'If he left you the house instead of your mum or your brother and sister.'

The unfairness of that act caught in Luce's chest every time she thought about it. 'It wasn't that, exactly. He relied on me to take care of them. The house needs a lot of work, and I don't think he thought they'd manage it. They all know it's still their home, too.'

'So you even give them your house?' Ben's eyes opened wide to stare at her. 'You really do give up everything for them, don't you?'

The cosy warmth of the fire started to cool and Luce pulled away a little. 'I don't expect you to understand,' she said, leaning back against the arm of the sofa.

Ben shrugged. 'Like I told you, home for me was hotels, after Mum left and Dad gave up the house. I used to think maybe I'd missed out, when I was a kid away at boarding school. But I like moving on—finding new things, new places.'

'But you bought this cottage,' Luce pointed out. 'You did it up, made it a home. You brought me here.'

She regretted the words as soon as they were spoken. She knew she shouldn't read more into that than a whim, an emergency pit stop in the snow. But it was so hard not to.

When she looked up his face was closed, his eyes staring over her head. 'The cottage is an investment. I'll probably sell it soon.'

The thought of Ben giving up his escape, the closest

thing he'd had to a home in years, without even realising what it meant, was too depressing to contemplate.

Looking away into the fire, she said, 'Doesn't look like the power's going to come back on tonight.'

'Yeah, I doubt it.' Ben gave her a look she couldn't quite read, then added, 'We'll have to see how the roads look in the morning.'

No. No way. Maybe she understood him a little better now, but that didn't mean she could stay here any longer and not go crazy. 'I'm sure they'll be fine.' Getting to her feet, she added, 'And a good night's sleep will do us both some good before the drive. I'll see you in the morning.'

She didn't look back, didn't check his expression, didn't wait for him to wish her goodnight. Even so, she barely made it to the door before the sound of his voice stopped her in her tracks.

'What if I said you were worth breaking my rule for?' he asked, so low she almost thought she must have misheard.

She turned back to face him, her heart thumping against her ribcage. 'But I'm not. I'm just the same Lucinda Myles you made fun of at university.'

Ben shook his head. 'You're so much more than I ever saw.'

Luce gave him a half-smile. 'So are you.'

And then, before she could change her mind, she shut the bedroom door behind her and climbed, fully clothed, into the freezing bed.

CHAPTER TWELVE

BEN HAD PASSED a fitful night on the sofa, his dreams filled with dark hair and brick walls. But at least he'd been warm, he reasoned. Luce must have been half frozen in her lonely bed, if the way she'd appeared in front of the freshly banked fire before the sun had risen was any indication.

'Happy Christmas Eve,' she murmured as she held her hands out to the flames. Her suitcase leant beside the front door, just as it had in Chester, waiting to leave.

He sat up, blankets falling to his waist, and motioned at the case. 'You're still hoping to make it back to Cardiff today, then?'

'I have to.'

'To cook dinner for your family,' he said, a little disbelievingly.

'To spend Christmas with them,' she corrected. 'Don't you want to get back to London to spend it with your brother?'

'I think Seb wants me there for a business meeting rather than to sing carols round the piano.' Come to think of it, what *did* Seb want him there for? He'd been so preoccupied with Luce he'd barely given the strange conversation with his brother another thought.

'Fine. Maybe you don't care about family, or home, or Christmas. But I need to get back. Will you drive me?'

She looked down at him, eyes wide and dark, her hair curling around her face, and Ben knew he couldn't say no to her.

'If the roads are clear.' It wasn't a promise, but it felt like one all the same.

Luce nodded. 'I'll pack up the car.'

The roads weren't clear, not by anyone's definition. But the snow had stopped, and by lunchtime the tractors were out clearing some of the local thoroughfares. Once Ben had spent another hour digging his four-by-four out of the snow that had built up around it, and reversed onto the track, the journey looked manageable.

Still, it wasn't until they got out of the Brecon Beacons National Park and onto larger roads that Ben finally felt his shoulders start to relax as he settled into the drive. He'd driven through worse weather, especially up in the hills in France, by the château, but that didn't mean it was his preferred time to travel. Didn't mean he wasn't still annoyed with Luce for making him.

That's why. That's the only reason. Nothing to do with her leaving me.

Something he wasn't going to think about until this drive was over.

As they entered Cardiff Luce gave quiet, monotone directions to her house and Ben could feel his time with her slipping away. Being wasted. But what was the point? Her family would always be more important than him. And he would never be able to give her enough to make her stay. Neither one of them was going to change now, if they hadn't already. Why put himself through that?

Eventually he pulled up outside a row of townhouses, most of them converted into flats. Luce had the car door open almost before he'd switched the engine off, so he got out and went to open the boot for her.

'Want me to carry this in for you?' He hefted her suitcase out of the car and rested it on the pavement, his fingers still on the handle.

Luce shook her head. 'I can manage.'

And wasn't that her all over? 'Fine,' he said, relinquishing his hold.

She paused, biting down on her lip again, and Ben tried to ignore the heat that flooded through him at the sight.

'Thank you,' she said, finally. 'For this week.'

'I know it wasn't what you planned. But I hope you found the time away...useful.'

'I did, actually.' She sounded surprised.

'Good.'

What else was there left to say?

Awkward silence stretched between them until Luce motioned towards her front door and said, 'I'd better go and get ready.'

'The dinner party.' Ben nodded, his neck feeling stiff. 'Of course.'

'I know it doesn't seem like—'

'It's your life,' he interrupted, too tired to have the argument again. 'Do whatever you want, Luce.'

As he got back into the car he could have sworn he heard her say, 'That's the problem.' But by the time he turned round she'd already gone inside.

He thought about going straight back to the cottage, but he knew the memory of her would linger there. He'd call his usual cleaning lady, get her to clear the place out so that all reminders would be gone by his next visit.

He could check into a hotel, he supposed, if any had a spare room on Christmas Eve. But suddenly he wanted to see his brother. He wanted to know what Seb had planned

next for the business. Something about this time with Luce
had left him unsettled, unsure. And he needed something
to throw himself into.

Decision made, he climbed back into the car and headed
east, watching the snow that had disrupted his life thin and
finally disappear as he sped along the M4.

He drove straight to Seb's office, figuring—correctly—
that even late on Christmas Eve his brother would still be
hard at work.

'You look terrible,' Seb said, as Ben sprawled in the visitor's chair on the opposite side of their dad's antique desk.

The usual unease and uncertainty rose up in Ben, just
as it always had when Dad had been in residence behind
the desk, but he clamped down on it, folded his ankle up
on one knee and leant back, arms spread along the arms of
the chair. Disrespectful and uncaring. Because Seb didn't
need good posture to know he had his respect, and his dad
wasn't there to care any more.

Neither is Luce.

'Hell of a drive in,' Ben said. 'Hills are practically snowbound.'

Seb's eyebrows pulled down into a frown. 'This could
have waited, you know. Until the weather cleared, at least.'

Ben shrugged. 'Needed to get back anyway.'

With a knowing look, Seb settled back in his chair. 'Ah.
Time to let the latest girlfriend know she was only tempo-
rary, right? I'm just amazed you managed more than one
night. Time to retire your rule at last?'

'No,' Ben said, shortly. 'The rule stays. And it's Christmas Eve. She had some family thing she had to get back
for.'

Ben stared out of the window, trying to ignore the sense
of wrongness that filled him when Seb talked about Luce
as one of his girlfriends. Why did it feel so different?

Hadn't it followed the exact same pattern it always did? A bit of fun, discovering they were entirely different people, and then going their separate ways. Except this time they'd known just how different they were before they even went out to dinner. They'd wanted each other anyway.

Seb hadn't said anything, Ben realised. When he drew his attention back to his brother he found Seb watching him, a contemplative look in his eye.

'What?' Ben asked, shifting to sit properly on the chair.

'Nothing. Just…she was different? This girl?'

'Luce,' Ben said, automatically. 'And I don't know what you mean.'

'You said she was an old friend,' Seb clarified, and a sense of relief came over Ben.

'Yeah. We knew each other in university. So what?'

'Nothing,' Seb said again.

Ben didn't believe him. Time to change the subject. 'So—come on. I've driven through snowstorms and London traffic to get here. What did you want to meet with me about?'

Seb blinked, tapping a pen against his desk as if trying to remember. Finally he said, 'I've got a new job for you. If you're interested.'

'A "your mission, should you choose to accept it" type thing?' He hoped so. Preferably something far away, completely absorbing and with no reminders of Luce. That sounded pretty much perfect.

'Sort of.' Seb sighed. 'Look. I'm trying to find the right way to say this.'

'Sounds ominous.'

'I don't want you thinking you're not good at your job.'

'I am excellent at my job,' Ben said. 'And since when do you worry about my ego?'

'Since when do you take women to your cottage?' Seb countered.

'Just say it. Whatever it is.'

'Okay. So… Although you are passably good at your job—'

'Excellent at, I think I said.'

'You don't love it.'

Ben looked at his brother in surprise. 'It's a job, Seb. I don't have to love it. I just have to do it.'

'Maybe not. But I think you could love it.'

Things started to fall into place for Ben. 'I know what this is. You're worried that I'm still angry Dad left control of the business to you. I told you—I don't want it. Too much responsibility for me. I like the travel. I like the money. I like making things happen. I don't want to be stuck behind that desk for the rest of my life.'

'Like you think I will be?' Seb looked at him. 'You think I'm going to turn into Dad.'

'Not if you choose not to.' Ben shrugged. 'Besides, it's different. You haven't got a wife and kids like Dad did.'

'Maybe I'd like to have those things, though. One day.'

'Really?' Ben shook his head. 'Nah—can't see it. You'll sit there and manage the business, I'll go out and about and make things happen, and neither of us will drag any kids from boarding school to hotel for their entire childhood. It's all good.'

'And that would be enough for you?'

'Yeah. Of course it would. What are you thinking? That I need a private jet to make my life complete?'

'Honestly? I think you need a home. I think you need someone to come home to. I know everything with Mum screwed up that ideal for you, and maybe it was easier for me, being away at boarding school already. But it wasn't your problem to fix. You can't fix problems, only situations. And, Ben, it's time to move on. Time to grow up at last.'

But Seb hadn't seen it. Hadn't seen their mother falling apart day by day. He'd already been away, engrossed in school and friends and sport. He'd already moved on before Mum had.

Ben had been the only one there to try to make things right for her. And he hadn't been able to.

'I think you're crazy.' Pushing against the arms of the chair, Ben stood up. 'And if that's all you wanted to talk to me about—'

'I haven't finished.' When Ben remained standing, Seb sighed. 'Just sit down, Ben. I promise to stay on topic. Business only. Your shambles of a private life is your own.'

'Yeah, like yours is any better,' Ben grumbled. But he sat.

'I'm working on it,' Seb said with a lopsided smile.

'Really? Am I missing something here? Did something happen while I was away?'

'Business only, right?' Seb grabbed a folder from the corner of his desk and handed it across to Ben.

Opening the file, Ben felt his heart lurch against his ribcage at the sight of the reception desk at the Royal Court Hotel, Chester. *So much for a distraction from Luce.* Slamming the folder shut, he said, 'Been there. Done that. What's next?'

'I want you to go back.'

'Why? It's fine. It's running well. I've made my recommendations for streamlining some processes, making things more effective. Other than that…' He shrugged.

'I want to try something new.'

Against his better judgement, curiosity welled up in Ben. Something new. Something different. That was something they'd never been able to do while their father was alive. He'd had an unalterable system. Buy the hotel, make it look and run like all the others in the chain, move on to the next project. Every time.

'New how, exactly?'

Seb gave him a slow smile. 'Knew that would catch your attention. Trust me, you're going to like this plan.'

Ben wasn't so sure about that. But he was willing to give his brother the benefit of the doubt. 'Okay. I'm listening.'

Luce barely had time to toss her suitcase in her room before her phone rang. Glancing at the display, she saw it was her mother and let it go to voicemail. *Sorry, Mum, but if you want dinner tonight you'll have to wait for me to call you back.*

Okay, it was almost five in the afternoon. Two hours until her guests arrived. Long enough to cook something fantastic if she had any food in the house—which, having missed her supermarket delivery, she didn't. Long enough to clean and tidy the house if she didn't have to do anything else—which she did. And long enough to make herself look presentable if she could bring herself to care what she looked like—which she couldn't.

Collapsing into her favourite armchair, Luce pulled out her organiser and started her list. The most important thing about the evening was that it go well for Tom. After his break-up with Hattie, and the misery and depression that had followed, he'd not introduced them to a new girlfriend in two years. This was big. This was a turning point. Luce needed to make it as successful as she could. And pray that the turkey she'd yanked out of the freezer the moment she walked in defrosted in time for tomorrow.

Obviously at this stage a gourmet feast was out of the question. Instead Luce raided the corner shop for whatever was left at this point in the Christmas panic buying—

mostly mismatched canapés and mince pies. Halfway to the till she remembered to grab vegetables for the next day. She'd just have to hope she had enough of everything else in to make do.

The house itself wasn't in too bad shape—after flinging everything that didn't belong in the lounge, dining room or kitchen into the bedroom, Luce figured it would serve. Candles and cloth napkins on the table, lamps instead of overhead lights, and they were set to go.

Of course by that point it was seven, and she was still wearing the skirt and jumper she'd travelled home from Brecon in. A shower was out of the question, she supposed, but she'd hoped to at least change and put some make-up on. The ringing doorbell suggested she was out of luck.

'Are you running late?' Dolly asked, looking her up and down as she answered the door.

'However did you guess?' Luce ushered her sister in. 'I just got back a couple of hours ago. You're lucky I'm here at all.'

'Tom's lucky, you mean. I had plans for tonight, you know. This new girl of his had better be worth the effort. Does this mean you didn't have time to make the chocolate pots?'

Luce glared, and Dolly held up her hands in self-defence. 'Okay, okay. Next time. You go and get changed and I'll get us something to drink. Is there wine in the fridge?'

'As always,' Luce called back as she went to try to excavate something from her wardrobe that didn't need dry cleaning.

In the end the best option she had turned out to be the purple dress she'd worn to dinner with Ben in Chester. Luce tugged it on, trying not to notice the way his scent still clung to the fabric. Shoving her feet into low heels and pulling a cardigan over it made it feel a little less dressy—

more suitable for a family occasion. *And it matches the culinary sophistication level better. Or maybe I should put on jeans...*

By the time she'd run a brush through her hair and thrown on the minimum amount of make-up her mother would let her get away with, the doorbell had rung twice and Luce could hear voices in the lounge, along with clinking glasses. 'Showtime,' she whispered to herself, and tried not to wish she was still at the cottage.

Five hours later, as Dolly watched her load the dishwasher while eating the leftovers she was supposed to be putting in the fridge, Luce had to admit it had been worth coming back for. Even with her mum's pointed comments about the food.

'Did you think she seemed nice?' Dolly asked.

Since the others had already left, Luce didn't bother hiding the surprise in her voice. 'I did.'

Dolly laughed. 'I know. I wasn't sure whether to expect another monster, or what. But, no, she's nice. A little bossy, maybe. It'll be weird not having Tom here for Christmas Day, though.'

'It will. But he seemed happy.' That was by far the most important part. Tom hadn't been remotely happy for a very long time.

'He did.'

Dolly paused, and Luce looked up at her, forehead creasing.

'You don't.'

'I'm fine,' Luce lied.

Dolly boosted herself up onto the kitchen counter. 'What happened this week?'

'I went away. To a conference. And ended up taking a bit of a detour home, what with all the snow.'

'And were you alone?' Dolly pressed, eyebrows raised.

'Not entirely.' The memory of Ben kissing her against the castle wall invaded her mind and she bit her lip and tried to concentrate on her little sister, in the here and now.

'I knew it! Who did you go with? Oh, no—it wasn't Dennis, was it? That would explain why you're so miserable.'

'It was *not* Dennis,' Luce said, with feeling. 'Wait—I thought you liked Dennis?'

Dolly rolled her eyes. 'Mum liked Dennis. And only because she thought he was what you wanted. Boring, staid and uneventful. But if you weren't with Dennis…'

'My train got cancelled and an old university friend offered me a lift home. We got stuck in the snow and holed up at a cottage in the hills for a couple of days.' She shrugged. 'That's all.'

But Dolly wasn't content to leave it at that. The same curiosity that drove Luce to discover the past had made her sister incurably nosy about the present. 'And was this friend male or female?'

'Does it matter?'

'Yes!' Dolly bounced down from the counter, her eyes bright and intense. 'If you're finally getting a life I want to know all about it. Hell, I want to throw a party in celebration.'

'It's not… There's nothing to celebrate.' Because she was probably never going to see Ben again.

Dolly's mouth turned down at the corners, her eyes full of sympathy. 'Do you want to—? Ooh, I bet that's him!' she interrupted herself as Luce's phone rang.

'I doubt it— *Oh*.' Ben's name flashed across the screen. Of course he'd have programmed his number in on one of the many occasions when he'd stolen her phone. No respect for personal boundaries, that man.

Dolly had already swept up her coat and bag and was halfway out through the door. 'I'll be along tomorrow for my Christmas dinner,' she said with a wave.

Luce stared at the phone again. And then she pressed 'answer'.

CHAPTER THIRTEEN

IT WENT AGAINST all his usual rules about women and re-
lationships, but Ben needed to talk to someone. And for
some reason the only person he wanted to talk to was Luce.

He sprawled across his bed, waiting for her to answer,
wondering if she would just ignore it. It was late, after all.
Gone midnight. She might be asleep. Or maybe her dinner
party was still going on. Maybe Dennis of the annoying
e-mails was there. Maybe—

'Hello?'

Maybe she would answer after all.

'Hey. Merry Christmas. You okay?'

'Happy Christmas to you, too.' There was a rustle of
fabric on the other end of the phone. Was she in bed? 'I'm
okay. Tired.'

'How did dinner go?' That was what you did, wasn't
it? When you wanted someone to stay in your life even if
just as a friend? You asked about stupid things you didn't
care about.

'You can't tell me that you're suddenly interested in my
family gatherings after all the time you've spent malign-
ing them this week.'

Luce's voice was amused, but Ben could hear a sharper
edge under it. He'd hurt her, even though he'd tried so
hard not to.

'No, not really.' Ben sighed. 'I just don't understand why it was so much more important to you than…everything else.'

'Because you never asked,' Luce responded promptly.

She had a point. Unfortunately, he'd found, she usually did. 'Okay, then, I'm asking. What was so important about this dinner?'

'Hang on,' she said.

Ben heard the click of her phone being put down somewhere. There was more rustling, then she picked up the phone again.

'Were you just getting undressed?' Ben asked, the image waking up his exhausted body instantly.

Luce gave a low laugh. 'It's gone midnight and I am more than ready to be out of this dress. Besides, if we're going to have this conversation I want to be comfortable while we're doing it.'

'What conversation?' The word made Ben nervous. He usually tried to avoid being in any situation with a woman that required him to have a serious conversation.

'The one about my family and why you're so offended by my taking care of them. And don't think I didn't notice that we managed to *not* have this conversation at any point where we couldn't just hang up on each other.'

'Well, we were a little preoccupied at certain points.'

'Ben?'

'Yeah?'

'We are not having phone sex.'

Damn. 'I know that. So—go on. Tell me about this dinner.'

Luce sighed. 'It wasn't just a dinner. It was for my brother Tom. He's had a rough time of it the last few years. Longer, really. But when his marriage broke down a couple of years ago he totally fell apart. And because he was in such a state my mother was beside herself, too. It was just when Dolly was applying to drama schools and, well…'

'You got stuck trying to hold everyone together?'

'Yeah. Anyway, this was the first time since then that Tom's met someone he's wanted to introduce us to. First time he's seemed interested in anything, let alone anyone, since Hattie left him.'

'And you didn't want to risk it not happening?'

'I just… It was a big deal for my family. And he'll be with her tomorrow. This was our only chance to be all together.'

'I get that.' Ben thought about Luce, alone in that big house, trying to make her family happy so that she could finally relax enough to find some happiness herself. 'I guess I just don't get why they're all *your* responsibility.'

'Who else would look after them?'

It was a throwaway comment, Ben knew. Self-deprecating, accepting the inevitable. But could he hear a real question under it? Was she ready to cast off some responsibility?

'Maybe it's time they learned to look after themselves.'

'Maybe.' She didn't sound entirely convinced, but it was a start. 'Did you make your meeting with your brother in the end?'

'I did.' It was the reason he'd called, actually. 'He has some new ideas for the business. A new role he wants me to take on.'

'Sounds interesting.'

'It is.'

'You don't sound sure.'

'It's a lot to take on.'

'A big responsibility.' To her credit, she didn't mock him for that. 'Tell me about it.'

How to explain? 'Well, you have to understand when my dad ran the business it was all about turnover. He bought up a hotel, made it a functional and decent place for businessmen, then moved on to the next one. Over time they became higher and higher end, with more amenities and luxurious surroundings, but the basis was the same. It was somewhere to work.'

'And that's where you grew up?' Luce said, surprising him with the sympathy in her voice. 'That must have been—'

'It was fine,' Ben interrupted. 'I got to travel the country before I was ten and the world before I was twenty. Not many kids had that chance.'

'No, but most kids had a home instead of a hotel.'

She sounded as if she wanted to ask more questions, and Ben really wasn't in the mood to be psychoanalysed, so he moved on quickly.

'Anyway, Seb wants to change the model. He wants us to look at adding more boutique hotels to our chain. Maybe even some family-friendly ones.'

'That sounds great. He wants *you* to run this?'

She sounded surprised, but Ben was too tired to be offended. 'Starting with the Royal Court in Chester.' Ben closed his eyes, remembering Seb saying, *Just because you're good at doing what Dad did, it doesn't mean it's what you have to do. It doesn't always have to be about the quick fix and moving on. I think you'll enjoy the challenge of long-term development more.'*

Was he right? Ben supposed he'd find out soon enough.

'So you're heading back to Chester?' Luce asked.

'Not yet. Got to visit some of our hotels on the continent first. But I should be able to get there in a few weeks.'

'So you'll be away a while?'

'About a month.' Normally the idea of getting away, of waking up in a different city every few days, would be appealing. Especially after an interlude with a woman who was getting too close for comfort. But today…it seemed too long.

There was a lengthy pause, and Ben cast around for something else to say to keep her on the phone. It had been so much easier when they were in the cottage, shut away from the rest of the world. Where he'd had her all to himself without having to share her.

'Should I…?' He took a deep breath and started again. 'Can I call you when I get back?'

Luce's voice was soft as she replied, 'Yes, please.'

Luce was surprised, in a way, at how easily she slipped back into her old life. Her pre-Ben life. There was no reason to be, she supposed. After all, she'd lived without Ben in her life for a lot longer than when he'd been there. But still, those few days at the cottage had been transformative, somehow. She wasn't the same person she'd been before she went. Even if it wasn't obvious in her everyday life.

'What are these files?' Dolly asked, poking at a stack of folders on the dining room table a few weeks later, when she came over to indulge in Luce's tea—and her biscuit tin.

Luce glanced over. 'Just some stuff Dennis wants me to sort through for him.'

Dolly raised her eyebrows. 'And this is more important than your own work because…?'

'It isn't.' Luce swept the files into a box on the nearby dining chair. 'That's why I haven't done them yet.' Besides, Dennis was still sulking about her missing the lecture in Chester. Given the way she'd snapped at him when he whined, he probably wouldn't be asking her to do anything else for him any time soon.

'Good.' Dolly settled herself onto one of the other chairs, tipping it back to rest against the wall behind her. 'You've changed, you know. In a good way,' she added hurriedly. 'But you definitely seem different since you went away last month.'

Luce stopped tidying. 'Do I?'

'Yeah.' Dolly slanted her head to the side and looked her up and down for long enough to make Luce blush. 'Maybe more self-assured, I guess. Which is good.'

'More self-aware, I think.' Luce bit her lip as she considered her sister.

She needed to tell someone her news, and Ben was still away. She'd thought about calling a few times, always late at night when she was tucked up in bed, but she couldn't tell him this over the phone. It wasn't fair. But Dolly... She seemed more of an ally than she ever had before lately. She'd always been the baby, the one who needed the most looking after, but recently she'd been more of a friend than an obligation. Someone who cared about Luce rather than just needing things from her. She could tell Dolly.

'What's going on?' Dolly let her chair tip onto four legs again, leaning forward to rest her wrists on her knees. 'Come on—tell me. It's obviously something big. You're actually blushing.'

Luce's face grew immediately hotter in response. 'Okay. But you can't tell Mum. Or Tom. Or anybody just yet.'

Dolly's eyes widened. 'Now I'm *really* intrigued.'

Gripping the edge of the table, Luce summoned her courage and said it out loud for the first time. 'I'm pregnant.'

For a long moment Dolly just stared at her in silence. Then she clapped her hand over her mouth, not quite muffling the squeak that came out.

Luce sank into a chair. 'I know. I know. It's absurd.'

'It's wonderful!' Jumping up, Dolly wrapped her arms around her, and Luce relaxed into the hug. 'I'm going to be an aunt!'

'You are,' Luce said firmly. She'd considered the other options—of course she had. But this was her baby— hers and Ben's—and it might be her only chance. She was financially capable of looking after it, she had her family around her...

'God, how the hell are you going to baby-proof this place?' Dolly asked, looking around.

...and she lived in a death trap.

'That's on my list of things to figure out,' Luce said. 'To be honest, given the length of the list, it might take me a while to get around to it.'

Dolly perched on the table beside her, looking down through her long dark hair. 'Okay, I'm not asking the obvious question, because I figure you'll tell me when it's right. But just promise me it's not Dennis's.'

Luce laughed. 'Trust me. The father is about as far from Dennis as you can imagine.'

'In that case, I really want to meet him,' Dolly said. 'I take it it's the old university friend, then? The one you got snowed in with?'

Luce nodded. 'That's him.'

'Funny...I didn't even know you were still in touch with any of your friends from then.'

'You mean, you didn't know I had any in the first place.' She hadn't, really. Mandy had been her housemate, but had only been friendly when it suited her.

'That, too.'

'We weren't...close then.' Understatement of the year.

Dolly nudged her with her shoulder. 'You obviously are now. Have you told him?'

God, how had things changed so that Dolly was the one asking sensible questions? Luce had imagined this conversation the other way round all through Dolly's teenage years. 'Not yet. He's away on business. I don't want to tell him over the phone.'

'Fair enough. How do you think he'll react?'

Luce thought of Ben recounting his life rules over dinner in Chester, his explanation of the one-night rule, and said, 'Badly.'

Really, who wouldn't? Yes, he'd asked if he could call her when he got back from his business trip, but that wasn't the same as having a lifetime tie to another person and the responsibility of a baby thrust upon him. Of course he was going to react badly. It was what he did next, once he'd calmed down, that mattered. How would he try to fix her life this time? Because if his answer was to throw money at the problem, rather than time or love, she was done with Ben Hampton.

'Then he's an idiot. Clearly having you in his life would be the best thing to ever happen to him.'

Luce looked up, astonished. 'Thank you.'

'And, anyway, it doesn't matter what he says. Auntie Dolly will be here to make things brilliant every step of the way.'

To her surprise, Luce found that made her feel a whole lot better.

Ben stared up at the building of the Royal Court Hotel, the February wind whipping down the cobbled streets and through his coat. How the hell was he going to look at this place objectively, think about changing anything, without thinking about Luce? Hell, she was all he'd thought of for over a month. In every Hampton & Sons hotel he'd visited there'd been something to remind him of her. A bedspread or a cushion in the same soft fabric she loved. A gin and tonic at the bar. Shining dark hair glimpsed across a room. She was haunting him, and he couldn't even figure out why. Was it because he'd left her as broken as he'd found her? Maybe more so? Or was it as simple as a bruised ego? He'd offered to break his rules for her and she'd turned him down.

He'd considered finding someone else—someone to prove the validity of his one-night rule—but none of the women he'd met seemed to appeal. Nothing did. Not the New Year's Eve party he'd found himself at in New York, nor the cutting-edge restaurant in Sydney. And as the jobs dragged on and delays crept in all he wanted was to be back in his cottage. With Luce.

He'd even thought about calling, asking her to join him, but he couldn't bear to hear her say that she couldn't leave her family, her job, whatever else it was that mattered more than he did.

The woman might think she wanted to settle down, find true love, but until she cut those ties—or at least slackened them a little—no man stood a chance.

Besides, it wasn't as if *he* was looking to settle down anyway. His job—his life—still involved travelling the world, getting out there, and what woman would put up with that long-term?

She could come with me. Write on the road... Except she wouldn't. And so he wouldn't ask. Even if the thought of waking up next to Luce Myles every morning was incredibly tempting.

Shivering, Ben pushed open the door at last, and memories made him grit his teeth at the sight of the lobby. The desk where he'd first seen her. The bar where he'd stolen her diary. And, upstairs, the suite where she'd taken that long, long bath. God, knowing what he knew now, he wished he'd just walked in on her then. All that time wasted...hours and hours when he could have had her in his arms and hadn't.

And even more of them ahead.

'Mr Hampton!'

The blonde behind the reception desk beamed at him and Ben tried desperately to remember her name.

'It's so wonderful to have you back so soon.'

Which meant that the entire hotel staff were panicking about why he needed a repeat visit, and wondering if it was a sign that their jobs were in danger. *Great.* 'It's lovely to be back...'

'Daisy.'

'Daisy. Right.' Ben rubbed a hand over his aching forehead. 'Sorry—long flight.'

A look of carefully schooled concern settled onto her face. 'Why don't we get you checked in, then, sir? I've put aside the King James Suite for you again, if that's okay?'

'Wonderful,' Ben said, taking the key. Not a chance in hell of getting any sleep there without Luce beside him. *Great.*

Even the walk to the lift was full of memories. Ben distracted himself by watching the other guests instead, trying to observe them in a professional manner, figure out their wants and needs and how the hotel could meet them.

The businessmen by the bar were easy; Ben's father had known exactly what they needed. A comfortable room, with a desk or table to work at, all-night concierge and room service, meeting rooms and wireless internet access, a business centre with photocopiers and fax machines, and admin assistants they could hire by the hour. A well-stocked bar and well-served restaurant. All done. The Royal Court had them covered. Of course so did every other business hotel in every city.

But what about the couple canoodling by the pot plant? What did they want?

Well, if they were anything like him and Luce…privacy, a sturdy bed, champagne in the mini-bar, a big, deep bath. Maybe a romantic restaurant for dinner, breakfast from room service. Nothing unusual. And, honestly, the couple by the plant were so wrapped up in each other that it didn't look as if it mattered where they were, as long as they had each other.

Which just left him wondering why he and Luce had never managed that. Which was depressing. Time to move on.

But the family waiting by the lift, with two huge suitcases and a small boy with an oversized rucksack… They didn't look happy.

The father was in a suit, tie knotted tightly, jacket still on, briefcase in hand. This wasn't a man who'd left work and gone straight on holiday with his family. This was a man who was still working. And, from the frown creasing his wife's forehead, she wasn't too happy about it. The boy just looked miserable.

Ben knew that look. That was the *another day, another hotel* look. The *will I get to see my dad between meetings?* look. The *did I bring enough books to read?* look. That boy knew his family weekend was going to be spent watching his parents arguing, then his mother putting on a brave face while his father disappeared to yet more meetings.

Ben had been that boy. And Ben knew what would happen when the mother couldn't take any more.

He couldn't change another family's future—couldn't explain to every father dragging his wife and kids to business hotel after business hotel instead of actually taking a holiday what could happen and how it felt. But maybe he could make it a little more fun for the families waiting for their husbands, wives, mothers or fathers to finish their meetings.

Pulling his mobile from his pocket, he called his brother. 'Seb? That new style of hotel you wanted? I've got an idea.'

CHAPTER FOURTEEN

IT HAD BEEN eight weeks. He'd said he'd be away for a month, and now it was nearly two. Luce dropped her bag by the front door and collapsed onto the sofa, preparing herself for another evening of not hearing from Ben.

Damn him.

She should have known better than to believe him when he said he'd call. Hadn't he made it perfectly clear what they were? One night only. He wasn't going to call again.

But eventually she'd have to call him. He deserved to know.

Her head ached, her body was exhausted, and constant low-level nausea left her weak and miserable—and, damn it, she wanted to tell him! Wanted the secret off her shoulders. Wanted to share it with someone else.

Dolly knew, of course, and had been more wonderful than Luce had imagined possible. Her little sister had grown up unexpectedly, and Luce loved seeing this new, responsible side to her. Having her onside made things bearable. But soon she would have to tell other people—her boss, her mother, Tom. God, she'd even have to tell Dennis eventually. But Ben had to know first.

She'd have to call him. If he wasn't back soon she'd have to tell him over the phone. Except then she wouldn't be able to see his face, his reaction, the truth about how he felt.

She'd imagined it a dozen different ways. Sometimes, if she was feeling excessively romantic, he fell down on one knee and proposed instantly. Most of the time he looked shocked, stunned and slightly horrified. That was okay. She expected that. But sometimes, after that, her imagination had him take her in his arms and tell her they'd figure it out together. And sometimes it had him walk out without looking back.

She'd cope, whatever his reaction—she knew that. She just needed to know what it was. If he wanted to be involved in his child's life or not. Then she could start making plans. Until then…this horrible limbo persisted.

Time to move the action back into her own hands. *Take responsibility. Take control.* 'If he doesn't call tonight I'll phone him.'

'You've been saying that for weeks,' Dolly said from the door.

Sad, but true. 'Yeah, but now I'm desperate. I'll do it.'

Dolly sighed, shut the front door behind her and came to sit on the sofa, lifting Luce's feet to rest them on her lap.

'Has it occurred to you that you might be better off without him? I mean, he's basically disappeared off the face of the earth for two months now, Luce.'

'I know. And it has.' Luce sighed. 'Chances are he'll run like the wind when I tell him anyway. But he needs to know. And *I* need to know.'

'This is all because you can't write your "To Do" list before you tell him, isn't it?'

Luce chuckled. 'Partly.'

Dolly tilted her head to look at her. 'Are you in love with him?'

Rolling her eyes, Luce gave her sister a shove to the shoulder. 'You've asked the same question every day for two months now. What on earth makes you think my answer might have changed? No, I'm not in love with him. But he's the father of my child, and the responsible thing is to let him know that and have a conversation about whether he wants to be involved. That's all.'

Dolly's smile was sad. 'I think you're getting less convincing every time you say that. Come on—I'll make us some tea.'

The worst thing was Dolly was right. As ridiculous as Luce knew it was to have fallen in love with someone based on three days in a cottage in the middle of nowhere, she was starting to be very afraid that was what had happened.

She missed him. More than she'd thought she possibly could. When he'd called that first night she'd hoped that maybe they'd speak again while he was away. Then, when he hadn't called, she'd been grateful for a while—after she took the pregnancy test and realised she had to tell him in person. She hadn't been sure she could keep it from him if they spoke.

But now? Now she just ached to see him. She fell asleep wishing she had his arms around her and woke up missing his morning kisses and the way, the one morning they'd woken up together, the first thing he'd done was pull her closer, kissing her neck. She missed the way he told her she had to stop working sometimes, to relax and have fun.

And she really wished he was around to help her figure out what to do about Tom.

Dolly brought the tea tray back to the coffee table: thick slices of ginger cake on a plate next to the teapot, milk jug and cups. 'I picked this up from the deli down the road. They said the ginger should be good for nausea.'

'Smells wonderful.' Luce picked up her plate and took a slice. Still warm.

Once she'd poured the tea Dolly settled into the armchair on the other side of the armchair. 'Okay. Now that you're fed and watered we need to talk.'

'Look, Doll, I'm going to tell him. But—'

Dolly put up a hand to stop her. 'Not about that, for once. We need to talk about Tom.'

Luce sank back against the cushions and ate some more cake. 'I know we do. I just—'

'Don't want to. I understand.' Dolly took a deep breath. 'I think you need to tell him about the pregnancy.'

'How on earth would *that* help?'

'He's talking to Mum about how he and Vanessa should have the house. Since she's got kids already and they need the space.'

Luce blinked. 'But it's *my* house. Grandad left it to me. And besides, they've been together—what?—three months? And they're already talking about shacking up in *my* home with *her* kids?' Luce could hear her voice getting higher and squeakier as she talked, but she couldn't seem to stop herself.

'Okay, you need to calm down. Think of the baby.'

Luce rolled her eyes, but settled back obediently against the cushions. 'As if I think about anything else.' Except the baby's father.

'Look, I don't know if he's just testing the waters, or what. But Mum's so happy to see him settled with someone that I think she'll go for anything that keeps him that way.'

'But it's my house,' Luce repeated, calmer this time.

'I know. But you've always given in to them before. To me, too.'

'You make it sound like I'm a doormat.'

'It's not that. It's just that you're always working so damn hard to make sure we're all happy and okay.'

'And that's a bad thing?'

'Not in itself, no. But Mum and Tom…they expect it now. They can't imagine it any other way.'

Everything Ben had ever said about giving in to her family, about giving up her life for them, came back in a rush. He was right. He'd been right all along. This was her life, and she needed to live it for herself. And she'd have someone else even more important to live it for when the baby came. She'd have her own little family to be responsible for. She couldn't let her mother and brother run her life any more.

'You honestly think they expect me to give up the house?'

Dolly shrugged. 'Mum and Tom both treat this place like it's theirs anyway, when it's convenient.'

'Not when the roof almost caved in or the stairs needed replacing.' Funny how they'd been nowhere to be seen when she'd needed money or time to help fix the place up.

'Exactly.'

'Exactly…what?'

'They have no idea what they'd be taking on. But Tom's so used to you doing whatever he needs I don't think it's crossed his mind that you won't just happily move out into some little flat somewhere while he moves his instant family in here.'

'That's crazy!'

'Luce…' Dolly put her cup and saucer back on the tray, and leant forwards. 'You've never said no to him before. No one has—except Hattie, and look what happened then.'

'So you're saying I should give him my house to avoid his mental breakdown?'

'Hell, no!' Dolly shook her head violently, her long dark hair flying across her face. 'I'm saying it's time you *did* say no. Unless you want to get the hell out of this crumbling museum before the baby comes. In which case, make him buy it from you.'

Luce looked around her at the antique furniture, the threadbare rugs and the splintering floorboards. Yes, the place was falling apart. But it was her home—would be her baby's home. It was all she had left of her grandfather. He'd left it to *her*, not to Tom or Dolly or their mother, and he'd done that for a reason.

No way in hell she was parting with it.

'No. It's my home. I'm staying.'

'Fine. Then we need to make that clear to Tom. And then we need to go and buy some yellow paint for the nursery.'

Dolly clapped her hands together with excitement. Luce wasn't sure whether it was the painting or the standing up to Tom that was filling her with glee. It didn't matter.

'There's something else I need to do first,' she said. 'I need to tell Ben.'

Ben was wrestling with the hotel key card when his phone rang. As the door fell open he dropped his suitcase and put the phone to his ear.

'How did it go?' Seb asked.

Ben kicked the door shut behind him. 'It went well, I think.' Meetings with investors were usually Seb's domain, but he'd insisted Ben take this one. It was his baby, after all.

'Good. Full debrief when I get there tomorrow? I got Sandra to book us a meeting room.'

'Sure. Just need to get some sleep first.'

Seb laughed. 'Welcome to the world of real work, brother.'

The cell was cut off as Seb hung up, and Ben tossed the phone onto the coffee table. There was truth in Seb's words. This was *real* work—trying to expand and transform a hotel chain that had been stuck in one mindset for too long. It was work Ben would never have been allowed to do while their father was alive—work he hadn't even known he wanted to do until Seb had suggested it to him.

But now? He was good at this. Better than he'd used to be. Because he cared about making these hotels right for their guests. Not just the businessmen or the couples. He wanted a chain of boutique hotels that felt like a home away from home for the families that stayed in them. That made the kids feel safe and happy—not scared of another sterile white room with a too-big bed. Not a free-for-all family hotel with everything in red plastic either, though. This was a hotel for grown-ups, too. It just didn't exclude or alienate children.

He had a plan, and he had convinced the backers, but he had a hell of a lot of work ahead of him.

But first he needed to sleep.

The phone rang again before he could make it to the bedroom. He intended to ignore it until he saw the name flashing across the screen.

Luce.

Snatching the phone up, he said, 'Hey, I was going to ring you. I just got back into the country and I'm in Cardiff for a few days.' He didn't mention that he'd scheduled this particular leg of the trip in the hope of getting to see her.

'That's lucky,' she said, her voice warm and familiar. 'I really need to talk to you.'

'Okay. Want to do it over the phone? Or meet me for lunch tomorrow?'

'Um…neither. Look, could I come over? Where are you staying?'

Ben felt ready to drop. His eyes itched with grit and his very bones ached with tiredness. But the thought of Luce in his arms again… 'Of course. I'd love to see you.'

There was a sigh of relief at the other end and Ben felt the first pang of concern at the sound. What did she want to talk about, anyway? He *had* hoped whatever it was was an excuse—just a reason to see him. He'd have to wait and see, he thought as he rattled off the hotel's details for Luce. She'd be here soon enough, and he really needed to shower first.

He barely made it. The knock on the door came as he towelled off his hair. Pulling a tee shirt over his head, he padded barefoot to the door in the comfiest jeans he'd packed and hoped Luce wouldn't be too disappointed if he wasn't up to hours of bedtime fun tonight.

When he opened the door he stopped worrying about that and started worrying about her instead. Her hair was scraped back from her face and he could clearly see the redness around her eyes, the puffiness of her skin.

'Are you okay? You look dreadful.' He ushered her in, keeping an arm around her shoulders as he guided her to the sofa.

Luce gave a watery chuckle. 'Just what every girl likes to hear.'

'Sorry. But…what's happened?'

'God—everything.' She sighed. 'Um…my brother Tom.'

'The one you rushed back to cook a dinner for?' Ben tried to keep the censure from his voice. He wasn't sure he was entirely successful, though.

'Yeah, that was… I shouldn't have. I know that now.'

Ben blinked at the unexpected victory. Except if she'd changed her mind *that* thoroughly… 'What did he do?'

'He wants my house.'

'What?'

Luce rubbed at her eyes. 'He and his new partner want to move in together, with her two kids, and Tom thinks it's only fair that *they* get the family house, since there's more of them.'

'That's crazy. It's your home.'

'That's what I'm going to tell him. And...'

She trailed off, and Ben felt fear clutch at his insides. What else had her brother done? 'Go on. Tell me.'

Luce looked up at him, holding his gaze with her own. Her eyes still looked tired and watery, but they were clear as she said, 'I need to tell him I'm pregnant. But I couldn't do that until I'd told you. That's why I wanted to see you tonight.'

'You need to tell him... Wait—what?' The world seemed to have gone fuzzy. Luce's voice was buzzing in his ear, making it impossible to make out the words. 'But... What?'

'I'm pregnant.' The words cut through the haze of confusion, clear as a bell, but still Ben couldn't make sense of them.

'Pregnant?' he repeated numbly.

'Yeah. I know we used protection, but that first time...'

'I was too desperate for you.' Stumbling to his feet, Ben moved to lean against the back of the sofa, hands braced against the edge, staring down at the cream leather. 'God, this is just...'

'I know it's not what either of us planned,' Luce said from behind him.

She sounded brave, calm—but then, she'd had more time to figure all this out, hadn't she? How long had she known? Long enough to make a twenty-five-point plan for dealing with it, he was sure. Whereas here he was, half-asleep and dead on his feet, trying to get his mind around the idea that in seven months he would be a *father*.

God, how could he be? When he'd just promised Seb he'd take on the whole new business? He couldn't drag Luce and a baby from hotel to hotel with him, like his father had. He'd lose them in a heartbeat. And Luce would never trail around after him while he worked anyway. She had her own career, and her own family tying her to Cardiff. He wasn't foolish enough to think she'd give those up for a man she barely knew and had spent just a few days with, even if she was mad at her brother right now.

So what did that leave?

Luce touched him on the shoulder and he flinched in surprise, spinning round to see her watching him with wide eyes. 'Look, I know this is a surprise—'

'Surprise?' Ben shook his head. 'It's a shock. A disaster.'

Her face hardened at that, and he wanted to take it back, but it was the truth, after all. What was he going to *do*?

'Okay. Fine. I just wanted you to know so you could decide what involvement you want in your child's life. Obviously the answer to that is clear. So I'll just—'

'Wait. No. I just… I need a little time here, Luce.'

She nodded. 'That's understandable. Why don't I meet you for lunch, later in the week, and we can talk? Come up with a plan?'

'No! I don't want you to go. And I don't want to come up with a plan! This is our whole lives being turned upside down. A "To Do" list isn't going to fix that.'

'It's a start.'

'It's an end. It's giving up on any other options.'

Her face turned stony. 'Options?'

Ben stared at her, his eyes widening when he realised what she thought he meant. 'Not that. No, never that. I just… I don't know how we could make this work right now. The business… There's a lot going on right now, and Seb needs me to do it…'

Luce took a step back, her mouth twisted in a cruel smile. 'So now your work matters to you? Right.'

'There's a new project,' Ben started, but it sounded weak even to his own ears.

How could he explain to her again, in a way she'd understand, that he couldn't be the man his father had been? He couldn't lose her and his child that way, have them hating him for never being there. But he still had too much to do. He couldn't give up his dreams for a life in an office, nine to five, never going anywhere or seeing anything. Where would they even live? A never-ending series of hotel rooms would be terrible for a child, despite the new project, and by all accounts her house was falling apart. They didn't even have a home—how could they be a family?

'I just need some time, Luce.'

She shook her head. 'No. You've made your priorities very clear, thanks. I can do this on my own. I have my family to help me.'

'Would that be the same family that's trying to take your home away from you? And how the hell are you going to look after a baby in that place anyway?'

'What? You think we'd be better off here?'

She glanced around her and Ben knew she was taking in the sharp corners and sterile white and metal furnishings. Nothing like the cottage at all.

'I think you'd be better off with me.'

'Living out of hotel rooms? Never settling down? Isn't that what you said you'd *never* do to a child?' The words stung as she bit them out. 'Or will it be you, gone for months on end, sleeping with every woman who smiles at you in a hotel bar? No, thanks. A family takes more than a one-night rule, Ben.'

He swallowed back an angry denial, not least because he knew everything she said was true. His father hadn't been able to do it, and Seb wasn't even trying, for all his talk. Ben wasn't content to be one of those once-a-month visiting dads. So maybe Luce was right. Maybe there was no place for him at all.

'I can help. Financially.'

She threw him a scathing look. 'I don't want it,' she said.

Ben heard, *I don't want you.*

'Money isn't going to give you a quick fix this time.'

Why was he even surprised? he wondered as Luce walked out, slamming the door behind her. He'd never expected his father to love him more than his work, or his mother to love him more than her freedom. He certainly couldn't expect Luce to love him more than her child.

Their child.

'Hell,' he whispered, and went to pour himself a very large whisky from the mini-bar.

CHAPTER FIFTEEN

LUCE REFUSED TO CRY.

She stayed resolutely dry-eyed while flagging down a taxi. She remained calm as they drove through the dark Cardiff streets and as she paid the driver. She didn't even give in while she fumbled with the keys to get into her house.

But at the sight of Dolly, asleep on her sofa with a blanket over her knees, having obviously failed in waiting up for her to get home, Luce fell apart and sobbed.

Dolly awoke with a start, jerking upright and tossing back the blanket even as she stumbled to her feet. 'What happened?' she asked, her voice bleary.

Luce shook her head and pulled Dolly down to sit on the sofa with her. 'I can't... Just...don't ask, please.'

'Idiot,' Dolly whispered. 'Tell me he wasn't more of an idiot than Tom?'

'It's a toss-up.'

'Useless. All of them. We should run away to some women's commune and raise her there.'

'It might be a boy.'

'Doesn't matter. We'll dress him in skirts.' Dolly shook her head. 'Except then Tom would just steal the house while we were gone, and that's no good. So we'll stay here.'

'We?' Luce blinked up at her sister

Dolly took a deep breath. 'I thought I could move in and help you. If you want me. And not at all in a house-stealing sibling way. Because you already have one of those. I know I haven't always been much help in the past, but I think it might be time for me to grow up and take care of myself.'

Luce tilted her head to look at her sister. 'You *have* grown up. I don't know what changed.'

Dolly shook her head. 'Doesn't matter. The only thing that does is that I want to be here to help you with the baby. To look after you for a change.'

'That would be wonderful.' Relief started to seep into her chest. She didn't have to do this alone. Even if Ben wasn't there she still had Dolly.

'And besides, I thought the rent money might help you with doing this place up a bit. Making it safe for the baby.'

Luce stared at her. 'You don't have to pay rent. You're still my baby sister.'

'And I'm a grown-up now, remember? I can pay my own way.' Dolly smiled a lopsided smile. 'Maybe we can help look after each other. Because it seems to me that there's going to be someone soon who needs your love and care a lot more than me or Tom or Mum.'

'Especially if I'm the only parent it's got.' Luce slumped back against the arm of the sofa.

'Idiot,' Dolly muttered again. 'But it doesn't matter. You'll be the best mum any child could hope for. And I'll be the coolest auntie.'

'Of course.'

There was a pause, then Dolly asked, 'What did he say?'

'He's got a lot of work on at the moment. He offered me money.' That was a reasonable summary, Luce felt.

'How dare he!' Dolly's voice grew ever more vehement.

'The thing is, he's not a bad man. He…he looked shell-shocked at the whole thing. Trapped. Like he couldn't see a way out.'

Dolly shook her head. 'Doesn't matter. He should have manned up and supported you.'

'Yeah, I know.' Luce twisted her hands in the blanket. He should have. Of course he should. And she couldn't quite believe that he hadn't.

'But…?'

Luce looked up at her sister. 'The thing is, I think I might be a little bit in love with him.'

Dolly laughed and pulled her into a hug, her arms warm and comforting around her. 'Oh, Luce. Of course you are. I've known that for weeks.'

'Then how come I only just figured it out?'

'Because you were too busy trying to come up with a sensible plan for all this. Except love isn't sensible, and it can't be planned.'

'Is that why you fall in love so often? Because you're not sensible and can't be planned either?'

'Exactly.'

How had her baby sister grown up so smart? Luce laid her head against Dolly's shoulder and stared out into the darkened room. She knew where every stick of furniture was, exactly where each painting hung on the wall. They'd been there her whole life, after all. 'What do I do now, Doll?'

'You just take each day as it comes. It gets easier, I promise. And I'll help you.'

Luce nodded. Time to try life without a 'To Do' list for a while.

Ben woke feeling jet-lagged and hung-over, and cursed his alarm clock before he'd even opened his eyes. A headache pounded behind his temples, beating a rhythm that sounded like a door slamming over and over again. Still, he had work to do. And since, after last night, work was all he had, he supposed he'd better make the most of it.

Dragging himself out of bed, into the shower and then into a suit took twice as long as normal. He skipped breakfast, his stomach rebelling at the idea. How much had he drunk after Luce had left? The mini-bar looked suspiciously empty.

Seb was waiting for him in the meeting room and raised his eyebrows at the sight of him. 'Jet-lag?' he asked, pouring Ben a coffee.

Ben dropped into an empty chair and pulled the saucer closer. 'Amongst other things.'

'Thought you'd be immune to that by now.'

'Twelve time zones in eight weeks is hard on anyone's body.' Which was true. It just wasn't why Ben felt so awful.

Seb tilted his head, looking sympathetic. 'You need some time off?'

Ben shook his head. 'I need to work.'

'Why?' Seb's brow furrowed. 'What's going on, Ben? You've been different lately. First your trip away with your "university friend" then a sudden desire to revamp our hotels for the family market. Anything you need to tell me?'

'She's pregnant,' Ben said, his voice flat.

Seb's eyebrows shot up. 'Really? Well, that explains a lot. When did you find out?'

'Last night.'

'Oh. So the hotel thing was…?'

'Coincidental. I hadn't seen her since we came back from the cottage. She stopped by last night and told me. I…reacted badly.'

'You were exhausted last night, Ben. I'm sure if you call her, talk to her…'

'No. She's right. It's better that I'm not a part of the baby's life.'

'She said that?' Seb shook his head. 'That can't possibly be true.'

Ben shrugged. 'What could I give a child? I have no idea how to be a father, my job means travelling pretty much all of the time, and I won't force a kid to come along with me like Dad did. This is something I can't fix. She told me as much.'

'You mean you won't try.' Seb's tone was flat. Disappointed.

Ben glared up at him. 'You don't think I would if I could?'

'I think you're scared. I think you've got so used to swooping in and solving a crisis before retiring victorious you've forgotten that some things take more than that. Some things are worth more than that. More than just throwing money at a problem, or hiring and firing people.'

'That's my *job*,' Ben snapped.

'Yeah, and this is your life. Your future. It deserves more than a quick fix. Your child deserves more.' Seb stared until Ben flinched. 'You need to decide right now that you're in this for the long haul.'

The long haul. For ever.

With Luce.

After the last couple of months of being miserable without her, how could he give that up without a fight?

Ben swallowed. 'Okay. Say I'm in. What the hell do I do? She still thinks I'm the same person I was at university, with no sense of responsibility. She thinks I've never grown up.'

'Then maybe it's time to prove her wrong,' Seb suggested.

Ben blinked at his brother. 'What do you mean?'

Seb got to his feet, coming round to lean against the front of the conference table, next to Ben's chair. Ben appreciated the gesture. It made it easier to remember that Seb was his brother, not just his boss, and definitely not their father all over again. Brothers. That was good.

'You're not that kid any more. I remember you at university. You're miles away from that now. You work hard, you value your friends, you want to make a home—'

'Where did you get that one from?' Ben asked with a laugh. 'I live in hotel rooms.'

'Maybe. But I've heard you talk about your cottage. About your plans for the château. What are they, if not homes?'

An image of Luce, leaning against the kitchen counter in the cottage while he cooked, flashed into his mind. Then one of her curled up on the sofa with a book and a blanket. Working at the desk. Sprawled across his bed, smiling at him, waiting for him to join her.

The buildings weren't home. Whatever he did to them, however he filled them, they couldn't be—not on their own.

They needed Luce there. *Luce* was home. Luce and their child.

'Oh, God,' he said, collapsing back in his chair. 'I'm in love with her.'

'Well, I thought that was obvious,' Seb said. 'Now, what do you want to do about it?'

'What *can* I do? She thinks I'm an idiot, and I still can't imagine how I could have a family right now.'

Seb picked up the phone. 'Business Services? Could you get us some more coffee in here, please? And we're going to need the room a little longer than anticipated. We need to have an important planning meeting. Right now.'

'Do you want me to send in some pastries, too?' came the muffled reply.

'Definitely,' Seb said, looking at Ben. 'Now, come on. Let's find a way to make this work.'

'I can help with that, you know,' Luce called up the stairs, behind the struggling Dolly and her suitcase. 'I'm pregnant. Not an invalid.'

'You're trying to save me again,' Dolly yelled back.

'No, I'm not. I'm...' But Dolly had already reached the top of the stairs and disappeared into her new bedroom. Since she wasn't allowed to help with any of the fetching and carrying, Luce decided to go and make tea instead. At least that was useful.

As she entered the kitchen her phone rang, as if it had known she was coming. Luce stared at it, sitting on the counter, with Ben's name scrolling across the screen. Just the sight of those three letters made her heart clench. She'd need to talk to him eventually, she knew. Give him another chance for some sort of involvement—with the baby, not her. She was all set without him, thank you. She had her own not-a-plan and she was sticking to it. Just her, Dolly and the baby.

Ben had been right about one thing—even if he was wrong about almost everything else. She needed priorities and she needed to stick to them. And for the foreseeable future her priority was her child, and staying healthy and stress-free so she could look after them.

Neither Ben nor her brother were conducive to that.

The phone stopped ringing and Luce went to put the kettle on. She'd talk to him soon. Just not yet.

'Anyone home?'

Luce's shoulders tensed at the sound of Tom's voice. She hadn't heard his key in the lock, but maybe Dolly had left the door open while she was dragging in her assorted bags and boxes.

'In the kitchen,' she called back, and schooled her face, ready for the showdown.

'Oh, good. I'd murder a cup of tea,' said Tabitha.

Luce bit her lip. She hadn't expected Mum, too. Oh, well, maybe it was best to get it all over with in one go, anyway.

'I'll make a pot,' Luce said. Maybe she could busy herself with the teacups and cake until Dolly came down. Moral support was always appreciated.

'I think that's the last of it,' Dolly said as she entered the kitchen. 'And just in time, too. Hi, Mum. Tom.'

Luce placed the tea tray on the kitchen table. 'Help yourselves,' she said, and settled into the chair at the head of the table.

'Now, Lucinda,' Tabitha said, taking a tiny sliver of cake. 'We wanted to talk to you about Tom's idea. He says you dismissed it rather out of hand, but I don't think you can have listened to all the details. He's put a lot of thought into this, you know.'

'He wants to live in my house with his new girlfriend and her children,' Luce summarised.

'Well, yes. But we thought that you could have Tom's flat in exchange! Wouldn't that be nice? This house is far too big with just you rattling around in it, anyway.'

'Tom's flat is rented,' Luce pointed out. Best to address all the problems with Tabitha's statement in turn, she decided.

'Well, yes, but the rent's very affordable for you on your salary. And, after all, you've been able to live here rent-free for the last few years. Isn't it time Tom had the same opportunity?'

Luce blinked and looked over at Dolly, who appeared

equally baffled by their mother's attempt at reasonable argument.

'She's lived here rent-free because it's *her* house,' Dolly said.

'Only because Grandad left it to her,' Tom put in. 'But it's always been the family house, hasn't it? Luce always says it belongs to all of us, really.'

'Except for the part where it's *her* house. Grandad left you other stuff. And me.'

Dolly's voice grew louder. Her grasp on staying restrained and reasonable wasn't going to last long, Luce suspected.

'Not a house, though,' Tom said, his tone perfectly reasonable.

Luce frowned. 'Is that what this is really about? You're jealous because Grandad left me more valuable property than you?'

Tom straightened his back and stared at her. 'It's not about jealousy. It's about fairness. I need the house more than you, that's all. We're a family. We share.'

The really scary part, Luce thought, was that he truly believed this was a reasonable demand. She'd spent her entire life giving and giving to these people, and now they couldn't imagine that there might be something she wasn't willing to hand over to them.

But Dolly had grown up, grown out of that dependence. She'd changed when Luce had never really believed it was possible.

And that meant Tom could, too.

'Do you know why he left it to me?' Luce asked, mildly. Tom shook his head.

'He left me a note in the will explaining. He said, *"You're going to spend the rest of your life looking after the lot of them, because God knows they can't do it them-*

selves. Think of this as your salary." And I think I've more than earned it over the last few years.'

Tom stared at her, his eyes wide and disbelieving, and Luce squashed down a pang of guilt. She needed to do this. For all their sakes.

'Sounds fair to me,' Dolly said gleefully. 'And that's another reason I have no problem paying you rent.'

'Rent?' Tabitha said, faintly.

'Yep. I'm moving in with Luce. Figure that the rent I pay can help her fix up this place. Trust me, Tom, you wouldn't want the house if you'd seen the damp in the attic.'

Tom finally found his voice. 'But I told Vanessa we could—'

'Well, you shouldn't have,' Luce interjected. 'This is my place, Tom. And while you, and Mum—and Vanessa, if she sticks around—are always welcome here, this is *my* house, *my* home. And I'm afraid all of you are going to have to get better at looking after yourselves. I'm going to have bigger concerns for the next decade or two.'

'Like what?' Tom asked.

'Like my own family. I'm pregnant.'

'You're...? Well... That's lovely, darling, I'm sure.' Tabitha's brows were furrowed, as if she were missing some vital part of the conversation.

Luce wondered if hearing what Grandad had really thought of her had sent Tabitha even further into her own world, reliving past events with new eyes. She was sure her mother would catch up later and demand answers and information. But for now Luce was glad of the respite.

Tom, however, had no such reserve.

'Pregnant! You can't be. Who's the father? Or is this some desperate attempt to find love from a child instead of actually falling in love? Some "must start a family by the age of thirty" plan?'

Anger bubbled in Luce's stomach, acid and biting. She'd known Tom wouldn't take the change in the status quo well, but to hear such words from her own brother—the brother she'd tried so hard to look after and protect—it made her heart ache. And told her it was past time to cut him off. Fighting to keep her voice even she said, 'That's none of your business. Now, get out of my house.'

'I thought we were always welcome here?' Tom said, sneering.

'Not when you talk to her like that, you're not,' Dolly said, grabbing his arm. 'Come on—time to go. Mum, I think you might be better off at home this afternoon, too. We'll see you soon.'

Luce collapsed back in her chair as she heard Dolly bundle their relatives out of the house. Reaching for a piece of ginger cake, she said, 'I can't believe I just kicked them out.'

'I can't believe it took you this long,' Dolly said cheerfully as she sat down and helped herself to her own slice. 'Buck up, sis. You know they'll be back. Tom will calm down and beg for forgiveness, then pretend he never said that stuff. But they need to stand on their own four feet for a while. You did the right thing. And besides, you still have me!'

'Yes, I do,' Luce said. 'And everyone needs an adoring sister to run them a bubble bath from time to time…'

Dolly rolled her eyes. '*Another* bath? Really? Okay. But only because you're pregnant. This stuff stops once the baby's here.'

'That's okay. You can bath the baby then, instead.'

Dolly laughed as she headed off to the bathroom, and Luce thought that maybe, just maybe, things would be okay after all. Not great, perhaps. They couldn't be—not without Ben. But she'd be okay. And that was enough for now.

* * *

Just one more try. Ben stared at the phone in his hand for a minute before taking a deep breath and pressing 'call'. Just because she'd ignored his last four phone calls, that didn't mean she'd definitely ignore this one, did it?

Still, as the phone rang and rang, Ben started to have his doubts.

'Hello?'

'Luce?' The voice didn't sound quite right, but international phone lines did that sometimes.

'No, it's Dolly.' The sister. *Great.* 'You must be the "old university friend".'

'Ben Hampton. Is Luce there?'

'She's in the bath. In there all the time now she's pregnant.'

'She was bad enough before.' Ben took a breath, and took a chance. 'Look, I know she's avoiding my calls. I was…'

'An idiot?'

'Last time we spoke. Yes. But I was jet-lagged and exhausted—and stupid, mostly. I've had a chance to let the news sink in, and I'm ready to make it up to her.' Ready to make her the centre of his world if she'd let him.

'Convince me,' Dolly said, her voice firm.

Ben blinked at the phone. 'What?'

'Convince me you're worthy of my sister. Make me want to help you.'

Dolly spoke slowly, as if she thought he was an idiot. Which, actually, she probably did.

'I don't know how.'

'Then try. Or you're on your own.'

Ben stared out across the gardens of the château and thought. He needed this. Needed Dolly's help if he was ever going to get Luce out here and convince her that they could be a real family. But convince her he was worthy of Luce? Impossible.

'I'm not,' he said, finally. 'I'm not worthy of her. No-body could be.'

'Right answer,' Dolly said. 'Now, tell me your plans and I'll see what I can do. Because, I'm telling you, she's absolutely miserable without you.'

Ben smiled for the first time in a week and told Dolly his plan.

CHAPTER SIXTEEN

'AT LEAST TELL me where I'm going,' Luce said as Dolly threw more clothes into her suitcase. 'And how long I'll be gone. I need to call work…' Which would be fun. Dennis was still speechless over the pregnancy thing.

'Already done,' Dolly said. 'I told them you'd be back next week. If you decide not to… Well, call them once you're there.'

'Where, exactly?' Luce asked, frustrated. 'And if I'm there longer than a few days that skirt won't fit me any more. Three months and I'm already starting to show.'

'You're glowing,' Dolly said. Then she stopped and looked at her. 'Well, sort of. Right now you just look stressed.'

'I can't imagine why.'

Dolly slammed the lid of the suitcase shut and fastened it, leaning hard on it with her elbow to keep it closed. 'Look, just trust me on this one. It's for the best, and everything's going to work out fine. You need a break. You need looking after. And, most importantly, you need to not be in the house while they're fixing the attic. God only knows what they're going to find up there, and all that dust would be bad for the baby. Even the builder's told you to get out for a few days.'

'I could have just booked into a hotel round the corner for the weekend,' Luce pointed out.

'Except I know you.' Dolly gave her a look. 'You'd be back here every five minutes, wanting to check on things. No. This is my first chance to be the grown-up and in-charge sister, and I'm taking it. I have booked you a long weekend and you are going. End of story. I'll take care of everything here, so you don't need to worry at all.'

Luce opened her mouth to speak, and then closed it again. Telling Dolly she couldn't go, that she'd worry too much, was tantamount to telling her she didn't trust her to look after things. How could she do that when Dolly was trying so hard?

'And, look,' Dolly said, pointing to the carry-on bag next to the suitcase. 'I'm letting you take your research notes and your laptop, aren't I? I know how close you are to finishing the revisions on your book. So it can be a working holiday. Perfect.'

Luce bit her lip at the memory of her last accidental, snowy working holiday. 'Thanks, Doll. I just…'

'You just need to relax. Come on—let's get you to the airport.'

In the end Luce decided it was easier just to cave in to Dolly's boundless enthusiasm and go. A weekend away did sound wonderful, and it was nice to have someone else take care of the planning for a change.

Or so she thought until her plane landed in Nice and there was no one there to meet her.

This was why she took care of things herself. As hard as Dolly was trying, organisation and responsibility still didn't come naturally to her. And now Luce was stuck in an airport with no idea where she was supposed to be going.

Fishing her phone out of her bag, she called Dolly. 'I

thought you said there'd be a car here to meet me? With, you know, a driver? To take me to the hotel?'

'He's not *there*?' Dolly's incredulous voice screeched down the line. 'Hang on. I'll call you back.'

Luce took her bags and sat down on a nearby bench to wait. The Arrivals lounge began to empty out a bit, waiting for the next influx of passengers from the following flight, and she glanced around her, trying to see if she'd missed a sign with her name on it or something. Dolly had been so sure it was all arranged...

The doors in front of her opened with a bang, and Luce looked up to see Ben Hampton—paint on his face, jeans, shirt and in his hair—running towards her just as her phone rang.

'Dolly.'

'He's on his way,' Dolly said quickly. 'There was a mix-up—'

'He's already here.'

'Oh.' Dolly paused. 'Are you cross?'

'Possibly. I'll let you know later.'

'Okay.'

Luce hung up. 'You and Dolly came up with a plan. You and Dolly. Together.' The two people least likely to work together or to come up with a coherent, responsible plan.

Wincing, Ben said, 'Yeah. Guess it's no surprise it didn't quite work. I thought you weren't due in for another hour.'

'And you still dressed for the occasion?'

Ben glanced down at his paint-splattered clothes. 'I lost track of time. Come on—let me take your bags.'

'Where are we going?' Luce asked as she followed him out to where his car was parked at a wildly illegal angle on the kerb. 'Another hotel?'

Ben shook his head. 'We're going home.'

* * *

She looked incredible. Three months pregnant, straight off an aeroplane, annoyed with him—and she was still, by far, the most beautiful thing he'd ever seen.

'Where is home, exactly?' Luce asked as they pulled out of the airport.

'I told you about my grandmother's château?'

'That's where we're going? So—what? You're moving to France?'

Ben sighed. 'If you just wait—just a little bit—I promise I can do grand apologies and romantic gestures in style once we get there. And maybe once I've changed clothes.'

'It's not your clothes I'm worried about you changing. And I'm not interested in romantic gestures.'

She had her arms crossed over her chest, her creamy breasts pushing against the silk of her top. Were they bigger? *Not the time, Hampton.*

'Just the apology, then?'

Luce nodded. 'And I'd rather have that sooner than later.'

Ben smiled despite himself. 'No patience at all, have you?'

'Oh, I don't know. I think I've waited quite long enough.'

She had a point. 'I made a plan and everything, you know. There was a list.'

'Dolly's been telling me for weeks that plans need to be flexible. That's why we're painting the nursery yellow.'

'You and Dolly?'

'She's moved in. She's paying rent so we can fix up the house and make it baby-safe. And it means I won't have to be alone when the baby comes.'

Ben clenched his jaw. She wouldn't be alone. She shouldn't ever have thought she had to be alone. *Never mind the plan.*

'I'm sorry, Luce. For reacting the way I did.' Ben glanced across at her. She stared out of the window, intently focusing on something in the distance, or maybe on nothing at all. Either way, she wasn't looking at him, which was all Ben cared about. 'I was an idiot. I know that. Seb told me, and Dolly told me.'

'She wrote a song about how much of an idiot you are, you know.'

Ben laughed. He was starting to actually like Dolly, against the odds.

'The thing is, I knew I was wrong. I knew losing you, and our baby, would be the worst decision I ever made. I just couldn't see any way out of it.'

Now Luce looked at him, eyebrows raised, and Ben looked away and concentrated on the road again, just to avoid the anger in her gaze.

'You couldn't just say, *We'll figure it out together*?'

Ben winced. 'Apparently not. I was jet-lagged, tired, not thinking straight. But mostly I just didn't want to turn into my father.'

'You can't let your parents' marriage define your life.'

'I know. But Seb wanted me to take on this new work, travelling all the time, and I couldn't drag you and a kid around with me—hell, you'd never let me. And even if you did you'd hate it so much you'd leave me eventually. But I couldn't see myself staying in one place either. And I don't want to be one of those dads who's never around and then shows up for a couple of days in a whirlwind before disappearing again.'

'So you made all these decisions for me and our child without talking to me about it?'

Luce's words were cold and hard, and Ben turned off the *autoroute* with relief. Nearly home. If he could just get her to the château...

'I'm trying to make up for it now,' he said. 'Just give me the chance.'

Luce shook her head. 'I'm not sure that you can, Ben.'

The pain in her voice made his heart clench. 'Let me try.'

They drove the rest of the way in silence, and by the time Ben pulled up in front of the château the sky was growing dark. Grabbing her bag from the boot, he opened the door to help her out, and watched her as she stared up at the building.

'It's beautiful,' she said.

'It's nothing compared to you.' She turned to him in surprise, and he shrugged, moving away towards the front door.

'You know flattery isn't going to win this one for you?'

'It's not flattery if it's true,' Ben called back. And besides, he'd try every trick he could think of if it meant getting Luce to stay.

Inside, the château was cool and dark. The spring evening had turned chilly, and Luce wrapped her cardigan tighter around her as Ben flicked on the lights. Lamps around the walls flared into life, lighting the wide entrance hall and sweeping staircase.

'You want the tour?' Ben asked, and Luce nodded.

She followed him through the first door on the left.

'Drawing room,' Ben said, waiting while Luce looked around.

Everything looked dusty, unloved. Sheets lay over the chairs and sofas and the candlesticks and brassware were tarnished. There was none of the careful design of his hotel rooms, or even the cosy decoration of his cottage. This was somebody else's home—not Ben's. Not yet, anyway.

'When did you get here?' she asked as he led her back into the hall and through the next door.

'A week ago,' Ben said. He flipped on the light switch, revealing case after case of dusty leather books. 'Library, obviously.'

'You flew straight here the day after I told you?'

'I had work to do.'

Of course. For someone who said he didn't want to turn into his father, Ben seemed to be doing his damnedest to become exactly the same sort of workaholic.

He led her across the hallway to show her a front sitting room and a formal dining room. More antique furniture, more dustsheets. More floral wallpaper and heavy curtains.

'This place doesn't seem very *you*,' she commented.

'It isn't yet. Lot of work to do.'

'Is that why you came straight here as soon as you got back from your work trip? Or is there a hotel nearby you're looking at acquiring?'

'Always with the questions…' Ben took her arm, tucking her hand into the crook of his arm just as he had that night in Chester. 'Come see the kitchen, then I'll explain everything.'

The kitchen stretched across the back of the house, with huge full-length windows leading out to the garden. The units were old and battered, but Luce could see what a fabulous space it could be, redone properly. The whole house had huge potential. Small for a château, she supposed, but plenty big enough for any modern family.

Not that she would be moving to France, of course. Ben hadn't even suggested it. In fact she had no idea at all what he wanted from her.

'It's a lovely kitchen,' she said, rounding on him. 'Now, talk.'

Ben smiled, and the love in his eyes as he looked at her shocked her. He looked…open. Free.

'I spoke to Seb,' he started. 'The morning after I saw you. Told him what an idiot I'd been. Told him I couldn't see how I could fix it—having you and a family—with my job. But without the job I couldn't support you, and being stuck in an office five days a week would drive me crazy.'

'I know that. I'd never ask you to do that.' Luce pulled away from him. 'I told you—you don't have to be involved if you don't want to be. But why you dragged me out here to tell me this again—'

'I didn't,' Ben said, grabbing her hands. 'Just listen—please. Actually, come upstairs with me.'

'Only if you talk as we go,' Luce said, hating the burning tears she could feel forming in her eyes. Damn hormones. They confused everything. She just wanted answers. No need to get upset.

'Okay,' Ben said with a laugh. 'You've been very patient with me.'

Holding her hand, he walked them back into the hallway and up the staircase.

'Seb asked me what I really wanted,' he said. 'And I realised it was the same question I'd kept asking you. You hadn't been able to answer it. But suddenly I could. The only thing in the world I wanted that morning, and every morning since, was you in my life. You and our child. No one-night rules. No running away. Just you. Always. However you'll have me.'

Luce looked up in surprise and the stair carpet slipped under her foot. Ben wrapped a strong arm around her waist and she grabbed at his shoulders as she found her balance and tried to get her heartbeat back under control.

Ben smiled at her, carrying on as if nothing had happened. 'So Seb ordered coffee, and we worked out a plan

to make it all work. A long-term, lasting plan. You'd have
been so proud of us.'

'I already am,' Luce murmured. He'd made the right
choice. It had taken him a couple of days, maybe, but he'd
chosen to stay, to fight. Chosen responsibility and grown-
up life over running away like a teenager. 'So, what was
the plan?'

'We tackled work first, because I was so worried about
making the same mistakes Dad did. I offered to quit, but
Seb had a better plan. I'm going to keep developing our
new hotel line—family-friendly, boutique business hotels—but I'm going to get help to do it. You can come with
me, whenever you want, and we'll structure it so I'm not
away more than two weeks in every month.'

Luce blinked. 'So—wait. You want to be with me—
with us—when you're in the country?'

Ben grinned and pulled her up the rest of the stairs. 'I
love you, Luce. I want to be with you all the time. Did I
miss that part out?'

'Yes.'

'Well, I do. I want to be a real family with you. And I
know now what a real family needs.'

'What's that?'

'A home. Or, in our case, several.' He threw open a door
off the landing and Luce looked in to see sunny yellow
walls and boxes of nursery furniture piled in the centre of
the room. 'I'd hoped to get at least the crib put together before you arrived. Painting took longer than I remembered.'

Luce bit her lip. 'You want us to live here?' That would
mean leaving Dolly—and Tom and Mum. Leaving Cardiff.
Leaving her job. Giving up everything she loved. Would
he really ask her to do that?

'Sometimes.' Ben wrapped his arms around her waist
and pulled her against him. 'I figure we'll fix up your Car-

diff house and live there most of the time. I mean, I don't imagine you're going to want to suddenly give up your home and your work or anything, but we can spend summers here at the château.'

Hope flared up inside her. Maybe he did understand after all. 'And any time we need a weekend to get away from it all we can go to the cottage?'

'Exactly.'

Ben smiled down at her and Luce tried to remember if she'd ever seen him looking so happy. She didn't think so. Not even after making love.

It all sounded perfect. More than she'd ever hoped or dreamed for. To be with him, just their little family, all the time. Except... 'I told you Dolly moved in, right?'

'I don't care. As long as I get to be with you. Besides, we might need a babysitter.'

Luce laughed. 'Very true.'

'So you'll do it?' Ben asked. 'You'll take the chance that I've changed? Grown up?'

Luce smiled up at him. 'I love you, you idiot. Of course I will.'

Ben lowered his lips to hers and kissed her softly. 'That's okay, then.'

'Well, seeing the château did make a bit of a difference. And I like the idea of homes in two countries...'

Ben shook his head. 'That's what I realised. These buildings aren't home. *You* are. You and our baby. That's home to me.'

Luce's shoulders relaxed as she tucked her head against his chest. That was what she'd needed to hear.

Things weren't just going to be okay any more, she knew. Their life together would be magnificent.

* * * * *

PROPOSAL AT THE LAZY S RANCH

PATRICIA THAYER

Patricia Thayer was born and raised in Muncie, Indiana, the second in a family of eight children. She attended Ball State University before heading west, where she has called Southern California home for many years. There she's been a member of the Orange County Chapter of RWA. It's a sisterhood like no other.

When not working on a story, she might be found travelling the United States and Europe, taking in the scenery and doing story research while enjoying time with her husband, Steve. Together, they have three grown sons, four grandsons and one granddaughter, whom Patricia calls her own true-life heroes.

CHAPTER ONE

SHE WAS A COWARD.

Josefina Slater jumped into her BMW and drove away from the Lazy S Ranch, her childhood home. Before she'd left California two days ago for Montana, she'd told herself she would be able to come back here and help with her father's recovery from a stroke. But when she'd arrived at the house and saw her older sister, Ana, she found she wasn't ready to face Colton Slater, or her past.

When Josie had arrived at the ranch house and was greeted by her older sister, Ana, she froze right there on the spot. She needed more time. She told her sister she wasn't ready and got back into her car and started driving. To where, she had no idea.

She'd grown up here on the ranch with a man who didn't want the daughters Lucia Slater left behind when she walked out. Outside of her siblings, her twin, Tori, and older sister, Ana, and younger sister, Marissa, there hadn't been much else to keep her here. This was Josie's first time back in nearly ten years.

About two miles down the road, she opened the window. The air was brisk, reminding her that winter was fast approaching. With the quiet hum of the engine mingled with soft music from the radio, she finally started to relax.

She glanced out the windshield at the rolling green pastures that seemed to go on for miles and was framed by the scenic Rocky Mountains. Tall pines covered the slopes as the majestic peaks reached upward to the incredible blue sky.

Quite a different landscape from her home in Los Angeles, or her life. Success in her career as an event planner came with a lot of hard work and little sleep. Except she'd been told if she didn't stop her hectic pace, her health could be in serious trouble. To help ease her stress, her doctor suggested she take time off. Tori, her twin sister and partner in Slater Style, had been the one who'd insisted she come back here to the ranch and try to relax.

Sure, returning here was going to ease her stress. Right. She couldn't even get through the front door.

Her grip tightened on the steering wheel. No. she wouldn't let Colt Slater turn her back into that insecure little girl. She shook her head. "Not again." She wouldn't let any man do that to her.

She continued to drive down the road until she could see part of the Big Hole River. Memories flooded her head, reminding her how she and her sisters used to sneak off and swim there. That brought a smile to her lips. It was also where Ana was building the new lodge along with some small fishing cabins. They'd hoped to add income to help the other problem, the Lazy S's struggling finances.

Curiosity had Josie turning off onto a dirt road and driving the half mile to where several trucks were parked. She pulled in next to a crew cab pickup that had GT Construction embossed on the side.

Why not check out the progress? Anything to delay her going back to the house. She climbed out, glad she'd worn her jeans and boots, and pulled her lined jacket closer to her body, shielding her from the late-October weather.

Feeling excitement for the project she'd helped create

with Ana, she headed across the grass toward the river to observe the progress of the two-story log cabin structure taking shape about thirty yards from the water's edge.

"Good job, Ana," she breathed into the cool autumn breeze.

Suddenly someone called out, but before she could turn around she felt something hit her in the back, sending her flying. Josie let out a cry as she hit the hard ground.

Garrett Temple felt pain shoot through his body as he cradled the small woman under him. It took a few breaths to get his lungs working from the impact, but at least he'd kept her from getting hit by the lumber truck. He managed to roll off her as his men started to gather around.

"I didn't see her, boss," Jerry said as he leaned over them. "You okay?"

Garrett nodded, but his attention was on the still woman facedown on the grass. He knelt beside the petite body and traced over her for any broken bones or visible injuries.

"You want me to call the paramedics?" someone asked.

"Give me a minute," Garrett said as he gently brushed back the long whiskey-colored hair from her face. He froze as recognition hit him. The olive skin, the delicate jawline, long dark lashes. He knew that underneath those closed lids were mesmerizing blue eyes. His heart began to pound even more rapidly. "Josie?"

She groaned, and he said her name again. "Josie. Can you hear me?"

With another groan, she started to raise her head. He stopped her, but caught a whiff of her familiar scent. Hell, how could he remember what she smelled like? He drew back, already feeling the familiar pull to this woman. It had been nearly ten years.

She rolled to one side.

"Take it easy," he told her. "Do you hurt anywhere?"

"My chest," she whispered. "Hard to breathe."

"You got the wind knocked out of you."

She blinked and finally opened her eyes, and he was hit with her rich blue gaze. She looked confused, and then said, "Garrett?"

He rose to his knees. "Hello, Josie."

Josie felt as if she were in a dream. Garrett Temple? It couldn't be… She blinked again, suddenly realizing it was reality. She pushed him away, sat up and groaned at the pounding in her head. "What are you doing here?"

He didn't look any happier to see her. "Trying to save your neck."

"Like I need your help for anything." She glanced up and saw several men peering at them. "I'm fine." She brushed off her sweater and jeans, trying to act as if nothing was wrong. "I just need a minute."

The crew didn't move away until Garrett stepped in. "Everyone, this is Ana Slater's sister Josie."

The guys mumbled a quick greeting, and then headed back to their jobs.

Once alone, Josie turned to the man she'd never expected to see again. The man who'd smashed all her dreams and the last person she needed to see right now.

"Do you hurt anywhere?" he asked again.

A broken heart. "No, I'm fine," she lied. Her ankle was suddenly killing her.

Garrett got to his feet and reached down to offer her some help. She got up under her own power, trying to ignore her light-headedness and her throbbing ankle.

"Still as stubborn as ever, I see."

She glared at the large man. He was well over six feet. Nothing had changed in the looks department, either. He was still handsome with all that black wavy hair, not a bald spot in view. Her attention went to his mouth to see that sexy grin, and her stomach tightened in awareness. Well, dang it. She wasn't going to let him get to her again.

She tested some weight on her tender ankle. Not good. "I know why I'm here," she began, "but…why are you?"

He folded his muscular arms over his wide chest. So he'd filled out from the thin boy she once knew in high school.

"I own GT Construction. Ana hired me."

No. Her sister wouldn't do that. Not when she knew how much Garrett had hurt and humiliated her. "We'll see about that." She started to walk off but her ankle couldn't hold her weight and she started to fall.

"Whoa." He caught her in his arms. Big strong arms. "You are hurt."

"No, I just twisted my ankle. I'll be fine when I get back to the ranch."

"You aren't going anywhere until I get you checked out."

"You're not doing anything—" She gasped as he swung her up into his arms as if she were a child. "Put me down," she demanded, but he only drew her closer and she had no choice but to slip her arm around his neck to keep her balance.

He carried her the short distance to his truck. One of the men rushed over and opened the passenger door. Garrett set her down in the seat.

"You can't kidnap me, Garrett." He was so close to her, she could inhale that so-familiar scent of the man she'd once loved more than anything. "Just take me home."

He shook his head. "You were hurt on my construction site, so I'm responsible for you. We're going to the E.R. first, then I'll take you back to the ranch."

She started to speak, but the door got shut in her face.

A few minutes later, he appeared in the driver's seat. He handed her purse to her. "You might want to call your sister and tell her where you're going."

"No. She'll get all worried and she has enough on her mind." She stole a glance at the man beside her, unable to stop studying his profile. Okay, so she was curious about him, darn it. "What about my car?"

"I'll have one of the men drive it back to the house."

She folded her arms over her chest.

Garrett started the engine and began to back up, then headed for the highway. "Josie…maybe this would be a good chance to talk."

She glared at him. "What could we possibly have to say to each other, Garrett? I got the message nine years ago when you said, 'Sorry Josie, I'm going to marry someone else.'" She hated that his words still hurt. "So don't waste any more words."

Josie managed to fight back tears. She had to concentrate on getting through this time with a man who broke her heart once. She wasn't going to let it happen again, so she decided to head back to Los Angeles as soon as possible.

An hour later at the emergency room in Dillon, Garrett sat with Josie while they waited for the doctor. Even in the silly gown they had her put on, she still looked good. There was no denying that seeing her again had affected him, more than he thought possible.

From the moment when he noticed Josie Slater in Royerton High School and saw her big blue eyes, he'd been a goner. They'd been a couple all through school, even after he graduated and went off to college. Josie finished high school and went to college locally two years later. Then one weekend he'd come home to tell her about his apprenticeship. They had a big fight about him being gone all summer, and they broke up. Josie refused to talk to him for months. Then he met Natalie....

Now all these years later, Josie was back here. Seeing her today had been harder than he could imagine. But her reaction toward him was a little hard to take. He didn't have to worry about her having any leftover feelings for him.

Garrett stood outside of the cubicle and the curtain was drawn as the doctor examined Josie.

"So, Ms. Slater," the doctor began, "you're getting a nasty bruise on your forehead." There was silence for a moment, and the middle-aged man continued, "You're lucky. It doesn't seem you have a concussion."

Grateful, Garrett sagged against the wall, knowing he shouldn't eavesdrop, but he still listened for more information.

"I want you to take it easy today," the doctor told her. "Your ankle is swollen, but the X-ray didn't show any broken bones. But you'll need to put ice on it." He paused. "Do you take any medications?"

Garrett heard Josie rattle off a few. He recognized one was for anxiety and the other for sleeping. What was wrong with her?

The doctor came out from behind the curtain. "She'll be fine, although she'll have some bruises."

"Thank you, Doctor."

He nodded. "Just make sure she rests today and have her stay off her feet."

"I will."

The doctor walked away, and Garrett called, "You decent?"

"Yes," she grumbled.

He went behind the curtain and found her sitting on

the bed, not looking happy. "I got a clean bill of health, so can we go home?"

He nodded, suddenly wishing she was home. But he had a feeling that Josie was headed back to California real soon, and he'd lose her for the second time.

It was another forty minutes before Garrett pulled up in front of the Slater home. Josie's pulse started racing once again as she looked up at the big two-story brown house with the white trim. It was a little faded and the porch needed some work. So a lot of things around the ranch hadn't been cared for in a while.

Garrett got out of the truck and walked around to her side. He pulled the crutches out of the back, but propped them against the side of the truck as he reached in and scooped her into his arms. Instead of setting her down on the ground, he carried her toward the house.

"Hey, I can do this myself."

"It's crazy to struggle with these steps when I can get you in the house faster."

She wasn't going to waste the effort to argue. Soon she'd be inside and he'd be gone.

Garrett paused at the heavy oak door with the cut-glass oval window. She drew a quiet breath and released it. It was bad enough that the man she'd once loved was carrying her around in his arms, but she still had to face the other man in her life. Her father.

"You okay?" Garrett asked.

"Yeah, I'm just peachy."

He stared at her, but didn't say a word. Wise man. He managed to turn the knob and open the door.

Inside, she glanced around. This had been part of the house she hadn't seen much as a child. Everyone used the back door off the kitchen. This was the formal part of the house.

Nothing much had changed over the years, she noted, as Garrett carried her across glossy honey-colored hardwood floors and past the sweeping staircase that led upstairs. He continued down the hall where the living room was closed off by large oak pocket doors. She tensed. Her father's new living quarters since coming home from the hospital.

They finally reached Colt's office. "She's home," Garrett announced as he carried her inside.

Ana Slater glanced up from the computer screen and froze. Her older sister was tall and slender with nearly black hair and blue eyes.

"Josie! Oh, God, what happened?"

"I had a little collision at the construction site."

Garrett set her down in the high-back chair across from the desk. "She'd gotten in the path of a truckload of lumber," he told her. "I pushed her out of the way. She landed funny."

"You mean, *you* landed on me."

Ana glanced back and forth between the two. "When you called me, you said nothing about being injured." She looked concerned. "But you're all right?"

"Yes!"

"No!" Garrett said. "The doctor wants her to rest."

"I need to stay off my ankle, but I have crutches to help get around."

"I'll go get them," Garrett said, and walked out of the room.

Josie turned to her big sister. "So when were you going to tell me that Garrett Temple was building the lodge? Or was it going to remain a secret?"

Ana tried to look innocent and failed. "Okay, how was I supposed to tell you?"

"By telling me the truth."

Josie glanced around the dark paneled room that had been Colt's sanctuary. They'd never been allowed in here, but that didn't seem to bother Ana these days. By the looks of it she'd taken over.

"I'm sorry, Josie. I thought since you said you weren't coming home, I didn't need to say anything."

Josie had trouble hiding her anger. "There have to be other contractors here in town you could have used."

"First of all, Garrett gave us the lowest bid, and some of our own ranch hands are working on the crew. Secondly, he's moved back here and now lives at the Temple Ranch to help out his father."

Josie closed her eyes. It was enough having to deal with her father but now, Garrett. "Then I'm going back to L.A."

"Josie, please. I need you to stay, at least for a little while. We can make it so that you and Garrett don't have any contact." She hesitated, then said, "And Colt, he definitely wants you here. He was so happy when I told him you came home."

Her father wanted her here? That didn't sound like the cold, distant man who'd raised her.

"We all need you here, sis." Ana continued her pitch. "I can't tell you how wonderful it is to have you here, even if it's only for a short time. So please, give it a few days. At least until your ankle is better."

The Lazy S had been her home, once. If Colt had changed like Ana said, she wanted to try and have some sort of relationship with the man. Was it crazy to hope? At the very least, she wanted to help Ana with the financial problems. It was no secret they needed outside income to survive.

Ana and her fiancé, Vance Rivers, the ranch foreman, had already opened the property on their section of the river to anglers. It brought in a nice profit. That was why they were expanding on the business.

Her sister spoke up. "The lodge was your idea to help with income for the ranch. Don't you want to stick around to see your vision come true?"

It had been Josie's idea to build housing to rent out. As an event planner she knew the large structure could be used for company retreats, family reunions and even small weddings. It was to bring in more revenue to help during lean years.

Maybe a little while here wouldn't be so bad. "How soon is this wedding of yours?"

"As soon as possible," came the answer from the doorway.

They both turned and saw Vance Rivers smiling at his future bride.

Ana's grin was just as goofy. "Oh, honey, I don't think I can pull it off that soon."

The sandy-haired man walked across the room dressed in his cowboy garb, including leather chaps. "I'm glad you're home, Josie," he told her. "Ana has missed her sisters."

Josie fought a smile and lost. "Seems to me my big sis has been too busy to miss anyone."

Ana came around the desk and slipped into Vance's arms. Josie couldn't miss the intimate look exchanged between the two. "Yeah, she's miserable all right."

That brought a smile from the handsome man. "A few weeks ago, she was ready to string me up and hang me out to dry."

Josie frowned as she looked at her older sister. "A misunderstanding," Ana said. "It was all resolved and we're all working hard to help the Lazy S and Dad."

"So that was why you hired Garrett?"

"At first I offered to be their partner."

Josie swung around to see Garrett standing in the doorway with her crutches. She stiffened, hating that he still got to her.

Josie didn't want to hear any more from Garrett Temple. "I don't think that will be necessary."

He walked into the room, and Ana and Vance walked out, leaving her alone with the man she once loved more than anything, until he betrayed her. Now, she didn't want to be around him.

With her bum ankle, she was stuck here. That didn't mean she would fall all over this man again.

"I was trying to help out a friend," Garrett said. "And I believe it's a good investment. A lot of ranches have to go into other business to help stay afloat."

"I might be stuck working with you, Temple, but I'm not the same girl who was falling all over you. I've grown up."

"Come on, Josie. What happened between us was years ago."

Eight years and eleven months, she silently corrected. She could still recall that awful day. She'd been so eager to see him when he returned home. It had been months since their argument. She'd finally agreed to see him, then he broke the devastating news.

He stared at her with those gray eyes, and she still felt the old pull. "I was hoping enough time has passed so…"

"So I'd do what? Forgive you? Forgive you for telling me you loved me, then going off and getting another woman pregnant?"

Later that afternoon in the parlor converted into a first-floor bedroom, Colt Slater sat in his chair in front of the picture window. He squeezed the rubber ball in his right hand. He knew his strength was coming back since the stroke. Just not fast enough to suit him. His therapist, Jay McNeal, kept telling him to have patience. He would get his strength back.

Right now, Colt's concern was for his daughter, Josie. He had watched her drive away from the house and prayed that she would come back, but he wouldn't have bet on it. Not that he could blame her; he hadn't been the best father in the world.

Then a truck pulled up about an hour ago. He held his breath and watched Garrett Temple get out, then lift Josie out of the passenger seat and carry her into the house. He heard the footsteps that went right past his room.

He tensed. What had happened? Had she been in an accident? Finally, Ana came in and explained about Josie's mishap at the construction site with Temple. He wasn't sure he was happy that those two were together again. That man had hurt Josie so badly. He'd wished he could have been there for her back then.

"Will you stop worrying? You're going to end up back in the hospital."

Colt glanced at his friend, Wade Dickson in the chair next to his. Dressed in his usual business suit with his gray hair cut and styled, his friend and lawyer knew all the family secrets.

"I can't stop worrying about Josie," Colt admitted.

"Hey, things worked out with Ana, so there's hope with Josie, too." Wade stood up. "I'll go see what's going on, then I need to get back to my office. Some of us have to work."

Colt nodded. "Thanks for everything, Wade."

"I love those girls, too. It's about time you realize what you have." He turned and walked out.

Alone again, Colt started having doubts again. Would Josie finally come to see him now?

He stood, grabbed the walker and made his way to the sideboard in the dining room. Now it was his exercise area, since he'd been released from the rehab center. He pulled open the drawer and dug under the stack of tablecloths until he found the old album.

Setting it on top, he turned the pages, trying to ignore the ones of his wife, Lucia. He should have burned those years ago, but something kept him from erasing all the past.

He made it to the picture of his four daughters together. The last one taken before their mother walked out the door. His hand moved over the photo. Josie was the one who was a miniature version of her mother, petite and curvy, although her hair was lighter and her eyes were definitely Slater blue.

He frowned, knowing he'd been unfair to his girls. He couldn't even use the excuse of being a single parent. Kathleen, the longtime housekeeper, handled most everything while he worked the ranch. He sighed, recalling those years. Since the day Lucia left, he'd closed up and couldn't show love to his four daughters.

He studied the photo. Analeigh was the oldest. Then came the twins, Josefina Isabel, followed five minutes later by Vittoria Irene. The memory of him standing next to his wife, and encouraging her as she gave birth to their beautiful daughters, Ana, Josie, Tori and Marissa.

He felt tears gathering in his eyes. Would he get the chance to fix the damage he'd done?

"Hello, Colt."

He turned and saw his beautiful Josie leaning against a crutch in the doorway. He'd just been given a second chance, and he wasn't about to throw it away.

CHAPTER TWO

JOSIE FELT STRANGE, not only being back in this house, but seeing her father after all these years.

"J…Josie. I'm gl…glad you're home."

Colt still stood straight and tall as he had before his stroke. Thirty years ago, he'd been a rodeo star, winning the World Saddle Bronc title before he retired when he married Lucia Delgado and brought her back to the Lazy S to make a life, raising cattle and a family.

Now in his mid-fifties, he was still a good-looking man, even with his weathered skin and graying hair. His blue eyes were the one thing she'd inherited from him. Her dark coloring was what she'd gotten from her Hispanic mother.

"This hasn't been my home for a long time." With the aid of her crutch, she bravely made her way into the room.

"You had an accident," Colt said.

"It seems I got in the way at the construction site." She nodded to her ankle. "In a few days I'll be as good as new. Looks like you're stuck with me for the duration anyway."

"Hap…happy to have you."

His words gave her a strange feeling, making her realize how badly she wanted to be here.

She began to examine the rehab equipment to hide her nervousness. "Looks like I don't need to go to a gym to exercise. You have everything right here."

"You're welcome to u…use it," he told her. "When you're able to."

She sat down on the weight bench and eyed the parallel bars, then Colt. Outside of some weight loss, he looked good. "Is all this helping you?"

He nodded. "Been working hard. I hope to get a lot better s…soon." He studied her. "Thank you for coming home."

That was a first. Her father actually thanked her. "Don't thank me yet. I'm not sure how much I can help, or how long I can stay."

Colt smiled.

Another first, Josie thought, not to mention he was actually carrying on a conversation with her. How many times had she tried to get some attention from this man? She felt tears gathering.

"Just glad you're here," he told her.

Suddenly her throat tightened so she nodded. "I should go and unpack." She got up, slipped the single crutch under her arms and headed for the door, but Colt's gravelly voice made her turn around.

"M…made a lot of mistakes, Josie. I would like a s…second chance."

His words about threw her over the edge. She raised a hand. "I can't deal with any more right now. We'll talk later."

She managed to get out the door and headed toward the staircase. She hopped up the steps on her good leg until she got to the second floor. Using her crutch, she made her way down the familiar hall to the third door on the left that had been her and Tori's bedroom. She stepped inside and froze. It looked the same as it did when she'd left here.

The walls were still pale lavender and the twin beds had floral print comforters with matching dust ruffles.

She walked to her bed against the far wall and sank down onto the mattress. Taking a toss pillow from the headboard, she hugged it close against the burning acid in the pit of her stomach.

Great, this trip was supposed to help relax her. This time when tears welled in her eyes she didn't stop them. Colt wanted to rebuild their relationship. What relationship? They'd never had a father/daughter relationship.

Memories of the lonely times welled in her chest. She'd been grateful for her sisters, especially Tori. When something wonderful happened to them, they'd been each others cheerleaders, along with Kathleen, the housekeeper and their surrogate mom, replacing the mother who'd disappeared from her kids' life when Josie had been only three years old. It had been pretty clear that neither parent wanted their children.

Josie wiped a tear from her cheek. Dang it. She thought she'd gotten over all this. Leaving here and the pain behind, she'd gone off to L.A. and worked hard on a career, building a successful business, Slater Style.

She got up and hobbled to the window and looked out at the ranch compound. From this room, she had a great view of the glossy white barn with the attached corral. There were many outbuildings, some old, plus some new ones that had been added over the years. Her attention turned to the horses grazing in the pasture. There were mares with their foals, frolicking around in the open field.

Smiling, she pressed her hand against the cool glass, knowing cold weather was coming, along with unpredictable Montana snows. Surprisingly, that had been what she'd missed since moving to L.A.

She caught sight of her car coming down the road and watched as it pulled up in front of the house. Good, she had her vehicle back.

Then she caught sight of two men stepping off the porch below her, Vance and Garrett. She felt a sudden jolt as she got the chance to observe the man she had once called her boyfriend. Both men were about the same height, and drop-dead handsome.

Josie hadn't been surprised at all when she learned Ana and Vance had fallen in love and planned to marry soon. The guy had been crazy about Ana for years, since he'd come to live at the Lazy S when he was a teenager.

She smiled, happy for her sister.

Josie looked back at Garrett. She couldn't help but take notice of the man. He'd filled out since college, and he still had those incredible eyes and sexy smile. And she hated the fact that just seeing him again still had an effect on her. She released a breath, recalling how it felt when he carried her in his arms.

After Vance shook hands with Garrett, her future brother-in-law headed off toward the barn. Garrett went to her car and spoke to the driver, one of the men on his crew.

Then as if Garrett could sense her, he looked up. Their eyes locked, and suddenly she felt her heart pounding in her chest. She finally moved out of his sight and went to lie down on the bed.

What was she doing? She didn't need to rehash her past. All there was here were the memories of the pain and heartache over her father. Now she also had to deal with Garrett. It had taken her a lot of time to get over him. She'd only been back a few hours and he was already involved in her life again.

Why, after all these years? Normally she never let men distract her, mainly because she hadn't met anyone who could stir her interest. She hadn't met anyone in L.A. she wanted to have a relationship with. She thought about the times she'd tried to find a man. Problem was she'd compared them all to Garrett Temple.

She thought back to the kind and considerate man who'd showed her in so many ways how much he loved her. How Garrett had told her they were going to marry and build a life together after they'd graduated college. Then all too quickly she learned that all those promises were lies when it all came crashing down around them that day....

There was a knock on the door.

She wiped away tears as she rolled over on the bed. "Come in," she called, thinking it was Ana.

The door opened and Garrett stepped inside, carrying her suitcases. "I figured you might need these."

Her heart leaped into her throat. She sat up. "You didn't need to bring my things up."

He set the bags over by the closet. "I told Vance I would. He needed to check on one of his horses."

She nodded. She wasn't sure she believed him. "Thank you."

"How are you feeling?" he asked as he crossed the room.

"I'm fine."

Garrett paused, his gaze searching her face. "I'm sorry I pushed you so hard. I was only trying to get you out of the way." He frowned. "I was worried the truck would hit you."

She nodded. "I should have been paying attention. But I'm fine now, so you can stop feeling guilty."

He still didn't leave. "Some habits are hard to break."

She knew what he was talking about, but their past was the last thing she wanted to rehash. "Well, stop it. I'm a big girl."

He studied her for what seemed to be forever. "Since you're still angry, maybe it's time to clear the air."

"I don't think anything you have to say will change a thing."

He was big and strong, and he seemed to take up a lot of space in the room. "Josie, I don't blame you for not wanting to see me again."

She raised a hand, praying he would just disappear. "I don't want to talk about this, Garrett."

"Well, if you want me to leave then you're going to have to hear me out first."

His gray gaze met hers, causing her pulse to race through her body. Darn the man. "Okay, talk."

"First, I'm sorrier than I can say for what happened all those years ago. I regret that I hurt you. But we broke up, Josie. We hadn't been together all summer, and you wouldn't even talk to me."

Just as it had been all those years ago, Garrett's words were like a knife slicing into her heart. "Feel better now?"

He released a breath. "Although I have many regrets about how things happened between us, what I'll never regret is my son. He's the most important thing in my life."

A son. She had to remember the innocent child. "I'm glad, Garrett. I'm glad you're happy."

He gave a nod. "I just want us to be able to work together on this project."

She wasn't even sure she could stay here. "Is that all?"

He nodded, then turned to leave, but for some reason she needed to know. "Was she worth it?"

Garrett paused and glanced over his shoulder. "I take it you're talking about my wife."

Another pain shot through Josie. "Yes."

"Natalie was my son's mother, so yes, the choice was worth it." She saw the pain flash through his eyes. "But our marriage didn't survive."

* * *

The next day at the Temple Ranch, Garrett forced himself out of bed after a sleepless night. Josie Slater was back. He knew he couldn't let her mess with his head, or his heart. Not again.

Why was he even worrying? There was no room for her in his life. So for both their sakes, he hoped she was headed back to California soon.

He walked down the stairs of his father's home. Now, not only had it been Garrett's for the past year, it was Brody's, too. And this morning he'd taken off work from the construction site to spend time with his son. Soon the boy would be starting a new school, so today was going to be just for them. With Brody's recent move to Royerton, he knew it was going to take some time to make the adjustment. And for Garrett to win his son's trust.

Since the divorce two years ago, it had been difficult on his child. Then his ex-wife's recent death in a car accident had struck Brody yet another blow. Garrett hoped that a stable home at the ranch would help the eight-year-old. As his father, he was going to spend as much time as possible with his son now that he was the sole parent.

Garrett finished tucking in his shirt as he walked into the kitchen. He found Brody sitting at the counter, eating a bowl of his favorite cereal.

"Good morning, Brody."

He was rewarded with a big smile. "Morning," his son murmured.

Garrett smiled at the boy who was his image at the same age.

Brody was tall and lanky, with a headful of unruly dark curls and big green eyes. The thing that tore at Garrett's heart was knowing that his son would have struggles without having a mother around. As Brody's father he'd vowed from the day he'd been born that he'd always be there for him.

He walked to the counter and took the mug of coffee from the housekeeper, Della Carlton.

"Thanks, Della." He took a sip. "Sorry I wasn't down earlier, but I needed to phone my crew foreman. How has Brody been this morning?"

"A sweetheart. He does need his routine, though."

Garrett nodded. "Change is hard for all of us."

The short stocky woman had gray hair pulled up into a ponytail. "It's so wonderful you brought him here. It's been good for your father, too."

Garrett glanced around. "Speaking of Nolan, where is he?"

"Jack Richardson came by and took him to a horse auction."

He frowned, thinking about his father's arthritis. "Dad was up to it?"

Della nodded as they watched Brody carry his bowl to the sink. "The new medication seems to be helping him a lot."

The main reason Garrett had moved back to the ranch was to help out his father. Relocating his construction company took longer, but business was picking up, and with his foreman, Jerry, they could still put in bids on long-distance projects. And now, Brody would be raised here, too.

"Can we go get my horse now?" Brody asked.

Garrett smiled. "Give me a minute."

"Okay. I'm going outside to wait." The boy took off toward the back door.

Garrett glanced at Della. The Temple men were lucky to have her here to help fill in with Brody. "We should be back from the Lazy S by lunch. If plans change I'll call you."

The middle-aged widow nodded. "You just have a good time today."

Garrett knew today Brody would be meeting new people. He'd been so withdrawn since his mother's death. "You think he's ready for his own horse?"

Della smiled. "I'm not an expert, but it seems to me this is the first thing I'd seen the boy get excited about since he's come here to live. I'd say that's a good sign, and isn't horseback riding therapeutic?"

"Dad!" Brody's voice rang out.

"Okay, I'm coming."

"You're doing the right thing by the boy," Della said. "You're a good man, Garrett Temple."

Garrett felt a sudden rush of emotion, but managed a nod. He caught up with his son and headed toward his truck. They were going to see Vance to get a suitable mount.

They climbed in the vehicle, and after buckling up, Garrett drove off toward their closest neighbor.

Since Nolan Temple's health had deteriorated most of the barn stock had been sold off. One of the jobs Garrett had taken on was to get the operation up and going again. Thanks to the ranch foreman, Charlie Bowers, and neighbor Vance Rivers, they now had a herd that was twice the size as last year's, along with an alfalfa crop for the spring.

Even his dad was feeling good enough to want to participate in the operation. Garrett enjoyed it, too, and he hoped the same for his son. He wanted a place where his boy would feel safe and secure again. He wanted that for himself, too.

He glanced at the boy sitting next to him. "Vance has three horses for you to see, but that doesn't mean you have to pick one of them. We can keep looking if you don't find what you want."

Brody shrugged, looking down at his hands. "Okay."

Garrett was eager to get his son something to distract him from the loss of his mother. There had also been some big changes in his life. He just wanted Brody to know that he was his top priority. Not even work was going to distract him from rebuilding a life with his son.

Then he'd seen Josie yesterday.

All these years and she was back here. Seeing her again had been harder than he could imagine. But by her reaction toward him, he didn't have to worry about her being interested in him. Besides, she was probably headed back to California really soon.

Josie had slept in until eight o'clock. After she'd tested the tenderness of her ankle, she managed to shower and rewrapped it. She dressed and was even able to put on a pair of canvas sneakers. Making her way downstairs, she went to the kitchen and was greeted by Kathleen's big smile and hug.

"Where is everyone?"

"Your father is with his therapist, Jay McNeal." The fiftysomething housekeeper glanced at the kitchen clock. "It'll be about another hour. Afterward, Jay helps him shower and get dressed."

"How is Colt really doing? I mean, Ana hadn't given a lot of details." Maybe Josie just hadn't been eager to listen. "Only that he's improving."

"He is improving and very quickly. We're all happy about that." Kathleen sat down across from her. "But your sister still wants your help. She won't ask you to, but she needs you to stay as long as you can spare the time."

Josie felt bad, knowing how much her older sister had taken on by herself. "I should have come sooner."

"Under the circumstances, I can't blame you all for not

wanting to come home," she told her. "But I'm sure glad you're here now. Please tell me you're staying awhile." The older woman squeezed her hand. "I missed you, Josie."

"Ah, Kathleen, I've missed you, too." But two weeks was about all she could handle with Garrett. "I said two weeks. After that…" She hesitated. "Remember, Tori is handling my end of the business while I'm here."

"Maybe she'll decide to come back, too."

Josie smiled. "As soon as I get back there, she can come home."

"So you still think of the Lazy S as home?"

Josie shook her head. "Don't start, Kathleen. Let's just take this slow. I've been away a long time." She finished her coffee. "Where's Ana?"

"She went out to the barn with Vance. They have someone coming to look at some horses this morning." Kathleen checked the clock. "Then she had to go to work at the high school."

Josie nodded, knowing the reason she came home was because of Ana's job as high school counselor.

She stood and tested her ankle. "Maybe I'll walk down to have a look around, then come back to see Colt." This was all so new to her. She was actually going to see her dad.

Josie kissed Kathleen's cheek. Grabbing her coat, she headed out the door and slowly made her way down the same path she used to take as a kid. Not that she'd been invited into the barn much. Colt had pretty much kept his daughters out of any ranch business. Even when they got older, he didn't want them around. It had been some of the ranch hands who taught them to rope and ride. When Colt learned of it, he made sure they learned to muck out stalls, too.

She stepped inside the large structure, where the scent

of straw and animals hit her. She smiled, thinking a few days here might not be so bad. She looked down the rows of stalls where several horses were housed. She liked this. Walking down the center aisle, she passed the stall that had the name Blondie on the gate. *Ana's buckskin,* Josie thought as she walked up and began to stroke the animal. Then she went to another stall with a big chestnut, Rusty.

"Well, aren't you a good-looking fella."

"That's Vance's horse."

Josie swung around when she heard a child's voice. She found a boy who was about eight or nine. He must be the buyer's son. "And I bet he's fun to ride, too," she said.

The child didn't make eye contact with her, but he wandered toward her. "Vance says he can chase down calves, too. That's what he's best at."

"We all have to be good at something." Who was this child? "I'm Josie, Ana's sister. And you are?"

"Brody. Vance said my horse can be like Rusty if I train him."

Where was her future brother-in-law? "You have your own horse, Brody?"

Josie watched the child nod, wondering why he looked so familiar. He nodded. "My dad's buying me one. He's brown with a black tail and mane. That means he's a bay. His name is Sky Rocket."

"Cool name."

The child nodded, causing his cowboy hat to tip back. "I'm going to teach him to run really fast."

Josie smiled. "That sounds like a lot of fun."

She was about to say something to the boy when she heard another voice calling out from the other side of the barn. "Brody!"

Josie looked at the boy. "Seems someone is looking for you."

The boy jerked around just as Garrett and Vance came walking down the aisle. "Brody Temple."

Temple. This was Garrett's child. Oh, God, she needed to leave. The last thing she wanted was to see the man again.

"Oh, no," Brody said as he stepped closer to Josie. "My dad is mad."

Suddenly Garrett and Vance came up to them, and she knew she couldn't ditch the boy.

"Brody, you were told not to wander off," his father said. "You're too young to be around horses without someone older."

Suddenly, the kid threw her under the bus. "It's okay. I was with Josie."

CHAPTER THREE

GARRETT WAS BOTH relieved and surprised to find Brody standing beside Josie. His son didn't usually approach strangers.

He looked down at the boy. "Son, you know you can't leave like that."

Brody stiffened. "I was careful," he said defensively, but that changed when Vance walked up to the group. "You sure have a lot of horses here."

"We hope to have a lot more in the spring," Vance said. "So we can keep selling them to other kids." He looked at Josie. "Josie. What brings you out here?"

"I came to find Ana." She looked at the boy and managed to smile. "And found Brody instead."

That smile quickly died when she turned to Garrett. "Seems you spend a lot of time at the Lazy S. I thought you were busy building a lodge."

So she was going to stay angry at him. "I am. My foreman has everything under control." He placed his hands on Brody's shoulders. "I was taking the morning off to spend with my son. We're picking out his first horse."

"I know. We were talking about Sky Rocket." She sighed. "Look, I should get back to the house to check on Colt. It was nice to meet you, Brody."

Vance stepped in. "Don't go yet, Josie, I was going to show Brody the new foal."

"Yeah, go with us," Brody pleaded.

Garrett knew it was inevitable he'd see Josie, but today he wanted to focus on his son, not his ex-girlfriend.

He could see her indecision, but she finally relented. "I can stay a few minutes."

Brody looked at Vance. "Where is it?"

Grinning, Vance pushed his hat back. "Down a few stalls." They all began walking. Garrett stayed back and let Brody and Josie take the lead, but once they got to the oversize stall, the boy waited, a big grin on his face, until the adults arrived before he got too close. He saw happiness in his child that he hadn't seen in a long time.

Garrett looked over the railing to find a dark chestnut mare. Close by was her pretty brown filly with four white socks just like her mama.

"Oh, she's so little," Brody said as he looked through the stall railings. "How old is she?"

Vance walked up and began to stroke the mare's nose. "Just two weeks."

Josie asked Vance, "Do you think the mama will let us pet her?"

Garrett enjoyed seeing the light in her eyes, the excitement in her voice. It had been a long time since he'd seen this carefree side of Josie.

"Sure. Sugar Plum is a sweetheart." He opened the gate, went inside and nudged the mare back and stood in front of her so the group could see the long-legged filly.

"So what do you think of her, Brody?" Vance asked.

Garrett knelt down away from the new mother, then reached out a hand to coax the filly, turning to Brody. "Come here, son."

The boy walked inside the stall and mimicked his dad. "She's so little."

His son seemed to have no fear of animals as he reached out his hand to the foal. Surprisingly, the horse sniffed it and allowed the boy to touch her. Brody grinned. "She likes me. Josie, she likes me."

Josie moved in next to Brody. "Animals are trusting as long as you don't hurt them."

Garrett couldn't take his eyes off the exchange between his son and the foal, also between Josie and Brody. He felt a tightening in his chest. Josie always had an easy way, a knack to make people feel comfortable.

Josie stood up and let Brody interact with the foal. There was a bond growing already. She glanced at Garrett, seeing the love and protectiveness he had for his child. She felt tears welling in her eyes as she thought about past regrets. What could have been if only… She quickly blinked them away.

"Hey, Brody," Vance said. "Can you think of a name for our filly?"

The child shrugged. "I don't know any names for a horse."

Josie saw the boy begin to withdraw. "Maybe," she suggested, "'cause her mom's name is Sugar Plum, you can call her 'Sweet' something." She shrugged. "You know, like Sweet Pea. Sweet Georgia Brown. Sweet Caroline. Sweetheart. Sweet Potato."

"Sweet potato?" Brody giggled. "That's a silly name."

"Well, come up with something better," she told him.

The child continued to stroke the animal. "How about Sweet as Sugar," he said. "My mom used to say that to me when I was little." His voice faded out. "Before she died."

Oh, God. Josie's heart nearly stopped as she shot a look

at Garrett. He didn't make eye contact with her. His gaze stayed on his child as he went to the boy. "I think your mom would really like that name."

Vance spoke up. "I think that's a perfect name. It's got her mother's name in it, too. We'll call her Sweetie for short. How do you like that, Sugar?" The horse whinnied and bobbed her head.

Brody flashed a big grin and his green eyes sparkled.

Josie felt a tug at her heart. "Yeah. That's a good name. Sweetie."

Vance patted the mare's neck as he winked at Josie. "Thank you. Good idea."

"Anytime, soon-to-be brother-in-law." She smiled and glanced at Garrett. He was watching her, and she felt the familiar feelings, that warm shiver as his gaze locked on hers. She hated that he still had an effect on her, but she refused to let him see it. "I should get back to the house and Colt."

"We all need to leave," Garrett said. "The mama has been patient long enough with her visitors."

Brody stood up, "Bye, Sweetie. Bye, Sugar."

After the stall gate closed, Josie turned to the child. "It was nice to meet you, Brody."

"Nice meeting you, Josie," the boy said, then when she started to walk out, he asked shyly, "Will I see you again?"

She was caught off guard. "Oh, probably. We're neighbors. And your dad is building a lodge for us."

"I know. My dad builds a lot of stuff."

She smiled, trying desperately to get away. "Enjoy your new horse." She stole a look at Garrett. "Goodbye." She tried not to run out of the barn, not that her sore ankle would allow it anyway.

Twenty-four hours home, and this man had been everywhere she turned. She knew one thing. She needed to get out of Montana as soon as possible.

She didn't need Garrett Temple messing up her life… again.

An hour later, Josie sat at the desk in her father's office talking on the phone with Tori. "How did the meeting go with Reed Corp?" she asked her sister, who'd pretty much taken over Josie's event business while she was here.

"It went well. They were disappointed that you weren't at the presentation. I think Jason Reed has a thing for you."

Josie shook her head. "He also has a wife and two kids." The short, balding fortysomething man liked all women. "I don't share well, remember?"

She glanced around Colt's private domain as she listened to her sister. The den walls were done in a dark wood paneling, and against one of those walls was a floor-to-ceiling bookcase filled with books, old rodeo buckles and trophies along with blue ribbons for Lazy S's award-winning cattle and horses.

The furniture was worn leather and the carpet needed to be replaced. How long had the ranch finances been bad?

Tori's laughter came over the speakerphone. "That's right, you were pretty stingy when we were growing up, not sharing your dolls or your boyfriend. Speaking of which, how is Garrett?"

Josie froze. Why did everything come back to that man? "How would I know?"

"Because Ana said you've been spending time with him."

"That's not by choice."

"So how does he look? Please tell me he's gotten fat and gone bald."

Josie had only confided in her twin what really happened the day Garrett confessed that he'd planned to marry another woman. Later she'd learned he'd gotten her pregnant. "No, he pretty much looks the same."

"Ana also told me that he's moved back to the Temple Ranch with his son." Tori paused. "If you want, Josie, you can come back to L.A., and I'll take your place."

"No, I can't keep running away from my past. We both decided that we'd help Ana and Vance. Besides, I want to find out if Colt's new attitude toward his daughters is for real."

"You have doubts?"

Josie wasn't sure, still leery of the man's sudden change of heart. "He's nothing like the man we remember, Tori. He actually talked to me this morning at breakfast. Since the man had pretty much ignored us when we were growing up, I'm not sure how to handle the new Colt Slater."

Tori joined in. "Like I said, we can change places if you want to come back here."

Josie was a little worried. Why was Tori so eager to come to Montana? "Is there something you're not telling me?"

"No, I've just been working a lot of hours."

"You're being careful, aren't you? Have you heard from Dane again?"

"No."

Tori's ex-boyfriend, Dane Buckley, had abused her. Josie shivered, recalling the night her sister had showed up on her doorstep with the bruises and busted lip. When she wanted to call the police, Tori begged her not to, not wanting anyone to know. They'd settled on getting a restraining order.

"You need to call Detective Brandon if Dane comes anywhere near you."

She heard the hesitation. "What aren't you telling me?"

"It's just a feeling… Dane's around. I saw a car like his down the street by the town house."

Josie leaned her arms on the deck, fighting her anger. "Then tell that to the detective. He can check around to make sure you're safe. That's their job."

"Okay, I will."

"No, I mean it, Tori. You don't want to take any chances with that jerk."

Josie looked up and saw Garrett standing in the doorway. She quickly picked up the receiver, taking the phone off speaker. "Just listen to me about this. Please, promise me."

She heard the exaggerated sigh. "I said I would. Right after I hang up I'll call Detective Brandon."

"Good. I better go, but could you send your samples for the lodge's website design?"

"Sure. Bye, Josie."

"Bye, Tori." She hung up the phone and looked across the room at the man who seemed to be everywhere she was. "Is there a problem, Garrett?"

"I was about to ask you the same thing," he said. "Is Tori all right?"

Josie shrugged. "She's fine."

Garrett walked to the desk. "Look, Josie, if someone is stalking your sister, it's serious. Maybe I can help."

Josie didn't want to talk to Garrett about this, or anything else. "Thank you, but we have it under control."

Garrett watched for a moment, and then finally nodded. "Okay, but the offer stands."

"Fine. So what brings you here?"

"I just got a call from my foreman from the lodge. He has questions about the bathroom locations."

Josie shook her head. "I have nothing to do with that. You need to ask Ana."

"I would, but Ana's not available. She's tied up in meetings all day and can't get away. If you want to keep this project on schedule, the rough plumbing problems need to get resolved before any walls go up."

"Fine. The last thing I want is any delays." She stood. She found she was excited about getting involved in the project. She'd always been a natural-born organizer. She just didn't want to spend any time with Garrett. "How soon do you need me there?"

"Right now. I can drive you out, but Brody will be going with us. Then I can come back here to trailer his horse."

Josie hated the idea, but what choice did she have? "Okay." She grabbed her jacket off the back of the chair. She headed out, but Garrett's voice stopped her.

"Brody's in the kitchen. Kathleen is feeding him some lunch."

Josie felt her own stomach protest from lack of food. "That's not a bad idea. I could use some nourishment."

They walked down the hall to the bright kitchen and heard laughter. At the big table sat Brody and her father. Kathleen was at the stove stirring a pot of soup. "Sit down, you two," the housekeeper said. "And I'll fix you something to eat."

Colt looked up at them, as did the boy. Both smiled mischievously.

"Hey, Dad, did you know that Colt used to be a World Saddle Bronc champion?"

Garrett nodded. Who would have thought, gruff, strictly business Colton Slater could make his son smile?

"I might have heard it somewhere." He nodded at the older man across from his son. "Hello, Colt. How are you doing these days?"

Colt looked at Josie. "Not bad. T…two of my daughters are home."

"Colt's learning to talk again," Brody explained. "'Cause he had a stroke. But he's getting better."

Garrett sat down at the table. "That's good news." He looked at Colt. "Did Brody tell you we just bought one of your horses?"

"Yeah, Sky Rocket," Brody said. "I'm going to learn to ride him really fast."

Colt frowned. "I'm s…sure you are. But f…first you have to learn to take care of your animal so he'll trust you."

A confused Brody looked at his dad.

"It means when you get an animal you have to take responsibility for it. You need to feed and clean up after Rocket."

He glanced back at Colt, his green eyes worried. "But I'm just a kid."

Kathleen brought two more bowls of potato soup to the table. Josie reluctantly took her seat beside her father.

"You'll learn some now, and as you get older you'll do more," Garrett told him. "You live on a ranch now. That means everyone does their share."

Brody took a hearty spoonful of soup, then said, "If I do all that stuff, will you teach me how to ride a bucking bronc?"

Colt watched out the window as the threesome drove off to the lodge site. He had to admit that he'd enjoyed sharing lunch with them.

"See, that wasn't so bad, was it?" Kathleen said. "Too bad you didn't get cozier with your kids a lot sooner."

Colt turned and made his way back to the kitchen table, but didn't say anything. Nothing to say. He'd messed up big-time when it came to his girls.

Kathleen placed two mugs filled with coffee on the table, then sat down across from him. "Looks like you're getting another chance at being their dad. I hope you realize how lucky you are."

Colt hated that it had taken him so many years to learn that. He thought about his girls. Why had it taken him so long to realize what they meant to him? Josie was home, but so was Garrett Temple. How was she handling seeing him again? He recalled how badly she'd been hurt by their breakup. Now Garrett had returned and brought his son with him. He could see being around the man bothered Josie, in more ways than he knew his daughter would ever admit.

"Did you see Josie with Garrett?"

Kathleen set down her mug. "That girl has a lot of you in her. If Garrett comes sniffing around again, I doubt she's going to make it easy for him." She shook her head. "Of course that little boy has to come first. From what I hear from Della, Brody's had a rough few years with the divorce and lately with his mother's death."

Colt nodded. "A horse would be good for him."

Kathleen smiled. "And maybe some time with you. He sure didn't have any trouble talking with you."

Colt would always regret that he never took time to console his own daughters. He couldn't get past his own anger. "Sometimes it's easier with strangers."

Thirty minutes later, Josie sat in the front seat as Garrett pulled his truck into his makeshift parking area at the site. He pulled his hard hat off the dashboard, then reached in the back and found one for Brody, then another for Josie.

"Keep these on for your safety," he told them both.

"Good idea," Josie said and put it on. "Let's go check out this place." She climbed out as Garrett opened the back door and helped Brody out.

Even though the circumstances weren't ideal, she was

eager to see the lodge. She pulled her coat together against the chill and waited for Brody and Garrett to catch up to her.

Together, they walked across the wet ground to the sheets of plywood covering the mud caused by last night's rain.

They reached the front door. Well, it was where the door was going to be. This was still a two-story log cabin shell. The outside logs were up, along with the roof, but not much more. She inhaled the scent of fresh-cut wood as they walked through the wide doorway into what would be the main meeting room. More like an open area with high ceilings of tongue-and-groove oak.

Josie glanced around at the huge picture windows that overlooked the river. Drawn to the beautiful scenery, she walked over. This was a perfect spot. In her head, she was already figuring out different events that could be held here.

The first was the Slater/Rivers wedding right in front of these windows. She began to visualize the number of chairs that the room could handle, leaving room for an aisle. She turned to the men working on the floor-to-ceiling fireplace made out of river rock. It took her breath away.

"How do you like it so far?"

She swung around to see Garrett and Brody. She couldn't help but smile. "It's really nice. In fact, it's better than I thought possible. There's a lot we can do with this space. Are the floors going to be hardwood?"

When Garrett nodded, she looked toward the roughed-in stairs to the second floor. It was going to be left open, a mezzanine level for the bedrooms upstairs. She hated that anglers would be using it. She could really promote this for high-dollar functions.

"Okay, I see your mind working," Garrett said. "Tell me what it is."

Josie turned toward him. "It would be nice if we didn't have to use it for anglers."

Garrett arched an eyebrow. "Before we open to the public there's going to be a wedding here."

She tensed, recalling when she was planning her own wedding, until her groom betrayed her.

She wiped the picture from her mind. "I know. I'll go over those details with Ana." She released a breath. "Okay, where are these bathrooms that need my attention?"

He glanced around. "I need to find Jerry."

When Garrett went off to find the foreman, Josie realized she had to find a way to get over her resentment toward him. It would be the only way this project would get completed.

Her cell phone rang and she reached inside her purse to answer it. "Hello."

"Josie, it's Ana."

"Hey, Ana. Are you planning to come out to the site?"

"No. I'm at the house, but we need to discuss the lodge."

"What about it?" she asked, and walked away from the group.

"I found out today that I'm going to a teacher's conference in Helena," Ana told her. "The school principal is sick and he asked me to take his place. I have to go out of town for three days."

Three days. She looked at Garrett talking with the foreman. "You're leaving me here alone?"

Ana paused. "I'm not doing this on purpose, Josie. It's only for a few days. Since you helped with the building plans, I figured this should be easy."

Josie glanced across the room. She was going to have

to spend more time with Garrett. Hadn't she already been doing that over the past twenty-four hours?

"Come on, I've seen you organize and delegate," Ana said. "This will be easy."

What could she say? "Okay, have a safe trip. But expect a lot of phone calls, because I'm still going to need your help."

"You've got Garrett."

That was what she was afraid of. Already her stomach began to hurt. She said goodbye and hung up as Garrett walked over.

"Is there something wrong?" he asked.

"Ana has to go out of town. Looks like you're stuck working with me."

A smile twitched at the corners of his mouth. "I can handle it, but can you?"

She wanted to wipe that smile off his face. "This is business. I can handle it with ease." Garrett Temple, the man, she wasn't so sure.

CHAPTER FOUR

GARRETT COULD SEE how hard Josie worked to hold her temper, but the frown lines between her eyes, and her clenched hands gave her away.

"Hey, don't be angry at me. I didn't send Ana out of town."

"I didn't say you did. I'm just saying, I'm not that sure about what's going on here at the site."

He glanced around at the work going on. "I don't believe that. Wasn't this lodge your idea?"

"A general idea is far from making decisions on the design," she argued. "Shouldn't you be doing that?"

"I could, but in order to save money on this project, your sister was going to handle that."

Before she could say anything, Brody walked toward him.

"Hey, Dad, Jerry said if it's all right with you he'll take me to look at the bulldozer. Can I go, please?"

Garrett glanced at his foreman to see him give the thumbs-up. Since Jerry had three of his own kids, he knew that his son would be taken care of.

"Sure. Just do what Jerry says." He tapped his son's head. "And keep your hard hat on."

"Okay," the boy yelled as he shot off toward Jerry.

Garrett turned back to Josie. She still wasn't happy.

"Come on, let's go upstairs so we can discuss this in private." He grabbed her hand, surprised that she didn't fight to get it back.

He led her through the crew working on the inside walls, then up the makeshift steps to the second story.

"Be careful," he told her. Once on the plywood floor upstairs, he still didn't let go of her small hand. Even with the flood of memories that reminded him how easily he could get mixed up with Josie Slater again, he held on tight to her hand.

Once safely on solid ground, he released her hand and went over to his plumber, Pete Saunders. "Hey, Pete, how's it going?"

The stocky-built man turned around, and seeing Josie, he smiled. "Hey, Garrett."

"Pete, this is Ana's sister Josie Slater. Josie, Pete."

She nodded. "Hi, Pete. I hear you have some problems."

"Well, not exactly problems, but more or less, a design issue. I'd rather get it right the first time than have to redo any work. It saves time and money."

"A man after my own heart." Josie smiled at him, and the plumber smiled back. "So, Pete, what do you need from me?"

"Well, there are four bedrooms upstairs. Each has its own bath." Pete walked her through a framed room and into a smaller area. "This is one of the bath spaces." He pushed his hard hat back. "My question is, do we put in bathtubs with showers, or a tub with a separate shower stall? I know that most fishermen could care less about a tub, but you want this lodge to be multifunctional. So I thought you should be the one to choose."

Garrett watched Josie, and without missing a beat, she said, "We definitely are going for the bigger clientele base here. They'll want a retreat." She glanced at Garrett. "I know we're trying to save on the budget, but since we're hoping to add on to the structure later on, I feel the upgrades would be a good investment now."

Garrett gave her a nod, agreeing, too.

Josie turned back to Pete then pointed to where everything was going. "So, a spa tub here, then a separate double shower with several sprays, here and here. Can you get in a vanity with two sinks?"

Garrett didn't hear anything else after double shower, big enough for two people—lovers. He glanced at Josie in her slim jeans and turtleneck sweater that showed off her curves. The picture quickly reminded him that he hadn't been with a woman in a long time. He'd been divorced for two years. His dating life had been virtually nonexistent because he wanted to spend as much time as possible with his son.

Now he'd been thrown together with the one woman who could cause him to regret what he'd been missing.

"Garrett, what do you think?" Josie asked. "Is there money in the budget for what I want?"

Get your head back on business. "What? Oh, I think so. If you shop for some good bargains on the fixtures and cabinets, the budget can handle it."

Josie looked thoughtful. He could see her mind working. She was no doubt planning out her strategy to get the job done. It seemed she wasn't thinking about going back to California just yet. Great. Just what he needed—another complication in his life right now.

Two hours later, after a complete tour of the lodge, and going over the progress and building details, Garrett drove Josie back to the house. Was it her, or did it seem easier to talk to him? At least when the subject was business. She only hoped that she didn't physically need to be by the man's side to make more decisions.

Garrett pulled up and stopped in front of the house. Josie reached for the door handle and paused to say, "If you'll point me in the direction of the wholesale plumbing house I'll go see what I can find."

"I'll come up with a list of places. We have some time before they're needed."

With a nod, Josie looked in the backseat at Brody. "Have fun with Sky Rocket, Brody."

The boy didn't look happy. "I can't because I have to start school."

Josie smiled. "Oh, that's good. You'll make all kinds of new friends there. It's a nice school."

"Is that where you knew my dad?"

Josie felt the heat move up her neck. "Yes, we were friends, but it was a long time ago."

Brody looked at his dad. "Was that before you knew Mom?"

Josie's breath caught as she glanced at Garrett. She could see he was uncomfortable with the question. Good.

"Yes, I knew Josie in high school." He rested his hand on the steering wheel. "I played football and she was a cheerleader. When we got older we used to go out with other friends, too." Garrett grinned. "If my memory serves me, Josie used to like to dance and sing karaoke."

She gasped. How could he remember that? "That was one time," she told him. "And as I recall, I did it on a dare."

He continued to smile, knowing he'd been the culprit.

She glanced at Brody again. "Give me some time and I'll tell you stories about your dad that will make you laugh your head off."

She got a smile from the kid. "Oh, boy," he said.

"I've got to go now." Josie waved. "Bye, Brody and Garrett." She opened the door and climbed out, knowing she couldn't get chummy with Garrett Temple and his son. No matter how cute, or how charming. It would lead nowhere.

She headed up the steps, opened the front door and walked inside to see her father coming out of his downstairs bedroom. He was using a cane today.

"Well, look at you. You seem to be getting around like a pro."

He stopped and waited for her. "It's all the great nursing."

They started a slow walk toward the kitchen. She was surprised he was doing so well. "It's good that you're recovering so fast."

"And th...thank you for coming home to help." He paused. "I gave you plenty of reasons never to come back here. I'm sorry."

Whoa. This was too much to handle. "Is the apology for bringing me here now, or for all the years you ignored your daughters?"

"F...for all the above. I know there isn't anything I can do to change the past, but if p...possible, I want to try and change how things are between us now."

Josie tried to speak, but emotions swamped her.

"It's okay." Colt put his hand on her arm. "I don't expect an answer, or your trust. I just want a chance to get to know you while you're here."

Josie nodded and went into the kitchen. Kathleen was preparing supper. "Hey, you two, what are you up to?"

"Just talkin'," Colt said.

Josie walked to the large bay window that overlooked the barn, where Garrett's truck was hooked to the horse trailer. She eyed the man as he led Sky Rocket to the ramp and up into the trailer. Brody stood by and watched as his father latched the gate, then he placed his hand on his son's shoulder and helped him into the truck.

"Nice boy."

Josie didn't turn when she heard her father.

"He's had a rough time," Josie said.

"Seems they both have," Colt answered.

Josie gave her father a sideways glance. "He brought on his troubles himself."

"I know. He hurt you badly. I wish I could have protected you all those years ago."

It surprised her that her father had known what happened. "I wish you'd have been there, too," she admitted.

She'd hurt more than she could tell anyone. More than she ever wanted to remember. But Garrett hadn't been the only man in her life to hurt her.

Monday morning Garrett drove Brody to school. He wanted to take his son on his first day. He glanced down at his solemn-looking eight-year-old. Six months ago when Natalie was killed in the automobile accident, he let his ex-in-laws keep the boy while he finished his move from Butte to Royerton. Although he'd visited Brody as much as possible, he knew that the move would be difficult for the boy. His son had to leave his home, friends and grandparents to move to a new place. That was tough for a kid, especially a kid who'd recently lost his mother.

"Look, Brody, being the new kid in school is never easy, but Royerton is your home now. It's a new start for both of us."

"But I liked my old school."

"I know, but I couldn't stay there. Grandpa Nolan needs us here to help with the ranch."

He pulled into the parking lot and they got out and walked toward the large complex that housed the community's school-aged children from kindergarten through eighth grade. The other building was the high school.

Standing in front of the elementary building was Brody's new teacher, Miss Lisa Kennedy. She looked about eighteen. Garrett had met with her last week, and was confident that she would do everything possible to help his son adjust to his new school.

"Mr. Temple," she said with a smile as she looked at Brody. "Good morning, Brody. I'm so happy that you'll be joining my class."

"Morning, Miss Kennedy," he murmured.

She kept eye contact with Brody. "I know it's tough starting a new school, so Royerton Elementary started the buddy system. And I have someone who's been anxious to meet you." The teacher looked toward the playground and motioned to someone. A small, redheaded boy about eight years old came running to them. "Brody, this is Adam Graves. Adam, meet Brody."

"Hi, Brody," Adam said. "You're going to be in my class." The freckled-faced boy smiled. "I was new last year, so I wanted to be the buddy this year."

Brody didn't say anything.

The boy looked at his teacher and when he got a nod, he said, "I hear you got a new horse."

The question got his son's attention. "Yeah, Sky Rocket. Do you have a horse?"

Adam shook his head. "Not anymore because we moved into town. But when my dad was around, I used to have a pony, Jodie."

Brody studied the boy. "Hey, maybe…you can come out to my house and see Sky Rocket sometime." He glanced up at his father. "Can he, Dad?"

Garrett felt a weight lift on seeing his child's enthusiasm. "Sure. Maybe after I talk with Adam's mother." He wanted to make sure he followed the right protocol for playdates. "Right now I think Miss Kennedy wants you to go to class."

The pretty teacher nodded as the bell rang. "Adam, why don't you take Brody to the classroom and show him where his desk is?"

"Okay, Miss Kennedy. Come on, Brody."

"Bye, Dad." Brody took off with his new friend.

"Bye, son. Have a good day," he called, but knew Brody wasn't hearing him. That was a good thing, right?

"He's going to be fine, Mr. Temple."

He nodded. "I know, but it's been a rough few months." It had been for him, too. He hadn't known how to handle his son's sadness.

"I'll call you if there are any problems."

"Thank you." Garrett walked off toward his truck and grabbed the lodge plans off the seat. Since he was here, he could catch Ana up on the progress and see if he could steal her for a few hours to help him with some design decisions.

He walked across the same school yard that a dozen years ago he once attended, and memories flooded back. He'd liked school. He had friends and was a good student. The girls liked him, too. But on that first day of his junior year when he walked though the front doors and literally ran into the new freshman, Josefina Slater, he was a goner.

He'd known the Slater sisters all his life, but that summer something changed with her. Josie's eyes were a richer blue, her face was prettier, and her body... Oh, God, her body.

He shivered, recalling how beautiful she looked. If only she still didn't have that effect on him.

He pulled open the door to the high school, and was quickly brought back to the present when he was nearly knocked over by a rush of teenagers.

Garrett removed his cowboy hat and headed to the office as his thoughts returned to Josie. He had to stop thinking about her because nothing could start up between them.

Not that she wanted anything to do with him. What they once had, had to stay a fond memory. He needed to concentrate on the future. Brody needed him full-time and so did his dad.

He opened the door and smiled at the receptionist, Clare Stewart. He remembered her from school. Of course, in a town of six thousand people, everyone knew most of the citizens.

"Hey, Garrett, it's been a few years."

He shook her hand. "Hello, Clare. It's good to see you again."

"So what brings you to the principal's office?"

"I'm not here to see the principal, but Ana Slater. Is she in her office?"

The pretty blonde shook her head. "No, she's in there." She pointed to the door that read Principal.

"Is she in a meeting?"

"No, she's with her sister, Josie." Clare raised an eyebrow. "You remember Josie, don't you?"

Garrett didn't answer. Everyone in school pretty much knew that they'd been a couple. With Josie's return home, no doubt there would be gossip around town. He knocked on the door and opened it to find the two Slater sisters in a heated discussion.

Josie swung around and glared at him. "What are you doing here?"

So much for getting along, he thought. He ignored her and closed the door behind him. "I came to see Ana, but good, I got both of you."

The last person Josie wanted in on this discussion was Garrett. She wanted to walk out, but she knew it wasn't the professional thing to do. She counted to ten to calm her racing pulse, then asked, "Did you need something?"

"Yeah, a project manager." He looked from Ana to her. "There needs to be someone around to make the decisions."

Ana turned to Josie. *Oh, no, this wasn't going to land in her lap.* "I thought I answered your questions Friday," she told Garrett.

"There are still more decisions to make. If either of you could stop by the site daily so there aren't any holdups that would be nice. When I have to chase down someone, it causes delays and costs money."

Josie turned to her sister. "Well, Ana?"

Her older sister shook her head. "Josie, I explained to you already." She then turned to Garrett. "My principal is in the hospital with pneumonia. I've been asked to take his place for the next few weeks. I've already taken so much time off as it is, and with my wedding coming…"

Ana sighed. "I'm sorry, Garrett. I never planned for this to happen. Like I was trying to tell Josie, I need her to take my place on the project."

"And I've told you, I'm not going to be in town that long," Josie shot back.

Josie could see Garrett was losing patience. "Seems that's been your tune since you've arrived here. Fine, you want me to have all the control? I can make the decisions and the hell with you wanting your corporate retreat."

He turned and started for the door. Curse that man. "Hold up there, Temple."

Garrett stopped and waited for her to speak.

"Are you headed out there now?" she asked.

Garrett nodded. "Yeah, I just dropped Brody off at school."

Josie walked toward him. "Okay, but I don't have my

car. I needed to get my brakes fixed. I'll have to ride out with you, but that also means you'll have to drop me off at the ranch." She'd get one of the men to bring her back to town later to get her car from Al's Garage.

After saying goodbye to Ana, Josie hurried to get outside. The air was downright cold today. She pulled her sweater coat tighter.

"You're going to need a warmer coat if you stay around much longer. My dad's predicting an early winter."

At the mention of Nolan Temple, Josie got all soft inside. "How is your Dad?"

"He's been doing better on this new medication, but his arthritis gets worse in the colder weather."

They reached his truck, and Garrett opened the passenger door, but he knew better than to help her in. A flash of memory took him back to how he used to swing the teenage Josie up in his arms and set her down on the seat. He used to be rewarded with a kiss.

A sudden ache constricted his chest as he watched her climb into the pickup. She did just fine without him, like she had for all these years. Maybe that had been their problem, her stubborn independence.

After he shut the door, he hurried around to the other side and got in behind the wheel. He immediately started up the engine and turned on the heat. The soft sounds of country-Western music filled the cab. He caught a whiff of her scent. It was the same perfume she'd worn years ago.

He needed a distraction. "Are you up for a drive into Butte?"

She looked at him, her eyes leery. "Why?"

"I thought we could pick out the bathroom and kitchen tiles along with the sinks and tubs. We can get it out of the way now…before you have to go back to California."

He checked his watch. "I have until three o'clock when I pick up Brody from school."

She hesitated as their gazes locked. It seemed to be a battle of wills. Even years ago, Josie liked to be in control. "Sure."

Hiding his surprise, Garrett put the truck in gear and pulled out onto Main Street and headed for the highway out of town. "You know this working together would be so much easier if you weren't always ready to fight me all the time."

She didn't say anything.

"Josie, what happened between us was a long time ago. I'm not saying you have to like me, but can't we put what happened aside? We were kids. It's time to move on."

"You're right, Temple. I need to think about the River's Edge project and nothing else." She glared at him as he turned onto the highway. "But that doesn't mean we can be friends."

Her words hurt him more than he wanted to admit. At one time, Josie Slater had been his best friend and his girl. They shared everything, but then that summer everything changed and not for the good.

"I'm sorry to hear that, Josie."

By noon, Josie was enjoying herself. They'd gone to a builders supply house and looked over cabinets and sinks for the kitchen and baths. She also realized that Garrett had good taste when it came to colors for tiles and flooring. The store's designer, Diana, was more than willing to help them. The way she looked at Garrett, Josie suspected the two had more than a business relationship. She hated that the other woman's attention toward Garrett bothered her.

After the order had been placed and a delivery date set, they walked back out to the truck.

"You seem to be well-known around here," she said.

"I built my construction company in this area. It's a good idea to be nice to everyone because most of my work is from word of mouth. I worked years to build a good reputation and I've done most of my trade here."

They climbed in the truck. "So why did you move everything back to Royerton?"

"Dad. He can't handle the ranch on his own." He released a breath. "And since my divorce and only getting to see Brody twice a week, I could spend more time at the ranch."

Josie didn't want to talk about his marriage. It wouldn't matter anyway. Garrett had given up on her years ago.

"How is the business since moving to Royerton?"

Garrett stopped at the light and glanced at her. "Not bad. I'm lucky that my foreman is willing to bid on jobs here in Butte. My crew is pretty mobile and they'll go almost anywhere for work."

Garrett drove down the street, then pulled his truck into the parking lot of the local café and shut off the engine. "Come on, I'll buy you some lunch."

He got out before she could argue. Since she was hungry, she didn't put up a fight. She hurried to catch up with him. Okay, so he was treating her like one of the guys. Wasn't that what she wanted him to do?

He stopped at the entrance and held open the door. She went inside first and glanced around the mom-and-pop place, with ruffled curtains and floral wallpaper.

"They've got the best food around." He smiled as an older woman came over. "Hi, Dolly."

The fortysomething woman looked at him and smiled. "Well, well, if it isn't Garrett Temple. Where is that sweet boy of yours?"

Garrett removed his cowboy hat. "He's in school in Royerton."

She moved across the café, her blond ponytail swinging back and forth. "So you got him settled in?"

"I'm trying. He's still a little sad about the move."

"He's lucky to have you." The woman turned to Josie. "Hi, I'm Dolly Madison." She raised a hand. "I've heard every joke there is. And if that guy cooking in the kitchen there wasn't about perfect, I wouldn't have married him and put up with the headache."

Josie smiled. "Nice to meet you, Dolly. I'm Josie Slater."

"Welcome to Dolly's Place." She grabbed two menus and led them to a table in the corner. Once they were seated, Dolly brought over two mugs of coffee, and the busboy filled their water glasses. After they ordered a club sandwich and a hamburger, Dolly left them alone.

Josie looked at him. She hated that she was so curious about Garrett's past. "You seem to have a nice life here."

His gray eyes were distant. "It's funny how looks can be deceiving."

Later that night, Colt had retired to his room, but he couldn't sleep. He thought about Josie and how quiet she'd been at supper. She had started to open up, to talk to him, but tonight she was quiet again. He knew she'd spent the day with Garrett. Had something happened between them?

He fought to keep from phoning the Temple Ranch and having a word with the man. Colt stood and went to the window and looked out into the night. The security lights were on, so he could see all the way to the barn and into the empty corral.

It was all quiet.

Problem was he wanted to be the one who did the last walk through the barn to check on the horses.

So many things had changed in the past few months. Two daughters had come home, one was engaged to marry. He smiled at the thought of Vance officially becoming a part of the family. Vance Rivers was a good man.

Colt sobered. If he wasn't careful, he could lose another daughter. Josie just might head back to California if she decided she couldn't deal with her past.

He knew everything about dealing with his past. He still couldn't let go of their mother. Lucia had nearly destroyed him. He walked slowly back to his bed and sat down. He worked the buttons on his Western-cut shirt and then pulled it off. He kicked off slippers, and couldn't wait until he was sure-footed enough to put on his well-broken-in Justin boots again. He stood and stripped down his jeans. He managed it all without Jay's help. He might not get to cowboy much these days, but he still liked to dress like one.

He turned off the bedside light, pulled back the blanket and got in. He laid his head against the pillow and stared at the outside lights making a pattern on the ceiling.

He shut his eyes as the familiar loneliness washed over him. He'd had the same feelings for a lot of years, but hard work helped him fight off the worst times. He closed his eyes, hoping sleep would take it away.

He must have dozed off when he heard the pocket door to his room open. It was probably one of the girls checking on him. When the figure moved to the bed, he caught a whiff of her fragrance. His eyes opened and his breath caught. "Lucia…"

"Yes, *mi amor*. I am here," she said, her voice soft and throaty. Her hand reached out and touched his face. Colt shivered as he looked at the woman he'd given his heart to so many years ago. Her face was in the shadows, but he saw the silhouette, the delicate features and the black hair that caressed her shoulders.

He knew it was her. His Lucia.

He blinked several times to get a better look, but his eyes grew heavy and he couldn't keep them open any longer. He didn't fight it, not wanting to disturb this wonderful dream.

CHAPTER FIVE

IT WAS ABOUT six the next morning when Josie awoke to the sound of voices outside her bedroom. She got up, realized how cold it was and pulled her sweatshirt over her head then went to the door.

Outside in the hall were Ana and Vance. "Hey, what's going on?" She rubbed the sleep from her eyes. "Is there a fire or something?"

The twosome didn't smile.

"Sorry to disturb you, sis," Ana began, "but Vance needs to move the herd in from the north pasture."

"There's a blizzard headed our way," Vance added. "And we're going to need every willing body we can get our hands on to help." He glanced over her pajama-clad body. "Think you're able to ride with us?"

Ana gasped. "Vance, no. Josie hasn't been on a horse in years. And it's cold out there."

Vance grinned. "So our California girl can't take the Montana cold?"

The two were talking and leaving her out. "Hey, I can speak for myself."

They both looked at her. "I remember how to ride, and if someone loans me a pair of long johns and a heavy coat, sure I'll join you."

"No, Josie. It's not safe."

"Ana, you'd be riding out if you weren't needed at the school."

Ana started to argue, then said, "You're right, but if this storm is as bad as they say, the high school will be shut down tomorrow. So I need to go in today. But I want you to take Blondie. She's a good mount and knows how to work cattle." She glanced at her soon-to-be husband. "You better take care of her, or you'll be moving back into the barn."

Josie left the couple to finish the argument and went into the shower. When she got back to her bedroom, she found thermal underwear, a winter coat, scarf and gloves on the bed and fur-lined boots next to the chair.

Josie dressed quickly, then went down to the kitchen, where she found Colt and Kathleen at the table.

"Hey, I hear there's a storm coming," she said as she poured some coffee.

Her father turned to her. "I wish you didn't have to go out in it. I sh…should go."

She sat down and began to eat the plate of eggs Kathleen put in front of her. "You will. Just keep getting better, and the next blizzard is yours."

She watched as a smile appeared on his face. Her chest grew tight and her eyes filled. Colt Slater smiling?

"That's a deal, but I'd like you to ride with me."

This was killing her. "If you get back on a horse, then I'll go with you." Why did it matter so much that her dad wanted to go riding with her? "Deal?"

Colt's blue gaze met hers as she stuck out her hand. "Deal."

They finished breakfast in silence, and she put on her coat, wrapped the scarf around her neck and chin and hurried out to the barn. She found Vance had finished loading four horses into a trailer.

Once finished, he gave her a hat, and she climbed into

the passenger side of the pickup as two more men got in the backseat. "We're meeting the other men at the pasture gate." The ride was slow over the dirt road and across Slater land as snow flurries blew, and she looked up at the dull gray sky with concern.

They finally made it to the gate and saw the other trucks. One stood out. Garrett's pickup. Of course he would be here to help a neighbor.

She could deal with him for the sake of the cattle. The men unloaded the already-saddled horses. Josie went to Blondie and waited for Vance to give out the orders.

"It's a precaution, but I don't want anyone riding by themselves," he said. "We'll work in teams. When visibility gets bad, we quit and go back to the house."

Everyone climbed on their mounts and Garrett headed toward her. "Looks like we're a team."

Garrett knew that Josie wasn't happy, but he didn't care. He wanted to finish this and get back to his house and Brody. He was thankful he'd moved his herd yesterday.

"We'll take it slow," he told her as he directed his roan, Pirate, through the gate behind her. At first, she looked a little awkward on her horse, but soon found her stride.

"I can keep up with you," she told him.

She proved she was a woman of her word as she quickly rode behind the herd and managed to do her part.

It was slow going over the next few hours as the mamas and calves resisted going along with the move and kept trying to run off, but the worst part was the size of the snowflakes, and the snow was sticking, even with the wind.

Garrett kept thinking about a warm fire, some hot coffee and... He glanced at Josie. Why couldn't he stop thinking about her? He spotted a stray calf and got him back to the herd. He hated that she'd been distracting him ever since she'd showed up in Montana.

He pulled his scarf over his nose as the cold burned his skin. He turned to Josie and called out to her, "You okay?"

She nodded. "Just cold."

When suddenly another calf shot off, Josie kicked into Blondie's sides and went after it. Garrett waited about five minutes, but Josie didn't return.

"Dammit." With a call to Vance to let him know where he was going, he tugged Pirate's reins and headed in the direction she'd gone.

It wasn't long before the visibility turned bad. Dammit, he knew this wasn't good. He knew where he was, but did Josie?

He cupped his hand around his mouth. "Josie!"

With his heart pounding, he waited for some answer, but heard the roar of the wind. "Josie."

Finally, he heard his phone and pulled it out of his pocket. "Josie?"

"Hey, I might be lost," she said.

"Can you see any landmarks?"

"I'm next to a big tree. I passed over the creek a ways back."

"Stay there, I'm coming for you. Listen for my voice."

He adjusted his direction and kept calling out to her. He walked his horse through the snow building on the ground. Worry took over, and he knew he had to find her fast.

After a few minutes he was about to call for Vance when he yelled out her name again. This time he got an answer.

"Keep talking," he told her, and he finally found her. She had roped a small calf. "What the hell?" He climbed down and reached for her. "Are you crazy?"

"I thought I was doing my job."

"Well, going after one small calf isn't worth losing your life, or mine." He glanced around, knowing they had to get out of the weather. "Come on, I know where we are."

He helped her back on her horse, then he climbed back on Pirate and pulled out his compass again.

"Think you can make it about a quarter of a mile to find shelter?"

She nodded and wrapped the rope attached to her calf and followed Garrett. He took out his phone and let Vance know that he'd found Josie and they were headed for the homestead cabin.

Garrett prayed they were headed in the right direction. There wasn't much visibility left as the storm intensified, but finally he saw the black stovepipe peeking out of the cabin's roof.

He stopped in front of the porch and lifted her down from the horse, and began to carry her inside.

"Hey, I can walk," she argued.

"This is easier," he told her as he opened the door to the dark cabin and sat her down in a chair.

"I'll be right back as soon as I take care of the animals."

Shivering, she nodded. "I'm okay."

Garrett went back out and got the horses in the lean-to along with the calf. They were out of the weather, so he got some feed from the bin and pumped some water into the trough. He hurried back inside and found Josie had lit the lantern on the table and was putting wood into the stove. "Here let me do that."

She relented and sat back down in the chair. "I'm never going to hear the end of this, am I?"

He kept working. "Probably not." Once the fire caught, he turned back to her and took hold of her hands. "How are your hands, fingers?"

"They're fine."

"What about your feet. Do you still feel them?"

"Yes, they're fine. And no, I don't feel sleepy. I'm feeling great." She pulled her hands away. "So you can quit playing doctor."

"I didn't realize I needed to play keeper."

"Hey, that could have happened to anyone. The storm decided at that moment to get worse."

Just then, Garrett's cell phone rang. "Hey, Vance. Yes, we made it to the cabin."

"Then stay put," the foreman told him. "We barely made it back to the truck with the men."

"How'd the herd survive?" Garrett asked, knowing Josie wasn't going to be happy.

"They're safe as possible in these conditions."

"Well, count one more calf because we have him up here with us."

That got a laugh. "Stay warm. We'll come dig you out tomorrow."

Garrett hung up the phone and looked at Josie.

"So are they coming to get us?"

He shook his head. "Not until morning if the storm stops."

"What do you mean, tomorrow?"

"Josie, you were out in it. You saw that the visibility was close to zero. Do you really want to risk someone's life to come and get you because you can't stand to be anywhere near me?"

The small room was finally getting warm, but Josie was still miserable. Not because of the cold, but for the trouble she'd caused Vance and the men. She shouldn't have been so set on going after the calf.

"I'm sorry. I had no idea the storm was so bad, or how far the calf led me."

"Not a problem. I found you. Besides, this is a freak

storm." The wind roared. "We have enough wood to keep us warm until someone comes for us."

That wasn't Josie's biggest problem. They were going to spend the night here. Together.

She sighed and looked around the rustic cabin that her great-grandparents built when George Slater brought his bride, Sarah Colton, here from Wyoming. There was the double bed against the wall with a nice quilt covering it. There was a small table and two chairs and a lantern in the center, also some personal items, candles, dishes and an assortment of canned food on the shelves. She had no doubt that someone had taken advantage of the cabin as their personal retreat. Ana and Vance?

Josie got up, went to the one window over the sink in the cabin and pulled back the curtains. A little more light came into the space. But there was nothing to see but blowing snow. She glanced across the room to find Garrett watching her.

"It's a good thing that Ana and Vance have made this place livable."

She folded her arms and nodded. "It doesn't look too bad. And there's some food. Some canned stew and soup."

"And coffee," Garrett added. "But sorry, no inside facilities."

His words nearly made her laugh except she could really use a bathroom right now. "How far away is it?"

He did smile, and her heart took a little tumble. "Just a few feet around back behind the lean-to." He buttoned his sheepskin-lined coat and waited for her to do the same.

Once bundled up, he said, "Earlier, I strung a rope from the porch railing to the lean-to. We'll string another line to the outhouse."

Suddenly the seriousness of the storm hit her. She paused. "You can't see that far?"

"I'm not taking any chances if the storm gets worse. Call it a safety net."

She gave him a nod, and he opened the door to a gust of wind. Once outside, he took her by the arm and escorted her to the edge of the porch and the lead rope. Together they made their way to the lean-to. After checking the animals, they trudged on, fighting the strong winds and biting temperature as they found the small structure. They finished their business quickly, then headed back to the cabin.

He opened the door, and she practically tumbled into the warm room. "Oh, man, it's crazy out there," she breathed, feeling the cold burning her lungs. "How much worse is it going to get?"

"I can't answer that. We're safe here, though. Vance knows where we are, and we have enough firewood and food to keep us for a few days."

She went to the stove to warm up. "A few days? We're going to be here that long?"

Garrett pulled off his gloves and put his hat on the table, but left the hood to his thermal up. He was chilled to the bone. He walked to the heat.

"I can't say, Josie. This is a big storm front moving through. It's the reason we were moving the herd. And since we don't have a radio, I'm not wasting the charge on my phone to find out." He stood next to her. "In fact, you should shut off your phone, too."

She took it from her coat pocket. Her hands were shaking, so he took it from her and pressed the button. "Thanks."

He saw the fear in her eyes. "It's going to be okay, Josie. I'm just glad I found you."

She didn't look convinced. "If I hadn't taken off on my own, you'd be safely home in a warm bed."

"We can't change that. Besides, there's a bed here, and we'll be warm."

In the shadows of the fire, he could see her eyes narrow. "You're crazy, Temple, if you think I'm sharing a bed with you."

He knew ten years ago she'd have been eager to steal time away with him. He shook off the memory. "Why don't we find something to eat?" He went to the group of shelves and found a large can of stew. He also found some bowls and flatware. "Looks like Vance and Ana have all the conveniences of home."

Josie glanced around. "I recognize her touches."

"The old homestead looks good."

He worked the can opener. "They're going to build a house not far from here."

"Let me guess—you're going to build it for them."

He smiled. "We're working on some of the details. But not until the lodge is finished, and revenue starts coming in, then they'll break ground. I'd say late spring."

"That will be nice." Josie glanced at her watch. Two o'clock. It seemed later. She went to the window and looked out, but there wasn't anything to see through the blowing snow.

"Are you returning for their wedding?" he asked.

"Of course. Ana's my sister."

He dumped the contents of the stew in the pan, then took it to the cast-iron stove and placed it on top. "It shouldn't take too long."

He wasn't sure if that was a true statement. Being alone with Josie Slater wasn't a good idea, not the way she still made him feel.

He released a long sigh. It was going to be a long night.

Later, with a mug of coffee in hand, and only the sounds of the wind and the crackling fire, Josie was still uncomfortable. She knew that she had to start up a conversation just to save her sanity.

"How long ago did your wife die?" Wonderful. Why not get personal, she thought.

He turned from the stove, where he'd just added wood. He walked to the shelves, looked inside and pulled out a bottle of wine. "Natalie died six months ago in a car accident, but she hadn't been my wife for two years."

"I'm sorry. I'm sorry that Brody lost his mother."

He went through the silverware bin and took out a corkscrew. "It's been tough on him, especially with our move here," he said. "Brody had been living with Natalie's parents since the divorce, so when I wanted to bring him here, I got a lot of resistance."

"It's tough for them to lose their daughter and now, their grandson moving away."

He opened the bottle and poured two glasses of wine. Setting them on the table, he returned to stir the stew. "It didn't help the situation when they tried to fight me for custody of my own son."

She felt a tugging on her heart as she retrieved some bowls and brought them to the table along with spoons. "I'm sorry, Garrett. I can see how much you love Brody."

He nodded and filled the bowls. He put the pan in the sink and came back to the table and sat down across from her. "Dig in."

She took a bite and realized she was really hungry. "This isn't bad." She took another bite.

He was eating, too. "Anything would taste good at this point." He sat back and took a sip of wine. "Now, this is good." He looked across the table at her. "What about you, Josie? Is there anyone special in your life?"

Whoa. She needed the wine now, and took a drink. "What is this? Secret confessions in a blizzard?"

"No, just curious how your life's going. We were a couple for a long time."

"Back when we were kids." She glanced away, then back at him. "What do you want me to say, Garrett? That there hasn't been anyone since you? Well, there have been, several, in fact."

Garrett didn't doubt that. Josie Slater was a beautiful woman. He could lie all he wanted, but truth was he'd never gotten over her. "You're too special to settle, Josie."

She glared at him. "Funny you'd be the one to tell me that. You didn't have any trouble walking away and finding someone else."

He leaned forward. "Your remembrance of that time seems to be a little different than mine. We broke up. Correction, you broke up with me."

"Because you weren't coming home for the summer," she argued. "We had plans."

"And as I explained back then, I was offered an apprenticeship with a large construction company. It was too good an opportunity to turn down."

She took a drink from her glass. "You didn't even discuss it with me."

"I tried. You weren't willing to listen to anything I had to say."

"So you went off, found someone and slept with her."

He froze at her words, but he quickly recovered. "Let's get that story straight, too. You broke up with me in May, saying we were finished for good if I took the job. Those were your exact words. When I tried to call you, you refused to talk to me. I met Natalie in July."

He was right. "Then why did you call me in September and tell me you loved me?"

Garrett remembered that night. It had been the night

Natalie had told him she was pregnant. He stood and walked to the window. "I was drunk."

He heard her intake of breath. "That makes me feel so much better."

Hours later, neither one of them were talking much. Garrett had gone out again to check the horses. He'd asked her if she needed the facilities again. She went, but only to break up the boredom.

Once they returned, Josie looked around for something to read, but there was nothing, not even a magazine. Why would her sister need reading material with Vance around? No, she didn't want to think about how the two were lovers.

She went to the cupboard, thinking she could open another bottle of wine, but that wouldn't help. She didn't need to add to her problems. Somehow she had to get through this night and keep away from Garrett. And not just tonight but at the site, too. Maybe she could handle all the business with the job foreman, Jerry. Then Garrett wouldn't have to put up with her, either.

Garrett finished adding wood to the stove and the room was nice and warm. He went to the bed and drew back the quilt and blanket. Then he sat down and started pulling off his boots.

"What are you doing?" she asked.

"I'm going to bed."

She stared at him. "But—"

"We're going to share, Josie. Sorry, but I'm not sleeping on the floor." He lay back against the pillow and pulled the blanket up over his large body. "Oh, this feels good," he said, patting the spot next to him. "Join me. I promise to behave."

She was either too tired, or too mellow from the wine, to care. She walked over and sat down on the other side.

Pulling off her coat and boots, she slipped under the blankets. It did feel good.

Garrett sat up and pulled the quilt over them. "It's going to get a lot colder later."

Not from where she was. Garrett's body was throwing off some serious heat. She had to resist curling into him.

"I'm sorry, Josie," he whispered into the darkness. "I shouldn't have said those things to you. We were kids back then, and I didn't always think clearly about all my choices."

The cabin was dim. Only the lantern on the table shed any light. Maybe that was what made her brave. "We were both wrong," she admitted. "You needed that apprenticeship. I just didn't want you to leave me. But you did anyway," she whispered. "You found someone else."

He turned toward her, his eyes serious. "There was never anyone except you, Josie. But things didn't work out for us." He paused. "When I married Natalie, I wanted my son to have a family, and I did everything possible to make that happen."

She started to speak, but he stopped her.

"Right now, Brody is my life. My focus is on his future. Also my dad needs me."

"You're a good father, Garrett," she told him, wishing she could turn back the clock for them.

His gaze met hers. He was too close and too tempting. "I've made a lot of mistakes, Josie, but I can't with Brody."

This was hard. They were supposed to have children together. "Of course he's got to be your first concern."

He leaned closer; she could feel his breath against her cheek. "I lied to you earlier."

She swallowed hard. "About what?"

"I did remember calling you that night. I missed you so much back then." He inched closer. "I didn't realize how much until I saw you again." Then his head lowered to hers, capturing her mouth in a kiss, so tender, so sweet that Josie was afraid to move.

She'd dreamed about this for so long. Slowly, her arms went around his neck, and she parted her lips. Garrett slipped his tongue into her mouth, and she couldn't help but groan as her desire for the man took over. It had been so long, but the familiarity was still there.

He pulled her closer against his body, and her need intensified. He released her, but rained kisses over her face. "Josie, you feel so good. This is such a bad idea, but I don't care." His mouth took hers again, and he showed her how much he wanted her.

She was gasping for a breath by the time he broke off the kiss again. "Garrett," she whispered against his mouth, wanting more and more.

He finally released her. "God, Josie. I'm sorry."

She tried to push away, but he held her close. "Gosh, woman, I'm not sorry I'm kissing you. I'm sorry that I'm taking advantage."

"I'm a big girl, Garrett. I'll let you know if you're taking advantage."

He grinned and she saw his straight white teeth. "Maybe the best idea is to try and get some sleep." He turned her on her side and spooned her backside. "But we need to share body heat."

She didn't care what kept them close. She just loved the feeling and sharing the intimacy with this man. Maybe she wasn't truly over him.

CHAPTER SIX

JOSIE FELT A strong body pressing into hers, cocooning her in warmth. It felt so good. She was too comfortable, too relaxed to move, and she snuggled in deeper.

That was when she heard voices. "I really hate to wake them. They look so…cozy."

Recognizing the man's voice, Josie struggled to open her eyes and blinked at the two figures. Finally, she managed to focus on Ana and Vance standing next to the bed.

Bed? "Oh, Ana. Vance."

She tried to sit up and quickly realized that she was pinned down by a strong arm. She glanced over her shoulder to find Garrett. Oh, God, a stream of memories flooded back. The snowstorm, the wine, Garrett's kiss… She felt the blush rise to her cheeks. Okay, this didn't look good.

"Garrett, wake up." She fought to separate them. "We've been rescued."

He refused to let her go. "Too cold to get up." He tightened his grip and snuggled against her.

Vance grinned. "We can come back if you need more time."

Ana swatted at her husband-to-be. "Stop it." She looked back at her sister. "Josie, are you okay?"

Josie managed to untangle herself from Garrett and sat up. "Yes, even better since you're here." She looked around and saw the sunlight coming through the window. "What time is it?"

"It's about eleven."

"Eleven in the morning?"

Her sister nodded. "The storm finally died out about 5:00 a.m. I was so worried about you two, I convinced Vance we should come and look for you." Ana eyed Garrett. "I'm just glad you found shelter when you got caught in the storm yesterday."

"It's a good thing we fixed up this place so you could enjoy the amenities," Vance said as Garrett finally sat up. "Hey, buddy, I see you survived." He glanced at Josie. "I'd say you two must have called a truce."

Josie practically jumped out of the bed. "We were only trying to keep warm." She tried not to make eye contact with Garrett, but she lost the battle. He, too, was remembering what had happened during the storm. "Unless you wanted us to freeze to death."

Garrett knew they'd been far from freezing last night. They'd gotten pretty heated up. "I had to wrestle her down to get her to cooperate. And her claws are sharp."

Ana went to the table and held up the empty wine bottle. "Looks like you had some help."

Garrett grinned and caught Josie's blush. "We ate in candlelight so…why not some wine?"

Ana started to reply when Vance said, "We better get you all back to the ranch. There's more snow coming."

Garrett pulled on his coat and followed Vance out to give the women a chance to straighten up the cabin while they got the horses ready. On the porch Garrett was greeted with a beautiful winter wonderland scene.

"This is quite a view." He nodded toward the mountains. "It's no wonder you want to build your house here."

Vance glanced at his friend. "There's not a prettier piece

of land. So you better come up with a house design to do it justice."

Garrett placed his hat on his head. He'd already had some ideas. "I'll do my best."

They trudged through the snow to the lean-to and found the horses along with the calf had survived the storm just fine.

"So this is the little guy who caused all the trouble?" Vance asked as he knelt down to see the baby red Angus and looked for an ear tag or brand. "He must have been dropped late and missed the last roundup." The calf bawled in answer. "Okay, guy, we'll get you back home and get you something to eat."

They readied the horses, and Garrett led them to the front of the cabin as Ana and Josie came outside. Vance was carrying the calf.

Josie smiled, and Garrett felt the familiar stirring. "Oh, good, Storm's okay."

Vance looked at Josie. "Since when did you start naming livestock?"

She petted the calf. "He's had a rough time, and I doubt we'll find his mama."

"So does that mean you'll bottle-feed him?" Vance asked her.

Josie nodded. "I can."

"What about when you go back to California?"

Josie shrugged. "Maybe one of the ranch hands can take over."

Garrett swung up into the saddle and reached for the small animal as Vance lifted him up and helped lay the calf across Garrett's lap. He watched as Josie climbed on her horse, and for a second there he regretted having to return to reality instead of staying here with her. He wouldn't mind at all continuing those sweet, heated kisses and close out the rest of the world and make love all night.

Vance rode up beside him. "Something wrong?"

He shook his head. "No. Just thinking about what I need to do." First on the list was to stop thinking about Josie Slater. "I just want to get home."

"Then let's go."

They walked the horses through the deep snow for about a mile until they reached the road where a four-wheel-drive pickup with a horse trailer was waiting for them. Although the road had been plowed, it was still slow going back to the Lazy S especially with a bawling calf in the truck bed.

The backseat was tight, making Garrett very aware of the woman next to him. It was hard not to think about how her body was pressed against his all night. It had been a long while since he'd shared time or a bed with a woman. Not just any woman; someone who'd once been the love of his life. He'd quickly discovered there were still sparks between them.

They finally arrived back at the ranch, and Vance pulled up in front of the barn. When they got out of the truck, Garrett heard, "Dad! Dad!"

He turned toward the house and saw Brody running down the steps and across the yard, struggling to get through the high snow.

Garrett hurried toward him and as soon as he got close enough, his son launched himself into his arms. "Dad, you're okay." Those small arms wrapped around his neck, and he caught his son's sob against his ear.

"Hey, Brody, I'm fine. Didn't Vance tell you that?"

The boy raised his head, wiped his eyes and nodded. "But the storm was so bad, and if you got really cold you could freeze to death."

Garrett swallowed back his emotions, seeing his son's

fear of being left again. "Hey, I didn't. We were in a warm cabin that belonged to Ana and Josie's great-grandfather. We had a wood-burning stove and…" He started to say *bed,* but he saw his own father walking toward him. "And plenty of food."

"I'm glad. I thought you might never come home."

Garrett shook his head. "No, son, I was going to do everything to get back to you." He tried to lighten the mood. "It's you and me."

Brody smiled. "And Grandpa Nolan."

"And Grandpa Nolan," Garrett agreed, and set his son down on the plowed driveway as the man in question appeared and pulled him into a big hug.

"It's good you're safe," Nolan said.

"Yeah, it is." He searched his father's worried look. "Is everything okay? How did we fare at home?"

"Not too bad, but we lost electricity during the night, and service hasn't been restored yet, so there isn't any heat. Charlie and two of the hands took out some feed for the herd. They got a generator in the bunkhouse to keep them warm."

"We came here to wait for you," Brody said. "Mr. Colt invited us to stay here to stay warm. We sat in front of a big fire, ate popcorn and watched some movies."

Josie listened to the conversation, surprised that Colt would invite anyone into his house. She walked back to the truck bed while the ranch hands unloaded the horses from the trailer and took them into the barn for a well-deserved feed and brush down.

Vance got her calf down, and Brody came up to her and said, "Wow, is he yours?"

"I guess he is since he lost his mama. We'll have to feed him with a bottle."

Those so-like-his-father's green eyes lit up. "Can I help?"

Josie didn't want to do anything to keep Garrett here any longer, but how could she turn down this boy? "Sure, just check with your father."

She handed the calf's rope to Brody so she could greet the elder Temple. "Hello, Mr. Temple."

A big smile appeared on the man's weathered face. "Well, aren't you a sight for these old eyes." He grabbed her in a tight bear hug. "It's so good to see you, Josie."

"It's nice to see you again, too."

He released her. "It's about time you came back home. Although, I'm betting right now, you'd like some of the warm California weather."

"It would be nice right about now." She shivered. "But I have missed the snow, just not this much of it."

"And not getting lost in a blizzard." He sobered. "So glad that Garrett found you."

"Ah, I would have found my own way home eventually."

They laughed and heard someone calling to them. She looked up to the porch to see her dad waving at her.

"Come up to the house where it's warm."

She waved back. "Okay. As soon as we get the calf settled in."

Brody came up to them. "Dad, can I help Josie feed him?"

Ana spoke up. "I'm going to have to put my foot down. Everyone up to the house," she ordered, then turned to Vance. "Could Jake handle the calf until Josie gets something to eat and a warm shower?"

Okay, so she could use a shower. Josie realized she must look a mess. She turned to Brody. "It seems the boss has spoken. Maybe after we eat, I'll bring you down a little later."

The boy smiled. "Okay. I helped Kathleen make cookies and hot chocolate."

"Why didn't you say so earlier?" Josie smiled. "Come on." They headed to the porch where her father stood. "Dad, it's too cold for you out here."

"I can handle it." His blue eyes showed his concern. "I was w…worried about you." He reached for her hand and pulled her close and whispered, "I'm glad you're safe."

She closed her eyes and let the unfamiliar feeling wash over her. "I'm glad, too, Dad. I'm glad, too." She pulled back and smiled. "Now, I could use some coffee." She took his hand and together they walked into the house. It was good to be home.

An hour later, Josie was refreshed from a shower and feeling like a new person. Dressed in clean jeans and a sweater, she came downstairs to find Garrett and the rest of the Temple men sitting around the kitchen table with her father and Vance. She had no idea where Ana was.

She noticed that Garrett had on different clothes and looked like he'd showered and shaved. She couldn't help but think about last night. The feel of Garrett's body pressed against her, holding her during the long night.

"Josie." Brody spotted her first. He got up and came to her. "Are you going to go feed the calf now?"

"Brody," Garrett called as he stood. "Let Josie eat something first."

"I'm fine," she told him, then looked down at the boy. "How about we go in about an hour?" She had no doubt that the guests would still be here, so she might as well get used to it. "I'm sure Storm will be ready for another bottle by then."

Brody looked back at his father and got a nod. "Okay.

Do you want something to eat? Kathleen left a plate in the refrigerator."

She didn't have an appetite right now. "I think coffee and maybe a few cookies would tide me over for a while."

Brody went to the cupboard and got her a mug and set it in front of the coffeemaker. "I can't pour it yet, not until I'm nine. My birthday isn't until May. May 19."

Josie didn't want to think about the child's conception, but she couldn't stop the addition. The boy was conceived sometime in August. She poured her coffee, trying not to let her hand shake. She and Garrett had been broken up nearly three months.

She shook away the thought and took a sip. "Are you going to have a party?" she asked.

Brody shrugged. "I don't know. I don't have any friends here, 'cept Adam. He's in my class."

She could feel for the child. She always had her twin sister to be her best friend. "Well, you've only been in school a few days. And you still have six months to make more."

His eyes brightened and then he grinned at her. "Will you be my friend and come to my party?"

He was killing her. "I would love to be your friend, Brody. And thank you for the invitation, but I live in California. I don't know if I'm going to be here then."

Suddenly the smile disappeared. "Oh."

Great, she was breaking the boy's heart. "We'll see." She glanced at the table to see that she had an audience. Her gaze went from her father to Garrett. She wasn't going to answer any more questions from this group.

"Hey, Brody, I think feeding Storm might be a good idea."

"Now?" His eyes brightened once again.

With her nod, he went to his dad. "Dad, can I go and feed the calf?"

Garrett's gaze locked on Josie. "Sure. In fact, I'll go with you."

She didn't need this. She wanted to get away from the man. "Sure, the more the merrier." She walked off to get her coat.

Garrett got his son bundled up and put on his own jacket as Josie met them at the back door and they all left together.

Colt watched the threesome walk out together, then he turned back to Nolan. Over the years they hadn't exactly been friends. Of course, over the years, Colt Slater hadn't been friends with too many people.

Nolan and he had a falling-out years ago, but when Colt had called him to tell him about Garrett and learned about his lack of heat, he invited him to the house to wait out the storm. They'd managed to bury any bad feelings.

"Do you think there's any chance for them?" Nolan asked.

Colt picked up his mug and took a sip. "If the way they're looking at each other is any indication, I'd say yes. Only problem is, my daughter is pretty stubborn."

"As is Garrett," Nolan said. "He's been burned once." The man shrugged. "Of course, in my opinion he picked the wrong girl to start with. He's always belonged with Josie."

Colt nodded in agreement, but he also knew that loving someone didn't mean you could keep them. He glanced at Nolan. He'd been happily married to Peggy for thirty years before she died from cancer a few years back.

Colt hadn't been as lucky to have that many years with Lucia. Only about a half dozen, and he'd thought they'd been happy ones, then she'd left him. Now he had his daughters—that was, if he could convince them to give him another chance.

He sighed. "Okay, what are we going to do to nudge them along?"

Nolan gave him a slow smile. "Well, I'd say this blizzard is helping the cause. I wonder if my son was smart enough to take advantage of last night." The man raised his hand. "Sorry, I didn't mean it like that."

"No offence taken. Josie has been an adult for a while, and I can't interfere in her business. But I heard from Vance that some wine was consumed and that they'd shared a bed—to keep warm of course."

Nolan shook his head. "And they think we're too old not to remember what it's like to be with someone you care about."

Colt remembered far too much. "So what do we do to help them?"

Out in the warm barn, Josie stood outside the corner stall as Garrett helped show Brody how to feed the calf.

"Keep the bottle tilted up," Garrett instructed the boy.

Brody giggled as he struggled to hold on to the bottle of formula. "He's wiggling too much."

"That's because he's hungry. You were like that, too. You couldn't get enough to eat."

"Did I drink a bottle like this?"

Garrett grinned. "Not this big, but yes, you drank from a bottle sometimes."

Josie had trouble thinking about Garrett sharing that experience with another woman. A woman who had his child, a child that she was supposed to have. *Stop it,* she told herself. That was another lifetime. She didn't get the guy or a child.

Brody looked at her. "You want a turn, Josie? It's fun."

"Sure." She took the bottle and immediately felt the strong tug. "Hey, this guy is a wrestler."

"Maybe you should rename him Hulk Hogan," Garrett said.

Josie couldn't help but laugh, recalling how Garrett used to watch wrestling on television. "Hey, Brody, did you know that your dad loves wrestling? He was a big Hulk Hogan fan."

The boy frowned. "Who's Hulk Hogan?"

She stared at Garrett. "You haven't taught your son the finer points of the WWF?"

"What's the WWF, Dad?"

Garret was shocked that Josie remembered that about the past. "The World Wrestling Federation. I'll tell you about it later." He leaned closer to Josie. "You enjoyed watching as much as I did."

She rolled those big blue eyes that had haunted him for years. "I was a teenage girl. I would enjoy just about anything my boyfriend liked."

She'd done that for him. She'd cared that much about him. It also surprised and saddened him that she'd pushed him out of her life. "So it wasn't Hogan's muscles?"

Josie's calf gave another long pull, this time throwing her off balance. He grabbed for her, but lost his balance, too, and all three went down in the fresh straw.

Brody began to giggle, then Garrett caught on and soon Josie joined the laughter. The white-faced calf cocked his head as if to say they were all crazy.

Garrett looked at Josie and mouthed a thank-you. He loved to see his son laugh as he tried to adjust to the move here. "Well, Brody, we better head for home." Garrett climbed to his feet and offered a hand to Josie and helped her up. "There's more snow coming."

The boy stood. "But our house is cold. We gotta keep Grandpa warm. You said it's not good for his arthritis."

"The electricity should be back on by now." Brody

didn't look too happy as they walked out of the stall and went outside the barn to see more gray clouds and snow flurries in the air. His son ran ahead toward the house as Garrett walked beside Josie.

"Well, we've managed to survive the past twenty-four hours without killing each other." If he ever got a hand on her again, it definitely wouldn't be to harm her.

"Speak for yourself, Temple. I've had a few wayward thoughts."

He stopped. "I can't believe you remembered about Hulk Hogan."

She opened her mouth, and all he could think about was kissing her. Instead, he placed a gloved finger over it. "Too late to deny it."

"Okay, you got me." She blinked those incredible eyes at him. "Thank you again for finding me in the storm yesterday."

He shrugged. "Anytime, especially when we find accommodations as nice as the cabin." With a big bed, he added silently. "About those kisses…"

She froze, then quickly shook her head. "Hey, so we got a little nostalgic."

"Yeah, nostalgic," he mimicked, but all he could think about was capturing her lips once again. Bad idea.

Suddenly, they broke apart, hearing Brody calling to them. "Hey, Dad, guess what?"

"What, son?"

"Grandpa Nolan said we have to stay here tonight. The electricity still isn't fixed." A big grin appeared. "We're going to have so much fun."

Garrett looked at Josie. "Yeah. Fun."

CHAPTER SEVEN

THE DAY WAS a long one. Having to stay inside with the blizzard raging across the area made it worse. Everyone was uneasy as they stayed glued to the television news channel telling of the destruction.

Josie watched her dad and Vance either pace around, or call down to the barn to check on the men and the animals. Garrett held his cell phone to his ear, talking with his foreman at the Temple Ranch. She saw the concern on his creased brow.

This storm was deadly serious. Herds could be wiped out. That had been the reason they'd moved the cattle closer to the house so they could at least get feed to them.

She went to Garrett. "Is everything okay?"

He shrugged and put his phone back into his pocket. "We won't know until the storm is over. My men are okay, though. They have generators running in the bunkhouse and the barn. I don't know why the one for the house isn't working." He nodded to Nolan. "I'm just glad Dad thought to bring Brody here."

Once again, she hated that she caused this problem. Garrett could have been home taking care of things if she hadn't gotten lost. "I'm sorry I caused all these problems for you."

He frowned. "You didn't cause the storm."

"But I was foolish enough to get lost. You would have been home dealing with your ranch."

He gave her that slow, sexy smile she remembered from so long ago. "And miss being with you last night?"

She gasped. "Stop making it sound improper. We didn't do anything."

He took a step closer. "You ever wonder what might have happened if Ana and Vance hadn't showed up? If we could finally have our night together?"

Only for the past eight years, she thought, then quickly shook off any memories. "Well, we're back here now, with family. There's plenty of room here, and because of Kathleen, we won't go hungry."

He looked at her, his eyes locked on hers. "Seems the elements are bent on throwing us together."

She glanced away. "It's a storm, Garrett, nothing more."

"Hey, Dad," Brody called.

Garrett started off, but stopped. "Maybe we should continue this discussion later."

She shook her head. "We can't look back, Garrett. Your son needs you."

He didn't move for a second or two, then he finally went to see what Brody wanted from him. She released a breath, glad he didn't push the issue. After last night, it would be easy to give in to her feelings. Wait. Wasn't that what got her hurt all those years ago?

The morning turned into a glum afternoon as the snow continued to fall. Josie tried to stay busy catching up with her work and went off to the den for some privacy.

About ten minutes later a young visitor showed up. Brody. The cute, inquisitive boy was polite and talked her into playing hooky. That was when she learned he was also a cutthroat video game player, beating her at everything.

"I give up," she cried. "You win."

The eight-year-old pumped his fist in the air. "I'll teach you to play better if you want." Those big green eyes sparkled in delight. "You can be good, too, Josie."

The boy was a charmer like his father. Watch out, all females, another Temple was coming soon. "And what happens when I get hooked on games and I spend all my days playing instead of working?"

Garrett stood outside the office door, listening to the conversation between his son and Josie. He was surprised at Brody. The boy hadn't been outgoing, especially with strangers, and it got worse since his mother's death. But something was happening between Brody and Josie.

Join the group, son. She's a real heartbreaker. He thought back all the years ago to that summer. He'd loved Josie, but he hated being so far away at college, and only getting to see her every few months. Getting married was the only solution, and that meant a job and working all summer to make enough money. When he'd gotten the apprenticeship with Kirkwood Construction it was so he could afford a wife and also get his college credits. Before he had a chance to propose marriage, Josie broke up with him.

Then that summer Garrett met Joe Kirkwood's daughter, Natalie. Four months later she was pregnant and they were married. He closed his eyes and thought how he should have worked harder on their marriage. He'd always regret that. Natalie might have wanted the divorce, but only because she knew that there was someone else who had his heart.

He closed his eyes. Did Josie still have his heart? He thought back to last night and how she felt in his arms. The familiar feelings…that he'd buried so far down that he didn't think they could ever surface, until last night when he'd held Josie again.

The sound of laughter brought him back to the present. His son's laughter. He pushed away from the wall and walked inside. He found Brody sitting across from Josie. They were playing some kind of card game.

Brody looked up. "Hey, Dad, Josie is teaching me to play War."

His gaze connected with Josie's. "Come on, Temple, join us. Unless you're afraid a girl will beat you."

Her eyes danced with mischief. He smiled. "That will be the day. Deal me in."

By afternoon, the daylight faded into darkness. Once again Garrett would be staying over, and although she hated to admit it, his presence made her restless.

She kept replaying their time together at the cabin. The kisses they'd shared. How his body felt against her. How secure she'd felt with him as the wind howled outside. She'd been far too eager to fall right back into Garrett Temple's arms. Storm or no storm, not a good idea.

She sighed and stole a glance across the room when Garrett got up from the sofa and walked through the wide doorway to the kitchen and the coffeemaker. After filling his mug, he leaned his hips against the counter and crossed his booted feet at the ankle then took a sip of coffee. Oh, yeah. The man was hard to resist.

Her gaze ate him up. He was tall with wide shoulders and a torso that narrowed to his waist and flat stomach. He was just long and lean. There wasn't anything about the man that she could complain about. And he still took her breath away.

Against her better judgment, Josie stood and walked

into the kitchen. She told herself she wanted coffee, but mostly she wanted the man standing beside it.

"You don't have to spend your entire evening entertaining my son," he told her.

She poured a cup of coffee. "Brody's not a problem. You've done a fine job with him, Garrett."

"Thank you." His eyes met hers. "I wasn't always there for him like I should have been. I was busy building my business. I made money, but I think I lost the connection to my family." His sad gaze caught hers. "Sometimes you can't get that back. That's why Brody is so important to me. He deserves the best father I can be."

Unable to stop herself, she touched his arm. "I can see how much you love him. And he loves you, too."

This time she saw the emotion in his eyes. "Sometimes we're lucky enough to get a second chance."

She didn't know how to answer that, but was grateful she didn't have to. A belly laugh escaped Brody as he rolled on the carpeted floor watching a cartoon video. She couldn't help but smile, too. Yet, she knew this child was a strong reminder of why she needed to keep her distance.

That little boy needed his father, and someone who could take over as a mother. That dream flew out the window a long time ago when the man she'd loved chose another woman over her.

Garrett's marriage to Natalie had broken her heart, and when she learned about the baby that nearly killed her. She shook away the sudden sadness. Another dream that had died was her hope of a life with Garrett. She turned to her career instead, and Slater Style had become her life. End of story.

After supper that evening, Josie decided to give up trying to work, but she still couldn't sit around, trying to avoid

Garrett. So she went back to her Dad's office and found Ana there.

Her sister glanced up from the computer. "Hey, I'll be done in a few minutes."

Josie shook her head. "It's okay, take your time." With her tablet cradled in her arms, she sat down in the big leather chair across from the desk.

"Okay, I'm done," Ana announced, and turned away from the screen. "I emailed all the parents about tomorrow's school closures." She smiled. "Although, I think they can figure that out without me telling them."

"So you're staying home tomorrow?"

Ana raised an eyebrow. "I know you've lived in sunny California for a long time, but yeah, this storm will keep everyone indoors, but hopefully not for very long."

"Hope so, too," Josie said, not realizing she spoke out loud.

Her sister studied her. "Did you come in here because of our guests?"

Josie frowned. "Of course not. Besides, we can't send them home in this storm and without heat in their house."

Ana smiled and leaned back in her chair. "Of course there's always body heat. That seemed to work for you last night."

Don't blush, Josie told herself. It didn't work as she felt her cheeks heat up. "We didn't have much of a choice."

"I can't help but be curious about what happened between you two last night."

"Nothing," Josie denied and stood up. "I was stupid enough to get lost yesterday, and Garrett rode after me. He knew where the cabin was, thank God. We stayed there until you came by this morning. End of story."

Ana stood up, too. "Hey, I know you're having a rough time with Garrett being here, but I'm grateful he was there when you got lost. As for the rest of what happened at the cabin, it's none of my business," her sister said, then grinned. "And if sharing a bottle of wine helped make the night more bearable, more power to you."

There was no way she was ready to admit anything to Ana, nor did she want to analyze what happened between her and Garrett.

Time to get off this subject. "Since you'll be home tomorrow, maybe we can look at wedding dresses on the internet. It's only about six weeks until the big day."

Ana got all dreamy-eyed. "We're not planning anything too elaborate with the financial problems and all." She smiled. "Besides, I already found this incredible dress. It's at a consignment shop in Dillon. It's slim fitted and done all in creamy satin, covered with antique lace. The owner, Carrie Norcott, promised to hold it for me a few weeks."

A consignment shop? "This is your big day, Ana. It's my job to make it special, and on a budget. We can afford to get you a new dress."

"I know. Vance said the same thing, but wait until you see this one. It came out of an estate sale from Billings. It looks like something out of the 1930s and it's perfect for me. Besides, we don't have time to order a new dress and get it here in time."

Josie knew she wouldn't win this. "If it's what you want then that's one more thing off our list. Since we have the location locked down, the rest will be aisle runners, seating and decor."

Ana frowned. "Now with this early storm, I'm worried that the lodge won't be finished in time."

Josie hoped that Garrett wouldn't let them down, either. "All we need completed is the main room, one bathroom and the kitchen. We can do that. And as for decorations, it will be Christmastime. How do you feel about a Winter

Wonderland theme? We place several pine trees on either side of the big picture window and add some poinsettias for color. An archway where that good-looking guy of yours can stand in his Western-cut tux. He'll have a perfect view of his bride coming down the aisle."

"Oh, Josie, it's perfect." Ana's eyes filled as she nodded, then pulled her sister into a big hug. "Thank you for coming home. You'll never know how much it means to me."

Josie pulled away, fighting her own tears. "I wouldn't miss it for anything."

Ana grew serious. "Then would you consider being my maid of honor?"

Josie felt tears welling in her eyes. "Oh, Ana. I'd love to." She hugged her sister.

Josie pulled back, wiping away tears, when she saw Vance and Garrett; both were bundled up in their coats. It was obvious they'd been outside.

"Oh, Vance. Josie was talking about the wedding. She's going to be my maid of honor." She went to her future husband. "And it's going to be a Christmas theme."

He kissed her. "Just tell me it's going to be this Christmas and I'm a happy man."

Ana laughed, and Josie turned her attention to Garrett. Once their eyes locked, she felt the pull. She couldn't help but think about being stranded in the cabin with the man's arms wrapped around her.

Josie heard her name. "What?"

"I wondered if you'd like some hot chocolate?" her sister asked.

"Sure, but I need to get some work done."

"I'll bring it to you here." She started out and stopped. "Oh, and Vance asked Garrett to be his best man." The couple walked out, but Garrett stayed.

Great. The last thing she wanted or needed was more time with this man. "Do you need something?"

"You don't want to talk about our duties as maid of honor and best man?"

She glared at him.

"Okay, how about we talk about the lodge. I was thinking when this weather clears we should get back to work on it. If the electrical is roughed in, then we can get the heat on and begin to drywall the inside."

She frowned. "I thought when the electrical was finished, your job was done and we take over."

Garrett shrugged. "I don't mind helping out so the wedding will come off on schedule. I'd hate to have them move the ceremony to the courthouse."

Josie shook her head. "I won't let that happen, but there isn't much extra money right now for the work."

Garrett walked toward her, and she had to fight to stand her ground. "I didn't say I would charge. I'll be doing the work myself, not my men."

"You?"

"Hey, I can still hang Sheetrock, even tape and mud the seams. And my carpenter skills are pretty good, too." She watched his delicious mouth twitch at the corners. "I still have a tool belt."

Oh, God. She didn't need to picture Garrett in a tool belt. "What about the time? Surely you have other jobs to do."

"With this weather there isn't much work right now, just a few small residential jobs that Jerry can handle. What do you say, Josie? You want to be my helper?"

No! She didn't need to spend any more time with this man, but the sooner the job got done the better. First the wedding, then the lodge could open for paying custom-

ers. Then she could go back to California and forget all
about Garrett Temple. "Apprentice. I like that title better."

About midnight, Colt sat by the fire in the family room and
watched the flames dance, holding a glass of whiskey in
his hand. He was probably breaking all the rules drinking
alcohol, but right now he didn't give a damn. Sometimes
a man needed a stiff drink. He was tired of his solitary
bedroom and more dreams about Lucia.

The house was quiet even though there were three
guests. Ana and Vance had gone off to the foreman's house
across the compound to spend the night. They'd given up
their bedroom upstairs to Garrett and Brody. Nolan had
been assigned to his youngest daughter, Marissa's, bedroom. He smiled, hoping his neighbor liked pink.

Josie had gone upstairs to her room hours ago. He had
no doubt that had been to keep the distance between her
and Garrett. The two had spent most of the day trying to
stay out of each other's way. But there were sparks flying everywhere.

"Mind if I join you?"

Colt looked up and saw Nolan standing in the doorway.
He still wore his jeans and the shirt he had on earlier, but
the boots had been replaced with a pair of moccasins.

"Not at all. Come in and pour yourself a drink."

That got a smile from the sixtysomething neighbor.
"Don't mind if I do." Nolan walked to the bar, took down
a glass from the shelf and poured a splash of bourbon. He
made his way to the other overstuffed chair across from Colt.

Nolan's dark gaze met his. "Couldn't sleep?" he asked.

"Seems that's all I do these days," Colt murmured. "I
hate it." He smacked the cane beside his chair. "Can't wait
until I lose this, too."

"Hey, you might be losing one, but I'll probably be taking up one soon with this dang arthritis." He ran a hand over his thinning gray hair. "But I can't say I'm unhappy that my son and grandson moved back home. He's doing a great job of running the operation." He smiled. "I have to say that my grandson really lights up that old house."

Colt knew his neighbor had been lonely since his wife, Peggy, died. Colt was ashamed he hadn't stayed in touch with his neighbor. "I love having Ana back, and now Josie's home." But soon Ana would marry Vance and Josie would go back to L.A.

Nolan took a drink and nodded. "I've sure enjoyed spending time with that sweet Josie of yours. I've noticed that Garrett liked it, too." He sighed. "I wish I could have helped those two out years ago. Maybe if I'd stepped in, things would have turned out different."

Colt sighed. "Did any of us listen to common sense when we were young? We had all the answers. Maybe they'll find a way to get together this time around."

Nolan nodded. "Got any more ideas?"

"Well, since this storm is expected to move out tomorrow, you can't use that excuse any longer to stay here."

"We might not have to," Nolan said. "Garrett told me that Josie is going to work with him on the lodge."

"Well, dang. That's not going to help much with the crew around."

Nolan shook his head. "No, the men won't be there. They have another job. They both decided this was going to be a wedding gift for Vance and Ana. They want to make sure the lodge is finished in time for the wedding."

Colt nodded. "That's a lot of time together. If your boy doesn't take advantage, there's no hope."

Garrett lay on the bed until he heard Brody's soft snores. The kid had been hyped up most of the day. Of course, he'd gotten a lot of attention. He'd even let his son go out to bottle-feed the calf.

Garrett stood and slipped on his jeans and shirt, but didn't bother with the buttons. He grabbed his shaving kit that his dad had brought over to the Slaters earlier and went down the hall to the bathroom. He quickly went through his nightly routine. Once he'd brushed his teeth, he put everything back, but left the small leather bag on the counter next to Josie's things.

He paused a moment to inhale the scent of her shampoo and soap that were so her. He wasn't going to get much sleep tonight. He stepped out into the hall and nearly ran into a petite body—Josie. He reached for her as she gasped.

"Sorry, I didn't know anyone was in here," she whispered.

"I just finished up." He watched as her tongue began to lick her lips. The memories of last night flooded his head. Josie in his arms, his mouth covering hers, hearing her soft moans.

"It's all yours," he finally managed to say, but he didn't move. He glanced down at her flannel pajamas and thought how sexy she looked.

As if she could read his mind, she said, "They keep me warm."

"Last night, I kept you warm."

She frowned, but he saw the blush. "That was an emergency."

"So is this." He gripped her arms and walked her backward into her bedroom, then his mouth covered hers.

It was heaven. Oh, God, he couldn't get enough of her as he drew her close, loving the feeling of her lush body sinking into his. Last night he'd been a fool to turn her away. He broke off the kiss, only to trail kisses down her jaw.

"Garrett…"

He pulled back, hearing her plea, but desire overtook him. His mouth returned to hers; he angled her face and deepened the kiss.

"I'd wanted to do this all day," he breathed against her lips in between teasing nibbles.

Then reality quickly intervened with the sound of someone out in the hall. He broke off the kiss and pulled her close.

They waited in the dark bedroom until the bathroom door opened and closed. He looked down at her, still feeling her heavy breathing. Then she pulled away and hugged herself. He suddenly realized what might have happened if they hadn't been interrupted. Not wise.

This wasn't the time to continue this. "I should get back to my room. Good night, Josie."

He left her, knowing there wasn't any future in starting up something with Josie or any woman right now, especially a woman who had a home and career in California. Over a thousand miles away.

So now he had to figure a way to keep his distance for another few weeks. He should be able to do that. So why had he asked her to work with him? Was he crazy? He groaned. Yeah, he was crazy about Josie Slater.

It took two days for the ranch to get back to operating as usual. The storm had taken its toll with downed fences and lost cattle. Not too bad, considering the intensity of the blizzard's destruction, Josie thought as she pulled up to the construction site.

She'd spent the past forty-eight hours trying not to second-guess her decision to help Garrett with the inside of the lodge. She thought back to the other night and the breathtaking, toe-curling kiss. What frightened her more was what might have happened if Brody hadn't gotten up.

Would things have gone further than just a kiss? No! She couldn't let the man back into her life. There was no future with Garrett Temple.

Josie parked Colt's four-wheel-drive pickup next to Garrett's truck. She stepped out onto the still-frozen ground, wrapped her scarf around her neck and made her way down the plowed path to the lodge. She smiled at the two-story rough-log structure with the green metal roof. The chimney stacks were covered in river rock and the wrap-around porch also had rough-log railings, adding to the rustic look.

"You do good work, Garrett Temple."

She walked up the steps to the double doors with the cut-glass insert that read River's End Lodge. That one extravagance was well worth it. She ran her fingers over the etched letters.

She felt her excitement build as she opened the door and stepped inside. It was hard to take it all in. So many things drew her attention as she glanced around the nearly finished main room. The dark-stain hammered hardwood floors, partly covered for protection in the traffic areas were well-done. She moved on to the huge river rock fireplace. The raised hearth had room for a dozen people to sit down and warm themselves.

She walked past the staircase, arching up toward the second-floor landing, a wrought-iron railing with the Lazy S brand symbol twisted in the design. Okay, another splurge. Her gaze continued to move around the room, seeing special touches that made this place more cozy and comfortable. It could almost be someone's home. At the wall of windows, she looked at the river and the mountain range. Amazing view. Okay, she was definitely going to push this place for weddings.

She heard a noise upstairs, then a loud curse. Garrett.

Hurrying to the steps, she made her way to the second floor and went on to search room to room. She started to call out his name when she spotted him and froze.

His back was to her and what a sight. A tool belt was strapped low on his waist and he wore faded jeans that hugged his slim hips and long legs. Her gaze moved to his dark T-shirt emphasizing his wide shoulders and muscular arms.

He was balancing a sheet of wallboard and trying to reach for a tool. Then he glanced at her. "Well, are you going to stand there or help me? Hand me that screw gun."

Josie shot across the large bedroom and reached for the electrical tool he'd pointed at. Once he had it in his hand, he said, "Here, hold this up." He nodded to the large sheet of wallboard. Once she pressed against it, he began to work on adding screws into the edges. "There, that does it." He looked at her. "So you finally decided to come to work."

"You said I could come when I had time. I need to check in with my office, and there's a few hours' difference between here and Los Angeles. If you wanted me here at 7:00 a.m., you should have told me."

Garrett hated that he'd snapped at Josie. He'd almost called her and told her not to come at all. After the other night and that kiss, he didn't need to spend any more time with her. He should have gotten one of his men. No matter what it cost.

"Sorry. I'm an early riser and just take it for granted everyone else is."

"I am, too. But I'm trying to run my business long-distance. There's a big wedding I'm coordinating a few weeks from now. My assistant is doing a great job, but she still has to run everything by me."

He walked over to the drywall compound and seam tape. "Sounds like your business is doing very well."

She shrugged. "I do well enough, but long-distance is hard, especially since I'm not able to do bids on jobs."

He nodded, loving the look of her in her jeans and sweatshirt. He liked her better in her pj's. *Don't go there,* he warned. "Okay, you ready to go to work?"

"Sure, what can I do?"

He handed her a long, narrow pan partly filled with a white compound and a putty knife. "We need to fill all these screw holes."

She glanced around the room. He knew that she was silently counting the thousands of screw heads. "Okay. I'm not sure how good I'll be."

"You'll be great."

He gave her a quick lesson, put her in front of one wall, and he went to the other end.

It wasn't long before they met in the middle. He was surprised at the progress they'd made. But it was only one room.

"Garrett," she began. "Not to complain, but how many rooms do we have to do?"

"Actually, all the rooms have been drywalled."

She turned to him, and he could see spots of compound on her cheek. "Wait, I thought you said that wasn't in our contract with GT Construction."

He shrugged. "It wasn't that much more in cost. Besides it was going to be a lot more work for us. It was easier to have one of my men do the hanging."

"Then I want to pay for half," she argued.

"Josie, that's not necessary."

She glared at him. "You can't take all the cost. I want to pay, too."

"Why are you being so stubborn about this?"

Her eyes widened. "Because you asked me to help with

this project and we agreed to work together." She paused. "If I were a man, you'd gladly take my money."

"If you were a man, I wouldn't be thinking what I'm thinking right now."

Josie worked hard to keep her composure. She couldn't let Garrett know how his words affected her, but she didn't want to deal with this all the time. She put down her mudding pan, grabbed her coat off the sawhorse and headed for the door. She never got there because Garrett grabbed her by the arm and turned her around.

"You want me to apologize for kissing you the other night? Why, Josie? You didn't stop me then." His gaze was heated. "Are you going to stop me now?" He leaned toward her and his mouth closed over hers.

Josie was ready to push him away, but the second his lips touched hers everything changed. She moaned and her arms wrapped around his neck, holding him there, afraid he would stop. Then he drew her against him, and she could feel his desire, his need for her.

He broke off the kiss. "God, Josie… What you do to me. What you've always done to me."

She hated how he made her feel vulnerable again. "I guess this isn't getting much work done. Besides, your tool belt is digging into me."

Grinning, he released her. "I can take it off."

Keep it light. "Thanks for the offer, but we need to get to work. We have a wedding in a month."

She caught his look, but ignored the pain she'd felt remembering their own wedding plans so long ago. She'd learned the hard way they were foolish dreams.

CHAPTER EIGHT

OVER THE NEXT five days Josie worked long, hard hours at the lodge with Garrett, then spent evenings with Ana, Vance and her father. Exhausted, she slept very well at night. She valued those hours of slumber, but it didn't look like she was going to get many tonight.

It was her duty as maid of honor to do a bachelorette party for the bride. So on Friday afternoon, the celebration began. She'd gone with Ana to see her sister's wedding dress in Dillon. Josie fell in love with the gown and agreed it was the perfect choice.

Once finished with shopping they stayed in town, and the plan was to meet some of Ana's friends for dinner. The three women—Sara Clarkson, a longtime friend; Clare Stewart, another school friend; and Josie—all convinced Ana to go into the Open Range Bar and Grill.

If they were going to misbehave tonight they wanted it to be away from their small community. The surprise was they were headed off to a honky-tonk for a few drinks to celebrate the upcoming wedding. Josie hadn't expected her commonsense older sister, Analeigh, to be so eager to go.

Inside the bar, Josie looked around the rustic-looking room that was a little raunchier than she liked. Although, it didn't seem to bother anyone else but her. It was crowded with people, and a country-Western song was blaring from

the DJ booth. The dance floor was filled with couples
two-stepping to the latest Tim McGraw song. This wasn't
Josie's kind of fun, but seeing the look on Ana's face was
priceless.

Her sister leaned toward her and cupped her mouth.
"I've heard about this bar—I can't believe I'm really here."

"Every girl needs a send-off," Josie said, and glanced at
the bartender, Tony. She'd spoken to him earlier, and he'd
been happy to help out. "Come on, let's go find a table."

She took her sister's hand and pulled her through the
crowd until she spotted a table that had a sign on the top.
Reserved for Slater Sisters.

"Oh, look." Ana sighed. "Did you do this?" she asked
Josie.

Josie smiled. "A phone call," she yelled over the music.

They sat down just as the music ended, and Clare said,
"Oh, my, look at all the guys."

"I'm not looking. I've already found mine," Ana said.

"You are so lucky to have Vance, Ana," her friend Sara
told her.

Her sister got that dreamy look again. "I know. And
he's been right under my nose for years."

Josie recalled the runaway boy, Vance Rivers, that their
father had taken in. Of course, back then she and her sister were jealous because Colt had paid more attention to
Vance than his own daughters. Josie realized now that it
wasn't Vance's fault.

The young waitress dressed in a little T-shirt, a pair
of jeans and boots took their drink order, margaritas all
around.

Clare drew their attention. "You know who else is a
really good-looking man? Garrett Temple." The blonde
looked at Josie. "Do you still lay claim on the man, or do
the rest of us get a chance with him?"

Josie stiffened as all eyes turned to her. She found she wanted to ward them off, but she hadn't the right to. "It's been years since Garrett and I were a couple. Besides, I'm headed back to L.A. soon."

The music started up again, and the waitress brought over their drinks. Josie handed over her credit card for the first round as Sara and Clare got up to go to the dance floor with two guys.

Ana leaned over and said, "Sorry, I don't want Clare to bring up bad memories."

Josie shook her head and took a drink and tasted the salt along the rim. "It's okay, Ana. Everyone here remembers Garrett and I together. I can handle that."

"Good." They drank and caught up on local news the past years. Soon the music turned to a fast-paced song, and everyone got up to do a popular line dance. Ana grabbed Josie's hand. "Come on, I want to dance."

Lined up on the floor next to Ana, Josie began to do the steps. She laughed as she messed up, but then finally caught on and got the rhythm. Maybe this night would be fun after all.

It was nearly eleven o'clock. This wasn't how Garrett wanted to spend his Friday evening as he walked into the Open Range Bar behind his friend Vance. He could smell sweat and liquor.

Vance had called him earlier and said his friend the bartender, Tony, had phoned him about a party with the Slater sisters and was worried about them driving home.

Garrett glanced around the crowded room and the couples dancing, or cuddled up together at tables. There were still guys lined up three deep at the bar looking hopeful they'd find that special girl, at least for tonight.

He'd never been the type to hang out in places like this.

He'd been married and had a child when he was barely the legal age to drink alcohol.

"You sure they're still here?" He wasn't too upset that he'd get a chance to see Josie. Would she be happy to see him? Would she be with another guy? She'd been keeping her distance at the lodge, making sure she worked in another area.

"Yes. Tony called and he's been watching the party for the past few hours. It seems they've been drinking tequila shots. He wanted to make sure they got home safely. Thanks for helping out, friend. I wasn't sure if I could handle all four of them."

"Not a problem." Garrett was more worried that Josie would be angry that he came to break up the party.

Vance pointed toward the table. "Hey, there they are." He started in that direction, and Garrett followed him.

When the girls spotted him they cheered, and Ana jumped up and threw herself into her future husband's arms. "Vance, you came to my party."

He kissed her. "I hope you don't mind. Garrett and I wanted to make sure you ladies got home all right. It's a long drive back."

"Oh, that's so sweet," Ana said. "But first you have to dance with me." She tugged Vance's hand, leading him onto the floor. Soon Ana was plastered against her man.

Garrett couldn't help but look around for Josie. He soon discovered her on the dance floor with some guy. He stiffened, seeing the man's hand moving lower on her hip. He immediately walked through the crowd. "Excuse me, but would you mind letting go of my...girlfriend?"

The shorter man with the wide-rim Stetson glared back.

Garrett stole a glance at Josie, then back at the guy. "Look, we had a big fight and she left. I went out looking for her to tell her how sorry I was." His gaze locked on hers again. "I'm sorry, darlin'. Will you forgive me for being such a jerk?"

Josie opened her mouth to speak, but instead, Garrett reached for her and planted a kiss on her lips to convince her dance partner of his intentions. When he'd released her—not that he cared—the stranger had disappeared.

"I guess he's gone," he told her, but he couldn't get himself to release her. She felt too good in his arms.

"What are you doing here?" she asked.

The music started up again with the Miranda Lambert song, "Over You." Garrett pulled Josie close and began to move to the slow ballad. The feel of her body against him had him groan in frustration. "Dancing with you."

"No, really, what are you doing here?" she whispered against his ear.

He wondered the same thing himself. "The bartender is a friend of Vance's. So we came to drive you ladies home," he told her as he led her around the dance floor to a secluded corner.

"I can manage getting everyone home," she told him. "And I can handle groping men."

He pulled back and looked in her eyes. "I guess I didn't need to kiss you to get rid of the guy."

"No, you didn't need to do that," she answered weakly, but he saw the desire in those cobalt-blue depths.

"What a shame, that was my favorite part." He placed another sweet kiss against her lips.

She swallowed hard, wanting more. "Garrett…"

Before she could finish, Ana and Vance danced toward them, and Ana said, "Oh, Josie, I'm having so much fun. This is the best bachelorette party I've ever been to."

Vance frowned at Ana. "Since when have you been to any other ones?"

Ana giggled. "I haven't, but this is still the best because

it's mine." She wrapped her arms around Vance's neck. "And you're going to be my husband. Oh, I love you so much." She planted a kiss on her groom.

Vance finally pulled back. "Hey, honey. Why don't I take you home?" He leaned in and whispered something in her ear that had her smiling.

Ana turned to Josie. "We're going home now." She wrapped her arms around her sister. "Thank you so much for the party. It was fun to spend time with you."

"You're very welcome," Josie said. "Don't worry, I'll make sure Clare and Sara get home."

She looked at Garrett. "You can go, too."

He shook his head. "Not on your life, darlin'. I'm you and your ladies' designated driver tonight. You got a problem with that?"

God help her. Josie shook her head and handed him her keys. "Not a single one."

The next morning, Josie slept in later than usual, but felt she'd earned the extra hour. After all, it was Saturday. She went down to the kitchen and had a quiet breakfast while Colt joined her with coffee, but there wasn't any sign of Ana or Vance.

She thought about Garrett and last night. He'd insisted that he drive her car, and then made sure that Sara and Clare had gotten home. During the ride back to the ranch, Josie realized she'd had more to drink than was safe to drive. Although she wouldn't admit it to Garrett, she liked that he'd taken care of her. She just couldn't let herself get too used to having him around, not when their futures were headed in different directions.

She only had to hold on a few more weeks. She needed to make it through Thanksgiving, then soon came the wedding.

Refilling her mug, she headed to the office to work. She knew the safe way to avoid temptation was to avoid Garrett altogether. She might just have a solution to the problem.

Josie walked in, sat down at the desk and dialed Tori for an update on upcoming events.

"Slater Style," her twin answered.

"So we're still in business?"

Tori groaned. "It's crazy here. Do know how many parties are scheduled for the holidays?"

Josie smiled. "Yes, I've been following the bookings Megan sent me, and we've gone over things."

Megan Buckner had been her assistant for over two years. The woman had really stepped up and taken over two jobs. Of course, Josie hadn't planned on being gone from L.A. this long.

"We need more help," Tori said. "I'm not sure I can do these parties myself."

Josie knew she'd put a lot on her sister's shoulders, but she figured there was something else on her mind.

"Tori, Megan has the list of regular employees we hire for big parties. What's really wrong, sis? Did something happen?"

She heard the long sigh. "No, it's not the business. It's just…"

"What? Is it Dane? Is he bothering you?"

There was a long silence.

This wasn't like her twin. "Tori, tell me."

"I have no proof it's him, Josie. I know he's watching me, but as far as I know, he hasn't violated the restraining order. And yes, I called Detective Brandon like you suggested. He said the police's hands are tied, too."

Josie closed her eyes. "I'm sorry, Tori. I shouldn't have left you alone. I called to tell you that I'm getting the next flight to L.A. At least I can take some of the business pressure off you."

There was a pause, then Tori said, "It's great you're coming back, but I don't want you to get involved with my trouble. Dane will just get angrier."

Josie was frustrated. "Fine, but we need to handle this situation, Tori."

"I know. Please, can we talk about something else? I'm worried about the wedding in Santa Barbara. Will you be here in time for that?"

Josie knew how important the Collins/Brimley wedding was to her. Both affluent families, they could bring her future business, or give her a bad name, and Slater Style would be finished. "Yes, I'll be there Friday."

Josie asked to speak with Megan. When her assistant came on the line, it wasn't long before Josie knew everything was under control, but the wedding party's families were concerned about Josie's absence. "Thanks for all your work, Megan. Will you put Tori back on the phone?"

"What do you need, sis?" Tori said.

Josie went over the flight time, then added, "I want you to be careful, Tori. Dane has already proved he can be violent. So don't go out alone at night and set the alarm in the house."

With Tori's promise, Josie said her goodbyes and hung up the phone. That was when she caught Garrett's large figure in the doorway. His sheepskin jacket was open, revealing a fitted Western-cut shirt and jeans over his slim hips and long legs. His cowboy hat in hand.

She ignored her racing pulse. "Garrett, is there something wrong?"

He held up her keys as he walked across the room, his gait slow and deliberate. He'd driven her car home last night, then used the vehicle to get himself back to his place. "And I stopped in to see how you were feeling this morning."

She shook her head, barely able to meet the man's gaze. "You don't have to babysit me." Then she quickly added, "I appreciate you taking me home last night. Thank you."

He smiled and it did things to her. "You're welcome," he told her, but didn't leave.

"Is there something else you need?"

"Just some input on the lodge. I have some countertop samples I need you to look at. Charlie's brought my truck, and the samples are inside."

"What happened with the ones we picked out two weeks ago?"

"They didn't have enough granite slabs to do the entire lodge."

"Okay." She glanced back at the computer screen. "Give me a few minutes. I need to book a flight to L.A. first."

He frowned. "You're leaving?"

She nodded. "Just for the weekend." She continued to scan through the flights. "I've been contracted to do a large wedding, and I need to be there."

Garrett already knew from the conversation it was more. "Is that the only reason?" He sat down on the edge of the large desk. "Is an ex-boyfriend bothering her?"

Josie hesitated, then nodded. "Dane hasn't broken any laws yet, but I'm worried about Tori's peace of mind. It's getting to her."

"My offer is still good. I can call my friend." Why did he keep getting mixed up in her life? "He's a private investigator and might be able to help."

"I appreciate your offer, Garrett, but when I go to L.A. I plan to bring Tori back here. She can work her web design business from here and help me with Ana's wedding." Her fingers worked the keyboard on the webpage.

Just leave, Garrett told himself. *She doesn't want your help.* "Book me a seat, too."

She jerked her head around to look at him. "You? You can't go."

He shrugged. "Why not? Someone's got to watch out for you two."

Her eyes widened. "For one thing, Tori and I have handled things on our own for a long time. Secondly, we're not your problem."

"I'm Vance's friend, and you're his family. Besides, there's a jerk out there who's making your sister's life miserable. What would Ana do if she knew?"

Josie shook her head. "She doesn't need this worry. I can take care of Tori."

His stomach tightened at the thought of some jerk possibly hurting her or her twin. "Josie, I can't just stand by and let someone hurt either you or your sister. What if I'm a deterrent for this guy? Wouldn't my presence help keep him away? Although I wouldn't mind taking a few jabs at him."

He watched her fight with his reasoning. "Okay, say it does, it still doesn't solve the problem."

"Let's just see the situation, then go from there."

"Wait, what about Brody? You can't leave him."

"Brody will be in Bozeman at his grandparents' house. It's a three-day weekend from school. So I'm all yours."

She didn't look convinced.

"This is your sister we're talking about, Josie. We wouldn't want to take any chances with her safety. We'll just tell Tori that I'm helping you with the event."

Those blue eyes bored into his. "This still isn't a good idea."

Hell, he already knew that, but it was too late to stop. He wanted to be with Josie.

* * *

Friday afternoon Josie found herself seated next to Garrett on an early-morning flight to Los Angeles. She'd been grateful he hadn't said much and she was able to get some work done. He'd slept.

When they'd landed at LAX, Garrett got a rental car, and knowing that Tori would be working at home, they drove straight to the town house that she shared with her twin.

Garrett pulled into her parking spot, but Josie hesitated before going inside. "I don't want you grilling Tori. She's been very secretive about her relationship with Dane, and when things turned abusive it made her more ashamed."

"It's not my place to tell her what to do. I only want to help her."

"She probably isn't going to want to share much of her personal life."

Garrett glanced away from the road. "Then you're going to let her think that you trust me, that we're friends again. More than friends."

She glared at him. "Garrett, I don't want to trick Tori into thinking anything like that."

He shook his head. "Look, Josie. This Dane guy seems like a loose cannon. He's already hit Tori, and now he seems to still be hanging around."

Josie knew what he said was true. This could be a dangerous game. "Okay, let's go inside and see how things are, but please don't mention anything about a private investigator."

He nodded. "Okay."

She didn't let go of his arm. "Have I told you how glad I am that you're here?"

He smiled. "You just did."

They got out of the car in an area off Los Feliz Ave.

This was old Los Angeles, where some structures were built in the 1930s. Their home was once an apartment that had been converted into town houses.

The Spanish-style building had original tile and archways, and that had been what drew Josie to the place. And nearly a year ago, Tori moved in with her after her breakup with Dane. She could still see her sister's battered face after he'd used her for a punching bag.

Josie used her key in the door, then immediately called out to Tori.

"Hey, is anyone home?"

In a few seconds, a petite woman came down the hall. Vittoria had glossy black chin-length hair and midnight eyes. Her twin had inherited their mother's Hispanic skin tone.

"Josie!" She picked up speed and soon the sisters were locked into a big embrace. "I'm so glad you're here."

Josie pulled back. "Why? Has something else happened?"

Tori quickly shook her head. "No, I'm fine. I just missed you these last few weeks." Her gaze shifted to Garrett, and she frowned. "Well, I'm surprised to see you here. Hello, Garrett."

"Hello, Tori. It's good to see you again."

Tori didn't smile. "Do you have business in L.A.?"

He glanced at Josie. "No, I just came to help your sister." He put their suitcase down on the tiled floor. "I hear there's a big wedding in Santa Barbara."

Tori placed her hands on her hips. "Okay, someone tell me what's going on here."

Garrett wasn't sure how much he should say. So the truth might be a good start. "Okay, truth is, I wanted to spend some time with Josie. At the ranch everyone has been watching us, and the same in town." He reached out and drew Josie to his side. "So when Josie needed to be in L.A. I offered to come along and help out. We thought if we came here we wouldn't have that pressure."

He felt Josie tense. "I think what Garrett left out is the fact that we aren't officially a couple." She turned those blue eyes toward him, and he suddenly wished for what he couldn't have.

"We're taking things slow," she added, not liking their made-up story.

Tori's dark eyes went back and forth between the two of them. "Yeah, like I believe that. Come on into the kitchen."

Garrett followed but took the chance to look around. The main living space was painted dark beige and had a sectional sofa in crimson. They passed a staircase that led to the second floor. The hall was tiled, but the rest of the floors were a dark hardwood. They walked through an archway into a big kitchen and family room area. The cupboards were painted a glossy cream color with colorful tiled counters.

"Wow, I really like your home. There's so much character."

Josie went straight to the large worktable in the family room with French doors leading to a patio. "That's the reason I bought the place, and it was a good investment at the time. It's been a lot of work." She smiled proudly. "Now that I know how to tape and mud drywall, I can do more remodeling."

"Or you can call your favorite handyman," he told her, and felt the heat spark between them.

"Hey, you two," Tori called.

They turned to Tori. "In case you've forgotten we've got a wedding to put together in two days. Isn't that the reason you came back?"

CHAPTER NINE

EARLY THE NEXT MORNING, there was little traffic on the 101 Freeway, so it had been a pleasant drive up from Los Angeles to Santa Barbara, especially with the springlike temperatures.

Occasionally, Garrett glanced at Josie, seated next to him in the car, but the conversation had been all but nil because she was either on her cell phone or working on her notes for the wedding later today.

Last night they hadn't talked much, either. They'd ordered pizza for dinner and discussed the details of the Santa Barbara wedding trip. Then Josie went up to her room, and Garrett went for a walk. Although the street was busy with traffic, he liked the older neighborhood. It seemed safe enough, but that could be the perfect cover for the ex-boyfriend, Dane. He still didn't feel good about leaving the two sisters alone with a crazy on the loose.

He thought about what Josie said to him a few days ago. "We're not your problem." What if he wanted her to be?

He glanced across the car at Josie. This could all end up badly if he got his heart involved…again.

Garrett shifted in the driver's seat and concentrated on following the white cargo van with Slater Style embossed on the sides as they made their way through the coastal town into the hills and the Collins Family Rose Farm.

It was 7:00 a.m. when they drove up the steep road through the rose-covered hillsides toward a huge white-washed barn. Standing in front was a group of workers, probably waiting for the next set of instructions.

"Good, the crew's here," Josie said more to herself than anyone else. "Looks like the tables and chairs have been delivered. And Mrs. Collins is here, too."

Practically before the car stopped, Josie grabbed her clipboard, was out the door and giving instructions to the crew. Then she took off again toward the older woman.

Garrett had trouble keeping up as he followed her toward the huge barn. He stood in awe of the hundred-year-old two-story structure as Josie talked to the mother of the bride. Using soothing hand motions, Josie assured the woman that nothing would go wrong on her daughter's special day.

"I assure you, Mrs. Collins, we'll have everything set up and ready hours before the first guests arrive for the ceremony."

The attractive older woman shook her head. "We could have had the wedding at a five-star hotel, but no, my daughter had to have it in a barn."

Josie's voice remained calm. "The renovations on this structure came out beautifully. Wait until you see it when I finish decorating the inside."

The mother of the bride didn't look convinced. "Nearly a hundred thousand dollars won't change the fact it's still a barn." She walked away and climbed into a golf cart and rode off toward the large house on the hill.

Garrett offered her an encouraging smile. "She's just nervous about the wedding."

Josie released a long sigh. "Welcome to my world."

He followed Josie inside the barn, but paused and looked around the huge open space. Along with a new concrete floor, a few horse stalls had been rebuilt along one side that would probably never see an animal. The beams overhead were massive and stained a rich walnut color.

Josie gave him a quick rundown on the Collins family history. The rose farm had been owned by them for over a hundred years. And great-granddaughter, Allison, wanted to be married in the barn her great-grandfather had built. "Of course after the renovations, it's perfect for what she wants."

"I think it's a great idea," Garrett said.

Before Josie could answer, her cell phone rang, and she quickly attached her Bluetooth to her ear and listened to her first crisis.

The portable bar collapsed, while workmen scurried around. Garrett got busy using his carpenter skills to get it fixed, then he went to look for Josie to get his next assignment. She directed him to stacks of chairs.

When that task was completed, he walked through the chaos to find Josie with Tori, and they were directing the florist about wrapping the greenery around the trellis that was placed in front of the open barn doors. It was where the ceremony would take place in the late afternoon.

Assured that Josie got her point across, she sent Tori off for another job, then made a call to the bride to remind her of the time for prewedding pictures. And that Megan would be there to help her.

Then she snagged Garrett to help dress the several round tables, adding burnt-orange-colored runners over the white linen. All the chairs had to be covered, too. By the time Garrett tied his last bow, he needed a break and grabbed two bottles of water and handed her one.

He stood next to Josie as they surveyed the area. The tables were now adorned with centerpieces of roses. Greenery had been draped over every stall, and baskets of multicolored flowers were everywhere. There was the sound of crystal and china being set out on long banquet tables. He was amazed how this production was all coming together.

"That was quite a workout," he admitted.

Josie was dressed in jeans and a sweatshirt, and her ponytail was askew. She took a hearty drink. He eyed her long slender neck as her throat worked to swallow. He felt the same familiar stirring he'd always had for her.

Her voice brought him back to the present. "It's the best workout, and you don't even need a gym membership." She glanced at her watch. "We need to get cleaned up. We have a wedding to go to."

Josie had to admit, Garrett had put in a hard morning without any complaint. She hadn't even had time to think about whether his coming this weekend was a good idea or not. She was just glad he'd been here to help out.

Back in the car, Josie directed Garrett to one of the guesthouses on the property that Mrs. Collins had supplied the Slater Style crew. It was more convenient, so they didn't have to keep running up and down the hill to a hotel, especially to shower and change for the event. Catch was, she had to share it with Garrett.

About two hundred yards away from the Collins home and the barn, they found the small house nestled in a group of trees. They parked in the gravel driveway, and Josie used the key as Garrett and Tori brought in the bags.

"Oh, this is nice," Tori said.

Inside, the main room was surprisingly large with an open kitchen that had all the luxuries of home. There were two bedrooms, each with their own bath. Josie and Tori chose the larger of the bedrooms. "Garrett, you can use this one," she said, avoiding any eye contact with him. If things were different maybe... No, she couldn't go back there.

With a nod, he carried his bag into the first room with two single beds.

Tori stared at her twin. "I thought you said you two were a couple?"

"I said we're going slow, too. Besides, this isn't a get-away weekend. I'm working, so today is for my bride." Josie tossed her bag on the bed, hoping she convinced her sister. "Now, do you want to shower first?"

Tori watched her for a moment, as if she would argue the point, but said, "Sure." She picked up her things and walked into the bathroom.

Josie sank down onto the king-size bed. Her sister could read her better than anyone, so she had to know that she and Garrett weren't a couple. She had no idea what they were. Old high school sweethearts? Friends?

Josie shook her head. *The wedding. Think about the wedding.* She wished now she'd changed places with Megan and taken the first bride duty.

Once she heard the shower turn on, she headed to the kitchen, wishing she could have a glass of wine, but that would have to wait until after the festivities.

She passed the living area and stopped short when she saw Garrett. He was bending down, getting something from the refrigerator, giving her a close-up view of his backside, slim hips and taut thighs. Then he stood, and she discovered he was shirtless.

She gasped and he quickly turned around. Oh, boy. His chest was impressive, too. Wide and well-developed and his arms...

"Is something wrong?" he asked.

"No. You...you just startled me. I didn't expect you... to be out here." *Stop rambling,* she told herself. "We don't have much time to get ready."

His gray eyes locked on hers. "Loosen up, Josie. We

have time." He reached out and touched her cheek. "It's going to be perfect. You've done a great job. You have to be proud of this, and the business you've created."

She tried to speak, but her throat grew tight and she swallowed hard to clear it. It didn't help.

"I am proud of you. But I always knew you'd be a success at anything you attempted," he breathed as his head descended toward hers.

Even knowing what was about to happen wasn't wise, she couldn't move away as his mouth brushed over hers. She sucked in needed air, but before she could protest, he pulled back and gave her a smile.

"I should get back to my room before I get us both into trouble." He stepped around her and headed down the hall.

She sagged against the counter and watched the man walk away. The way her thoughts were going, she was already in trouble. Big trouble.

It was midnight, so Josie's job was officially over. The wedding ceremony had gone off with only minor mishaps, including a five-year-old ring bearer who suddenly refused to participate. No amount of bribing would make the boy go down that aisle.

The best man's toast revealed a little too much about the groom's past, and the bride got a little too much cake on her face. Josie leaned against the stall gate next to the dance floor and watched the happy couple grooving to a fast-paced song, and smiled. Okay, she'd done a good job of putting this together, from the bride's spark of an idea to have her wedding on her family's estate.

She thought back to the project at the lodge. Could she put together a few wedding packages to help make it a successful venue and bring in money for the ranch?

"Looks like you can use this," a familiar voice said.

She looked over her shoulder and found Garrett holding two glasses of champagne. She accepted the crystal flute and took a sip of the Napa Valley vintage. Heavenly. She closed her eyes and savored the warm feeling the bubbly liquid gave her.

"You're a lifesaver."

She took a sip as she examined Garrett, dressed in his dark tailored slacks and wine-colored shirt with a dark print tie. Her heart went all aflutter gazing at the handsome man.

"At your service, ma'am."

Garrett leaned against the post on the stall and studied the beautiful woman in a basic black dress. Except there wasn't anything basic about Josie Slater. The knit material draped over her body, subtly showing off her curves. Her hair was swept up on top of her head, revealing her long graceful neck. Diamond studs adorned her sexy earlobes.

"I should have come to your rescue sooner, except I couldn't seem to catch up to you. I don't think anyone could."

"There's always a lot to do at these events. I'm actually off now, but until the bride and groom leave, anything can happen." She checked her watch. "I'm hoping that will be in the next thirty minutes."

The band ended one song and applause broke out in the crowd, then quickly died down when a ballad began, Al Green's "Let's Stay Together." Garrett didn't hesitate as he took the glass from Josie's hand and set it on the railing, then reached for her.

"I can't… I shouldn't, Garrett."

He shook his head as he drew her into his arms. "No one will even see us," he told her as they began to move to the music inside the privacy of the stall.

When he pulled her close, she didn't fight him. He bit

back a groan, feeling her body pressed against him. He could barely move, afraid to disturb the moment. The familiarity of her scent, her touch, churned up so many emotions, emotions he thought had died long ago. He was wrong. So wrong. He'd never gotten over her.

When his thigh brushed Josie's, she drew a breath. He tightened his hold, knowing this moment in time was fleeting for both of them. He knew he shouldn't want this so much. It couldn't last. Soon they had to go back to reality and their different lives. Just seeing her in action today proved that.

Slowly the music faded, but he didn't release her. He closed his eyes, feeling her softness molded to him. They were a perfect fit. Hearing people approach, Josie pulled back, her eyes dark and filled with desire.

"I need to get back to work."

When she started to leave, he reached for her. "Josie…"

She stopped but didn't look at him. "This isn't a good idea, Garrett."

"It felt pretty good a few seconds ago."

Before she could speak, someone called to her. "I can't do this right now, Garrett. I need to get back to work." She pulled away and hurried off.

Garrett walked to the edge of the stall. "This isn't over, Josie."

It was after one in the morning before the caterers finished cleaning up and left the premises. The band had packed up their equipment and driven off thirty minutes earlier.

The newlyweds had a formal send-off just after midnight, and the party finally began to wind down and the rest of the Collins/Brimley families went home, too. Josie pulled the sweater coat tighter around her shoulders to ward off the night's chill. She caught up with Tori and Megan while they finished packing up the Slater Style van.

"Thank you so much," she said and hugged them both. "Everything turned out wonderful."

"Wait until you get my bill," Tori teased, fighting a yawn.

"Then let's go to the cottage so we can get some sleep. Mrs. Collins said we can stay as late tomorrow as we want."

Tori shook her head. "I'm not staying. I'm going back with Megan."

"But the traffic," Josie said, trying to change her decision. She wasn't sure if she could handle Garrett as close as the next bedroom. "And what about Dane?"

"I'm not driving. And I haven't seen Dane in over a week. Besides, I'm going to spend the night with Megan."

"No need to stay with Megan, I'll go back, too. Give me fifteen minutes to pack up." She glanced around for Garrett. "I'm sure Garrett would be willing to drive back."

Tori took her sister's hand. "No, Josie. You stay here." She paused and pulled her away from the others for some privacy. "I've been watching you and Garrett dance around each other all day and this evening in the stall."

Josie released a breath. "That wasn't very smart of me."

"You need some time alone to figure out where to go with those feelings."

Josie knew that was the last thing she needed. Garrett could hurt her again. "I can't get involved with him again."

Tori hugged her. "Dear sister, that's the problem. You've never gotten uninvolved with the man. And if you look closely, he still has feelings for you. Maybe you should find out where it goes."

Josie shook her head. "This isn't a good idea. I can't let him hurt me again."

"How do you know that will happen? It's been nearly ten years. Maybe there's something there to build on, but at the very least you need closure." She kissed her, then started walking toward the van. "I'll see you tomorrow."

Josie watched Tori climb in, and soon they drove off. Her heart pounded in her chest as Garrett walked toward her. Did she really want to get involved with Garrett again?

"It seems we have this knack for getting stranded together." He reached out and cupped her cheek, then leaned down and brushed a kiss over her mouth. She shivered at his touch. Oh, God, she ached for him.

He pulled back. His dark gaze said so much. "Do you want me to take you back to L.A., too?"

Darn the man, he was leaving this up to her. "No, I want to stay here tonight. With you."

Garrett's hand was shaking as he took Josie's and they made their way along the path that led to the small cottage with a single light on the porch. The rush of excitement from being with her was even stronger than all those years ago when he'd first met her. He still cared about her.

He took out the key and inserted it into the lock, then pushed open the door, allowing her to go inside first.

He followed then closed the door, but quickly found himself pushed up against the raised panels with Josie's hands wrapped around his neck. She pulled his head down to meet her hungry mouth and didn't stop there. She went to work on seducing him with her lips, hands and her body.

He broke off the kiss. "I take it you're glad we're staying."

"Don't get cocky, Temple, or I won't let you get to first base, let alone make all your dreams come true tonight."

Well, well! He couldn't help but grin, remembering that first base had been as far as he'd gotten while they'd dated in school. He quickly sobered, and leaned down to whisper in her ear, "I want to make your dreams come true."

His mouth brushed over hers, so gently, so softly she nearly groaned in frustration. She told herself this was crazy, but it felt too good. It always felt good with Garrett.

Josie shivered at his words. "Oh, Garrett," she breathed.

His lips found hers again, and he angled her mouth to deepen the kiss, letting her know how much he wanted her. When he released her, they were both breathing hard. "Let's continue this somewhere we'll be more comfortable." He swung her up in his arms and carried her down the hall into her room.

"Good idea." She kicked off her shoes as they went to her bedroom.

It was dark, only the light from the hall illuminated the room, helping to direct him to the king-size bed. He set her down and kissed her again and again. "I thought you'd appreciate the bigger bed, since my room has singles."

Josie looked around the room. Her sister had straightened up the mess they'd left earlier with the rush to leave for the wedding. She looked back up at the man she'd wanted since the first day she'd met him in high school.

He leaned down and pressed his lips against her ear. "I want you, Josie Slater. More than you could ever imagine, but if you're having second thoughts…"

More like third and fourth, yet she reached out with shaky fingers to unbutton his dress shirt. With her heart beating wildly, she parted the material, and her hands came in contact with his chest. He sucked in a breath. "Only if you want to stop—"

His mouth came down hard on hers. This time slow and deeper, giving her his tongue and feasting on her until she was clinging to him. Her fingers tangled in his hair, holding him close. It left her no doubt what he wanted. The sensations that he created had her pressing against him as his hands worked the zipper at the back of her dress. Soon the soft fabric landed in a heap on the floor. Her pulse danced.

This time he sucked in a breath. "You are gorgeous." He dipped his head and kissed her. No man's touch had ever affected her like this.

"My turn," she said bravely. She pushed his shirt off those wide shoulders, then hungrily ran her fingers through the mat of dark hair that covered his beautiful chest. Next she used her lips to place kisses along his heated skin, causing him to tense.

"I'm not sure how much I can stand." He cupped her face and leaned down and kissed her. "I want you so much, Josie."

She looked into his eyes, seeing his need, his desire for her. "I want you, too, Garrett."

His mouth came down on hers, and true to his promise…he began to make her dreams come true.

CHAPTER TEN

IT WASN'T EVEN dawn yet, but Garrett was wide-awake. It might have something to do with the woman lying next to him. Last night had been incredible. Loving Josie had been only a dream, and now that dream had become a reality.

He wasn't naive enough to think she would wake up and want to continue what they'd started last night. But he had all morning to try and convince her. Even he wasn't sure how they could solve many of their problems. She had a life here, and she'd told him so many times that she didn't want to give it up. How could she give up a thriving business? He had a business, too, and so much more. There was his ailing father and a son to raise. Brody had to come first.

Josie moved beside him, then she rolled toward him, throwing her arm across his chest. He tensed, feeling her warm flesh against his, stirring him once again. He wanted her even more than he had all those years ago. He made the mistake then of giving up on her. There was no way he would do that again, not easily. Not when he knew Josie still had feelings for him.

He felt her cheek against his shoulder, her breast brushed his chest. Her legs tangled with his, inciting him further. Then her eyelashes fluttered and she finally opened them.

He froze and offered her a smile. "Hi, there."

She smiled back. "Hi, yourself."

She looked a little unsure and started to turn away. He wouldn't let her. Then he leaned down and opening his mouth against her throat, he kissed her, causing her to shiver. He wanted her to understand that whatever was happening, he wanted more than one night.

He raised his head and looked at her. "No hiding, Josie. Not after last night. You have to realize that there's still something between us."

She didn't say anything.

"Can you at least admit to that?"

"Okay, so you rocked my world. That doesn't mean it goes further than last night."

She was so stubborn. "It's not even up for discussion?"

"I thought we agreed that we had separate worlds, and there's no possible way we can combine them."

He felt the constriction in his chest. There had to be a way for them to be together. "I don't want you to walk away again."

She hesitated. Wasn't that a good sign? "Garrett, we talked about this. Our lives are so different…"

"The hell with our lives, what about what we feel?" He placed her hand against his bare chest. "Feel my heart pound, Josie. Only you can make that happen."

Josie had tears in her eyes as she moved his hand and put it against her chest so he could also feel the rapid rhythm. "Ditto."

Garrett rolled her onto her back and captured her mouth in a hungry kiss. He felt her palm against his chest starting to push him away, but not for long. Her arms wrapped around his neck and brought him closer. When her mouth opened on a groan, he pushed his tongue inside, stroking and teasing her. Soon, his hands moved over her body, caressing her warm skin.

"Garrett…"

He looked at her as the morning sun began to slowly illuminate the bedroom. He could see the desire in her eyes and he touched her cheek. He'd never felt such closeness with anyone, only with Josie.

"I love it when you say my name, especially when I'm doing something to please you." He felt like a teenager again. "Tell me what you want, Josie Slater."

She arched her back as his hand cupped her breast. "You. I want you."

"You've always had me, Josie," he said as his mouth captured hers just as a cell phone began to ring. It was Josie's.

She sat up, holding the sheet against her, and reached for her purse on the table next to her side of the bed. She checked the caller ID.

"It's Tori." She punched the button. "Tori, what's wrong?" Garrett watched her expression change to panic. "Get out of there and call the police." Josie nodded as she listened. "Okay, we'll be home as soon as possible." She hung up and looked at Garrett. "Someone broke into my house and trashed the place."

The trip back from Santa Barbara was fast. Josie didn't argue with Garrett about his speed, knowing she only wanted to get to her sister. By the time they pulled up in front of her condo, Josie was out and running to her sister, who was standing on the small lawn.

Josie grabbed Tori close and felt her trembling. "Oh, Tori, I'm so glad you're safe." She shivered. "Thank God you were staying with Megan and not here."

Tori nodded at Garrett then back to her. "I'm so sorry about your house, Josie."

"Why are you sorry? You didn't do any of this."

She saw the tormented look in her twin's eyes. "If I'd only pressed charges against him before…"

"No! That's in the past, Tori. Dane's not going to get off free this time." She glanced around. "Where's Detective Brandon?"

"He's inside," Tori said. "But he wants us to wait out here."

"Too bad." Josie marched up the two steps and through the doorway.

She bit her bottom lip, trying to hold back the emotion as she glanced around the entry. All the work she'd put into her home and some crazy had broken in and destroyed it.

She couldn't hold back a gasp as her gaze roamed toward the living room, where furniture had been turned over, cushions were sliced with a knife and stuffing was scattered all around. Pictures had been destroyed and thrown to the floor. In their place on the walls were spray painted messages. Horrible words.

Garrett cursed. "They'd better have this creep and bully in custody," he said.

Teary-eyed, Tori shook her head. "Detective Brandon said until they find proof that Dane did this, they have to treat it like a random break-in. We're not to touch anything."

Just then Josie saw a uniformed officer coming down the hall. He had on a pair of rubber gloves and was carrying a plastic bag. She fought back her anger that someone was going through her personal things.

"It's going to be okay," she told Tori, but wasn't sure she believed it.

"How can you say that? Look at this place," Tori said, barely holding it together.

Garrett stepped forward. "These are just things, Tori. It's you we're worried about." When Tori nodded, he hugged her. "We'll get to the bottom of this," he promised her.

He turned to Josie and pulled her close, too. She stiffened, hating that she wanted his comforting embrace. In a few weeks Garrett Temple wouldn't be around for her to lean on. He'd be back in Montana and she'd be here. And once again, she'd have to learn to live without him.

Their moment of quiet was interrupted when a middle-aged man dressed in dark slacks and a white shirt and a tie under a nylon jacket that read LAPD walked into the room.

"Miss Slater." Detective Brandon nodded in greeting. "I'm sorry we have to meet again under these circumstances."

She was working to hold on to her composure. "Sorry, doesn't cut it, Detective. You know Dane Buckley is behind this. A random thief doesn't leave personal messages," she told him, and pointed to the wall.

The detective nodded in agreement. "But until we have proof who did this, I can't arrest him or anyone. We are bringing him in for questioning. We're also talking to your neighbors. Maybe they saw him around." He frowned. "We should be finished with photos and fingerprints by the end of the day, so you can call your insurance company and make arrangements to clean and paint the place."

Josie knew that new paint and furniture wouldn't erase this memory. How could she ever feel safe here again?

After exchanging goodbyes, the detective walked out the door, and Garrett followed him, but it was difficult to stay calm.

"Detective, tell me you aren't going to just push this case aside and wait for Buckley to strike again."

He saw the frustration in the man's eyes. "Like I said, we find some proof, and I'll do everything I can to get this predator off the street. If you want to help, I suggest you get both sisters away from here. This guy's message is clear. He wants revenge."

Garrett already knew that. "How would you feel if I bring in some outside help?"

The cop watched him. "As long as you don't interfere with the investigation or do anything illegal, I don't have a problem."

Garrett shook the officer's hand before he walked away. He took out his cell phone, not intending to stand by and let anything happen to Josie or Tori.

He needed someone he could trust. Brad Richards had helped him out before when someone hacked into his business computer system. He punched in the number and after the third ring it was answered. "McNeely Investigations."

"Hey, Brad, it's Garrett Temple."

There was a pause, then the ex-Special Forces soldier said, "What can I do for you, Garrett?"

"I need you to look into someone's past. Someone who preys on women."

"When and where do you need me?"

Two days later, after contacting the insurance company and scheduling the cleanup, Garrett had finally managed to get Tori and Josie on a noon flight back to Montana.

Josie had put on a brave front, but he knew she'd been frightened by this lunatic. He'd hoped that she would lean on him. Instead, she'd done everything she could to avoid coming near him.

She had stayed busy dealing with all the mess, trying to gather up their things to take back to Montana. He'd at least gotten them to move into a hotel, and then their agreement to come back to the ranch until Ana's wedding. There was no way he was going to leave them behind.

He was just happy Josie was returning with him, but his

true wish was that they were still in Santa Barbara. Before her world had suddenly been turned upside down. Before reality invaded and threw yet another obstacle at them. Before she pulled away from him once again.

He drove under the archway to the Lazy S Ranch. The pastures were covered in layers of snow, but the roads had been cleared from the recent snowstorm. "We're almost home," he told them.

"This isn't my home," Tori murmured.

Garrett glanced in the rearview mirror. Tori was looking out the window.

It might not be her home any longer, but as long as Dane was on the loose they were in danger. He prayed both Tori and Josie would stay here for as long as it took for them to be safe again.

"It will be for the next few weeks."

He heard Tori's sigh. "As long as you don't tell anyone what happened, I'll stay."

He didn't like that deal. Everyone needed to be vigilant if a stranger showed up.

"Deal," he said, and looked at Josie. That meant she'd be going back, too. He honestly didn't want her to go. Would she even think about staying in Montana to give them a second chance? By the look of her body language, he had no chance at all.

Garrett pulled into the driveway and saw his dad's truck. He parked, then the front door opened and Brody came running out. He couldn't get out of the car fast enough. The bitter cold air stung his face, but he only saw his son.

"Dad!" The boy launched himself into his waiting arms. "You're home."

"I'm glad I'm back, too." He set his son down and pulled his jacket together to ward off the cold. "Did you have fun with Grandpa and Grandma Kirkwood?"

He nodded. "But I missed you."

Those were wonderful words to hear. "I've missed you, too, son."

Brody's attention went to the passengers. "Josie! You came back, too." He ran to her side of the car and hugged her. "Colt was afraid you might stay in California."

She ruffled the boy's hair. "No, I had to come back so I can get a video game rematch. You promised to teach me how to get to the next level." She directed him to the other side of the car. "Brody, this is my sister, Tori. She's going to be staying for a while."

"Hi, Tori. I can teach you how to play video games if you want."

"Great to meet you, Brody."

Garrett got the suitcases out of the trunk and urged the group toward the house. "Hey, let's take this conversation inside where it's warm."

Brody ran up ahead calling back to the sisters, "Yeah, Kathleen baked a cake."

Josie stopped on the porch and waited as Tori stepped across the threshold and into the entry. She was pretty sure she knew what was going through her sister's head. It was hard not to think about the past years here along with the father who'd ignored them. It had been a cold existence for the four girls growing up here.

Josie looked down the hall and saw Colt walking toward them. His gait was slow and maybe not as steady as it should be, but there'd been improvement since Josie had first come home over three weeks ago.

She watched her sister's reaction. Would she accept the changes in this man? Even Josie had been leery that maybe the cold, distant man would return. Over the past weeks, she'd seen changes in Colt. She was willing to give him a chance to be the father he'd said he wanted to be, but Tori had to make her own decision.

"Vittoria." He came to her and without hesitation reached out and took her hand in his. "I'm so glad you're home."

"Hello, Colt. I'm glad to see you're doing well."

Josie could see how hard it was for her sister to hold back the tears.

"It gets better each time one of my daughters comes home," Colt told her.

She shook her head. "I'm only staying until Ana's wedding." She glanced around. "Speaking of Ana, where is my big sister?"

"She's working at the high school," a familiar male voice answered.

They turned to see Vance coming toward them. "She'll be home soon. Hi, Tori. It's good to see you again."

Tori smiled. "Good to see you, too, Vance. How are you surviving the wedding plans?"

He grinned. "Anything Ana wants. I just hope it happens soon before she realizes I'm not such a great catch."

"Oh, I think Ana knows what a good man you are." Tears welled in her eyes. "And you've always treated her well."

"I love her and wouldn't intentionally do anything to hurt her."

Tori nodded. "Good." She stepped back as another woman hurried in.

"Kathleen," Tori cried as the older woman took her into her welcoming arms.

"Another of my babies came home." She wiped her eyes. "Praise the Lord."

Tori grinned and looked at the older woman. "I can't tell you how much I've missed you."

"I know, child. I always enjoyed your cards and presents." Those kind hazel eyes searched Tori's face. "Your heart is sad. I'm glad you came home."

Even Josie had to wipe away tears.

Tori nodded. "Would anyone mind if I went upstairs and rested?"

"Of course not," everyone chimed in. Tori looked toward the staircase. "Which room?"

"I put your suitcase in your old bedroom," Garrett told her.

Josie felt her cheeks redden and rushed on to explain. "Garrett and Brody stayed during the blizzard two weeks ago."

Tori gave her a knowing smile and walked off with Kathleen.

Josie looked across the entry at Garrett. He turned his gray gaze on her, and she felt that familiar jolt. He was a hard man to resist. She'd already let her defenses drop, but she couldn't let it happen again. She was L.A. bound.

At eleven o'clock the house was quiet, and everyone had settled in for the night. In his room, Colt stood in the darkness by the window. If there was one thing he enjoyed about having to move his bedroom downstairs, it was the view. He could see the entire compound, the corral, the barn. He could keep an eye on the operation.

He looked out at the foreman's cottage and saw the lights go off. He smiled to himself. Ana and Vance were probably heading to bed. His oldest daughter had no qualms about staying with the man she planned to marry. Colt didn't, either. Life was too short to waste; love was too fleeting.

Regrets. Colt closed his eyes against the memories. He had too many regrets to count. The biggest mistake had been turning away from his daughters when they needed him the most. No more.

Three of his four daughters were home now. Not for long, and somehow he needed to prove to them that he was worth the risk. Okay, Ana was happy with Vance, and they would be living close. Josie was a different story. He'd been watching the sparks fly between her and Garrett. He doubted that his girl was going to give the man a second chance easily. But he had hopes that they would work things out.

Then there was Tori. Something bad had happened to her in California. He didn't know what it was, and she didn't trust him enough to tell him. He hated to see the pain in her beautiful dark eyes. He had to help her.

Suddenly, fatigue hit him hard, and Colt closed the window shades and walked to his bed. When would he get his energy back? When would he get his life back? He opened the buttons on his shirt and stripped it off his shoulders and tossed it on the chair. He liked that his arm had regained strength. His therapy with Jay was tough, but it was paying off. He had good muscle tone.

He went for the button fly on his jeans when he caught a familiar scent. Roses. He glanced toward the door and saw a small figure standing there. He blinked once, then again.

"Who is it?" he asked, afraid to know. "Who are you?"

"Colt..." a woman's voice said.

He froze. No. It couldn't be. He felt his heart hammering in his chest as the figure stepped into the dim lamplight. The slender figure was dressed in black. Her hair was long, reaching her shoulders. Although her face was in the shadows, he knew her eyes were almond-shaped and as black as midnight. He forced himself to take a breath. "Lucia..."

CHAPTER ELEVEN

AFTER A RESTLESS NIGHT, Josie slept in later than usual. Tori was already up and gone from the room. Not surprising, since she'd heard her sister tossing around in the other bed most of the night. Not that she'd blamed her for feeling uneasy after the break-in. For now, they were both safe here. But how long could they hide out at the ranch when their lives were in California?

Of course, Montana had Garrett Temple. And now, after his visit to L.A., she knew firsthand how he would never fit into her life, any more than she'd fit into his. No matter how incredible their night together had been, it had to be a onetime thing.

Not that he would ever ask her for more. He had a child to think about. She smiled. Brody was a sweet boy, but his home was here, too.

She sighed. No more dreams about Garrett. She needed to focus on Ana's wedding, and enjoy her remaining time here with her family. She thought about Colt. She'd been surprised how much she liked spending time with him. He'd even taken an interest in her life and her work. The Colt Slater she'd remembered never had time for his daughters.

Could her father change that much?

After showering and dressing, Josie went downstairs to find Ana, Tori and Colt waiting for her in the kitchen.

"Good, you're finally awake," Ana said. "We want to drive out to the lodge. Garrett and Vance are already there finishing up any last-minute details. Also, Colt and Tori haven't seen the place."

"Do you think I have time for some coffee and toast?"

"Of course you do," Kathleen said, filling her cup.

As much as Josie wanted to delay the inevitable, she had to go. After her quick breakfast, they jumped into Colt's pickup and headed out to the river.

Ana chattered most of the way about wedding details. Josie took notes and asked even more questions, trying to concentrate on her job rather than on seeing Garrett again. When Ana pulled up to the construction site, Vance and Garrett's trucks were there, and her heart began to race.

"Good, the guys are already here. I can't wait to see all the finishing touches to the place." She turned to Colt. "Oh, wait until you see it, Tori, Dad. It's beautiful."

They climbed out and helped Colt while he used his cane to get over the plywood walkway toward the wide porch. Josie made more notes about some minor landscaping needs.

Colt stopped and gazed at the two-story log structure. "Land sakes, she's a beauty." He looked overwhelmed. "I'm glad Ana didn't listen to an old man's rantings and got this place built."

Ana grinned. "Actually, the lodge was Josie's idea."

"Well, I give you all the credit for coming up with ideas to help out. I'm so grateful."

They finally reached the front door, and Ana paused and brushed her ebony hair off her shoulders. "It's been a while since I've been here. Vance said he didn't want me to see it until it was completed. Dad, welcome to River's Edge Lodge." She swung open the doors, and the group walked across the threshold.

Ana let out a gasp as her gaze moved around the large open room with the massive floor-to-ceiling river rock fireplace. There were honey-oak hardwood floors and the far wall was all windows, overlooking the river and mountain range.

Tears came to Ana's eyes. "Oh, it's perfect."

"That's good to hear," a familiar man's voice said.

Josie swung around to find Vance and Garrett were right behind her. The handsome men wore tool belts to let the others know they'd been working this morning.

Ana ran to her man. Josie stood in her place, hating the fact she wished she could go to Garrett. Whoa. *He isn't yours to run to.*

"It's perfect," Ana said.

"Then it's worth all the work we put in." Vance looked at Colt. "How do you like it?"

Her father shook his head. "What's not to like?" He glanced at Garrett. "Thank you for all you've done."

"You're welcome, but your future son-in-law and Josie put in a lot of work, too."

Vance turned to Ana. "I know Josie worked really hard, and Garrett also logged in time he didn't bill us for. These two put in a long few weeks to make sure it was finished for our wedding."

Ana looked at her and mouthed, "T+hank you."

Josie didn't want any praise. "Hey, I'm the maid of honor, and besides, we need to get this place rented to start making some money."

"Well, then, let's start booking the place," Ana said.

Tori jumped in. "We'll need to take a few pictures for the website and then we can begin to advertise River's Edge Lodge." She turned to Colt. "Do we have your approval?"

Josie could see the emotion on her father's face. "My approval? But I didn't put in a lick of the work."

Ana stepped forward. "The Lazy S is your ranch, Dad. Vance and I had power of attorney while you were recovering, but you're still the head of this family, and we make decisions together."

Colt nodded as tears filled his eyes. "Let's have a wedding, and then start taking reservations."

Ana clasped her hands together. "I have another question to ask you, Dad." Ana paused a moment. "Would you give me away?"

The room grew silent. Josie glanced at Garrett. He caught her gaze, and she couldn't seem to look away until her father answered, "Oh, Analeigh, I'd be honored." He took her hand. "But I hate to give you away since I just found you."

"I think Vance would be willing to share me with you. And we'll be living practically outside your door in the foreman's house." She glanced at Vance and smiled. "Until we get our new home built this spring."

Colt tapped his cane. "I wish I could do more to contribute to the operation."

Vance patted him on the back. "Come spring, Colt, I have no doubt you'll be back on a horse. Until then we'll help each other because that's what families do."

Colt nodded.

Vance tugged on Ana's arm. "Come on, we want to show you the rest of the place."

Vance and Ana took Tori and Colt up the stairs.

Garrett stayed back watching Josie taking some notes for the wedding beside the big window. She'd been doing her best to keep her distance ever since they returned to Montana. They'd spent four days together while in California, and then yesterday they'd gone their separate ways. He'd found he'd missed her. Lying in bed last night, he couldn't sleep as memories of her flooded his head. He knew these feelings he had for her complicated his life. It would be disastrous if let himself fall in love with her again.

He wasn't listening to common sense when he walked up to her. "How'd you sleep last night?"

She swung around, looking startled. "Oh, fine. I was pretty tired after the flight."

He reached out and touched her cheek. "I miss you, Josie. Being with you in Santa Barbara was incredible."

He watched her eyes darken and knew she'd been just as affected by what happened between them as he was.

She closed her eyes a moment. "It was, but we can't go back there again."

He knew that. He heard the voices upstairs. "Maybe we could go somewhere and talk about that."

Josie shook her head. "Garrett, we had our night. A night that we should have had as teenagers, but we aren't those kids anymore."

Years ago, they'd planned to wait until they were married to have sex. He forced a smile. "We still have feelings for each other."

"I think we always will." She sighed and glanced away. "We have different lives now. I'm going back to L.A., and you're staying here because it's where you belong…with your son."

He felt tightness in his chest as his heart lodged in his throat. He was losing her again. He should be used to her rejection, but it still hurt like hell. "You're right. Brody has to be my main focus." Wanting her had made him forget that. "Then I guess there's nothing more to say."

Josie avoided his gaze. "I guess not." She finally looked at him. "If things were different—"

He raised his hand to stop from hearing her regrets. The familiar ache brought him back to all those years ago. He felt the pain again. "There's no need to explain. It's been over for a lot of years. It's best we stop now before—"

All at once the rest of the group appeared above them along the open staircase and started down the steps.

"We're all going to lunch at the Big Sky Café," Vance announced. "You two want to join us?"

"Sure," Josie said, lacking enthusiasm.

Garrett couldn't be with Josie and keep pretending. He looked at his watch. "I'll have to pass. I need to check on another job in Dillon."

After another round of thanks to him, the Slaters started out the door. Josie was the last to leave. She turned and looked at him. "This is for the best, Garrett. You'll see."

He nodded and she left. "Yeah, we'll always have Santa Barbara." Why wasn't that enough?

It was Thanksgiving morning, and Garrett had to start the celebration by breaking the bad news to his son. They weren't going to the Slaters' today.

"But we were invited," Brody said. "Why can't we go?" The child was close to tears.

"There's been a change in plans, son. They have family home from California and they should spend time together."

Brody jumped up from the kitchen table. "It's not fair. I wanted to be with Josie and Tori. We were going to play video games."

"I'll play games with you."

"I don't want to play with you." The boy glared at him. "What did you do to make Josie mad?"

He was taken aback by Brody's comment. "I didn't do anything."

"Yes, you did. You always made Mom mad."

Whoa, where did that come from? "It wasn't intentional, son. People argue sometimes."

The child didn't look convinced, so Garrett went on to say, "We're not Josie's family, and Josie, Tori and Ana need time with their dad."

"I don't believe you," the boy shouted before he ran from the room.

Garrett started to go after him, but walked to the kitchen window and looked out. They both needed to cool off. It was obvious he and his son had more to work through. Worse, Brody was getting too attached to Josie. When she went back to L.A., he knew his son would be hurt.

"You okay, Garrett?"

He turned to see his father and nodded.

Nolan Temple walked over to him. "Kids say things because they're hurt and disappointed."

"Maybe he's right," he began. "I wasn't the best husband."

"But you were always the best father to that boy," Nolan countered. "He had a rough time with the divorce, then his mother's passing not even a year ago, and the move here. Give him time."

"What if I do it all wrong?"

"Just keep loving that boy." His dad nodded. "But don't let your marriage to Natalie keep you from moving on."

Garrett sighed. He didn't want to think about his ex-wife or their bad years together. "I wasn't the man she needed. As you saw with Brody's attitude, I caused a lot of damage."

"Don't be too quick to take all the blame, son. It takes

two to make a marriage work." Nolan shook his head. "I'm sorry. I won't speak ill of the dead."

His father changed the subject. "When Josie showed up, I was kind of hoping you two would find each other again. You kind of gave Colt and I some hope when you went off to L.A. together."

He'd given himself some hope. Garrett shrugged, not wanting to rehash this. He hoped he'd been able to accept the fact that once again she'd leave and he'd stay here. "And she's returning to L.A."

His father nodded. "Have you asked her to stay?"

Garrett thought back to the wedding in Santa Barbara. He'd seen Josie at work. "She has her business there. I have my work here. We have the ranch and our home, and there's Brody."

"I guess you've thought this out."

"Look, Dad, I'm not that boy she left behind years ago. I have to think of my son. I'm not going to chase after someone who doesn't want me."

"Who said she doesn't want you?"

"She did, okay," he answered a little too loud. "Sorry."

His father reached out and placed a hand on his arm. "It's hard to give you advice, son. From the minute I saw your mother, I fell in love." His father's gaze settled on him. "I don't have any regrets except I didn't have enough time with her. Twenty-five years seems like a lifetime, but it's not. I miss her every day. I wake up missing her, and I go to bed every night missing her."

Garrett had always envied his parents and the affection they showed each other. He smiled. "You two were so loving."

"Josie and her sisters haven't been as lucky with their parents. Colt might be seeing the error of his ways since his stroke, but those girls never had a mother and father who were there for them growing up. It makes trust hard."

Garrett didn't say anything. He knew, outside of Kathleen, Josie and her sisters had been on their own growing up. He recalled the teenage Josie who was afraid of the passion they shared. Then he'd gone away to college and left her behind.

Garrett shook his head. No, he needed to move away from the past. How could he do that when all he wanted was in his past?

Josie never remembered having a Thanksgiving like this. The kitchen was filled with her sisters helping Kathleen prepare the large turkey. Laughing and joking went on all the while they worked on the food prep. It was almost the best Thanksgiving ever. Then she thought about Garrett, knowing he wasn't coming today because of her. It was for the best. In the long run, he would thank her.

Ana walked into the room carrying a large leather album.

"Did you find the silverware?" Josie asked.

Ana held up the book. "No, but look what I found."

Josie and Tori went to the table where Ana laid out the book. Ana sat down, and the twins looked over her shoulder. Her sister gasped as she turned to the first page that showed a young Ana. "That's me!"

Josie smiled as she looked at the toddler in her little cowgirl outfit and bright red boots and hat. "Oh, weren't you cute."

Ana turned to the next page and saw the twins, side by side wrapped in pink blankets. "Gosh, we look so much alike," Tori said. "I don't know who is who."

Ana pointed at the photo. "This is you, Josie, and this one is you, Tori."

They both stared at their older sister. "What? I was there so I know this. Our mother always put Tori on the left side because you, Josie, would fuss if she didn't." .

"You always liked being the boss, even back then," Tori said.

Ana turned to the next page and they all froze. There was a large picture of Lucia and Colton Slater staring back at them. "Oh, my, I didn't think Colt kept any of her."

"We can't even say her name?" Tori asked. "It's Lucia."

Josie studied the beautiful woman in the portrait, their mother. She could barely remember the woman with the long black hair that smelled like flowers. She and Tori had only been three years old, and Marissa had been a year old when their mother left the family.

In the picture Ana was standing next to Colt, and the twins were in between them and Lucia held a toddler in her arms. "That's Marissa."

"There are so few baby pictures of her," Ana said.

"Maybe that's the reason she became a photographer," Tori said.

Ana looked at Josie. "Have you talked to her recently?"

"No, I tried before we left L.A. I wanted her to know we'd be out of town. Have you spoken to her?"

"Just once," Ana admitted. "I wanted to make sure she's coming to the wedding, and I hoped she'd come early for Thanksgiving."

Josie thought about all the times she'd called Marissa. San Diego was less than three hours away, but somehow they couldn't seem to get together. "What was her excuse this time?"

"That she has to photograph a big magazine layout. I asked her if she'd do the pictures for my wedding. She's going to try to make it. That's all I can ask." Ana got another dreamy look. "My sisters home. That would be a perfect day."

Not so perfect for Josie, not with having to spend the entire day with Garrett. All she had to do was get through the rehearsal dinner and the wedding before she could cut her ties with Garrett for good. She'd done it before; she could do it again. She just couldn't come back, knowing he'd be here, reminding her of what she couldn't have.

At least she didn't have to see him today, but found she was disappointed that he and Brody weren't coming to Thanksgiving dinner.

There was a knock on the kitchen door, and Ana went to answer it. "Garrett. Oh, good, you've changed your mind about dinner."

He looked upset. "No, but I was hoping I'd find Brody here."

Josie felt a sudden panic. "No, he hasn't been here."

He removed his hat and ran his fingers through his hair. "He was upset with me for changing our dinner plans. He went to his room, but I discovered he took off on his bike. I was hoping he came here."

Josie gasped. "Garrett, we're over two miles from your house."

He shook his head. "Not if you take the shortcut along the river. Since the weather is so mild that road is pretty clear. It's the way I think he'd go." He started off the back stoop and grabbed his horse's reins. "I've got to go find him."

Dear God. Josie began to shake. "Then let's all go looking for him," she said.

Ana picked up the phone and dialed. "Vance is in the barn. I'll have him saddle up some horses."

"Have him saddle a mount for me, too," Josie said. "I'm

going." This man came after her when she'd gotten lost. She had to help him find his son.

Dinner forgotten, the sisters grabbed warm coats and hats, then headed down to the barn. Ana's Blondie was saddled along with Vance's Rusty. Jake had a gentle mare, Molly, ready for Josie.

They had daylight in their favor, but still nightfall came fast in November. They had to find the child because a freeze warning was predicted for tonight.

Temple and Slater land bordered each other, but that left a lot of land to cover.

"My three men are fanned out along the bank on our side," Garrett said. "I thought Brody might show up here since this was where he wanted to come today."

"Is there anywhere else he might go, a special place?" Vance asked.

"I've talked to him about the river and the old cabin. I thought I explained we'd have to wait to go there until spring."

The riders were all given an area to search, and equipped with cell phones. Josie was going with Garrett, whether he wanted her to or not. "We're going to find him, Garrett."

He didn't say anything.

"He's a smart boy," she told him, praying that she was right, realizing how much she cared the child.

Josie saw the pain on Garrett's face. She wished she could comfort him.

"Too smart for his own good," he blurted out. "Wait until I get…" He didn't finish the thought, just kicked his heels into Pirate's sides and took off.

She rode after him, knowing nothing else mattered but getting the child and his father back together.

An hour had passed, and the homestead cabin had been checked, but was found empty. Garrett was about to go out of his mind. "Dear God, where would he go?"

The wind had picked up, and the daylight was growing dim as clouds moved in.

Garrett looked ahead and side to side, knowing he had to phone the sheriff and get help in the air. Then he saw a shiny object flash in the sunlight. He rode closer and saw Brody's chrome bike just a few yards from the river. "It's his bike."

Josie climbed off her horse and reached for her cell phone to call Vance. "We found the bike, but no Brody." She gave her location as she led her horse along the rocky bank of the wide river behind Garrett.

"He's close by, Garrett. I just know it."

They walked about a quarter mile calling Brody's name. That was when she heard the sound. She stopped Garrett. "I heard him."

Again the sound of Brody's voice. She dropped the horse's reins and took off toward the big tree and found the boy sitting against it. "Brody!" she cried and hurried to him.

Garrett passed her and got to the boy's side and reached for him. "Son, it's okay. We're here."

"It hurts, Dad." The boy was fighting tears. "Really bad. I slipped on that big rock by the river. I couldn't ride my bike home."

Garrett quickly examined his arm, then his shoulder. "It's going to be all right, son. Just hang in there for a few minutes and we'll get you some help."

Josie took Garrett's place next to Brody and took the boy's hand. "It's okay, Brody. Your dad's here. He'll take care of you."

Garrett pulled out his phone and called to have some-

one bring a truck. He looked at Josie, raw emotion showing on his face.

She looked up at him with those big eyes. "He's safe
now, Garrett." She let her own tears fall. "Brody is safe."

CHAPTER TWELVE

THEY LEFT THE emergency room two hours later, after the doctor's diagnosis.

Brody had a hairline clavicle fracture. It wasn't a complete break, so the healing time would be shorter with less chance of losing any movement in his arm. Garrett breathed a sigh of relief.

After his son's arm had been put into a sling to keep his shoulder immobile, they headed back to the Slater house to drop off Josie and get Nolan.

It had been at Brody's insistence that she go along with him. And he was glad she'd been there to calm his son.

It was dark by the time Garrett pulled up, but before anyone got out of the truck, family filed out of the house. Brody was out of the vehicle before he could stop him.

After hugs all round, Ana coaxed them. "Come on Josie, Garrett. We have Thanksgiving to celebrate."

Josie saw that Garrett wasn't happy as everyone went inside ahead of them. "I know you're still upset about what happened to Brody, but now is not the time."

Garrett shook his head and started to speak, then stopped. He walked back to the truck and turned around. "I could have lost him today. What if we hadn't found him?"

Josie went to him, feeling his pain. "Oh, Garrett, there are so many what-ifs, but what really happened today i your son made a mistake in judgment. But he's safe now, and he's going to be sitting down to Thanksgiving dinner with you."

He turned to her. Even in the darkness, she could see his tears. "This is hard. I'm so angry with him, but all I want to do is hold him close and protect him from all harm. I didn't do that today."

Josie tried to stay back, but she, too, had been terrified of losing Brody. She felt her own tears. "I'm not an expert, but I think you did everything right. You're a wonderful dad, Garrett." She went into his arms and hugged him close. It seemed the most natural thing to do.

Thanksgiving dinner was a joyous event, something that Josie had never experienced in the Slater house. Everyone was seated at the large dining room table, her father at the head and Kathleen at the opposite end. Having the Temple family here added so much more to this day, more than she should allow herself to dream about. Although Nolan, Garrett and Brody had become a part of her life, it wouldn't be for much longer.

She glanced at the eight-year-old boy. Brody didn't seem to mind the discomfort in his shoulder. He was going to have a great story when he returned to class on Monday.

She turned her attention to Garrett, seated across from her. He looked tired, and there were still worry lines on his forehead. Again, she wanted to comfort him, and that was a mistake. Only days ago, they'd decided it was best to stay away from each other. Now look at them—they were acting like one big happy family.

Brody's laughter filled the room. "This is the best Thanksgiving ever," he said.

Garrett disagreed. "You might not think so when you receive your punishment for your stunt today."

The boy looked embarrassed as he glanced around the table. "I'm sorry that I caused so much trouble and spoiled everybody's Thanksgiving." He glanced at his father. "Did I say it right, Dad?"

Josie saw Garrett's pride. "You did it perfect, son. I'm proud of you for taking responsibility."

The boy perked up. "Do I get less punishment now?"

Everyone laughed, and Kathleen stood. "You better come with me, young man, and help me cut some pies. You can put on the whipped cream."

Colt called to the housekeeper. "Kathleen, could you hold off on dessert for about fifteen minutes?"

She nodded and took the boy's hand, and they walked into the kitchen.

Colt looked around the table. "I need to say a little something." He cleared his throat. "First of all, I'm very thankful that my daughters are here, also Vance and my friends—some old." He nodded to Wade. "Some new." He saluted Nolan and Garrett. "I'm not going to sugarcoat how bad things were through those years. If I apologize every day for the rest of my life, it still wouldn't make up for the hurt my daughters have lived through. I'm not going to make excuses… I am just going to say I'm sorry. I love you all, and I hope in time you girls can forgive me."

Josie felt the tears start. She glanced at her twin and saw the same. Vance put his arm around Ana and pulled her close.

"I made a vow when I was in the hospital that if I was given a second chance, I'd do whatever it takes to try and make it up to you girls." He sighed and pulled out an envelope from his pocket. "I need to start with some honesty. This here is a twenty-five-year-old letter…from your mother."

Ana gasped. Josie froze, not wanting to feel anything. She glanced at Tori.

"It was sent along with the divorce papers. At first I was so angry, I nearly threw it away. Then I decided to save it until you girls got older. I honestly forgot about it and just found it the other day."

"Why even tell us about it?" Tori threw out. "Bring up memories about a woman who abandoned us? I don't want to hear anything she had to say."

Garrett felt uncomfortable and started to get up and leave the room, but Colt asked him to stay.

"You'll understand in a minute," Colt told him.

"I opened it because I wanted to protect you all." He glanced at Ana. "The last thing I want is for your mother to hurt you any more than she already has."

Josie didn't want to feel anything for a woman she barely knew. She didn't even care enough about her own children to stick around. "We don't need her letter now. Her leaving us says it all."

Ana gripped Vance's hand. "Do you want us to read the letter? Open all those wounds again?"

Colt glanced around the table. "I blame myself for not showing this to you before. My main reason is, as I told you, I wanted to be honest with you girls. So I'm leaving the decision up to you."

"I don't want to hear her tell us stuff just to ease her conscience," Tori said.

Colt sighed. "Look, I still have no idea why she left. For years I was selfish enough to think it was all about me. I think I was wrong…. So maybe you should read the letter and judge for yourself."

Garrett followed Colt, Vance and the family lawyer, Wade Dickson, into the office. His dad took charge of Brody, and they were watching a video in the Slaters' family room. The sisters disappeared upstairs to discuss the mysterious letter.

Garrett needed to be home with his son tucked into his bed, but he couldn't help thinking about Josie and the letter she had to deal with.

After shutting the door, Colt made his way to the desk chair. "Honestly, I had forgotten about that letter."

"Maybe it should have stayed forgotten," Vance said. "None of the girls need to be reminded their mother left them."

"I know, but let me explain something first." He looked at Vance, then to Garrett. "I trust you two not to say anything to them just yet."

"You're asking a lot," Vance said. "I'm marrying your daughter in less than two weeks. I don't keep anything from her."

Garrett had no idea why he was here. "All we can promise is we'll hear you out, and then decide." He didn't want Josie hurt, either.

Colt nodded. "At first I thought it was the medication." He looked at Vance. "At the hospital after my stroke, someone came into my room late one night. She looked like Lucia."

"It probably was the meds," Vance told him. "They wanted you to rest and heal."

"I thought the same thing," Colt said. "But it happened again when I went into the rehab facility." He hesitated. "And then again when I returned home."

Garrett leaned forward. "Are you saying Lucia was here in this house?"

He nodded. "I'm as sure as I can be that the woman was in my room two nights ago."

"You talked to her?" Vance asked, looking skeptical.

"No, but she spoke to me. She said my name."

"What did you say to her?"

"When I said her name, she smiled. It made me angry, and I told her to get out. I turned around but when I looked again, she was gone."

Garrett wasn't sure what to think. "Do you think she's come back because she wants something? Money? Her daughters?"

Colt shook his head and looked at his friend, Wade. "I don't know. And it wasn't until I started looking at old pictures that I remembered the letter." He shook his head. "I knew I couldn't keep it from the girls. I want to be completely honest with them."

Vance began to pace then asked, "How could she get onto the ranch with no one knowing?"

Colt looked tired. "Hell, I don't know. And since I'm the only one who's seen her, I'm probably just going crazy." He waved a hand. "Maybe you should forget I said anything."

"No," Garrett said. "I think we need to check into it." He turned to Colt. "Do you know where Lucia went all those years ago?"

Colt shook his head. "Even though she was estranged from her family, I assumed she went back to Mexico." He got up and went to the wall safe and used the combination to open it. He pulled out a manila envelope and brought it back and tossed it on the desk. "Here are the divorce papers and the last correspondence we had through our lawyers."

He looked at Garrett. "Do you think your friend the P.I. can find out where Lucia is now?"

Vance put his hand on the papers. "Whoa, we aren't going to spoil Ana's wedding. She deserves her day."

Colt nodded. "Of course she does, and so do you. We can hold off with this until after the holidays."

Garrett nodded. Once again, he was getting involved in Josie's life. "I think the girls should decide if they want to find their mother."

Upstairs, the three sisters sat in Ana's room on the big bed with the letter. It was still in the envelope because a decision couldn't be made about what to do.

"What can she do to us now?" Josie asked. "The woman hasn't been in our lives for years." She glanced at Tori. "Besides, we barely remember her."

"I remember her," Ana said. "I loved her so much, I wanted to die after she left." Her voice was a hoarse whisper. "I never understood why she left and never even said goodbye." She took the letter. "Yes, I want to know what she wrote us. What we did that made her walk away from her family."

Ana got up from the bed and took out a single piece of paper from the yellowing envelope. She took a breath and released it, then read,

"'To my *bambinas,* Analeigh, Josefina, Vittoria and Marissa.

It is so hard to have to say these words to you, but I must. I cannot stay and be your mother any longer. It's not because I don't love you all, it's because I do. So I must leave you for a while. I'm needed back in Mexico to be with my family.

Please, know that I will think about you every day and pray that someday I will be able to return to you. For now, take care of your papa, and never forget me.

I vow, no matter how, I will find my way back to my *niñas.*

Love, Mama'"

Ana swallowed hard. "Oh, God. It sounds as if she didn't want to leave."

Josie wasn't so sure. "What else could she say? And where has she been all these years? Surely, if she wanted to come back, she would have been here before now. I don't want to do this." She got up from the bed and started to walk away.

"Wait, Josie," Ana called.

Josie turned around. "What?"

"Do you want to pursue this?"

"No! I don't know. Can we just wait a little while? I can't face this right now."

Ana nodded and said, "We'll decide after the wedding and the holidays."

All the sisters agreed, and Josie walked out of the room, her emotions in turmoil. She didn't need another rejection. Then a thought struck her. What if she wasn't even alive? Dear, God. What if Lucia Slater had died and she couldn't come back to them?

Trembling, she sank down on the top step, unable to stop the tears. She hated being weak. Her mother never mattered before. Why now? She'd never had her in her life. Why did she want her so badly now?

"Josie…"

She looked up from her perch on the step and saw Garrett. She saw the compassion in his eyes and knew she couldn't hold it together any longer.

"Oh, Garrett," she cried and went into his open arms. "She said she loved us. But she left anyway."

Garrett cupped the back of Josie's head and held her against his shoulder. She was heartbroken, and he couldn't help her. He couldn't stop her pain. "I'm here, Josie. I'll help you through this."

Suddenly, she pulled back and wiped at her tears. "I'm fine."

Garrett felt her pull away, both physically and emotionally. "There's nothing wrong with leaning on someone, Josie. I want to be there for you."

She shook her head. "You'll go away. Everybody always goes away." She got up and hurried down the hall to her bedroom.

Garrett started to go after her, but knew she wasn't ready to listen. "I'm not going anywhere, Josie. Not this time."

He was going to figure out a way for them to be together. He wouldn't lose her again.

Another week had gone by, and Colt had filled his days with his therapy routine so he could be strong enough to walk Ana down the aisle at her wedding.

He felt fatigued as he looked out the window of his room. Had that been the reason for his confusion, for imagining the mystery woman in his room last week?

Was this part of the brain damage from his stroke? All he wanted to do was rebuild a relationship with his daughters, and so far he'd caused more problems. Vance was right. He should have waited until after the ceremony to dredge up the past.

Colt closed his eyes. He hated remembering back to that time. The years of misery without the woman he loved, but there had been years of joy with her, too.

"Oh, Lucia. What have you done? If you were to come back, do you realize the problems you'd create?" Dear God, for a long time after Lucia had left, he would have sold his soul to have her back in his life again.

"I was hoping you'd let me explain," a familiar voice said.

He sucked in a breath and turned around. There was a

small figure standing in the shadow of the doorway. His heart was pounding in his chest.

"Then step out of the dark and tell me who you are and what you want here."

He held his breath as he prayed, but he didn't know what he was praying for until she came into the light.

She moved forward, and the dim light shone on the small, slender woman with inky-black hair as he remembered. Her face... She was still beautiful, with her perfect olive skin and high cheekbones. It was those eyes, ebony in color and so piercing.

He swallowed back the dryness in his throat. "Lucia?" Was she a dream?

"Yes, it's me, Colt. I came back as soon as I could get here."

He blinked several times, but she was still there. Suddenly, he felt his anger build, years' worth of anger. "Well, you're too late," he lied. "Too many years late."

The next week had been a blur of activities preparing for the wedding. When the day finally arrived, Garrett helped his son with his tie. They were both in the wedding party.

They'd spent the past two days decorating the lodge for the wedding, and the rehearsal dinner last night had him already exhausted. Today was going to be the end of it. Would it also be the end of his seeing Josie?

"Dad, do you want to get married again?"

Whoa, where did that come from? "I think I'm going to wait awhile for that, son. I have you and Grandpa, and that's enough for me now."

Brody wrinkled his nose. "But Grandpa says that it's really good to have someone to share stuff with. You know, like when you come home from work and she kisses you and makes supper."

"What are you getting at, son?"

The boy shrugged. "I was just thinking maybe it would be nice to have someone to live with us. Someone who gives hugs and kisses at bedtime. I mean, I know I'm almost too big for that, but having a mom again might be nice."

"But your mother…"

"I miss her, and Grandpa says I always will, but he says there's always more room in our hearts to love people. So can we love Josie?"

Boy, could he. He knelt down in front of his son. "If it were that easy, son, I would have figured out a way by now. Josie lives in California."

"Can't she live here?"

"She does weddings and other special parties. She needs a place like this lodge, but bigger."

Brody's green eyes searched Garrett's face. "Well, that's easy. Can't you build her a really big place for all her parties closer to our house?"

CHAPTER THIRTEEN

THE WINTER WONDERLAND scene was perfect for a December wedding.

At seven o'clock the music cued the wedding party to begin the procession down the River's Edge Lodge's staircase. Fresh garlands intertwined with white ribbon had been strung along the banister. Downstairs in front of the picture window were four pine trees decorated with twinkling lights and at the white arch stood pots of bright red poinsettias.

Josie glanced at Ana, dressed in her beautiful antique-white satin gown. The long veil was the perfect touch to highlight the bride's dark hair, pulled away from her pretty face.

Tori and Josie were dressed in dark green ankle-length dresses. Bridesmaid Tori started her descent down the staircase. The only one missing was their youngest sister, Marissa, who couldn't make it that day.

Josie handed Ana a bouquet of blush-colored roses, then blew a kiss before she made her way down. Immediately, she looked toward the front of the main area where the groom and the best man stood at attention. She smiled at the small group of friends seated on either side of the aisle, but she couldn't take her eyes off Garrett. He looked so handsome in his tux. His dark hair had been cut and styled. Their gazes locked, and she felt a warm tingle all the way to her open-toed heels.

Just make it through today and tomorrow, she thought, knowing she already had her flight booked to leave in two days. And then she could put this all behind her.

Josie arrived at her spot at the end of the aisle. She broke her eye contact with Garrett and smiled at Brody, standing beside his father, then went to her place next to Tori. She stole another glance at Garrett and found him staring at her. The pull was so strong she had to fight to look away. Leaving was getting harder and harder.

The music changed, and Ana appeared at the top of the staircase and walked down alone, then Dad met the bride at the bottom.

Colt Slater drew his eldest daughter into his arms and held her close. Seconds ticked off as the big man blinked away tears and he whispered something to Ana. Finally, he kissed her cheek then offered his arm to her, and together they made their way up the aisle toward her soon-to-be husband.

Once they began to exchange vows, Josie's gaze kept wandering back to Garrett. He was watching her, too. She looked away but felt the heat of his gaze.

Finally, the ceremony was over, and the bride and groom came down the aisle arm in arm. The wedding party was next. Garrett offered Josie his arm and they walked out.

Before he released her, he said, "It was a nice ceremony. You look beautiful, Josie."

"Thank you, but you should be telling the bride that." She loved hearing the words, but it didn't change anything. She was in love with a man she couldn't be with.

Brody rushed up to them. "You look so pretty, Josie. Doesn't she, Dad?"

He winked at her. "Yes, son, she does."

Josie smiled. "Okay, you two flirts, I need to supervise the reception. So I'm off." She headed toward the banquet room past the fireplace. Round tables had been set up, decorated with white linen and multicolored floral centerpieces. At the head of the room was the long bridal party table. She'd be seated with Garrett. She had to blink away the tears. For the last time.

An hour later, the reception was in full swing. Garrett watched as Vance took Ana in his arms and began to move around the small dance floor. Envy tore at him. His friend went after what he wanted, and he'd found the woman of his dreams.

He watched as Vance kissed Ana, then released her as Colt made his way out to the floor. "Father and daughter dance," the DJ announced. Colt took his oldest daughter in his arms and began to move to the song. It was touching to see how far the man had come to repair the relationship with his daughters.

Then the DJ called for the wedding party to join them. Garrett didn't hesitate and escorted Josie onto the floor. He closed his eyes and drew her against him and prayed he'd be able to find the words to keep her with him. He swayed to the soft ballad, then placed a soft kiss against her forehead.

He danced her off to a corner. "Josie…I need to talk to you."

She shook her head. "I can't, Garrett."

He held her close. "Can't you give me five minutes so I can tell you how I feel?"

"Please, Garrett. We've gone over this so many times."

"Then hear me out once more."

Just then the DJ came up to them. "It's time for the maid of honor and best man's toasts."

Josie took off, but Garrett was stopped by his son. "Dad, did you ask her yet?"

His son looked hopeful. "Look, Brody, I don't think this is going to work. Josie is set on going back to L.A."

"You can't let her. Tell her we love her. A lot. And we want to her stay." The boy squeezed his hand. "Don't be afraid, Dad, 'cause she loves us, too. I know she does."

Garrett nodded and watched as Josie took the microphone and began with a childhood story and then talked about how Vance came to the ranch. Josie also spoke about how much she loved her sister and how lucky Vance was to have her in his life.

After the applause, it was Garrett's turn, and he walked to the front of the room. He looked at Vance and Ana and smiled.

"I can't be any happier for the two of you. Of course, there were times, Ana, that this man was going half-crazy because you wouldn't give him the time of day." Everyone laughed. "I told him to be patient because you were worth it." Garrett sighed. "I hope you two know how lucky you are to find each other."

He turned and looked at Josie. "I know because it's hard to find that special person to love." His gaze met hers, and he was determined to make her hear this. "If you do find her, tell her how much you love her. Tell her how your life is so empty without her in it. Because you might not get another chance." He realized the guests were silent.

He raised his glass as Josie left the room. "To Vance and Ana, may your life together be a long and happy one." He took a drink of champagne, and then hugged the bride, then Vance.

"Go after her, Garrett," his friend said. "Don't let her get away this time."

* * *

Josie rushed upstairs into the bedroom they'd used as a dressing room. She paced in front of the window. She couldn't keep doing this. Garrett wanted her. Okay, she wanted him, too, but that didn't mean it would happen.

There was a knock on the door, and Colt peered inside. "If you'd rather be alone, I'll leave."

She fought tears and motioned for him to enter. Without a word she walked into his open arms and let the tears fall.

After a few minutes, he pulled back. "I hate seeing you hurting."

"Some things can't be helped."

"Do you love Garrett?"

"Yes, Dad, I love him. I don't think I ever stopped loving him, but when he found someone else and had a child… It hurt me."

Colt looked serious. "I'm new at this giving advice stuff, and you might not like what I have to say, but here goes. If my memory is correct, about ten years ago you sent Garrett away. And as for finding someone else, I believe that was months later, after Garrett made several attempts to talk to you." Her father's eyes grew tender. "And the man did the right thing and married the mother of his child. Now he's raising his son alone. Brody is a great kid." Colt tipped her chin up. "I take blame in this, too. I made you girls afraid to trust a man to be there because I was never there for you. I'm so sorry, Josie."

She nodded and wiped her tears.

"Just don't let what I did cloud your judgment toward Garrett. He's a good man and he loves you. You know those second chances are pretty sweet. At least give him that chance to tell you what he wants."

She wrapped her arms around this man. It felt so good. "I love you, Dad."

"I love you, too, Josie," he said in a gruff voice. "Now, go find your guy and put him out of his misery."

Could there be a chance for them? She had to find Garrett. Smiling, she opened the door and there stood Brody.

"Josie, please don't leave. Dad and I want you to stay here with us. He can build you a big building and you can do weddings and parties so you don't have to go back to California."

She pulled the boy into a hug, overwhelmed by a rush of feelings. "Oh, Brody, it's going to be okay. I just need to talk to your father."

Her wish came true, and Garrett appeared in the doorway. "I'm right here."

Her heart stopped then began to race. "Garrett…"

Colt slipped out behind her and took Brody's hand. "How about we let Josie and your dad work things out?" The two walked away, and Josie's fear almost had her running after them.

Garrett wasn't sure he could handle another rejection from her, but at least he wasn't going to do it in public. He guided Josie back into the room and closed the door. "I'm going to give it one more shot, then if you don't like what I have to say, I promise I won't bother you again." He prayed he could find the right words. "Josie, from the second I saw you in high school, you had me. We were both young back then, too young to know what we wanted. No, that's not true. I wanted you. I've always wanted you."

Her eyes were big and so blue. He had to glance away so he could concentrate.

"Ten years ago, when I took that job, I'd planned to make enough money that summer to buy you an engagement ring. I'd hoped we could be married and I'd take you back to college with me. I couldn't stand being without you."

A tear slid down her face, and he brushed it away. "I'm sorry." She raised a trembling hand to her mouth.

"When you refused to talk to me I nearly quit work and school to come home, but I needed the job for college credit. Natalie Kirkwood was my boss's daughter, so she was around a lot. The first time I went out with her it was to try and forget you." He glanced away again. "I was hurting so much…it just happened between us. But I'll never regret having Brody. My son is the best of me, and I love him."

"He's a wonderful boy," she whispered.

"I'll always care about Natalie because she's Brody's mom. But our marriage was doomed from the start because I still had feelings for you. I want another chance for us."

She blinked back more tears. "Maybe I should be asking for a second chance. I was the one who pushed you away." She shrugged. "I was afraid, Garrett. I knew you wanted to get married, and I panicked."

"Why didn't you tell me?"

Again she shrugged. "I thought you'd leave me." She gave a tiny laugh. "You left me anyway."

He brushed away the moisture from her cheek. "Like I said, you always had me, Josie." He felt the trembling, but didn't know if it was her or him. "How about we forgive ourselves for the past and start a clean slate?" He took her in his arms. "I love you, Josie Slater. I always have and always will."

"Oh, Garrett, I love you, too."

"I love hearing you say those words again." He dipped his head and covered her mouth in a soft kiss, making him only want more. He took several nibbles, then had to stop. There was so much that needed to be settled between them.

He drew back. "Now we have to find a way to be together. And I don't want a long-distance relationship."

She raised an eyebrow. "Brody said something about you wanting to build a place for my weddings and parties."

He couldn't help but smile. "So my son's been playing my pitchman. I had to talk to him about the future, Josie. We are a package deal."

Josie realized that she wanted Brody in her life as much as his father. "You are so lucky to have that boy. I'm already crazy about him."

Garrett hesitated, then finally said, "I'm asking a lot of you, Josie, to take on an eight-year-old child, my father and me. And if it was just us two, I'd follow you back to L.A. But I can't leave. So I'm offering to help you build a business here. I know Royerton might not be able to handle enough work for an event planner. Maybe Butte, or Bozeman, and I'll build you another lodge, a wedding chapel, a retreat. You name whatever you want, and I'll do what I can to get it for you."

She couldn't believe he was doing all this for her. "You. I want you…and Brody and Nolan in my life."

"God, I love you." He picked her up and swung her around, then finally put her down.

She raised a hand. "I'll still need to travel back and forth to L.A. until I finish out the contracts I've already signed. But I'm ready now to be with the man I love."

"That's music to my ears," he told her, then covered her mouth with his. He nudged her lips with his tongue, and she opened eagerly to welcome him. He finally broke off the kiss. "You are one big distraction."

She was too dazed to react to what happened next. He drew back and lowered to one knee.

"I hadn't planned to do this here, but I'm not about to let you get away again. Josie Slater, I love you with all my heart. Would you do me the honor of being my wife and the mother to my son and all the other children we may have together?"

Tears flowed again. "Oh, Garrett. Yes! Yes, I'll marry you."

He kissed her tenderly, and she melted into his arms, nearly forgetting where they were. That's when she heard the commotion downstairs.

"Oh, gosh, the wedding. We've got to get back."

Josie opened the door and, almost giddy, they rushed along the open railing to the top of the staircase. Looking down, she found the wedding party and guests in front of the picture window. Ana was standing alone with a line of ladies about twenty feet away. "Oh, she's going to toss the bouquet," Josie said.

Ana looked up and spotted them. "Josie you're just in time. Come on down, I'm going to throw my bouquet."

Josie looked at Garrett.

He grinned at her, then he addressed the crowd. "Josie Slater isn't going to be single for very much longer. She's just agreed to marry me."

The crowd cheered as Ana walked to the staircase. "Then this is rightfully yours." Her sister tossed the bouquet toward the balcony. Josie leaned forward and snatched it out of the air.

She blushed as everyone applauded and Garrett pulled her into his arms. "It's too late to back out now."

"No way. I have everything I've always wanted."

She touched her lips to his. She knew she didn't have to give up anything, because this man was what she'd always wanted and so much more.

EPILOGUE

THREE DAYS AFTER Ana and Vance's wedding, Colt was alone for the first time since his stroke. The newlyweds were off on their honeymoon, and Josie and Garrett had flown to L.A. to deal with her business and the town house cleanup. Tori had gone off to visit an old school friend in town, and it was Kathleen's day off.

It was all set. Colt was free to go to his meeting without any questions. Only his friend and lawyer, Wade, knew what had been going on. He had to confide in someone.

"Are you sure you want to do this?" Wade asked as he glanced away from the road leading to Dillon.

"Hell, no, I'm not sure of anything, except I have to see her." He looked at his friend. "I need to hear her reason for why she left."

"What about the girls?" Wade asked.

He felt a little traitorous for not telling his daughters. "I'm not going to tell 'em, yet. Not until Lucia convinces me she doesn't want to claim something that isn't hers."

"I think maybe you should wait until the P.I. has finished checking things out."

Colt sighed. That would be the wise thing, but when it came to Lucia Delgado, he hadn't always acted wisely. "All I'm doing is listening to what she has to say."

Wade stayed silent as they pulled into the chain hotel

parking lot. Colt and Wade got out of the car and walked through the double doors. He looked into the restaurant/ lounge to see it was nearly empty except for a woman seated at a corner booth.

Colt squared his shoulders as his stomach took a tumble. She looked across the room, then stood up. His breath caught. She was dressed in a leather jacket and a black turtleneck sweater with a bright scarf around her slender neck. Even though she was wearing jeans, there was no way this woman wouldn't turn heads.

"Damn…" Wade breathed from behind him. "It's like time has stood still. I'll be at the bar if you need me."

Colt started across the room, careful his steps were sure and true. The last thing he wanted was to fall on his face. He had some pride. He made his way through the empty tables until he stood in front of his ex-wife.

"Lucia." Even at the age of fifty-two, he was slammed in his gut by her beauty.

"Hello, Colt."

Even though he'd expected her, he couldn't believe she was really here. "We should get this over with." He motioned for her to sit, then he slid into the booth across from her.

Although it was dim in the room, he stared into those incredible dark eyes. "It's been a long time, Lucia."

Not counting the night she'd come into his room. Then she'd called him yesterday and asked to meet with him.

"Yes, it has." Her voice was soft and throaty.

He felt as shaky as a teenager. "Okay, I agreed to talk to you, so we should get started." The waitress appeared and he ordered some coffee. He wanted something stronger, but knew that wasn't wise. He needed a clear head.

The waitress came back with two coffee cups and a

cream pitcher. Lucia looked surprised when he pushed the creamer toward her.

"You remember how I like my coffee." The words came out in a soft voice.

"I remember a lot of things. The sound of your voice as you read stories to our babies. How you cuddled them in your arms, how you loved them."

He drew a breath and worked hard to release it. "I also remember the way it felt to make love to you, to hear your gasps of pleasure." He watched her eyes widen, her face flush. "I also remember you saying you loved me, that you loved the girls. Then the next day you disappeared from our lives."

She stayed silent for a long time, and then said, "I had no choice, Colton."

"There's always a choice, Lucia. You chose to leave your family…your *bambinas,* your *marido.*" *Husband.*

She shook her head. "You have to believe me, *mi amor.*"

"No! You can't call me your love. The woman I married, the woman I loved would never leave me. I don't know who you are."

Lucia stiffened and pulled back. So she still had a temper. "I never wanted to leave my family, *mi corazon.*" *My heart.* There was a fierce look in her ebony eyes, and his body betrayed him as he reacted to her.

"And you were my heart, too, Lucia. I gave you everything, but you left anyway."

"You don't understand," she insisted. "I gave up my *familia* to keep you from harm."

He frowned. "You're saying that someone wanted to harm us?"

He saw her hands shake as she nodded.

"Who was this person?"

"Vicente Santoya… My husband."

Her declaration was like a knife to his heart. Of course, she'd been with other men. Was Santoya the reason she'd left him?

"I don't want to hear about your lovers." He was unable to keep the anger out of his voice. "I've made a life without you. So you can just go back to him." Hell, he didn't need this. He'd learned to live without her before—he could do it again. He started to get out of the booth. Then she placed her hand on his and stopped him.

"*Por favor,* Colt! I can't go back there. It took me too long to get out. Vicente is dead. So I've broken most of my ties there. So I can safely come back...to you."

He didn't want to hear about her marriage. "What about your father?" Cesar Delgado never wanted his only child to marry an American, especially a broken-down, ex-rodeo cowboy. How did he feel about her return to Montana?

Lucia straightened and looked him in the eye. "My parents are gone. My ties and loyalty are only to this country. So please, I ask that you hear what I have to say before you send me away."

He wasn't going to be fooled again. Lucia had made a life for herself without him. "I don't see how anything that you have to say will change my mind."

She looked nervous, almost panicky. "What if it concerns your sons?"

He shook his head. "I don't have sons."

Lucia nodded. "Yes, you do. I was pregnant with twin boys when I left you."

Five days later, a happy Garrett and Josie arrived back in Montana. The only reason she'd wanted to stay in L.A. a little longer was because Josie had liked having her man all to herself. Still, she knew they needed to get back. She had a wedding to plan.

She was also able to start her life in Montana because she had a great assistant. That was why she'd offered Megan Buckner a partnership in the business. Megan had eagerly accepted the deal. So Josie would be able to wean herself from her L.A. projects and not cancel a single event.

Garrett reached across the seat and took her hand as he drove down the road. "Would you mind if we made a quick stop in town first?"

"Not a problem, but I want to be at the house so we can meet Brody's bus."

"I thought we could pick him up at school after I show you something."

She smiled. "I like that idea better." She was so anxious to see the child. She couldn't believe how easily she'd fallen in love with the eight-year-old boy. Of course all the Temple men were very appealing.

At the end of Main Street, Garrett turned into the driveway of a three-story Victorian house. The huge structure showed years of neglect with faded and peeling paint, and the wraparound porch needed a railing at the very least.

"Isn't this Mrs. Anderson's house?"

Garrett put the truck into Park and shut off the engine. "Yes, but she died last year and her daughter inherited it. She wants to sell the place." He rubbed his hand along the back of his neck. "I thought with a little rehab and TLC it would make a great office for Slater Style and maybe even a place to hold some small events. The large backyard could be landscaped for weddings."

Josie was suddenly excited. "I want to go see it." She jumped out of the car and rushed to the door. She tried the knob but it was locked.

"Hold on." Garrett came after her, put a key into the lock and got it open. "Now, don't get too excited," he warned. "It needs some work."

She kissed him. "I'm going to love it, but not as much as I love you for doing this," she said as she walked inside.

The entry was huge, with a crystal chandelier hanging from the high ceiling. The staircase was a work of art, with a hand-carved banister that ran up to the second floor, and stained-glass windows above the landing.

There were raised-panel pocket doors that could close off the three large rooms downstairs. The hardwood floors needed refinishing, but there would soon be a contractor in the family.

She was a little giddy as she walked down the hall to a kitchen that was in really bad condition.

Garrett came up behind her. "This needs a gut job, honey. But we can make it look like the era of the home. Anything you want."

"You're spoiling me."

"Get used to it." He turned her around and lowered his mouth to hers for a kiss that was slow and easy. The result had her breathless.

"I plan to make sure you're happy working here."

"I have you and Brody in my life, and that makes everything just about perfect."

She brushed another kiss on his tempting mouth, then went to check every nook and cranny of the area, which included a large pantry and sunroom off the kitchen. Then she opened the back door into a yard that seemed to go on forever. A high fence circled the property and there was a gazebo toward the back.

"Oh, Garrett, it's lovely."

Garrett came up behind her and wrapped his arms around her to ward off the winter cold. "I'm glad you like it. You've had to make all the sacrifices, Josie. So I wanted you to have this house." He loved her so much. "Your career is important."

She smiled at him, and his heart raced. "Being with you and Brody doesn't feel like a sacrifice to me. And I get to be around my family, too. Ana and Dad." She shook her head. "Can you believe I'm calling Colt, Dad?"

"You have to give him credit, Josie. He's trying hard with you girls."

"I know." She shook her head. "Now, if I can convince Tori to stay around for a while." She frowned. "At least until we're sure that Dane is out of her life."

"Richards is working on that. Until then, I promise I'll do everything possible to keep her here and keep her safe."

She smiled. "I love you so much, Garrett Temple. I can't wait to start our life together."

He pulled her into his arms. He wanted that to happen very soon. "About that. I was wondering when that special day is going to take place. I'm not happy about you still living in your dad's house."

They'd both decided because Brody was at an impressionable age, that they wouldn't live together until after the wedding.

"How soon can you get the renovations done here?" she asked.

"That depends on what you want done."

"The downstairs. The floors refinished and some new paint."

"A few weeks, maybe a month with a new kitchen. The crew can start renovations right after Christmas."

She sighed. "Christmas is only ten days away. I've always hated the holiday...." She glanced up at him. "Until now. Now, I get you, Brody and my family."

"I'm gonna make it special for you," he told her. "We'll start some good memories."

Josie held up her hand to inspect the diamond solitaire engagement ring he'd bought her in Los Angeles. "Oh, I do believe you've already made everything very special." She glanced back at the yard. "So how do you feel about having the wedding right here?"

Garrett arched an eyebrow. "Outside?"

"Oh, I'd love that. A garden wedding, but even I don't want to wait that long. How about Valentine's Day in the front parlor?"

"If that's what you want, I'll work day and night to get this place ready." He grinned. "And it will be great advertising for future weddings at Slater Manor."

Josie had trouble holding on to her emotions. "Slater Manor..." She repeated the name over in her head. "I like that, but how about Temple Manor?"

He shook his head. "No, Josie. You've worked hard to build a name with Slater Style. Slater Manor makes good business sense." He smiled. "I still want you to take my name for everything else."

"I've waited a long time for you, Garrett Temple. So only in business will I use Slater." She swallowed hard. She bravely went on, hoping he wanted the same thing. "And while you're doing the renovations, could you make a nursery upstairs?"

This time she watched him swallow hard. "A nursery? A baby nursery?"

She nodded. "So I can work and keep our babies with me."

"I would love that. But not as much as making a child with you," he whispered as he placed kisses along her jaw to her ear, finally reaching her mouth. The kiss was hungry, letting her know he desired her. When he released her, she could see he'd been as affected as she was.

"God, we're so lucky, Josie. We got a second chance." He cupped her face. "There's never been anyone I've loved as much as you. There's no one else I want to spend the rest of my life with."

She smiled. "Then it's a good thing you don't have to, because I'm not leaving you ever again."

"And this time, I'd just follow you, because you are my heart." He kissed her again, holding her close.

Josie held on, too. She'd stopped running away. She'd found everything right here. She would never feel alone again.

* * * * *

MILLS & BOON®

Why shop at millsandboon.co.uk?

Each year, thousands of romance readers find their perfect read at millsandboon.co.uk. That's because we're passionate about bringing you the very best romantic fiction. Here are some of the advantages of shopping at www.millsandboon.co.uk:

* **Get new books first**—you'll be able to buy your favourite books one month before they hit the shops

* **Get exclusive discounts**—you'll also be able to buy our specially created monthly collections, with up to 50% off the RRP

* **Find your favourite authors**—latest news, interviews and new releases for all your favourite authors and series on our website, plus ideas for what to try next

* **Join in**—once you've bought your favourite books, don't forget to register with us to rate, review and join in the discussions

Visit **www.millsandboon.co.uk**
for all this and more today!

The World of
MILLS & BOON®

HISTORICAL

*Awaken the romance
of the past*
6 new stories every month

*The ultimate in romantic
medical drama*
6 new stories every month

MODERN™

*Power, passion and
irresistible temptation*
8 new stories every month

By Request

*Relive the romance with the
best of the best*
12 stories every month

Have you tried eBooks?

With eBook exclusive series and titles from just **£1.99**
there's even more reason to try our eBooks today

Visit www.millsandboon.co.uk/eBooks
for more details